There were no preliminaries. The mighty flying reptile dove straight toward them. Tarzan loosed an arrow that drove true to its mark, burying its head in the breast of the pterodactyl. It rose suddenly upward and then, suddenly and with a speed incomprehensible in a creature of its tremendous size, wheeled like a sparrow hawk and dove straight at Tarzan's back.

So quickly did the creature strike that there could be no defense. The ape-man felt sharp talons half buried in his naked flesh and simultaneously he was lifted from the ground.

Thoar raised his spear and Tar-gash swung his cudgel, but neither dared strike for fear of wounding their comrade. In silence they stood watching until the creature passed out of sight beyond the summit of a distant peak, the body of the ape-man still dangling in its talons.

"Tarzan is dead," said Tar-gash . . .

By Edgar Rice Burroughs
Published by Ballantine Books:

THE TARZAN SERIES
Tarzan of the Apes (#1)
The Return of Tarzan (#2)
The Beasts of Tarzan (#3)
The Son of Tarzan (#4)
Tarzan and the Jewels of Opar (#5)
Jungle Tales of Tarzan (#6)
Tarzan the Untamed (#7)
Tarzan the Terrible (#8)
Tarzan and the Golden Lion (#9)
Tarzan and the Ant Men (#10)
Tarzan, Lord of the Jungle (#11)
Tarzan and the Lost Empire (#12)
Tarzan at the Earth's Core (#13)
Tarzan the Invincible (#14)
Tarzan Triumphant (#15)
Tarzan and the City of Gold (#16)
Tarzan and the Lion Man (#17)
Tarzan and the Leopard Men (#18)
Tarzan's Quest (#19)
Tarzan and the Forbidden City (#20)
Tarzan the Magnificent (#21)
Tarzan and the Foreign Legion (#22)
Tarzan and the Madman (#23)
Tarzan and the Castaways (#24)

COMPLETE AND UNABRIDGED!

And be sure to look for all 11 books of the *Mars* series and all 6
books of the *Pellucidar* series, also published by Ballantine!

By Edgar Rice Burroughs and Joe R. Lansdale:
TARZAN: THE LOST ADVENTURE

Books published by The Ballantine Publishing Group
are available at quantity discounts on bulk purchases
for premium, educational, fund-raising, and special
sales use. For details, please call 1-800-733-3000.

TARZAN AT THE EARTH'S CORE

Edgar Rice Burroughs

TARZAN THE INVINCIBLE

A Del Rey® Book
BALLANTINE BOOKS • NEW YORK

A Del Rey® Book
Published by Ballantine Books

Tarzan at the Earth's Core was originally published serially in *The Blue Book Magazine* from September 1929 to March 1930. *Tarzan the Invincible* was originally published serially in *The Blue Book Magazine* from October 1930 to April 1931 under the title "Tarzan, Guard of the Jungle."

http://www.randomhouse.com

Library of Congress Catalog Card Number: 97-91712

ISBN 0-345-41349-0

This authorized edition published by arrangement with Edgar Rice Burroughs, Inc.

Printed in Canada

First Edition: September 1997

10 9 8 7 6 5 4 3

Contents

TARZAN AT THE EARTH'S CORE

Foreword

PELLUCIDAR, AS EVERY schoolboy knows, is a world within a world, lying, as it does, upon the inner surface of the hollow sphere, which is the Earth.

It was discovered by David Innes and Abner Perry upon the occasion when they made the trial trip upon the mechanical prospector invented by Perry, wherewith they hoped to locate new beds of anthracite coal. Owing, however, to their inability to deflect the nose of the prospector, after it had started downward into the Earth's crust, they bored straight through for five hundred miles, and upon the third day, when Perry was already unconscious owing to the consumption of their stock of oxygen, and David was fast losing consciousness, the nose of the prospector broke through the crust of the inner world and the cabin was filled with fresh air.

In the years that have intervened, weird adventures have befallen these two explorers. Perry has never returned to the outer crust, and Innes but once—upon that occasion when he made the difficult and dangerous return trip in the prospector for the purpose of bringing back to the empire he had founded in the inner world the means to bestow upon his primitive people of the stone age the civilization of the twentieth century.

But what with battles with primitive men and still more primitive beasts and reptiles, the advance of the empire of Pellucidar toward civilization has been small; and insofar as the great area of the inner world is concerned, or the countless millions of its teeming life of another age than ours, David Innes and Abner Perry might never have existed.

When one considers that these land and water areas upon the surface of Pellucidar are in opposite relationship to the same areas upon the outer crust, some slight conception of the vast extent of this mighty world within a world may be dreamed.

The land area of the outer world comprises some fifty-three million square miles, or one-quarter of the total area of the earth's surface; while within Pellucidar three-quarters of the surface is land, so that jungle, mountain, forest, and plain stretch interminably over 124,110,000 square miles; nor are the oceans with their area of 41,370,000 square miles of any mean or niggardly extent.

Thus, considering the land area only, we have the strange anomaly of a larger world within a smaller one, but then Pellucidar is a world of deviation from what we of the outer crust have come to accept as unalterable laws of nature.

In the exact center of the earth hangs Pellucidar's sun, a tiny orb compared with ours, but sufficient to illuminate Pellucidar and flood her teeming jungles with warmth and life-giving rays. Her sun hanging thus perpetually at zenith, there is no night upon Pellucidar, but always an endless eternity of noon.

There being no stars and no apparent movement of the sun, Pellucidar has no points of compass; nor has she any horizon since her surface curves always upward in all directions from the observer, so that far above one's line of vision, plain or sea or distant mountain range go onward and upward until lost in the haze of the distance. And again, in a world where there is no sun, no stars, and no moon, such as we know, there can be no such thing as time, as we know it. And so, in Pellucidar, we have a timeless world which must necessarily be free from those pests who are constantly calling our attention to "the busy little bee" and to the fact that "time is money." While time may be "the soul of the world" and the "essence of contracts," in the beatific existence of Pellucidar it is nothing and less than nothing.

Thrice in the past have we of the outer world received communication from Pellucidar. We know that Perry's first great gift of civilization to the stone age was gunpowder. We know that he followed this with repeating rifles, small ships of war upon which were mounted guns of no great caliber, and finally we know that he perfected a radio.

Knowing Perry as something of an empiric, we were not surprised to learn that his radio could not be tuned in upon any known wave or wavelength of the outer world, and it remained for young Jason Gridley of Tarzana, experimenting with his newly discovered Gridley Wave, to pick up the first message from Pellucidar.

The last word that we received from Perry before his messages faltered and died out was to the effect that David Innes, first Emperor of Pellucidar, was languishing in a dark dungeon in the land of the Korsars, far across continent and ocean from his beloved land of Sari, which lies upon a great plateau not far inland from the Lural Az.

Contents

1

The O-220

TARZAN OF THE Apes paused to listen and to sniff the air. Had you been there you could not have heard what he heard, or had you you could not have interpreted it. You could have smelled nothing but the mustiness of decaying vegetation, which blended with the aroma of growing things.

The sounds that Tarzan heard came from a great distance and were faint even to his ears; nor at first could he definitely ascribe them to their true source, though he conceived the impression that they heralded the coming of a party of men.

Buto the rhinoceros, Tantor the elephant, or Numa the lion might come and go through the forest without arousing more than the indifferent interest of the Lord of the Jungle, but when man came Tarzan investigated, for man alone of all creatures brings change and dissension and strife wheresoever he first sets foot.

Reared to manhood among the great apes without knowledge of the existence of any other creatures like himself, Tarzan had since learned to anticipate with concern each fresh invasion of his jungle by these two-footed harbingers of strife. Among many races of men he had found friends, but this did not prevent him from questioning the purposes and the motives of whosoever entered his domain. And so today he moved silently through the middle terrace of his leafy way in the direction of the sounds that he had heard.

As the distance closed between him and those he went to investigate, his keen ears cataloged the sound of padding, naked feet and the song of native carriers as they swung along beneath their heavy burdens. And then to his nostrils came the scent spoor of black men and with it, faintly, the suggestion of another scent, and Tarzan knew that a white man was on safari before the head of the column came in view along the wide, well-marked game trail, above which the Lord of the Jungle waited.

Near the head of the column marched a young white man, and when Tarzan's eyes had rested upon him for a moment as he swung along the trail they impressed their stamp of approval of the stranger within the ape-man's brain, for in common with many savage beasts and primitive men Tarzan possessed an uncanny instinct in judging aright the characters of strangers whom he met.

Turning about, Tarzan moved swiftly and silently through the trees until he was some little distance ahead of the marching safari, then he dropped down into the trail and awaited its coming.

Rounding a curve in the trail the leading askari came in sight of him and when they saw him they halted and commenced to jabber excitedly, for these were men recruited in another district—men who did not know Tarzan of the Apes by sight.

"I am Tarzan," announced the ape-man. "What do you in Tarzan's country?"

Immediately the young man, who had halted abreast of his askari, advanced toward the ape-man. There was a smile upon his eager face. "You are Lord Greystoke?" he asked.

"Here, I am Tarzan of the Apes," replied the foster son of Kala.

"Then luck is certainly with me," said the young man, "for I have come all the way from Southern California to find you."

"Who are you," demanded the ape-man, "and what do you want of Tarzan of the Apes?"

"My name is Jason Gridley," replied the other. "And what I have come to talk to you about will make a long story. I hope that you can find the time to accompany me to our next camp and the patience to listen to me there until I have explained my mission."

Tarzan nodded. "In the jungle," he said, "we are not often pressed for time. Where do you intend making camp?"

"The guide that I obtained in the last village complained of being ill and turned back an hour ago, and as none of my own men is familiar with this country we do not know whether there is a suitable campsite within one mile or ten."

"There is one within half a mile," replied Tarzan, "and with good water."

"Good," said Gridley; and the safari resumed its way, the porters laughing and singing at the prospect of an early camp.

It was not until Jason and Tarzan were enjoying their coffee that evening that the ape-man reverted to the subject of the American's visit.

"And now," he said, "what has brought you all the way from Southern California to the heart of Africa?"

Gridley smiled. "Now that I am actually here," he said, "and face to face with you, I am suddenly confronted with the conviction that after you have heard my story it is going to be difficult to convince you that I am not crazy, and yet in my own mind I am so thoroughly convinced of the truth of what I am going to tell you that I have already invested a considerable amount of money and time to place my plan before you for the purpose of enlisting your personal and financial support, and I am ready and willing to invest still more money and all of my time. Unfortunately I cannot wholly finance the expedition that I have in mind from my personal resources, but that is not primarily my reason for coming to you. Doubtless I could have raised the necessary money elsewhere, but I believe that you are peculiarly fitted to lead such a venture as I have in mind."

"Whatever the expedition may be that you are contemplating," said Tarzan, "the potential profits must be great indeed if you are willing to risk so much of your own money."

"On the contrary," replied Gridley, "there will be no financial profit for anyone concerned insofar as I now know."

"And you are an American?" asked Tarzan, smiling.

"We are not all money mad," replied Gridley.

"Then what is the incentive? Explain the whole proposition to me."

"Have you ever heard of the theory that the earth is a hollow sphere, containing a habitable world within its interior?"

"The theory that has been definitely refuted by scientific investigation," replied the ape-man.

"But has it been refuted satisfactorily?" asked Gridley.

"To the satisfaction of the scientists," replied Tarzan.

"And to my satisfaction, too," replied the American, "until I recently received a message direct from the inner world."

"You surprise me," said the ape-man.

"And I, too, was surprised, but the fact remains that I have been in radio communication with Abner Perry in the inner world of Pellucidar and I have brought a copy of that message with me and also an affidavit of its authenticity from a man with whose name you are familiar and who was with me when I received the message; in fact, he was listening in at the same time with me. Here they are."

From a portfolio he took a letter which he handed to Tarzan and a bulky manuscript bound in board covers.

"I shall not take the time to read you all of the story of Tanar of Pellucidar," said Gridley, "because there is a great deal in it that is not essential to the exposition of my plan."

"As you will," said Tarzan. "I am listening."

For half an hour Jason Gridley read excerpts from the manuscript before him. "This," he said, when he had completed the reading, "is what convinced me of the existence of Pellucidar, and it is the unfortunate situation of David Innes that impelled me to come to you with the proposal that we undertake an expedition whose first purpose shall be to rescue him from the dungeon of the Korsars."

"And how do you think this may be done?" asked the ape-man. "Are you convinced of the correctness of Innes' theory that there is an entrance to the inner world at each pole?"

"I am free to confess that I do not know what to believe," replied the American. "But after I received this message from Perry I commenced to investigate and I discovered that the theory of an inhabitable world at the center of the earth with openings leading into it at the north and south poles is no new one and that there is much evidence to support it. I found a very complete exposition of the theory in a book written about 1830 and in another work of more recent time. Therein I found what seemed to be a reasonable explanation of many well-known phenomena that have not been satisfactorily explained by any hypothesis endorsed by science."

"What, for example?" asked Tarzan.

"Well, for example, warm winds and warm ocean currents coming from the north and encountered and reported by practically all arctic explorers; the presence of the limbs and branches of trees with green foliage upon them floating southward from the far north, far above the latitude where any such trees are found upon the outer crust; then there is the phenomenon of the northern lights, which in the light of David Innes' theory may easily be explained as rays of light from the central sun of the inner world, breaking occasionally through the fog and cloud banks above the polar opening. Again there is the pollen, which often thickly covers the snow and ice in portions of the polar regions. This pollen could not come from elsewhere than the inner world. And in addition to all this is the insistence of the far northern tribes of Eskimos that their forefathers came from a country to the north."

"Did not Amundson and Ellsworth in the Norge expedition definitely disprove the theory of a north polar opening in the earth's crust, and have not airplane flights been made over a considerable portion of the hitherto unexplored regions near the pole?" demanded the ape-man.

"The answer to that is that the polar opening is so large that a ship, a dirigible or an airplane could dip down over the edge into it a short distance and return without ever being aware of the fact, but the most tenable theory is that in most instances explorers have merely followed around the outer rim of the orifice, which would largely explain the peculiar and mystifying action of compasses and other scientific instruments at points near the so-called north pole—matters which have greatly puzzled all arctic explorers."

"You are convinced then that there is not only an inner world but that there is an entrance to it at the north pole?" asked Tarzan.

"I am convinced that there is an inner world, but I am not convinced of the existence of a polar opening," replied Gridley. "I can only say that I believe there is sufficient evidence to warrant the organization of an expedition such as I have suggested."

"Assuming that a polar opening into an inner world exists, by just what means do you purpose accomplishing the discovery and exploration of it?"

"The most practical means of transportation that exists today for carrying out my plan would be a specially constructed rigid airship, built along the lines of the modern Zeppelin. Such a ship, using helium gas, would show a higher factor of safety than any other means of transportation at our disposal. I have given the matter considerable thought and I feel sure that if there is such a polar opening, the obstacles that would confront us in an attempt to enter the inner world would be far less than those encountered by the Norge in its famous trip across the pole to Alaska, for there is no question in my mind but that it made a wide detour in following the rim of the polar orifice and covered a far greater distance than we shall have to cover to reach a reasonably safe anchorage below the cold, polar sea that David Innes discovered north of the land of the Korsars before he was finally taken prisoner by them.

"The greatest risk that we would have to face would be a possible inability to return to the outer crust, owing to the depletion of our helium gas that might be made necessary by the maneuvering of the ship. But that is only the same chance of life or death that every explorer and scientific investigator must be willing to assume in the prosecution of his labors. If it were but possible to build a hull sufficiently light, and at the same time sufficiently strong, to withstand atmospheric pressure, we could dispense with both the dangerous hydrogen gas and the rare and expensive helium gas and have the assurance of the utmost safety and maximum of buoyancy in a ship supported entirely by vacuum tanks."

"Perhaps even that is possible," said Tarzan, who was now evincing increasing interest in Gridley's proposition.

The American shook his head. "It may be possible some day," he said, "but not at present with any known material.

Any receptacle having sufficient strength to withstand the atmospheric pressure upon a vacuum would have a weight far too great for the vacuum to lift."

"Perhaps," said Tarzan, "and, again, perhaps not."

"What do you mean?" inquired Gridley.

"What you have just said," replied Tarzan, "reminds me of something that a young friend of mine recently told me. Erich von Harben is something of a scientist and explorer himself, and the last time that I saw him he had just returned from a second expedition into the Wiramwazi Mountains, where he told me that he had discovered a lake-dwelling tribe using canoes made of a metal that was apparently as light as cork and stronger than steel. He brought some samples of the metal back with him, and at the time I last saw him he was conducting some experiments in a little laboratory he has rigged up at his father's mission."

"Where is this man?" demanded Gridley.

"Dr. von Harben's mission is in the Urambi country," replied the ape-man, "about four marches west of where we now are."

Far into the night the two men discussed plans for the project, for Tarzan was now thoroughly interested, and the next day they turned back toward the Urambi country and von Harben's mission, where they arrived on the fourth day and were greeted by Dr. von Harben and his son, Erich, as well as by the latter's wife, the beautiful Favonia of Castrum Mare.

It is not my intention to weary you with a recital of the details of the organization and equipment of the Pellucidarian expedition, although that portion of it which relates to the search for and discovery of the native mine containing the remarkable metal now known as Harbenite, filled as it was with adventure and excitement, is well worth a volume by itself.

While Tarzan and Erich von Harben were locating the mine and transporting the metal to the seacoast, Jason Gridley was in Friedrichshafen in consultation with the engineers of the company he had chosen to construct the specially designed airship in which the attempt was to be made to reach the inner world. Exhaustive tests were made of the samples of Harbenite brought to Friedrichshafen by Jason Gridley. Plans were drawn, and by the time the shipment of the ore arrived everything was in readiness to commence immediate construction, which was carried on secretly. And six months later, when the O-220, as it was officially known, was ready to take to the air, it was generally considered to be nothing more than a new design of the ordinary type of rigid airship, destined to be used as a common carrier upon one of the already numerous commercial airways of Europe.

The great cigar-shaped hull of the O-220 was 997 feet in length and 150 feet in diameter. The interior of the hull was divided into six large, airtight compartments, three of which, running the full length of the ship, were above the medial line and three below. Inside the hull and running along each side of the ship, between the upper and lower vacuum tanks, were long corridors in which were located the engines, motors and pumps, in addition to supplies of gasoline and oil.

The internal location of the engine room was made possible by the elimination of fire risk, which is an ever-present source of danger in airships which depend for their lifting power upon hydrogen gas, as well as to the absolutely fireproof construction of the O-220; every part of which, with the exception of a few cabin fittings and furniture, was of Harbenite, this metal being used throughout except for certain bushings and bearings in motors, generators, and propellers.

Connecting the port and starboard engine and fuel corridors were two transverse corridors, one forward and one aft, while bisecting these transverse corridors were two climbing shafts extending from the bottom of the ship to the top.

The upper end of the forward climbing shaft terminated in a small gun and observation cabin at the top of the ship, along which was a narrow walking-way extending from the forward cabin to a small turret near the tail of the ship, where provision had been made for fixing a machine gun.

The main cabin, running along the keel of the ship, was an integral part of the hull, and because of this entirely rigid construction, which eliminated the necessity for cabins suspended below the hull, the O-220 was equipped with landing gear in the form of six large heavily tired wheels projecting below the bottom of the main cabin. In the extreme stern of the keel cabin a small scout monoplane was carried in such a way that it could be lowered through the bottom of the ship and launched while the O-220 was in flight.

Eight air-cooled motors drove as many propellers, which were arranged in pairs upon either side of the ship and staggered in such a manner that the air from the forward propellers would not interfere with those behind.

The engines, developing 5600 horsepower, were capable of driving the ship at a speed of 105 miles per hour.

In the O-220 the ordinary axial wire, which passes the whole length of the ship through the center, consisted of a tubular shaft of Harbenite from which smaller tubular braces radiated, like the spokes of a wheel, to the tubular girders, to which the Harbenite plates of the outer envelope were welded.

Owing to the extreme lightness of Harbenite, the total weight of the ship was 75 tons, while the total lift of its vacuum tanks was 225 tons.

For purposes of maneuvering the ship and to facilitate landing, each of the vacuum tanks was equipped with a bank of eight air valves operated from the control cabin at the forward end of the keel; while six pumps, three in the starboard and three in the port engine corridors, were designed to expel the air from the tanks when it became necessary to renew the vacuum. Special rudders and elevators were also operated from the forward control cabin as well as from an auxiliary position aft in the port engine corridor, in the event that the control cabin steering gear should break down.

In the main keel cabin were located the quarters for the officers and crew, gun and ammunition room, provision room, galley, additional gasoline and oil storage tanks, and water tanks, the latter so constructed that the contents of any of them might be emptied instantaneously in case of an emergency, while a proportion of the gasoline and oil tanks were slip tanks that might be slipped through the bottom of the ship in cases of extreme emergency when it was necessary instantaneously to reduce the weight of the load.

This, then, briefly, was the great, rigid airship in which Jason Gridley and Tarzan of the Apes hoped to discover the north polar entrance to the inner world and rescue David Innes, Emperor of Pellucidar, from the dungeons of the Korsars.

2

Pellucidar

J UST BEFORE DAYBREAK of a clear June morning, the O-220 moved slowly from its hangar under its own power. Fully loaded and equipped, it was to make its test flight under load conditions identical with those that would obtain when it set forth upon its long journey. The three lower tanks were still filled with air and she carried an excess of water ballast sufficient to overcome her equilibrium, so that while she moved lightly over the ground she moved with entire safety and could be maneuvered almost as handily as an automobile.

As she came into the open her pumps commenced to expel the air from the three lower tanks, and at the same time a portion of her excess water ballast was slowly discharged, and almost immediately the huge ship rose slowly and gracefully from the ground.

The entire personnel of the ship's company during the test flight was the same that had been selected for the expedition. Zuppner, who had been chosen as captain, had been in charge of the construction of the ship and had a considerable part in its designing. There were two mates, Von Horst and Dorf, who had been officers in the Imperial air forces, as also had the navigator, Lieutenant Hines. In addition to these there were twelve engineers and eight mechanics, a negro cook and two Filipino cabin boys.

Tarzan was commander of the expedition, with Jason Gridley as his lieutenant, while the fighting men of the ship consisted of Muviro and nine of his Waziri warriors.

As the ship rose gracefully above the city, Zuppner, who was at the controls, could scarce restrain his enthusiasm.

"The sweetest thing I ever saw!" he exclaimed. "She responds to the lightest touch."

"I am not surprised at that," said Hines; "I knew she'd do it. Why we've got twice the crew we need to handle her."

"There you go again, Lieutenant," said Tarzan, laughing; "but do not think that my insistence upon a large crew was based upon any lack of confidence in the ship. We are going into a strange world. We may be gone a long time. If we reach our destination we shall have fighting, as each of you men who volunteered has been informed many times, so that while we may have twice as many men as we need for the trip in, we may yet find ourselves shorthanded on the return journey, for not all of us will return."

"I suppose you are right," said Hines; "but with the feel of this ship permeating me and the quiet peacefulness of the scene below, danger and death seem remote."

"I hope they are," returned Tarzan, "and I hope that we shall return with every man that goes out with us, but I believe in being prepared and to that end Gridley and I have been studying navigation and we want you to give us a chance at some practical experience before we reach our destination."

Zuppner laughed. "They have you marked already, Hines," he said.

The lieutenant grinned. "I'll teach them all I know," he said; "but I'll bet the best dinner that can be served in Berlin that if this ship returns I'll still be her navigator."

"That is a case of heads-I-win, tails-you-lose," said Gridley.

"And to return to the subject of preparedness," said Tarzan, "I am going to ask you to let my Waziri help the mechanics and engineers. They are highly intelligent men, quick to learn, and if some calamity should overtake us we cannot have too many men familiar with the engines and other machinery of the ship."

"You are right," said Zuppner, "and I shall see that it is done."

The great, shining ship sailed majestically north; Ravensburg fell astern and half an hour later the somber gray ribbon of the Danube lay below them.

The longer they were in the air the more enthusiastic Zuppner became. "I had every confidence in the successful outcome of the trial flight," he said; "but I can assure you that I did not look for such perfection as I find in this ship. It marks a new era in aeronautics, and I am convinced that long before we cover the four hundred miles to Hamburg that we shall have established the entire airworthiness of the O-220 to the entire satisfaction of each of us."

"To Hamburg and return to Friedrichshafen was to have been the route of the trial trip," said Tarzan, "but why turn back at Hamburg?"

The others turned questioning eyes upon him as the purport of his query sank home.

"Yes, why?" demanded Gridley.

Zuppner shrugged his shoulders. "We are fully equipped and provisioned," he said.

"Then why waste eight hundred miles in returning to Friedrichshafen?" demanded Hines.

"If you are all agreeable we shall continue on toward the north," said Tarzan. And so it was that the trial trip of the O-220 became an actual start upon its long journey toward the interior of the earth, and the secrecy that was desired for the expedition was insured.

The plan had been to follow the Tenth Meridian east of Greenwich north to the pole. But to avoid attracting unnecessary notice a slight deviation from this course was found desirable, and the ship passed to the west of Hamburg and out across the waters of the North Sea, and thus due north, passing to the west of Spitsbergen and out across the frozen polar wastes.

Maintaining an average cruising speed of about 75 miles per hour, the O-220 reached the vicinity of the north pole about midnight of the second day, and excitement ran high when Hines announced that in accordance with his calculation they should be directly over the pole. At Tarzan's suggestion the ship circled slowly at an altitude of a few hundred feet above the rough, snow-covered ice.

"We ought to be able to recognize it by the Italian flags," said Zuppner, with a smile. But if any reminders of the passage of the Norge remained below them, they were effectually hidden by the mantle of many snows.

The ship made a single circle above the desolate ice pack before she took up her southerly course along the 170th East Meridian.

From the moment that the ship struck south from the pole Jason Gridley remained constantly with Hines and Zuppner eagerly and anxiously watching the instruments, or gazing down upon the bleak landscape ahead. It was Gridley's belief that the north polar opening lay in the vicinity of 85 north latitude and 170 east longitude. Before him were compass, aneroids, bubble statoscope, airspeed indicator, inclinometers, rise and fall indicator, bearing plate, clock, and thermometers; but the instrument that commanded his closest attention was the compass, for Jason Gridley held a theory and upon the correctness of it depended their success in finding the north polar opening.

For five hours the ship flew steadily toward the south, when she developed an apparent tendency to fall off toward the west.

"Hold her steady, Captain," cautioned Gridley, "for if I am correct we are now going over the lip of the polar opening, and the deviation is in the compass only and not in our course. The further we go along this course the more erratic the compass will become and if we were presently to move upward, or in other words, straight out across the polar opening toward its center, the needle would spin erratically in a circle. But we could not reach the center of the polar opening because of the tremendous altitude which this would require. I believe that we are now on the eastern verge of the opening and if whatever deviation from the present course you make is to the starboard we shall slowly spiral downward into Pellucidar, but your compass will be useless for the next four to six hundred miles."

Zuppner shook his head, dubiously. "If this weather holds, we may be able to do it," he said, "but if it commences to blow I doubt my ability to keep any sort of a course if I am not to follow the compass."

"Do the best you can," said Gridley, "and when in doubt put her to starboard."

So great was the nervous strain upon all of them that for hours at a time scarcely a word was exchanged.

"Look!" exclaimed Hines suddenly. "There is open water just ahead of us."

"That, of course, we might expect," said Zuppner, "even if there is no polar opening, and you know that I have been skeptical about that ever since Gridley first explained his theory to me."

"I think," said Gridley, with a smile, "that really I am the only one in the party who has had any faith at all in the theory, but please do not call it my theory for it is not, and even I should not have been surprised had the theory proven to be a false one. But if any of you has been watching the sun for the last few hours, I think that you will have to agree with me that even though there may be no polar opening into an inner world, there must be a great depression at this point in the earth's crust and that we have gone down into it for a considerable distance, for you will notice that the midnight sun is much lower than it should be and that the further we continue upon this course the lower it drops—eventually it will set completely, and if I am not much mistaken we shall soon see the light of the eternal noonday sun of Pellucidar."

Suddenly the telephone rang and Hines put the receiver to his ear. "Very good, sir," he said, after a moment, and hung up. "It was Von Horst, Captain, reporting from the observation cabin. He has sighted land dead ahead."

"Land!" exclaimed Zuppner. "The only land our chart shows in this direction is Siberia."

"Siberia lies over a thousand miles south of 85, and we cannot be over three hundred miles south of 85," said Gridley.

"Then we have either discovered a new arctic land, or we are approaching the northern frontiers of Pellucidar," said Lieutenant Hines.

"And that is just what we are doing," said Gridley. "Look at your thermometer."

"The devil!" exclaimed Zuppner. "It is only twenty degrees below zero Fahrenheit."

"You can see the land plainly now," said Tarzan. "It looks desolate enough, but there are only little patches of snow here and there."

"This corresponds with the land Innes described north of Korsar," said Gridley.

Word was quickly passed around the ship to the other officers and the crew that there was reason to believe that the land below them was Pellucidar. Excitement ran high, and every man who could spare a moment from his duties was aloft on the walking-way, or peering through portholes for a glimpse of the inner world.

Steadily the O-220 forged southward and just as the rim of the midnight sun disappeared from view below the horizon astern, the glow of Pellucidar's central sun was plainly visible ahead.

The nature of the landscape below was changing rapidly. The barren land had fallen astern, the ship had crossed a range of wooded hills and now before it lay a great forest that stretched on and on seemingly curving upward to be lost eventually in the haze of the distance. This was indeed Pellucidar— the Pellucidar of which Jason Gridley had dreamed.

Beyond the forest lay a rolling plain dotted with clumps of trees, a well-watered plain through which wound numerous streams, which emptied into a large river at its opposite side.

Great herds of game were grazing in the open pasture land and nowhere was there sight of man.

"This looks like heaven to me," said Tarzan of the Apes. "Let us land, Captain."

Slowly the great ship came to earth as air was taken into the lower vacuum tanks.

Short ladders were run out, for the bottom of the cabin was only six feet above the ground, and presently the entire ship's company, with the exception of a watch of an officer and two men, were knee-deep in the lush grasses of Pellucidar.

"I thought we might get some fresh meat," said Tarzan, "but the ship has frightened all the game away."

"From the quantity of it I saw, we shall not have to go far to bag some," said Dorf.

"What we need most right now, however, is rest," said Tarzan. "For weeks every man has been working at high pitch in completing the preparation for the expedition and I doubt if one of us has had over two hours' sleep in the last three days. I suggest that we remain here until we are all thoroughly rested and then take up a systematic search for the city of Korsar."

The plan met with general approval and preparations were made for a stay of several days.

"I believe," said Gridley to Captain Zuppner, "that it would be well to issue strict orders that no one is to leave the ship, or rather its close vicinity, without permission from you and that no one be allowed to venture far afield except in parties commanded by an officer, for we have every assurance that we shall meet with savage men and far more savage beasts everywhere within Pellucidar."

"I hope that you will except me from that order," said Tarzan, smiling.

"I believe that you can take care of yourself in any country," said Zuppner.

"And I can certainly hunt to better effect alone than I can with a party," said the ape-man.

"In any event," continued Zuppner, "the order comes from you as commander, and no one will complain if you exempt yourself from its provisions since I am sure that none of the rest of us is particularly anxious to wander about Pellucidar alone."

Officers and men, with the exception of the watch, which changed every four hours, slept the clock around.

Tarzan of the Apes was the first to complete his sleep and leave the ship. He had discarded the clothing that had encumbered and annoyed him since he had left his own African jungle to join in the preparation of the O-220, and it was no faultlessly attired Englishman that came from the cabin and dropped to the ground below, but instead an almost naked and primitive warrior, armed with hunting knife, spear, a bow and arrows, and the long rope which Tarzan always carried, for in the hunt he preferred the weapons of his youth to the firearms of civilization.

Lieutenant Dorf, the only officer on duty at the time, saw him depart and watched with unfeigned admiration as the black-haired jungle lord moved across the open plain and disappeared in the forest.

There were trees that were familiar to the eyes of the ape-man, and trees such as he had never seen before, but it was a forest and that was enough to lure Tarzan of the Apes and permit him to forget the last few weeks that had been spent amidst the distasteful surroundings of civilization. He was happy to be free from the ship, too, and, while he liked all his companions, he was yet glad to be alone.

In the first flight of his newfound freedom Tarzan was like a boy released from school. Unhampered by the hated vestments of civilization, out of sight of anything that might even remotely remind him of the atrocities with which man scars the face of nature, he filled his lungs with the free air of Pellucidar, leaped into a nearby tree and swung away through the forest, his only concern for the moment the joyousness of exultant vitality and life. On he sped through the primeval forest of Pellucidar. Strange birds, startled by his swift and silent passage, flew screaming from his path, and strange beasts slunk to cover beneath him. But Tarzan did not care; he was not hunting; he was not even searching for the new in this new world. For the moment he was only living.

While this mood dominated him Tarzan gave no thought to the passage of time any more than he had given thought to the timelessness of Pellucidar, whose noonday sun, hanging perpetually at zenith, gives a lie to us of the outer crust who rush frantically through life in mad and futile effort to beat the earth in her revolutions. Nor did Tarzan reckon upon distance or direction, for such matters were seldom the subjects of conscious consideration upon the part of the ape-man, whose remarkable ability to meet every and any emergency he unconsciously attributed to powers that lay within himself, not stopping to consider that in his own jungle he relied upon the friendly sun and moon and stars as guides by day and night, and to the myriad familiar things that spoke to him in a friendly, voiceless language that only the jungle people can interpret.

As his mood changed Tarzan reduced his speed, and presently he dropped to the ground in a well-marked game trail. Now he let his eyes take in the new wonders all about him. He noticed the evidences of great age as betokened by the enormous size of the trees and the hoary stems of the great vines that clung to many of them—suggestions of age that made his own jungle seem modern—and he marveled at the gorgeous flowers that bloomed in riotous profusion upon every hand, and then of a sudden something gripped him about the body and snapped him high into the air.

Tarzan of the Apes had nodded. His mind occupied with the wonders of this new world had permitted a momentary relaxation of that habitual wariness that distinguishes creatures of the wild.

Almost in the instant of its occurrence the ape-man realized what had befallen him. Although he could easily imagine its disastrous sequel, the suggestion of a smile touched his lips—a rueful smile—and one that was perhaps tinged with disgust for himself, for Tarzan of the Apes had been caught in as primitive a snare as was ever laid for unwary beasts.

A rawhide noose, attached to the downbent limb of an overhanging tree, had been buried in the trail along which he had been passing and he had struck the trigger—that was the whole story. But its sequel might have had less unfortunate possibilities had the noose not pinioned his arms to his sides as it closed about him.

He hung about six feet above the trail, caught securely about the hips, the noose imprisoning his arms between elbows and wrists and pinioning them securely to his sides. And to add to his discomfort and helplessness, he swung head downward, spinning dizzily like a human plumb-bob.

He tried to draw an arm from the encircling noose so that he might reach his hunting knife and free himself, but the weight of his body constantly drew the noose more tightly about him and every effort upon his part seemed but to strengthen the relentless grip of the rawhide that was pressing deep into his flesh.

He knew that the snare meant the presence of men and that doubtless they would soon come to inspect their noose, for his own knowledge of primitive hunting taught him that they would not leave their snares long untended, since in the event of a catch, if they would have it at all, they must claim it soon lest it fall prey to carnivorous beasts or birds. He wondered what sort of people they were and if he might not make friends with them, but whatever they were he hoped that they would come before the beasts of prey came. And while such thoughts were running through his mind, his keen ears caught the sound of approaching footsteps, but they were not the steps of men. Whatever was approaching was approaching across the wind and he could detect no scent spoor; nor, upon the other hand, he realized, could the beast scent him. It was coming leisurely and as it neared him, but before it came in sight along the trail, he knew that it was a hoofed animal and, therefore, that he had little reason to fear its approach unless, indeed, it might prove to be some strange Pellucidarian creature with characteristics entirely unlike any that he knew upon the outer crust.

But even as he permitted these thoughts partially to reassure him, there came strongly to his nostrils a scent that always caused the short hairs upon his head to rise, not in fear but in natural reaction to the presence of an hereditary enemy. It was not an odor that he had ever smelled before. It was not the scent spoor of Numa the lion, nor Sheeta the leopard, but it was the scent spoor of some sort of great cat. And now he could hear its almost silent approach through the underbrush and he knew that it was coming down toward the trail, lured either by knowledge of his presence or by that of the beast whose approach Tarzan had been awaiting.

It was the latter who came first into view—a great oxlike animal with widespread horns and shaggy coat—a huge bull that advanced several yards along the trail after Tarzan discovered it before it saw the ape-man dangling in front of it. It was the thag of Pellucidar, the Bos Primigenus of the paleontologist of the outer crust, a long extinct progenitor of the bovine races of our own world.

For a moment it stood eyeing the man dangling in its path.

Tarzan remained very quiet. He did not wish to frighten it

away for he realized that one of them must be the prey of the carnivore sneaking up on them, but if he expected the thag to be frightened he soon realized his error in judgment for, uttering low grumblings, the great bull pawed the earth with a front foot, and then, lowering his massive horns, gored it angrily, and the ape-man knew that he was working his short temper up to charging pitch; nor did it seem that this was to take long for already he was advancing menacingly to the accompaniment of thunderous bellowing. His tail was up and his head down as he broke into the trot that preluded the charge.

The ape-man realized that if he was ever struck by those massive horns or that heavy head, his skull would be crushed like an eggshell.

The dizzy spinning that had been caused by the first stretching of the rawhide to his weight had lessened to a gentle turning motion, so that sometimes he faced the thag and sometimes in the opposite direction. The utter helplessness of his position galled the ape-man and gave him more concern than any consideration of impending death. From childhood he had walked hand in hand with the Grim Reaper and he had looked upon death in so many forms that it held no terror for him. He knew that it was the final experience of all created things, that it must as inevitably come to him as to others and while he loved life and did not wish to die, its mere approach induced within him no futile hysteria. But to die without a chance to fight for life was not such an end as Tarzan of the Apes would have chosen. And now, as his body slowly revolved and his eyes were turned away from the charging thag, his heart sank at the thought that he was not even to be vouchsafed the meager satisfaction of meeting death face to face.

In the brief instant that he waited for the impact, the air was rent by as horrid a scream as had ever broken upon the ears of the ape-man and the bellowing of the bull rose suddenly to a higher pitch and mingled with that other awesome sound.

Once more the dangling body of the ape-man revolved and his eyes fell upon such a scene as had not been vouchsafed to men of the outer world for countless ages.

Upon the massive shoulders and neck of the great thag clung a tiger of such huge proportions that Tarzan could scarce credit the testimony of his own eyes. Great saberlike tusks, projecting from the upper jaw, were buried deep in the neck of the bull, which, instead of trying to escape, had stopped in its tracks and was endeavoring to dislodge the great beast of prey, swinging its huge horns backward in an attempt to rake the living death from its shoulders, or again shaking its whole body violently for the same purpose and all the while bellowing in pain and rage.

Gradually the saber-tooth changed its position until it had attained a hold suited to its purpose. Then with lightninglike swiftness it swung back a great forearm and delivered a single, terrific blow on the side of the thag's head—a titanic blow that crushed that mighty skull and dropped the huge bull dead in its tracks. And then the carnivore settled down to feast upon its kill.

During the battle the saber-tooth had not noticed the ape-man; nor was it until after he had commenced to feed upon the thag that his eye was attracted by the revolving body swinging above the trail a few yards away. Instantly the beast stopped feeding; his head lowered and flattened, his upper lip turned back in a hideous snarl. He watched the ape-man. Low, menacing growls rumbled from his cavernous throat; his long, sinuous tail lashed angrily as slowly he arose from the body of his kill and advanced toward Tarzan of the Apes.

3

The Great Cats

THE EBBING TIDE of the great war had left human flotsam stranded upon many an unfamiliar beach. In its full flow it had lifted Robert Jones, high private in the ranks of a labor battalion, from uncongenial surroundings and landed him in a prison camp behind the enemy line. Here his good nature won him friends and favors, but neither one nor the other served to obtain his freedom. Robert Jones seemed to have been lost in the shuffle. And finally, when the evacuation of the prison had been completed, Robert Jones still remained, but he was not downhearted. He had learned the language of his captors and had made many friends among them. They found him a job and Robert Jones of Alabama was content to remain where he was. He had been graduated from body servant to cook of an officers' mess and it was in this capacity that he had come under the observation of Captain Zuppner, who had drafted him for the O-220 expedition.

Robert Jones yawned, stretched, turned over in his narrow berth aboard the O-220, opened his eyes and sat up with an exclamation of surprise. He jumped to the floor and stuck his head out of an open port.

"Lawd!" he exclaimed; "you all suah done overslep' yo'sef."

For a moment he gazed up at the noonday sun shining down upon him and then, hastily dressing, hurried into his galley.

" 'S funny," he soliloquized; "dey ain't no one stirrin'—mus' all of overslep' demsef." He looked at the clock on the galley wall. The hour hand pointed to six. He cocked his ear and listened. "She ain't stopped," he muttered. Then he went to the door that opened from the galley through the ship's side and pushed it back. Leaning far out he looked up again at the sun. Then he shook his head. "Dey's sumpin wrong," he said. "Ah dunno whether to cook breakfas', dinner, or supper."

Jason Gridley, emerging from his cabin, sauntered down the narrow corridor toward the galley. "Good morning, Bob!" he said, stopping in the open doorway. "What's the chance for a bite of breakfast?"

"Did you all say breakfas', suh?" inquired Robert.

"Yes," replied Gridley; "just toast and coffee and a couple of eggs—anything you have handy."

"Ah knew it!" the man exclaimed. "Ah knew dat ol' clock couldn't be wrong, but Mistah Sun he suah gone haywire."

Gridley grinned. "I'll drop down and have a little walk," he said. "I'll be back in fifteen minutes. Have you seen anything of Lord Greystoke?"

"No suh, Ah ain't seen nothin' o' Ta'zan sence yesterday."

"I wondered," said Gridley; "he is not in his cabin."

For fifteen minutes Gridley walked briskly about in the vicinity of the ship. When he returned to the mess room he found Zuppner and Dorf awaiting breakfast and greeted them with a pleasant "good morning."

"I don't know whether it's good morning or good evening," said Zuppner.

"We have been here twelve hours," said Dorf, "and it is just the same time that it was when we arrived. I have been on watch for the last four hours and if it hadn't been for the chronometer I could not swear that I had been on fifteen minutes or that I had not been on a week."

"It certainly induces a feeling of unreality that is hard to explain," said Gridley.

"Where is Greystoke?" asked Zuppner. "He is usually an early riser."

"I was just asking Bob," said Gridley, "but he has not seen him."

"He left the ship shortly after I came on watch," said Dorf. "I should say about three hours ago, possibly longer. I saw him cross the open country and enter the forest."

"I wish he had not gone out alone," said Gridley.

"He strikes me as a man who can take care of himself," said Zuppner.

"I have seen some things during the last four hours," said Dorf, "that make me doubt whether any man can take care of himself alone in this world, especially one armed only with the primitive weapons that Greystoke carried with him."

"You mean that he carried no firearms?" demanded Zuppner.

"He was armed with a bow and arrows, a spear and a rope," said Dorf, "and I think he carried a hunting knife as well. But he might as well have had nothing but a peashooter if he met some of the things I have seen since I went on watch."

"What do you mean?" demanded Zuppner. "What have you seen?"

Dorf grinned sheepishly. "Honestly, Captain, I hate to tell you," he said, "for I'm damned if I believe it myself."

"Well, out with it," exclaimed Zuppner. "We will make allowances for your youth and for the effect that the sun and horizon of Pellucidar may have had upon your eyesight or your veracity."

"Well," said Dorf, "about an hour ago a bear passed within a hundred yards of the ship."

"There is nothing remarkable about that," said Zuppner.

"There was a great deal that was remarkable about the bear, however," said Dorf.

"In what way?" asked Gridley.

"It was fully as large as an ox," said Dorf, "and if I were going out after bear in this country I should want to take along field artillery."

"Was that all you saw—just a bear?" asked Zuppner.

"No" said Dorf, "I saw tigers, not one but fully a dozen, and they were as much larger than our Bengal tigers as the bear was larger than any bear of the outer crust that I have ever seen. They were perfectly enormous and they were armed with the most amazing fangs you ever saw—great curved fangs that extended from their upper jaws to lengths of from eight inches to a foot. They came down to this stream here to drink and then wandered away, some of them toward the forest and some down toward that big river yonder."

"Greystoke couldn't do much against such creatures as those even if he had carried a rifle," said Zuppner.

"If he was in the forest, he could escape them," said Gridley.

Zuppner shook his head. "I don't like the looks of it," he said. "I wish that he had not gone out alone."

"The bear and the tigers were bad enough," continued Dorf, "but I saw another creature that to me seemed infinitely worse."

Robert, who was more or less a privileged character, had entered from the galley and was listening with wide-eyed interest to Dorf's account of the creatures he had seen, while Victor, one of the Filipino cabin boys, served the officers.

"Yes," continued Dorf, "I saw a mighty strange creature. It flew directly over the ship and I had an excellent view of it. At first I thought that it was a bird, but when it approached more closely I saw that it was a winged reptile. It had a long, narrow head and it flew so close that I could see its great jaws, armed with an infinite number of long, sharp teeth. Its head was elongated above the eyes and came to a sharp point. It was perfectly immense and must have had a wingspread of at least twenty feet. While I was watching it, it dropped suddenly to earth only a short distance beyond the ship, and when it arose again it was carrying in its talons some animal that must have been fully as large as a good-sized sheep, with which it flew away without apparent effort. That the creature is carnivorous is evident as is also the fact that it has sufficient strength to carry away a man."

Robert Jones covered his large mouth with a pink palm and with hunched and shaking shoulders turned and tiptoed from the room. Once in the galley with the door closed, he gave himself over to unrestrained mirth.

"What is the matter with you?" asked Victor.

"Lawd-a-massy!" exclaimed Robert. "Ah allus thought some o' dem gem'n in dat dere Adventurous Club in Bummingham could lie some, but, shucks, dey ain't in it with this

Lieutenant Dorf. Did you all heah him tell about dat flyin' snake what carries off sheep?"

But back in the mess room Dorf's statement was taken more seriously.

"That would be a pterodactyl," said Zuppner.

"Yes," replied Dorf. "I classified it as a Pteranodon."

"Don't you think we ought to send out a search party?" asked Gridley.

"I am afraid Greystoke would not like it," replied Zuppner.

"It could go out under the guise of a hunting party," suggested Dorf.

"If he has not returned within an hour," said Zuppner, "we shall have to do something of the sort."

Hines and Von Horst now entered the mess room, and when they learned of Tarzan's absence from the ship and had heard from Dorf a description of some of the animals that he might have encountered, they were equally as apprehensive as the others of his safety.

"We might cruise around a bit, sir," suggested Von Horst to Zuppner.

"But suppose he returns to this spot during our absence?" asked Gridley.

"Could you return the ship to this anchorage again?" inquired Zuppner.

"I doubt it," replied the lieutenant. "Our instruments are almost worthless under the conditions existing in Pellucidar."

"Then we had better remain where we are," said Gridley, "until he returns."

"But if we send a searching party after him on foot, what assurance have we that it will be able to find its way back to the ship?" demanded Zuppner.

"That will not be so difficult," said Gridley. "We can always blaze our trail as we go and thus easily retrace our steps."

"Yes, that is so," agreed Zuppner.

"Suppose," said Gridley, "that Von Horst and I go out with Muviro and his Waziri. They are experienced trackers, prime fighting men, and they certainly know the jungle."

"Not this jungle," said Dorf.

"But at least they know any jungle better than the rest of us," insisted Gridley.

"I think your plan is a good one," said Zuppner, "and anyway as you are in command now, the rest of us gladly place ourselves under your orders."

"The conditions that confront us here are new to all of us," said Gridley. "Nothing that any one of us can suggest or command can be based upon any personal experience or knowledge that the rest do not possess, and in matters of this kind I think that we had better reach our decision after full discussion rather than to depend blindly upon official priority of authority."

"That has been Greystroke's policy," said Zuppner, "and it has made it very easy and pleasant for all of us. I quite agree with you, but I can think of no more feasible plan than that which you have suggested."

"Very good," said Gridley. "Will you accompany me, Lieutenant?" he asked, turning to Von Horst.

The officer grinned. "Will I?" he exclaimed. "I should never have forgiven you if you had left me out of it."

"Fine," said Gridley. "And now, I think, we might as well make our preparations at once and get as early a start as possible. See that the Waziri have eaten, Lieutenant, and tell Muviro that I want them armed with rifles. These fellows can use them all right, but they rather look with scorn upon anything more modern than their war spears and arrows."

"Yes, I discovered that," said Hines. "Muviro told me a few days ago that his people consider firearms as something of an admission of cowardice. He told me that they use them for target practice, but when they go out after lions or rhino they leave their rifles behind and take their spears and arrows."

"After they have seen what I saw," said Dorf, "they will have more respect for an express rifle."

"See that they take plenty of ammunition, Von Horst," said Gridley, "for from what I have seen in this country we shall not have to carry any provisions."

"A man who could not live off this country would starve to death in a meat market," said Zuppner.

Von Horst left to carry out Gridley's orders while the latter returned to his cabin to prepare for the expedition.

The officers and crew remaining with the O-220 were all on hand to bid farewell to the expedition starting out in search of Tarzan of the Apes, and as the ten stalwart Waziri warriors marched away behind Gridley and Von Horst, Robert Jones, watching from the galley door, swelled with pride. "All dem flyin' snakes bettah clear out de country now," he exclaimed. With the others Robert watched the little party as it crossed the plain and until it had disappeared within the dark precincts of the forest upon the opposite side. Then he glanced up at the noonday sun, shook his head, elevated his palms in resignation and turned back into his galley.

Almost immediately after the party had left the ship, Gridley directed Muviro to take the lead and watch for Tarzan's trail since, of the entire party, he was the most experienced tracker; nor did the Waziri chieftain have any difficulty in following the spoor of the ape-man across the plain and into the forest, but here, beneath a great tree, it disappeared.

"The Big Bwana took to the trees here," said Muviro, "and no man lives who can follow his spoor through the lower, the middle, or the upper terraces."

"What do you suggest, then, Muviro?" asked Gridley.

"If this were his own jungle," replied the warrior, "I should feel sure that when he took to the trees he would move in a straight line toward the place he wished to go; unless he happened to be hunting, in which case his direction would be influenced by the sign and scent of game."

"Doubtless he was hunting here," said Von Horst.

"If he was hunting," said Muviro, "he would have moved in a straight line until he caught the scent spoor of game or came to a well-beaten game trail."

"And then what would he do?" asked Gridley.

"He might wait above the trail," replied Muviro, "or he might follow it. In a new country like this, I think he would follow it, for he has always been interested in exploring every new country he entered."

"Then let us push straight into the forest in this same direction until we strike a game trail," said Gridley.

Muviro and three of his warriors went ahead, cutting brush where it was necessary and blazing the trees at frequent intervals that they might more easily retrace their steps to the ship. With the aid of a small pocket compass Gridley directed the line of advance, which otherwise it would have been difficult to hold accurately beneath that eternal noonday sun, whose warm rays filtered down through the foliage of the forest.

"God! What a forest!" exclaimed Von Horst. "To search for a man here is like the proverbial search for the needle in a haystack."

"Except," said Gridley, "that one might stand a slight chance of finding the needle."

"Perhaps we had better fire a shot occasionally," suggested Von Horst.

"Excellent," said Gridley. "The rifles carry a much heavier charge and make a louder report than our revolvers."

After warning the others of his intention, he directed one of the blacks to fire three shots at intervals of a few seconds, for neither Gridley nor Von Horst was armed with rifles, each of the officers carrying two .45 caliber Colts. Thereafter, at intervals of about half an hour, a single shot was fired, but as the searching party forced its way on into the forest each of its members became gloomily impressed with the futility of their search.

Presently the nature of the forest changed. The trees were set less closely together and the underbrush, while still forming an almost impenetrable screen, was less dense than it had been heretofore and here they came upon a wide game trail, worn by countless hooves and padded feet to a depth of two feet or more below the surface of the surrounding ground, and here Jason Gridley blundered.

"We won't bother about blazing the trees as long as we follow this trail," he said to Muviro, "except at such places as it may fork or be crossed by other trails."

It was, after all, a quite natural mistake since a few blazed trees along the trail would not serve any purpose in following it back when they wished to return.

The going here was easier and as the Waziri warriors swung along at a brisk pace, the miles dropped quickly behind them and already had the noonday sun so cast its spell upon them that the element of time seemed not to enter into their calculations, while the teeming life about them absorbed the attention of blacks and whites alike.

Strange monkeys, some of them startlingly manlike in appearance and of large size, watched them pass. Birds of both gay and somber plumage scattered protestingly before their advance, and again dim bulks loomed through the undergrowth and the sound of padded feet was everywhere.

At times they would pass through a stretch of forest as silent as the tomb, and then again they seemed to be surrounded by a bedlam of hideous growls and roars and screams.

"I'd like to see some of those fellows," said Von Horst, after a particularly savage outburst of sound.

"I am surprised that we haven't," replied Gridley; "but I imagine that they are a little bit leery of us right now, not alone on account of our numbers but because of the, to them strange and unfamiliar, odors which must surround us. These would naturally increase the suspicion which must have been aroused by the sound of our shots."

"Have you noticed," said Von Horst, "that most of the noise seems to come from behind us; I mean the more savage, growling sounds. I have heard squeals and noises that sounded like the trumpeting of elephants to the right and to the left and ahead, but only an occasional growl or roar seems to come from these directions and then always at a considerable distance."

"How do you account for it?" asked Gridley.

"I can't account for it," replied Von Horst. "It is as though we were moving along in the center of a procession with all the savage carnivores behind us."

"This perpetual noonday sun has its compensations," remarked Gridley with a laugh, "for at least it insures that we shall not have to spend the night here."

At that instant the attention of the two men was attracted by an exclamation from one of the Waziri behind them. "Look, Bwana! Look!" cried the man, pointing back along the trail. Following the direction of the Waziri's extended finger, Gridley and Von Horst saw a huge beast slinking slowly along the trail in their rear.

"God!" exclaimed Von Horst, "and I thought Dorf was exaggerating."

"It doesn't seem possible," exclaimed Gridley, "that five hundred miles below our feet automobiles are dashing through crowded streets lined by enormous buildings; that there the telegraph, the telephone and the radio are so commonplace as to excite no comment; that countless thousands live out their entire lives without ever having to use a weapon in self-defense, and yet at the same instant we stand here facing a saber-tooth tiger in surroundings that may not have existed upon the outer crust for a million years."

"Look at them!" exclaimed Von Horst. "If there is one there are a dozen of them."

"Shall we fire, Bwana?" asked one of the Waziri.

"Not yet," said Gridley. "Close up and be ready. They seem to be only following us."

Slowly the party fell back, a line of Waziri in the rear facing the tigers and backing slowly away from them. Muviro dropped back to Gridley's side.

"For a long time, Bwana," he said, "there has been the spoor of many elephants in the trail, or spoor that looked like the spoor of elephants, though it was different. And just now I sighted some of the beasts ahead. I could not make them out distinctly, but if they are not elephants they are very much like them."

"We seem to be between the devil and the deep sea," said Von Horst.

"And there are either elephants or tigers on either side of us," said Muviro. "I can hear them moving through the brush."

Perhaps the same thought was in the minds of all these men, that they might take to the trees, but for some reason no one expressed it. And so they continued to move slowly along the trail until suddenly it broke into a large, open area in the forest, where the ground was scantily covered with brush and there were few trees. Perhaps a hundred acres were included in the clearing and then the forest commenced again upon all sides.

And into the clearing, along numerous trails that seemed to

center at this spot, came as strange a procession as the eyes of these men had ever rested upon. There were great oxlike creatures with shaggy coats and wide-spreading horns. There were red deer and sloths of gigantic size. There were mastodon and mammoth, and a huge, elephantine creature that resembled an elephant and yet did not seem to be an elephant at all. Its great head was four feet long and three feet wide. It had a short, powerful trunk and from its lower jaw mighty tusks curved downward, their points bending inward toward the body. At the shoulder it stood at least ten feet above the ground, and in length it must have been fully twenty feet. But what resemblance it bore to an elephant was lessened by its small, piglike ears.

The two white men, momentarily forgetting the tigers behind them in their amazement at the sight ahead, halted and looked with wonder upon the huge gathering of creatures within the clearing.

"Did you ever see anything like it?" exclaimed Gridley.

"No, nor anyone else," replied Von Horst.

"I could catalog a great many of them," said Gridley, "although practically all are extinct upon the outer crust. But that fellow there gets me," and he pointed to the elephantine creature with the downward-pointing tusks.

"A dinotherium of the Miocene," said Von Horst.

Muviro had stopped beside the two whites and was gazing in wide-eyed astonishment at the scene before him.

"Well," asked Gridley, "what do you make of it, Muviro?"

"I think I understand now, Bwana," replied the black, "and if we are ever going to escape our one chance is to cross that clearing as quickly as possible. The great cats are herding these creatures here and presently there will be such a killing as the eyes of man have never before seen. If we are not killed by the cats, we shall be trampled to death by these beasts in their efforts to escape or to fight the tigers."

"I believe you are right, Muviro," said Gridley.

"There is an opening just ahead of us," said Von Horst.

Gridley called the men around him and pointed out across the clearing to the forest upon the opposite side. "Apparently our only chance now," he said, "is to cross before the cats close in on these beasts. We have already come into the clearing too far to try to take refuge in the trees on this side for the saber-tooths are too close. Stick close together and fire at nothing unless we are charged."

"Look!" exclaimed Von Horst. "The tigers are entering the clearing from all sides. They have surrounded their quarry."

"There is still the one opening ahead of us, Bwana," said Muviro.

Already the little party was moving slowly across the clearing, which was covered with nervous beasts moving irritably to and fro, their whole demeanor marked by nervous apprehension. Prior to the advent of the tigers the animals had been moving quietly about, some of them grazing on the short grass of the clearing or upon the leaves and twigs of the scattered trees growing in it; but with the appearance of the first of the carnivores their attitude changed. A huge bull mastodon raised his trunk and trumpeted shrilly, and instantly every herbivore was on the alert. And as eyes or nostrils detected the presence of the great cats, or the beasts became excited by the excitement of their fellows, each added his voice to the pandemonium that now reigned. To the squealing, trumpeting, and bellowing of the quarry were added the hideous growls and roars of the carnivores.

"Look at those cats!" cried Von Horst. "There must be hundreds of them." Nor was his estimate an exaggeration for from all sides of the clearing, with the exception of a single point opposite them, the cats were emerging from the forest and starting to circle the herd. That they did not rush it immediately evidenced their respect for the huge beasts they had corraled, the majority of which they would not have dared to attack except in superior numbers.

Now a mammoth, a giant bull with tail raised and ears upcocked, curled his trunk above his head and charged. But a score of the giant cats, growling hideously, sprang to meet him, and the bull, losing his nerve, wheeled in a wide circle and returned to the herd. Had he gone through that menacing line of fangs and talons, as with his great size and weight and strength he might have done, he would have opened a hole through which a stampede of the other animals would have carried the bulk of them to safety.

The frightened herbivores, their attention centered upon the menacing tigers, paid little attention to the insignificant man-things passing among them. But there were some exceptions. A thag, bellowing and pawing the earth directly in their line of march, terrified by the odor of the carnivores and aroused and angered by the excited trumpeting and squealing of the creatures about him, seeking to vent his displeasure upon something, lowered his head and charged them. A Waziri warrior raised his rifle to his shoulder and fired, and a prehistoric Bos Primigenus crashed to the impact of a modern bullet.

As the report of the rifle sounded above the other noises of the clearing, the latter were momentarily stilled, and the full attention of hunters and hunted was focused upon the little band of men, so puny and insignificant in the presence of the mighty beasts of another day. A dinotherium, his little ears up-cocked, his tail stiffly erect, walked slowly toward them. Almost immediately others followed his example until it seemed that the whole aggregation was converging upon them. The forest was yet a hundred yards away as Jason Gridley realized the seriousness of the emergency that now confronted them.

"We shall have to run for it," he said. "Give them a volley, and then beat it for the trees. If they charge, it will have to be every man for himself."

The Waziri wheeled and faced the slowly advancing herd and then, at Gridley's command, they fired. The thunderous volley had its effect upon the advancing beasts. They hesitated and then turned and retreated; but behind them were the carnivores. And once again they swung back in the direction of the men, who were now moving rapidly toward the forest.

"Here they come!" cried Von Horst. And a backward glance revealed the fact that the entire herd, goaded to terror by the tigers behind them, had broken into a mad stampede. Whether or not it was a direct charge upon the little party of men is open to question, but the fact that they lay in its path was sufficient to seal their doom if they were unable to reach the safety of the forest ahead of the charging quadrupeds.

"Give them another volley!" cried Gridley. And again the Waziri turned and fired. A dinotherium, a thag, and two mammoths stumbled and fell to the ground, but the remainder of the herd did not pause. Leaping over the carcasses of their fallen comrades they thundered down upon the fleeing men.

It was now, in truth, every man for himself, and so close pressed were they that even the brave Waziri threw away their rifles as useless encumbrances to flight.

Several of the red deer, swifter in flight than the other members of the herd, had taken the lead, and, stampeding through the party, scattered them to left and right.

Gridley and Von Horst were attempting to cover the retreat of the Waziri and check the charge of the stampeding animals with their revolvers. They succeeded in turning a few of the leaders, but presently a great, red stag passed between them, forcing them to jump quickly apart to escape his heavy antlers, and behind him swept a nightmare of terrified beasts forcing them still farther apart.

Not far from Gridley grew a single, giant tree, a short distance from the edge of the clearing, and finding himself alone and cut off from further retreat, the American turned and ran for it, while Von Horst was forced to bolt for the jungle which was now almost within reach.

Bowled over by the huge sloth, Gridley scrambled to his feet, and, passing in front of a fleeing mastodon, reached the tree just as the main body of the stampeding herd closed about it. Its great bole gave him momentary protection and an instant later he had scrambled among its branches.

Instantly his first thought was for his fellows, but where they had been a moment before was now only a solid mass of leaping, plunging, terrified beasts. No sign of a human being was anywhere to be seen and Gridley knew that no living thing could have survived the trampling of those incalculable tons of terrified flesh.

Some of them, he knew, must have reached the forest, but he doubted that all had come through in safety and he feared particularly for Von Horst, who had been some little distance in rear of the Waziri.

The eyes of the American swept back over the clearing to

observe such a scene as probably in all the history of the world had never before been vouchsafed to the eyes of man. Literally thousands of creatures, large and small, were following their leaders in a break for life and liberty, while upon their flanks and at their rear hundreds of savage saber-tooth tigers leaped upon them, dragging down the weaker, battling with the stronger, leaving the maimed and crippled behind that they might charge into the herd again and drag down others.

The mad rush of the leaders across the clearing had been checked as they entered the forest, and now those in the rear were forced to move more slowly, but in their terror they sought to clamber over the backs of those ahead. Red deer leaped upon the backs of mastodons and fled across the heaving bodies beneath them, as a mountain goat might leap from rock to rock. Mammoths raised their huge bulks upon lesser animals and crushed them to the ground. Tusks and horns were red with gore as the maddened beasts battled for their lives. The scene was sickening in its horror, and yet fascinating in its primitive strength and savagery—and everywhere were the great, savage cats.

Slowly they were cutting into the herd from both sides in an effort to encircle a portion of it and at last they were successful, though within the circle there remained but a few scattered beasts that were still unmaimed or uncrippled. And then the great tigers turned upon these, closing in and drawing tighter their hideous band of savage fury.

In twos and threes and scores they leaped upon the remaining beasts and dragged them down until the sole creature remaining alive within their circle was a gigantic bull mammoth. His shaggy coat was splashed with blood and his tusks were red with gore. Trumpeting, he stood at bay, a magnificent picture of primordial power, of sagacity, of courage.

The heart of the American went out to that lone warrior trumpeting his challenge to overwhelming odds in the face of certain doom.

By hundreds the carnivores were closing in upon the great bull; yet it was evident that even though they outnumbered him so overwhelmingly, they still held him in vast respect. Growling and snarling, a few of them slunk in stealthy circles about him, and as he wheeled about with them, three of them charged him from the rear. With a swiftness that matched their own, the pachyderm wheeled to meet them. Two of them he caught upon his tusks and tossed them high into the air, and at the same instant a score of others rushed him from each side and from the rear and fastened themselves to his back and flanks. Down he went as though struck by lightning, squatting quickly upon his haunches and rolling over backward, crushing a dozen tigers before they could escape.

Gridley could scarce repress a cheer as the great fellow staggered to his feet and threw himself again upon the opposite side to the accompaniment of hideous screams of pain and anger from the tigers he pinioned beneath him. But now he was gushing blood from a hundred wounds, and other scores of the savage carnivores were charging him.

Though he put up a magnificent battle the end was inevitable and at last they dragged him down, tearing him to pieces while he yet struggled to rise again and battle with them.

And then commenced the aftermath as the savage beasts fought among themselves for possession of their prey. For even though there was flesh to more than surfeit them all, in their greed, jealousy, and ferocity, they must still battle one with another.

That they had paid heavily for their meat was evident by the carcasses of the tigers strewn about the clearing and as the survivors slowly settled down to feed, there came the jackals, the hyaenodons, and the wild dogs to feast upon their leavings.

4

The Sagoths

A S THE GREAT cat slunk toward him, Tarzan of the Apes realized that at last he faced inevitable death, yet even in that last moment of life the emotion which dominated him was one of admiration for the magnificent beast drawing angrily toward him.

Tarzan of the Apes would have preferred to die fighting, if he must die; yet he felt a certain thrill as he contemplated the magnificence of the great beast that Fate had chosen to terminate his earthly career. He felt no fear, but a certain sense of anticipation of what would follow after death. The Lord of the Jungle subscribed to no creed. Tarzan of the Apes was not a church man; yet like the majority of those who have always lived close to nature he was, in a sense, intensely religious. His intimate knowledge of the stupendous forces of nature, of her wonders and her miracles had impressed him with the fact that their ultimate origin lay far beyond the conception of the finite mind of man, and thus incalculably remote from the farthest bounds of science. When he thought of God he liked to think of Him primitively, as a personal God. And while he realized that he knew nothing of such matters, he liked to believe that after death he would live again.

Many thoughts passed quickly through his mind as the saber-tooth advanced upon him. He was watching the long, glistening fangs that so soon were to be buried in his flesh when his attention was attracted by a sound among the trees about him. That the great cat had heard too was evident, for it stopped in its tracks and gazed up into the foliage of the trees above. And then Tarzan heard a rustling in the branches directly overhead, and looking up he saw what appeared to be a gorilla glaring down upon him.

Two more savage faces showed through the foliage above him and then in other trees about he caught glimpses of similar shaggy forms and fierce faces. He saw that they were like gorillas, and yet unlike them; that in some respects they were more man than gorilla, and in others more gorilla than man. He caught glimpses of great clubs wielded by hairy hands, and when his eyes returned to the saber-tooth he saw that the great beast had hesitated in its advance and was snarling and growling angrily as its eyes roved upward and around at the savage creatures glaring down upon it.

It was only for a moment that the cat paused in its advance upon the ape-man. Snarling angrily, it moved forward again and as it did so, one of the creatures in the tree above Tarzan reached down, and, seizing the rope that held him dangling in midair, drew him swiftly upward. Then several things occurred simultaneously—the saber-tooth leaped to retrieve its prey and a dozen heavy cudgels hurtled through the air from the surrounding trees, striking the great cat heavily upon head and body with the result that the talons that must otherwise have inevitably been imbedded in the flesh of the ape-man grazed harmlessly by him, and an instant later he was drawn well up among the branches of the tree, where he was seized by three hairy brutes whose attitude suggested that he might have been as well off had he been left to the tender mercies of the saber-tooth.

Two of them, one on either side, seized an arm and the third grasped him by the throat with one hand while he held his cudgel poised above his head in the other. And then from the lips of the creature facing him came a sound that fell as startlingly upon the ears of the ape-man as had the first unexpected roar of the saber-tooth, but with far different effect.

"Ka-goda!" said the creature facing Tarzan.

In the language of the apes of his own jungle Ka-goda may

be roughly interpreted according to its inflection as a command to surrender, or as an interrogation, "do you surrender?" or as a declaration of surrender.

This word, coming from the lips of a hairy gorilla man of the inner world, suggested possibilities of the most startling nature. For years Tarzan had considered the language of the great apes as the primitive root language of created things. The great apes, the lesser apes, the gorillas, the baboons, and the monkeys utilized this with various degrees of refinement and many of its words were understood by jungle animals of other species and by many of the birds; but, perhaps, after the fashion that our domestic animals have learned many of the words in our vocabulary, with this difference that the language of the great apes has doubtless persisted unchanged for countless ages.

That these gorilla men of the inner world used even one word of this language suggested one of two possibilities—either they held an origin in common with the creatures of the outer crust, or else that the laws of evolution and progress were so constant that this was the only form of primitive language that could have been possible to any creatures emerging from the lower orders toward the estate of man. But the suggestion that impressed Tarzan most vividly was that this single word, uttered by the creature grasping him by the throat, postulated familiarity on the part of his fierce captors with the entire ape language that he had used since boyhood.

"Ka-goda?" inquired the bull.

"Ka-goda," said Tarzan of the Apes.

The brute, facing Tarzan, half lowered his cudgel as though he were surprised to hear the prisoner answer in his own tongue. "Who are you?" he demanded in the language of the great apes.

"I am Tarzan—mighty hunter, mighty fighter," replied the ape-man.

"What are you doing in M'wa-lot's country?" demanded the gorilla man.

"I come as a friend," replied Tarzan. "I have no quarrel with your people."

The fellow had lowered his club now, and from other trees

had come a score more of the shaggy creatures until the surrounding limbs sagged beneath their weight.

"How did you learn the language of the Sagoths?" demanded the bull. "We have captured gilaks in the past, but you are the first one who ever spoke or understood our language."

"It is the language of my people," replied Tarzan. "As a little balu, I learned it from Kala and other apes of the tribe of Kerchak."

"We never heard of the tribe of Kerchak," said the bull.

"Perhaps he is not telling the truth," said another. "Let us kill him; he is only a gilak."

"No," said a third. "Take him back to M'wa-lot that the whole tribe of M'wa-lot may join in the killing."

"That is good," said another. "Take him back to the tribe, and while we are killing him we shall dance."

The language of the great apes is not like our language. It sounds to man like growling and barking and grunting, punctuated at times by shrill screams, and it is practically untranslatable to any tongue known to man; yet it carried to Tarzan and the Sagoths the sense that we have given it. It is a means of communicating thought and there its similarity to the languages of men ceases.

Having decided upon the disposition of their prisoner, the Sagoths now turned their attention to the saber-tooth, who had returned to his kill, across the body of which he was lying. He was not feeding, but was gazing angrily up into the trees at his tormentors.

While three of the gorilla men secured Tarzan's wrists behind his back with a length of buckskin thong, the others renewed their attention to the tiger. Three or four of them would cast well-aimed cudgels at his face at intervals so nicely timed that the great beast could do nothing but fend off the missiles as they sped toward him. And while he was thus occupied, the other Sagoths, who had already cast their clubs, sprang to the ground and retrieved them with an agility and celerity that would have done credit to the tiniest monkey of the jungle. The risk that they took bespoke great self-confidence and high courage since often they were compelled to snatch their cudgels from almost beneath the claws of the saber-tooth.

Battered and bruised, the great cat gave back inch by inch until, unable to stand the fusillade longer, it suddenly turned tail and bounded into the underbrush, where for some time the sound of its crashing retreat could be distinctly heard. And with the departure of the carnivore, the gorilla men leaped to the ground and fell upon the carcass of the thag. With heavy fangs they tore its flesh, oftentimes fighting among themselves like wild beasts for some particularly choice morsel; but unlike many of the lower orders of man upon similar occasions they did not gorge themselves, and having satisfied their hunger they left what remained to the jackals and wild dogs that had already gathered.

Tarzan of the Apes, silent spectator of this savage scene, had an opportunity during the feast to examine his captors more closely. He saw that they were rather lighter in build than the gorillas he had seen in his own native jungle, but even though they were not as heavy as Bolgani, they were yet mighty creatures. Their arms and legs were of more human conformation and proportion than those of a gorilla, but the shaggy brown hair covering their entire body increased their beastlike appearance, while their faces were even more brutal than that of Bolgani himself, except that the development of the skull denoted a brain capacity seemingly as great as that of man.

They were entirely naked, nor was there among them any suggestion of ornamentation, while their only weapons were clubs. These, however, showed indications of having been shaped by some sharp instrument as though an effort had been made to insure a firm grip and a well-balanced weapon.

Their feeding completed, the Sagoths turned back along the game trail in the same direction that Tarzan had been going when he had sprung the trigger of the snare. But before departing several of them reset the noose, covered it carefully with earth and leaves, and set the trigger that it might be sprung by the first passing animal.

So sure were all their movements and so deft their fingers, Tarzan realized that though these creatures looked like beasts they had long since entered the estate of man. Perhaps they were still low in the scale of evolution, but unquestionably they were men with the brains of men and the faces and skins of gorillas.

As the Sagoths moved along the jungle trail they walked erect as men walk, but in other ways they reminded Tarzan of the great apes who were his own people, for they were given neither to laughter nor song and their taciturnity suggested the speechlessness of the alali. That certain of their sense faculties were more highly developed than in man was evidenced by the greater dependence they placed upon their ears and noses than upon their eyes in their unremitting vigil against surprise by an enemy.

While by human standards they might have been judged ugly and even hideous, they did not so impress Tarzan of the Apes, who recognized in them a certain primitive majesty of bearing and mien such as might well have been expected of pioneers upon the frontiers of humanity.

It is sometimes the custom of theorists to picture our primordial progenitors as timid, fearful creatures, fleeing from the womb to the grave in constant terror of the countless, savage creatures that beset their entire existence. But as it does not seem reasonable that a creature so poorly equipped for offense and defense could have survived without courage, it seems far more consistent to assume that with the dawning of reason came a certain superiority complex—a vast and at first stupid egotism—that knew caution, perhaps, but not fear; nor is any other theory tenable unless we are to suppose that from the loin of a rabbit-hearted creature sprang men who hunted the bison, the mammoth, and the cave bear with crude spears tipped with stone.

The Sagoths of Pellucidar may have been analogous in the scale of evolution to the Neanderthal men of the outer crust, or they may, indeed, have been even a step lower; yet in their bearing there was nothing to suggest to Tarzan that they had reached this stage in evolution through the expedience of flight. Their bearing as they trod the jungle trail bespoke assurance and even truculence, as though they were indeed the lords of creation, fearing nothing. Perhaps Tarzan understood their attitude better than another might have since it had been his own always in the jungle—unquestioning fearlessness—with which a certain intelligent caution was not inconsistent.

They had come but a short distance from the scene of Tarzan's capture when the Sagoths stopped beside a hollow log, the skeleton of a great tree that had fallen beside the trail. One of the creatures tapped upon the log with his club—one, two; one, two; one, two, three. And then, after a moment's pause, he repeated the same tapping. Three times the signal boomed through the jungle and then the signaler paused, listening, while others stooped and put their ears against the ground.

Faintly through the air, more plainly through the ground, came an answering signal—one, two; one, two; one, two, three.

The creatures seemed satisfied and, climbing into the surrounding trees, disposed themselves comfortably as though settling down to a wait. Two of them carried Tarzan easily aloft with them, as with his hands bound behind his back he could not climb unassisted.

Since they had started on the march Tarzan had not spoken, but now he turned to one of the Sagoths near him. "Remove the bonds from my wrists," he said. "I am not an enemy."

"Tar-gash," said he whom Tarzan had addressed, "the gilak wants his bonds removed."

Tar-gash, a large bull with noticeably long, white canine fangs, turned his savage eyes upon the ape-man. For a long time he glared unblinkingly at the prisoner and it seemed to Tarzan that the mind of the half-brute was struggling with a new idea. Presently he turned to the Sagoth who had repeated Tarzan's request. "Take them off," he said.

"Why?" demanded another of the bulls. The tone was challenging.

"Because I, Tar-gash, say 'take them off,' " growled the other.

"You are not M'wa-lot. He is king. If M'wa-lot says take them off, we will take them off."

"I am not M'wa-lot, To-yad; I am Tar-gash, and Tar-gash says 'take them off.' "

To-yad swung to Tarzan's side. "M'wa-lot will come soon,"

he said. "If M'wa-lot says take them off, we shall take them off. We do not take orders from Tar-gash."

Like a panther, quickly, silently Tar-gash sprang straight for the throat of To-yad. There was no warning, not even an instant of hesitation. In this Tarzan saw that Tar-gash differed from the great apes with whom the Lord of the Jungle had been familiar upon the outer crust, for among them two bulls ordinarily must need have gone through a long preliminary of stiff-legged strutting and grumbled invective before either one launched himself upon the other in deadly combat. But the mind of Tar-gash had functioned with manlike celerity, so much so that decision and action had appeared to be almost simultaneous.

The impact of the heavy body of Tar-gash toppled To-yad from the branch upon which he had been standing, but so naturally arboreal were the two great creatures that even as they fell they reached out and seized the same branch and, still fighting, each with his free hand and his heavy fangs, they hung there a second breaking their fall, and then dropped to the ground. They fought almost silently except for low growls, Tar-gash seeking the jugular of To-yad with those sharp, white fangs that had given him his name. To-yad, his every faculty concentrated upon defense, kept the grinning jaws from his flesh and, suddenly twisting quickly around, tore loose from the powerful fingers of his opponent and sought safety in flight. But like a football player, Tar-gash launched himself through the air; his long hairy arms encircled the legs of the fleeing To-yad, bringing him heavily to the ground, and an instant later the powerful aggressor was on the back of his opponent and To-yad's jugular was at the mercy of his foe, but the great jaws of Tar-gash did not close.

"Ka-goda?" he inquired.

"Ka-goda," growled To-yad, and instantly Tar-gash arose from the body of the other bull.

With the agility of a monkey the victor leaped back into the branches of the tree. "Remove the bonds from the wrists of the gilak," he said, and at the same time he glared ferociously about him to see if there was another so mutinously minded as To-yad; but none spoke and none objected as one of the

Sagoths who had dragged Tarzan up into the tree untied the bonds that secured his wrists.

"If he tries to run away from us," said Tar-gash, "kill him."

When his bonds were removed Tarzan expected that the Sagoths would take his knife away from him. He had lost his spear and bow and most of his arrows at the instant that the snare had snapped him from the ground, but though they had lain in plain view in the trail beneath the snare the Sagoths had paid no attention to them; nor did they now pay any attention to his knife. He was sure they must have seen it and he could not understand their lack of concern regarding it, unless they were ignorant of its purpose or held him in such contempt that they did not consider it worth the effort to disarm him.

Presently To-yad sneaked back into the tree, but he huddled sullenly by himself, apart from the others.

Faintly, from a distance, Tarzan heard something approaching. He heard it just a moment before the Sagoths heard it.

"They come!" announced Tar-gash.

"M'wa-lot comes," said another, glancing at To-yad. Now Tarzan knew why the primitive drum had been sounded, but he wondered why they were gathering.

At last they arrived, nor was it difficult for Tarzan to recognize M'wa-lot, the king among the others. A great bull walked in front—a bull with so much gray among the hairs on his face that the latter had a slightly bluish complexion, and instantly the ape-man saw how the king had come by his name.

As soon as the Sagoths with Tarzan were convinced of the identity of the approaching party, they descended from the trees to the ground and when M'wa-lot had approached within twenty paces of them, he halted. "I am M'wa-lot," he announced. "With me are the people of my tribe."

"I am Tar-gash," replied the bull who seemed to be in charge of the other party. "With me are other bulls of the tribe of M'wa-lot."

This precautionary preliminary over, M'wa-lot advanced, followed by the bulls, the shes and the balus of his tribe.

"What is that?" demanded M'wa-lot, as his fierce eyes espied Tarzan.

"It is a gilak that we found caught in our snare," replied Tar-gash.

"That is the feast that you called us to?" demanded M'wa-lot, angrily. "You should have brought it to the tribe. It can walk."

"This is not the food of which the drum spoke," replied Tar-gash. "Nearby is the body of a thag that was killed by a tarag close by the snare in which this gilak was caught."

"Ugh!" grunted M'wa-lot. "We can eat the gilak later."

"We can have a dance," suggested one of Tarzan's captors. "We have eaten and slept many times since we have danced, M'wa-lot."

As the Sagoths, guided by Tar-gash, proceeded along the trail toward the body of the thag, the females with balus growled savagely when one of the little ones chanced to come near to Tarzan. The bulls eyed him suspiciously and all seemed uneasy because of his presence. In these and in other ways the Sagoths were reminiscent of the apes of the tribe of Kerchak and to such an extent was this true that Tarzan, although a prisoner among them, felt strangely at home in this new environment.

A short distance ahead of the ape-man walked M'wa-lot, king of the tribe, and at M'wa-lot's elbow was To-yad. The two spoke in low tones and from the frequent glances they cast at Tar-gash, who walked ahead of them, it was evident that he was the subject of their conversation, the effect of which upon M'wa-lot seemed to be highly disturbing.

Tarzan could see that the shaggy chieftain was working himself into a frenzy of rage, the inciting cause of which was evidently the information that To-yad was imparting to him. The latter seemed to be attempting to goad him to greater fury, a fact which seemed to be now apparent to every member of the tribe with the exception of Tar-gash, who was walking in the lead, ahead of M'wa-lot and To-yad, for practically every other eye was turned upon the king, whose evident excitement had imparted a certain fierce restlessness in the other members of his party. But it was not until they had come within sight of the body of the thag that the storm broke and then, without warning, M'wa-lot swung his heavy club and leaped forward toward Tar-gash with the very evident intention of braining him from behind.

If the life of the ape-man in his constant battle for survival had taught him to act quickly, it also had taught him to think quickly. He knew that in all this savage company he had no friends, but he also knew that Tar-gash, from very stubbornness and to spite To-yad, might alone be expected to befriend him and now it appeared that Tar-gash himself might need a friend, for it was evident that no hand was to be raised in defense of him nor any voice in warning. And so Tarzan of the Apes, prompted both by considerations of self-interest and fair play, took matters into his own hands with such suddenness that he had already acted before any hand could be raised to stop him.

"Kreeg-ah, Tar-gash!" he cried, and at the same instant he sprang quickly forward, brushing To-yad aside with a single sweep of a giant arm that sent the Sagoth headlong into the underbrush bordering the trail.

At the warning cry of "Kreeg-ah," which in the language of the great apes is synonymous to beware, Tar-gash wheeled about to see the infuriated M'wa-lot with upraised club almost upon him and then he saw something else which made his savage eyes widen in surprise. The strange gilak, whom he had taken prisoner, had leaped close to M'wa-lot from behind. A smooth, bronzed arm slipped quickly about the king's neck and tightened. The gilak turned and stooped and surging forward with the king across his hip threw the great, hairy bull completely over his head and sent him sprawling at the feet of his astonished warriors. Then the gilak leaped to Tar-gash's side and, wheeling, faced the tribe with Tar-gash.

Instantly a score of clubs were raised against the two.

"Shall we remain and fight, Tar-gash?" demanded the ape-man.

"They will kill us," said Tar-gash. "If you were not a gilak, we might escape through the trees, but as you cannot escape we shall have to remain and fight."

"Lead the way," said Tarzan. "There is no Sagoth trail that Tarzan cannot follow."

"Come then," said Tar-gash, and as he spoke he hurled his

club into the faces of the oncoming warriors, and turning, fled along the trail. A dozen mighty bounds he took and then leaped to the branch of an overhanging tree, and close behind him came the hairless gilak.

M'wa-lot's hairy warrior bulls pursued the two for a short distance and then gave up the chase as Tarzan was confident that they would, since among his own people it had usually been considered sufficient to run a recalcitrant bull out of the tribe and, unless he insisted upon returning, no particular effort was made to molest him.

As soon as it become evident that pursuit had been abandoned the Sagoth halted among the branches of a huge tree. "I am Tar-gash," he said, as Tarzan stopped near him.

"I am Tarzan," replied the ape-man.

"Why did you warn me?" asked Tar-gash.

"I told you that I did not come among you as an enemy," replied Tarzan, "and when I saw that To-yad had succeeded in urging M'wa-lot to kill you, I warned you because it was you that kept the bulls from killing me when I was captured."

"What were you doing in the country of the Sagoths?" asked Tar-gash.

"I was hunting," replied Tarzan.

"Where do you want to go now?" asked the Sagoth.

"I shall return to my people," replied Tarzan.

"Where are they?"

Tarzan of the Apes hesitated. He looked upward toward the sun, whose rays were filtering down through the foliage of the forest. He looked about him—everywhere was foliage. There was nothing in the foliage nor upon the boles or branches of the trees to indicate direction. Tarzan of the Apes was lost!

5

Brought Down

JASON GRIDLEY, LOOKING down from the branches of the tree in which he had found sanctuary, was held by a certain horrible fascination as he watched the feast of the great cats.

The scene that he had just witnessed—this stupendous spectacle of savagery—suggested to him something of what life upon the outer crust must have been at the dawn of humanity.

The suggestion was borne in upon him that perhaps this scene which he had witnessed might illustrate an important cause of the extinction of all of these animals upon the outer crust.

The action of the great saber-tooth tigers of Pellucidar in rounding up the other beasts of the forest and driving them to this clearing for slaughter evidenced a development of intelligence far beyond that attained by the carnivores of the outer world of the present day, such concerted action by any great number for the common good being unknown.

Gridley saw the vast number of animals that had been slaughtered and most of them uselessly, since there was more flesh there than the surviving tigers could consume before it reached a stage of putrefaction that would render it unpalatable even to one of the great cats. And this fact suggested the conviction that the cunning of the tigers had reached a plane where it might reasonably be expected to react upon themselves and eventually cause their extinction, for in their savage fury and lust for flesh they had slaughtered indiscriminately males and females, young and old. If this slaughter went on unchecked for ages, the natural prey of the tigers must become extinct and then, goaded by starvation, they would fall upon one another.

The last stage of the ascendancy of the great cats upon the outer crust must have been short and terrible and so eventually it would prove here in Pellucidar.

And just as the great cats may have reached a point where their mental development had spelled their own doom, so in the preceding era the gigantic, carnivorous dinosaurs of the Jurassic may similarly have caused the extinction of their own contemporaries and then of themselves. Nor did Jason Gridley find it difficult to apply the same line of reasoning to the evolution of man upon the outer crust and to his own possible extinction in the not far remote future. In fact, he recalled quite definitely that statisticians had shown that within two hundred years or less the human race would have so greatly increased and the natural resources of the outer world would have been so depleted that the last generation must either starve to death or turn to cannibalism to prolong its hateful existence for another short period.

Perhaps, thought Gridley, in nature's laboratory each type that had at some era dominated all others represented an experiment in the eternal search for perfection. The invertebrate had given way to fishes, the fishes to the reptiles, the reptiles to the birds and mammals, and these, in turn, had been forced to bow to the greater intelligence of man.

What would be next? Gridley was sure that there would be something after man, who is unquestionably the Creator's greatest blunder, combining as he does all the vices of preceding types from invertebrates to mammals, while possessing few of their virtues.

As such thoughts were forced upon his mind by the scene below him they were accompanied by others of more immediate importance, first of which was concern for his fellows.

Nowhere about the clearing did he see any sign of a human being alive or dead. He called aloud several times but received no reply, though he realized that it was possible that above the roaring and the growling of the feeding beasts his voice might not carry to any great distance. He began to have hopes that his companions had all escaped, but he was still greatly worried over the fate of Von Horst.

The subject of second consideration was that of his own escape and return to the O-220. He had it in his mind that at nightfall the beasts might retire and unconsciously he glanced upward at the sun to note the time, when the realization came to him that there would never be any night, that forever throughout all eternity it would be noon here. And then he began to wonder how long he had been gone from the ship, but when he glanced at his watch he realized that that meant nothing. The hour hand might have made an entire circle since he had last looked at it, for in the excitement of all that had transpired since they had left the O-220 how might the mind of man, unaided, compute time?

But he knew that eventually the beasts must get their fill and leave. After them, however, there would be the hyaenodons and the jackals with their fierce cousins, the wild dogs. As he watched these, sitting at a respectful distance from the tigers or slinking hungrily in the background, he realized that they might easily prove as much of a bar to his escape as the saber-tooth tigers themselves.

The hyaenodons especially were most discouraging to contemplate. Their bodies were as large as that of a full-grown mastiff. They walked upon short, powerful legs and their broad jaws were massive and strong. Dark, shaggy hair covered their backs and sides, turning to white upon their breasts and bellies.

Gnawing hunger assailed Jason Gridley and also an overpowering desire to sleep, convincing him that he must have been many hours away from the O-220, and yet the beasts beneath him continued to feed.

A dead thag lay at the foot of the tree in which the American kept his lonely vigil. So far it had not been fed upon and the nearest tiger was fifty yards away. Gridley was hungry, so hungry that he eyed the thag covetously. He glanced about him, measuring the distance from the tree to the nearest tiger and trying to compute the length of time that it would take him to clamber back to safety should he descend to the ground. He had seen the tigers in action and he knew how swiftly they could cover ground and that one of them could leap almost as high as the branch upon which he sat.

Altogether the chance of success seemed slight for the plan he had in mind in the event that the nearest tiger took exception to it. But great though the danger was, hunger won. Gridley drew his hunting knife and lowered himself gently to the ground, keeping an alert eye upon the nearest tiger. Quickly he sliced several long strips of flesh from the thag's hindquarter.

The tarag feeding fifty yards away looked up. Jason sliced another strip, returned his knife to its sheath and climbed quickly back to safety. The tarag lowered its head upon its kill and closed its eyes.

The American gathered dead twigs and small branches that still clung to the living tree and with them he built a small fire in a great crotch.

Here he cooked some of the meat of the thag; the edges were charred, the inside was raw, but Jason Gridley could have sworn that never before in his life had he tasted such delicious food.

How long his culinary activities employed him, he did not know, but when he glanced down again at the clearing he saw that most of the tigers had quitted their kills and were moving leisurely toward the forest, their distended bellies proclaiming how well they had surfeited themselves. And as the tigers retired, the hyaenodons, the wild dogs, and the jackals closed in to the feast.

The hyaenodons kept the others away and Gridley saw another long wait ahead of him; nor was he mistaken. And when the hyaenodons had had their fill and gone, the wild dogs came and kept the jackals away.

In the meantime Gridley had fashioned a rude platform among the branches of the tree, and here he had slept, awakening refreshed but assailed by a thirst that was almost overpowering.

The wild dogs were leaving now and Gridley determined to wait no longer. Already the odor of decaying flesh was warning him of worse to come and there was the fear too that the tigers might return to their kills.

Descending from the tree he skirted the clearing, keeping close to the forest and searching for the trail by which his party had entered the clearing. The wild dogs, slinking away, turned to growl at him, baring menacing fangs. But knowing how well their bellies were filled, he entertained little fear of them; while for the jackals he harbored that contempt which is common among all creatures.

Gridley was dismayed to note that many trails entered the clearing; nor could he recognize any distinguishing mark that might suggest the one by which he had come. Whatever footprints his party had left had been entirely obliterated by the pads of the carnivores.

He tried to reconstruct his passage across the clearing to the tree in which he had found safety and by this means he hit upon a trail to follow, although he had no assurance that it was the right trail. The baffling noonday sun shining down upon him seemed to taunt him with his helplessness.

As he proceeded alone down the lonely trail, realizing that at any instant he might come face-to-face with some terrible beast of a long-dead past, Jason Gridley wondered how the apelike progenitors of man had survived to transmit any of their characteristics however unpleasant to a posterity. That he could live to reach the O-220 he much doubted. The idea that he might live to take a mate and raise a family was preposterous.

While the general aspect of the forest through which he was passing seemed familiar, he realized that this might be true no matter what trail he was upon and now he reproached himself for not having had the trees along the trail blazed. What a stupid ass he had been, he thought; but his regrets were not so much for himself as for the others, whose safety had been in his hands.

Never in his life had Jason Gridley felt more futile or helpless. To trudge ceaselessly along that endless trail, having not the slightest idea whether it led toward the O-220 or in the opposite direction was depressing, even maddening; yet there was naught else to do. And always that damned noonday sun staring unblinkingly down upon him—the cruel sun that could see his ship, but would not lead him to it.

His thirst was annoying, but not yet overpowering, when he came to a small stream that was crossed by the trail. Here he drank and rested for a while, built a small fire, cooked some more of his thag meat, drank again and took up his weary march—but much refreshed.

Aboard the O-220, as the hours passed and hope waned, the spirit of the remaining officers and members of the crew became increasingly depressed as apprehension for the safety of their absent comrades increased gradually until it became eventually an almost absolute conviction of disaster.

"They have been gone nearly seventy-two hours now," said Zuppner, who, with Dorf and Hines, spent most of his time in the upper observation cabin or pacing the narrow walking-way along the ship's back. "I never felt helpless before in my life," he continued ruefully, "but I am free to admit that I don't know what in the devil to do."

"It just goes to show," said Hines, "how much we depend upon habit and custom and precedence in determining all our action even in the face of what we are pleased to call emergency. Here there is no custom, habit, or precedence to guide us."

"We have only our own resources to fall back upon," said Dorf, "and it is humiliating to realize that we have no resources."

"Not under the conditions that surround us," said Zuppner. "On the outer crust there would be no question but that we should cruise around in search of the missing members of our party. We could make rapid excursions, returning to our base often; but here in Pellucidar if we should lose sight of our base there is not one of us who believes he could return the ship to this same anchorage. And that is a chance we cannot take for the only hope those men have is that the ship shall be here when they return."

One hundred and fifty feet below them Robert Jones leaned far out of the galley doorway in an effort to see the noonday sun shining down upon the ship. His simple, good-natured face wore a puzzled expression not untinged with awe, and as he drew back into the galley he extracted a rabbit's foot from his trousers pocket. Gently he touched each eye with it and then rubbed it vigorously upon the top of his head at the same time muttering incoherently below his breath.

From the vantage point of the walking-way far above, Lieutenant Hines scanned the landscape in all directions through powerful glasses as he had done for so long that it seemed he knew every shrub and tree and blade of grass within sight. The wildlife of savage Pellucidar that crossed and recrossed the clearing had long since become an old story to these three men. Again and again as one animal or another had emerged from the distant forest the glasses had been leveled upon it until it could be identified as other than man; but now Hines voiced a sudden, nervous exclamation.

"What is it?" demanded Zuppner. "What do you see?"

"It's a man!" exclaimed Hines. "I'm sure of it."

"Where?" asked Dorf, as he and Zuppner raised their glasses to their eyes.

"About two points to port."

"I see it," said Dorf. "It's either Gridley or Von Horst, and whoever it is he is alone."

"Take ten of the crew at once, Lieutenant," said Zuppner, turning to Dorf. "See that they are well armed and go out and meet him. Lose no time," he shouted after the lieutenant, who had already started down the climbing shaft.

The two officers upon the top of the O-220 watched Dorf and his party as it set out to meet the man they could see trudging steadily toward the ship. They watched them as they approached one another, though, owing to the contour of the land, which was rolling, neither Dorf nor the man he had gone to meet caught sight of one another until they were less than a hundred yards apart. It was then that the lieutenant recognized the other as Jason Gridley.

As they hastened forward and clasped hands it was typical of the man that Gridley's first words were an inquiry relative to the missing members of the party.

Dorf shook his head. "You are the only one that has returned," he said.

The eager light died out of Gridley's eyes and he suddenly looked very tired and much older as he greeted the engineers and mechanics who made up the party that had come to escort him back to the ship.

"I have been within sight of the ship for a long time," he said. "How long, I do not know. I broke my watch back in the forest a way trying to beat a tiger up a tree. Then another one treed me just on the edge of the clearing in plain view of the ship. It seems as though I have been there a week. How long have I been gone, Dorf?"

"About seventy-two hours."

Gridley's face brightened. "Then there is no reason to give up hope yet for the others," he said. "I honestly thought I had been gone a week. I have slept several times, I never could tell how long; and then I have gone for what seemed long periods without sleep because I became very tired and excessively hungry and thirsty."

During the return march to the ship Jason insisted upon hearing a detailed account of everything that had happened since his departure, but it was not until they had joined Zuppner and Hines that he narrated the adventures that had befallen him and his companions during their ill-fated expedition.

"The first thing I want," he told them after he had been greeted by Zuppner and Hines, "is a bath, and then if you will have Bob cook a couple of cows I'll give you the details of the expedition while I am eating them. A couple of handfuls of Bos Primigenus and some wild fruits have only whetted my appetite."

A half hour later, refreshed by a bath, a shave, and fresh clothing, he joined them in the mess room.

As the three men seated themselves, Robert Jones entered from the galley, his shining face wreathed in smiles.

"Ah'm suttinly glad to see you all, suh," said Robert. "Ah knew sumpin was a-goin' to happen though—Ah knew we was a-goin' to have good luck."

"Well, I'm glad to be back, Bob," said Gridley, "and I don't know of anyone that I am any happier to see than you, for I sure have missed your cooking. But what made you think that we're going to have good luck?"

"Ah jes had a brief conversation with mah rabbit's foot. Dat ole boy he never fails me. We suah be out o' luck if Ah lose him."

"Oh, I've seen lots of rabbits around, Bob," said Zuppner. "We can get you a bushel of them in no time."

"Yes suh, Cap'n, but you cain't get 'em in de dahk of de moon where dey ain't no dahk an' dey ain't no moon, an' othe'wise dey lacks efficiency."

"It's a good thing, then, that we brought you along," said Jason, "and a mighty good thing for Pellucidar, for she never has had a really effective rabbit's foot before in all her existence. But I can see where you're going to need that rabbit's foot pretty badly yourself in about a minute, Bob."

"How's dat, suh?" demanded Robert.

"The spirits tell me that something is going to happen to you if you don't get food onto this table in a hurry," laughed Gridley.

"Yes suh, comin' right up," exclaimed the man as he hastened into the galley.

As Gridley ate, he went over the adventures of the last seventy-two hours in careful detail and the three men sought to arrive at some definite conjecture as to the distance he had covered from the ship and the direction.

"Do you think that you could lead another party to the clearing where you became separated from Von Horst and the Waziri?" asked Zuppner.

"Yes, of course I could," replied Gridley, "because from the point that we entered the forest we blazed the trees up to the time we reached the trail, which we followed to the left. In fact I would not be needed at all and if we decide to send out such a party, I shall not accompany it."

The others officers looked at him in surprise and for a moment there was an embarrassed silence.

"I have what I consider a better plan," continued Gridley. "There are twenty-seven of us left. In the event of absolute necessity, twelve men can operate the ship. That will leave fifteen to form a new searching party. Leaving me out, you would have fourteen, and after you have heard my plan, if you decide upon sending out such a party, I suggest that Lieutenant Dorf command it, leaving you, Captain Zuppner, and Hines to navigate the ship in the event that none of us returns, or that you finally decide to set out in search of us."

"But I thought that you were not going," said Zuppner.

"I am not going with the searching party. I am going alone in the scout plane, and my advice would be that you send out no searching party for at least twenty-four hours after I depart, for in that time I shall either have located those who are missing or have failed entirely."

Zuppner shook his head, dubiously. "Hines, Dorf, and I have discussed the feasibility of using the scout plane," he said. "Hines was very anxious to make the attempt, although he realizes better than any of us that once a pilot is out of sight of the O-220 he may never be able to locate it again, for you must remember that we know nothing concerning any of the landmarks of the country in the direction that our search must be prosecuted."

"I have taken all that into consideration," replied Gridley, "and I realize that it is at best but a forlorn hope."

"Let me undertake it," said Hines. "I have had more flying experience than any of you with the possible exception of Captain Zuppner, and it is out of the question that we should risk losing him."

"Any one of you three is probably better fitted to undertake such a flight than I," replied Gridley; "but that does not relieve me of the responsibility. I am more responsible than any other member of this party for our being where we are and, therefore, my responsibility for the safety of the missing members of the expedition is greater than that of any of the rest of you. Under the circumstances, then, I could not permit anyone else to undertake this flight. I think that you will all understand and appreciate how I feel and that you will do me the favor to interpose no more objection."

It was several minutes thereafter before anyone spoke, the four seeming to be immersed in the business of sipping their coffee and smoking their cigarettes. It was Zuppner who broke the silence.

"Before you undertake this thing," he said, "you should have a long sleep, and in the meantime we will get the plane out and have it gone over thoroughly. You must have every chance for success that we can give you."

"Thank you!" said Gridley. "I suppose you are right about the sleep. I hate to waste the time, but if you will call me the moment that the ship is ready I shall go to my cabin at once and get such sleep as I can in the meantime."

While Gridley slept, the scout plane, carried aft in the keel cabin, was lowered to the ground, where it underwent a careful inspection and test by the engineers and officers of the O-220.

Even before the plane was ready Gridley appeared at the cabin door of the O-220 and descended to the ground.

"You did not sleep long," said Zuppner.

"I do not know how long," said Gridley, "but I feel rested and anyway I could not have slept longer, knowing that those fellows are out there somewhere waiting and hoping for succor."

"What route do you expect to follow," asked Zuppner, "and how are you planning to insure a reasonable likelihood of your being able to return?"

"I shall fly directly over the forest as far as I think it at all likely that they could have marched in the time that they have been absent, assuming that they became absolutely confused and have traveled steadily away from the ship. As soon as I have gained sufficient altitude to make any observation I shall try and spot some natural landmark, like a mountain or a body of water, near the ship and from time to time, as I proceed, I shall make a note of similar landmarks. I believe that in this way I can easily find my way back, since at the farthest I cannot proceed over two hundred and fifty miles from the O-220 and return to it with the fuel that I can carry.

"After I have reached the farthest possible limits that I think the party could have strayed, I shall commence circling, depending upon the noise of the motor to attract their attention and, of course, assuming that they will find some means of signaling their presence to me, which they can do even in wooded country by building smudges."

"You expect to land?" inquired Zuppner, nodding at the heavy rifle which Gridley carried.

"If I find them in open country, I shall land; but even if I do not find them it may be necessary for me to come down and my recent experiences have taught me not to venture far in Pellucidar without a rifle."

After a careful inspection, Gridley shook hands with the three remaining officers and bid farewell to the ship's company, all of whom were anxious observers of his preparation for departure.

"Good-bye, old man," said Zuppner, "and may God and luck go with you."

Gridley pressed the hand of the man he had come to look upon as a staunch and loyal friend, and then took his seat in the open cockpit of the scout plane. Two mechanics spun the propeller, the motor roared and a moment later the block was kicked away and the plane rolled out across the grassy meadowland toward the forest at the far side. The watchers saw it rise swiftly and make a great circle and they knew that Gridley was looking for a landmark. Twice it circled above the open plain and then darted away across the forest.

It had not been until he had made that first circle that Jason Gridley had realized the handicap that this horizonless landscape of Pellucidar had placed upon his chances of return. He had thought of a mountain standing boldly out against the sky, for such a landmark would have been almost constantly within the range of his vision during the entire flight.

There were mountains in the distance, but they stood out against no background of blue sky nor upon any horizon. They simply merged with the landscape beyond them, curving upward in the distance. Twice he circled, his keen eyes searching for any outstanding point in the topography of the country beneath him, but there was nothing that was more apparent than the grassy plain upon which the O-220 rested.

He felt that he could not waste time and fuel by searching longer for a landmark that did not exist, and while he realized that the plain would be visible for but a comparatively short distance he was forced to accept it as his sole guide in lieu of a better one.

Roaring above the leafy roof of the primeval forest, all that transpired upon the ground below was hidden from him and it was tantalizing to realize that he might have passed directly over the heads of the comrades he sought, yet there was no other way. Returning, he would either circle or hold an exaggerated zigzag course, watching carefully for sign of a signal.

For almost two hours Jason Gridley held a straight course, passing over forest, plain, and rolling, hilly country, but nowhere did he see any sign of those he sought. Already he had reached the limit of the distance he had planned upon coming when there loomed ahead of him in the distance a range of lofty mountains. These alone would have determined him to turn back, since his judgment told him that the lost members of the party, should they have chanced to come this far, would by now have realized that they were traveling in the wrong direction.

As he banked to turn he caught a glimpse out of the corner of an eye of something in the air above him and looking quickly back, Jason Gridley caught his breath in astonishment.

Hovering now, almost above him, was a gigantic creature, the enormous spread of whose wings almost equaled that of the plane he was piloting. The man had a single glimpse of tremendous jaws, armed with mighty teeth, in the very instant that he realized that this mighty anachronism was bent upon attacking him.

Gridley was flying at an altitude of about three thousand feet when the huge pteranodon launched itself straight at the ship. Jason sought to elude it by diving. There was a terrific crash, a roar, a splintering of wood and a grinding of metal as the pteranodon swooped down upon its prey and full into the propeller.

What happened then, happened so quickly that Jason Gridley could not have reconstructed the scene five seconds later.

The plane turned completely over and at the same instant Gridley jumped. He jerked the rip cord of his parachute. Something struck him on the head and he lost consciousness.

6

A Phororhacos of the Miocene

W HERE ARE YOUR people?" Tar-gash asked again.
Tarzan shook his head. "I do not know," he said.
"Where is your country?" asked Tar-gash.

"It is a long way off," replied the ape-man. "It is not in Pellucidar"; but that the Sagoth could not understand any more than he could understand that a creature might be lost at all, for inherent in him was that same homing instinct that marked all the creatures of Pellucidar and which constitutes a wise provision of nature in a world without guiding celestial bodies.

Had it been possible to transport Tar-gash instantly to any point within that mighty inner world, elsewhere than upon the surface of an ocean, he could have unerringly found his way to the very spot where he was born, and because that power was instinctive he could not understand why Tarzan did not possess it.

"I know where there is a tribe of men," he said, presently. "Perhaps they are your people. I shall lead you to them."

As Tarzan had no idea as to the direction in which the ship lay and as it was remotely possible that Tar-gash was referring to the members of the O-220 expedition, he felt that he was as well off following where Tar-gash led as elsewhere, and so he signified his readiness to accompany the Sagoth.

"How long since you saw this tribe of men," he asked after a while, "and how long have they lived where you saw them?"

Upon the Sagoth's reply to these questions, the ape-man felt that he might determine the possibility of the men to whom Tar-gash referred being the members of his own party, for if they were newcomers in the district then the chances were excellent that they were the people he sought; but his questions elicited no satisfactory reply for the excellent reason that time meant nothing to Tar-gash. And so the two set out upon a leisurely search for the tribe of men that Tar-gash knew of. It was leisurely because for Tar-gash time did not exist; nor had it ever been a very important factor in the existence of the ape-man, except in occasional moments of emergency.

They were a strangely assorted pair—one a creature just standing upon the threshold of humanity, the other an English lord in his own right, who was, at the same time, in many respects as primitive as the savage, shaggy bull into whose companionship chance had thrown him.

At first Tar-gash had been inclined to look with contempt upon this creature of another race, which he considered far inferior to his own in strength, agility, courage, and woodcraft, but he soon came to hold the ape-man in vast respect. And because he could respect his prowess he became attached to him in bonds of loyalty that were as closely akin to friendship as the savage nature of his primitive mind permitted.

They hunted together and fought together. They swung through the trees when the great cats hunted upon the ground, or they followed game trails ages old beneath the hoary trees of Pellucidar or out across her rolling, grassy, flower-spangled meadowland.

They lived well upon the fat of the land for both were mighty hunters.

Tarzan fashioned a new bow and arrows and a stout spear, and these, at first, the Sagoth refused even to notice, but presently when he saw how easily and quickly they brought game to their larder he evinced a keen interest and Tarzan taught him how to use the weapons and later how to fashion them.

The country through which they traveled was well watered and was alive with game. It was partly wooded with great stretches of open land, where tremendous herds of herbivores grazed beneath the eternal noonday sun, and because of these great herds the beasts of prey were numerous—and such beasts!

Tarzan had thought that there was no world like his own world and no jungle like his own jungle, but the more deeply he dipped into the wonders of Pellucidar the more enamored he became of this savage, primitive world, teeming with the wildlife he loved best. That there were few men was Pellucidar's chiefest recommendation. Had there been none the ape-man might have considered this the land of ultimate perfection, for who is there more conversant with the cruelty and inconsideration of man than the savage beasts of the jungle?

The friendship that had developed between Tarzan and the Sagoth—and that was primarily based upon the respect which each felt for the prowess of the other—increased as each seemed to realize other admirable, personal qualities and characteristics in his companion, not the least of which being a common taciturnity. They spoke only when conversation seemed necessary, and that, in reality, was seldom.

If man spoke only when he had something worthwhile to say and said that as quickly as possible, ninety-eight percent of the human race might as well be dumb, thereby establishing a heavenly harmony from pate to tonsil.

And so the companionship of Tar-gash, coupled with the romance of strange sights and sounds and odors in this new world, acted upon the ape-man as might a strong drug, filling him with exhilaration and dulling his sense of responsibility, so that the necessity of finding his people dwindled to a matter of minor importance. Had he known that some of them were in trouble his attitude would have changed immediately, but this he did not know. On the contrary he was only aware that they had every facility for insuring their safety and their ultimate return to the outer world and that his absence would not handicap them in any particular. However, when he did give the matter thought he knew that he must return to them, that he must find them, and that sooner or later he must go back with them to the world from which they had come.

But all such considerations were quite remote from his thoughts as he and Tar-gash were crossing a rolling, tree-dotted plain in their search for the tribe of men to which the

Sagoth was guiding him. By comparison with other plains they had crossed, this one seemed strangely deserted, but the reason for this was evident in the close-cropped grass which suggested that great herds had grazed it off before moving on to new pastures. The absence of life and movement was slightly depressing and Tarzan found himself regretting the absence of even the dangers of the teeming land through which they had just come.

They were well out toward the center of the plain and could see the solid green of a great forest curving upward into the hazy distance when the attention of both was attracted by a strange, droning noise that brought them to a sudden halt. Simultaneously both turned and looked backward and up into the sky from which the sound seemed to come.

Far above and just emerging from the haze of the distance was a tiny speck. "Quick!" exclaimed Tar-gash. "It is a thipdar," and motioning Tarzan to follow him he ran swiftly to concealment beneath a large tree.

"What is a thipdar?" asked Tarzan, as the two halted beneath the friendly shade.

"A thipdar," said the Sagoth, "is a thipdar"; nor could he describe it more fully other than to add that the thipdars were sometimes used by the Mahars either to protect them or to hunt their food.

"Is the thipdar a living thing?" demanded Tarzan.

"Yes," replied Tar-gash. "It lives and is very strong and very fierce."

"Then that is not a thipdar," said Tarzan.

"What is it then?" demanded the Sagoth.

"It is an airplane," replied Tarzan.

"What is that?" inquired the Sagoth.

"It would be hard to explain it to you," replied the ape-man. "It is something that the men of my world build and in which they fly through the air," and as he spoke he stepped out into the opening, where he might signal the pilot of the plane, which he was positive was the one carried by the O-220 and which, he assumed, was prosecuting a search for him.

"Come back," exclaimed Tar-gash. "You cannot fight a

thipdar. It will swoop down and carry you off if you are out in the open."

"It will not harm me," said Tarzan. "One of my friends is in it."

"And you will be in it, too, if you do not come back under the tree," replied Tar-gash.

As the plane approached, Tarzan ran around in a small circle to attract the pilot's attention, stopping occasionally to wave his arms, but the plane sped on above him and it was evident that its pilot had not seen him.

Until it faded from sight in the distance, Tarzan of the Apes stood upon the lonely plain, watching the ship that was bearing his comrade away from him.

The sight of the ship awakened Tarzan to a sense of his responsibility. He realized now that someone was risking his life to save him and with this thought came a determination to exert every possible effort to locate the O-220.

The passage of the plane opened many possibilities for conjecture. If it was circling, which was possible, the direction of its flight as it passed over him would have no bearing upon the direction of the O-220, and if it were not circling, then how was he to know whether it was traveling away from the ship in the beginning of its quest, or was returning to it having concluded its flight.

"That was not a thipdar," said Tar-gash, coming from beneath the tree and standing at Tarzan's side. "It is a creature that I have never seen before. It is larger and must be even more terrible than a thipdar. It must have been very angry, for it growled terribly all the time."

"It is not alive," said Tarzan. "It is something that the men of my country build that they may fly through the air. Riding in it is one of my friends. He is looking for me."

The Sagoth shook his head. "I am glad he did not come down," he said. "He was either very angry or very hungry, otherwise he would not have growled so loudly."

It was apparent to Tarzan that Tar-gash was entirely incapable of comprehending his explanation of the airplane and that he would always believe it was a huge, flying reptile; but that was of no importance—the thing that troubled Tarzan being the question of the direction in which he should now prosecute his search for the O-220, and eventually he determined to follow in the direction taken by the airship, for as this coincided with the direction in which Tar-gash assured him he would find the tribe of human beings for which they were searching, it seemed after all the wisest course to pursue.

The drone of the motor had died away in the distance when Tarzan and Tar-gash took up their interrupted journey across the plain and into broken country of low, rocky hills.

The trail, which was well marked and which Tar-gash said led through the hills, followed the windings of a shallow canyon, which was rimmed on one side by low cliffs, in the face of which there were occasional caves and crevices. The bottom of the canyon was strewn with fragments of rock of various sizes. The vegetation was sparse and there was every indication of an aridity such as Tarzan had not previously encountered since he left the O-220, and as it seemed likely that both game and water would be scarce here, the two pushed on at a brisk, swinging walk.

It was very quiet and Tarzan's eyes were constantly upon the alert to catch the first sound of the hum of the motor of the returning airplane, when suddenly the silence was shattered by the sound of hoarse screeching which seemed to be coming from a point further up the canyon.

Tar-gash halted. "Dyal," he said.

Tarzan looked at the Sagoth questioningly.

"It is a Dyal," repeated Tar-gash, "and it is angry."

"What is a Dyal?" asked Tarzan.

"It is a terrible bird," replied the Sagoth; "but its meat is good, and Tar-gash is hungry."

That was enough. No matter how terrible the Dyal might be, it was meat and Tar-gash was hungry, and so the two beasts of prey crept warily forward, stalking their quarry. A vagrant breeze, wafting gently down the canyon, brought to the nostrils of the ape-man a strange, new scent. It was a bird scent, slightly suggestive of the scent of the ostrich, and from its volume Tarzan guessed that it might come from a very large bird, a suggestion that was borne out by the loud screeching of the creature, intermingled with which was a scratching and a scraping sound.

Tar-gash, who was in the lead and who was taking advantage of all the natural shelter afforded by the fragments of rock with which the canyon bed was strewn, came to a halt upon the lower side of a great boulder, behind which he quickly withdrew, and as Tarzan joined him he signaled the ape-man to look around the corner of the boulder.

Following the suggestion of his companion, Tarzan saw the author of the commotion that had attracted their attention. Being a savage jungle beast, he exhibited no outward sign of the astonishment he felt as he gazed upon the mighty creature that was clawing frantically at a crevice in the cliffside.

To Tarzan it was a nameless creature of another world. To Tar-gash it was simply a Dyal. Neither knew that he was looking upon a Phororhacos of the Miocene. They saw a huge creature whose crested head, larger than that of a horse, towered eight feet above the ground. Its powerful, curved beak gaped wide as it screeched in anger. It beat its short, useless wing in a frenzy of rage as it struck with its mighty three-toed talons at something just within the fissure before it. And then it was that Tarzan saw that the thing at which it struck was a spear, held by human hands—a pitifully inadequate weapon with which to attempt to ward off the attack of the mighty Dyal.

As Tarzan surveyed the creature he wondered how Tar-gash, armed only with his puny club, might hope to pit himself in successful combat against it. He saw the Sagoth creep stealthily out from behind their rocky shelter and move slowly to another closer to the Dyal and behind it, and so absorbed was the bird in its attack upon the man within the fissure that it did not notice the approach of the enemy in its rear.

The moment that Tar-gash was safely concealed behind the new shelter, Tarzan followed him and now they were within fifty feet of the great bird.

The Sagoth, grasping his club firmly by the small end, arose and ran swiftly from his concealment, straight toward the giant Dyal, and Tarzan followed, fitting an arrow to his bow.

Tar-gash had covered but half the distance when the sound

of his approach attracted the attention of the bird. Wheeling about, it discovered the two rash creatures who dared to interfere with its attack upon its quarry, and with a loud screech and wide distended beak it charged them.

The instant that the Dyal had turned and discovered them, Tar-gash had commenced whirling his club about his head and as the bird charged he launched it at one of those mighty legs, and on the instant Tarzan understood the purpose of the Sagoth's method of attack. The heavy club, launched by the mighty muscles of the beast man, would snap the leg bone that it struck, and then the enormous fowl would be at the mercy of the Sagoth. But if it did not strike the leg, what then? Almost certain death for Tar-gash.

Tarzan had long since had reason to appreciate his companion's savage disregard of life in the pursuit of flesh, but this seemed the highest pinnacle to which rashness might ascend and still remain within the realm of sanity.

And, indeed, there happened that which Tarzan had feared—the club missed its mark. Tarzan's bow sang and an arrow sank deep into the breast of the Dyal. Tar-gash leaped swiftly to one side, eluding the charge, and another arrow pierced the bird's feathers and hide. And then the ape-man sprang quickly to his right as the avalanche of destruction bore down upon him, its speed undiminished by the force of the two arrows buried so deeply within it.

Before the Dyal could turn to pursue either of them, Tar-gash hurled a rock, many of which were scattered upon the ground about them. It struck the Dyal upon the side of the head, momentarily dazing him, and Tarzan drove home two more arrows. As he did so, the Dyal wheeled drunkenly toward him and as he faced about a great spear drove past Tarzan's shoulder and plunged deep into the breast of the maddened creature, and to the impact of this last missile it went down, falling almost at the feet of the ape-man.

Ignorant though he was of the strength and the methods of attack and defense of this strange bird, Tarzan nevertheless hesitated not an instant and as the Dyal fell he was upon it with drawn hunting knife.

So quickly was he in and out that he had severed its windpipe and was away again before he could become entangled in its death struggle, and then it was that for the first time he saw the man who had cast the spear.

Standing erect, a puzzled expression upon his face, was a tall, stalwart warrior, his slightly bronzed skin gleaming in the sunlight, his shaggy head of hair bound back by a deerskin band.

For weapons, in addition to his spear, he carried a stone knife, thrust into the girdle that supported his G-string. His eyes were well set and intelligent. His features were regular and well cut. Altogether he was as splendid a specimen of manhood as Tarzan had ever beheld.

Tar-gash, who had recovered his club, was advancing toward the stranger. "I am Tar-gash," he said. "I kill."

The stranger drew his stone knife and waited, looking first at Tar-gash and then at Tarzan.

The ape-man stepped in front of Tar-gash. "Wait," he commanded. "Why do you kill?"

"He is a gilak," replied the Sagoth.

"He saved you from the Dyal," Tarzan reminded Tar-gash. "My arrows would not stop the bird. Had it not been for his spear, one or both of us must have died."

The Sagoth appeared puzzled. He scratched his head in perplexity. "But if I do not kill him, he will kill me," he said finally.

Tarzan turned toward the stranger. "I am Tarzan," he said. "This is Tar-gash," and he pointed at the Sagoth and waited.

"I am Thoar," said the stranger.

"Let us be friends," said Tarzan. "We have no quarrel with you."

Again the stranger looked puzzled.

"Do you understand the language of the Sagoths?" asked Tarzan, thinking that possibly the man might not have understood him.

Thoar nodded. "A little," he said; "but why should we be friends?"

"Why should we be enemies?" countered the ape-man.

Thoar shook his head. "I do not know," he said. "It is always thus."

"Together we have slain the Dyal," said Tarzan. "Had we

not come it would have killed you. Had you not cast your spear it would have killed us. Therefore, we should be friends, not enemies. Where are you going?"

"Back to my own country," replied Thoar, nodding in the direction that Tarzan and Tar-gash had been traveling.

"We, too, are going in that direction," said Tarzan. "Let us go together. Six hands are better than four."

Thoar glanced at the Sagoth.

"Shall we all go together as friends, Tar-gash?" demanded Tarzan.

"It is not done," said the Sagoth, precisely as though he had behind him thousands of years of civilization and culture.

Tarzan smiled one of his rare smiles. "We shall do it, then," he said. "Come!"

As though taking it for granted that the others would obey his command, the ape-man turned to the body of the Dyal and, drawing his hunting knife, fell to work cutting off portions of the meat. For a moment Thoar and Tar-gash hesitated, eyeing each other suspiciously, and then the bronzed warrior walked over to assist Tarzan and presently Tar-gash joined them.

Thoar exhibited keen interest in Tarzan's steel knife, which slid so easily through the flesh while he hacked and hewed laboriously with his stone implement; while Tar-gash seemed not particularly to notice either of the implements as he sank his strong fangs into the breast of the Dyal and tore away a large hunk of the meat, which he devoured raw. Tarzan was about to do the same, having been raised exclusively upon a diet of raw meat, when he saw Thoar preparing to make fire, which he accomplished by the primitive expedient of friction. The three ate in silence, the Sagoth carrying his meat to a little distance from the others, perhaps because in him the instinct of the wild beast was stronger.

When they had finished they followed the trail upward toward the pass through which it led across the hills, and as they went Tarzan sought to question Thoar concerning his country and its people, but so limited is the primitive vocabulary of the Sagoths and so meager Thoar's knowledge of this language that they found communication difficult and Tarzan determined to master Thoar's tongue.

Considerable experience in learning new dialects and languages rendered the task far from difficult and as the ape-man never for a moment relinquished a purpose he intended to achieve, nor ever abandoned a task that he had set himself until it had been successfully concluded, he made rapid progress which was greatly facilitated by the interest which Thoar took in instructing him.

As they reached the summit of the low hills, they saw, hazily in the far distance, what appeared to be a range of lofty mountains.

"There," said Thoar, pointing, "lies Zoram."

"What is Zoram?" asked Tarzan.

"It is my country," replied the warrior. "It lies in the Mountains of the Thipdars."

This was the second time that Tarzan had heard a reference to thipdars. Tar-gash had said the aeroplane was a thipdar and now Thoar spoke of the Mountains of the Thipdars. "What is a thipdar?" he asked.

Thoar looked at him in astonishment. "From what country do you come," he demanded, "that you do not know what a thipdar is and do not speak the language of the gilaks?"

"I am not of Pellucidar," said Tarzan.

"I could believe that," said Thoar, "if there were any other place from which you could be, but there is not, except Molop Az, the flaming sea upon which Pellucidar floats. But the only inhabitants of the Molop Az are the little demons, who carry the dead who are buried in the ground, piece by piece, down to Molop Az, and while I have never seen one of these little demons I am sure that they are not like you."

"No," said Tarzan, "I am not from Molop Az, yet sometimes I have thought that the world from which I come is inhabited by demons, both large and small."

As they hunted and ate and slept and marched together, these three creatures found their confidence in one another increasing so that even Tar-gash looked no longer with suspicion upon Thoar, and though they represented three distinct periods in the ascent of man, each separated from the other by countless thousands of years, yet they had so much in common that the advance which man had made from Tar-gash to Tarzan seemed scarcely a fair recompense for the time and effort which Nature must have expended.

Tarzan could not even conjecture the length of time he had been absent from the O-220, but he was confident that he must be upon the wrong trail, yet it seemed futile to turn back since he could not possibly have any idea as to what direction he should take. His one hope was that either he might be sighted by the pilot of the plane, which he was certain was hunting for him, or that the O-220, in cruising about, would eventually pass within signaling distance of him. In the meantime he might as well be with Tar-gash and Thoar as elsewhere.

The three had eaten and slept again and were resuming their journey when Tarzan's keen eyes espied from the summit of a low hill something lying upon an open plain at a considerable distance ahead of them. He did not know what it was, but he was sure that whatever it was, it was not a part of the natural landscape, there being about it that indefinable suggestion of discord, or, more properly, lack of harmony with its surroundings that every man whose perception has not been dulled by city dwelling will understand. And as it was almost instinctive with Tarzan to investigate anything that he did not understand, he turned his footsteps in the direction of the thing that he had seen.

The object that had aroused his curiosity was hidden from him almost immediately after he started the descent of the hill upon which he had stood when he discovered it; nor did it come again within the range of his vision until he was close upon it, when to his astonishment and dismay he saw that it was the wreck of an airplane.

The Red Flower of Zoram

JANA, THE RED Flower of Zoram, paused and looked back across the rocky crags behind and below her. She was very hungry and it had been long since she had slept, for behind her, dogging her trail, were the four terrible men from Pheli, which lies at the foot of the Mountains of the Thipdars, beyond the land of Zoram.

For just an instant she stood erect and then she threw herself prone upon the rough rock, behind a jutting fragment that partially concealed her, and here she looked back along the way she had come, across a pathless waste of tumbled granite. Mountain-bred, she had lived her life among the lofty peaks of the Mountains of the Thipdars, considering contemptuously the people of the lowland to which those who pursued her belonged. Perchance, if they followed her here she might be forced to concede them some measure of courage and possibly to look upon them with a slightly lessened contempt, yet even so she would never abate her effort to escape them.

Bred in the bone of The Red Flower was loathing of the men of Pheli, who ventured occasionally into the fastnesses of the Mountains of the Thipdars to steal women, for the pride and the fame of the mountain people lay in the beauty of their girls, and so far had this fame spread that men came from far countries, out of the vast river basin below their lofty range, and risked a hundred deaths in efforts to steal such a mate as Jana, The Red Flower of Zoram.

The girl's sister, Lana, had been thus stolen, and within her memory two other girls of Zoram, by the men from the lowland, and so the fear, as well as the danger, was ever present. Such a fate seemed to The Red Flower worse than death, since not only would it take her forever from her beloved mountains, but make her a low-country woman and her children low-country children than which, in the eyes of the mountain people, there could be no deeper disgrace, for the mountain men mated only with mountain women, the men of Zoram, and Clovi, and Daroz taking mates from their own tribes or stealing them from their neighbors.

Jana was beloved by many of the young warriors of Zoram, and though, as yet, there had been none who had fired her own heart to love she knew that some day she would mate with one of them, unless in the meantime she was stolen by a warrior from another tribe.

Were she to fall into the hands of one from either Clovi or Daroz she would not be disgraced and she might even be happy, but she was determined to die rather than to be taken by the men from Pheli.

Long ago, it seemed to her now, who had no means for measuring time, she had been searching for thipdar eggs among the lofty crags above the caverns that were the home of her people when a great hairy man leaped from behind a rock and endeavored to seize her. Active as a chamois, she eluded him with ease, but he stood between her and the village and when she sought to circle back she discovered that he had three companions who effectually barred her way, and then had commenced the flight and the pursuit that had taken her far from Zoram among lofty peaks where she had never been before.

Not far below her, four squat, hairy men had stopped to rest. "Let us turn back," growled one. "You can never catch her, Skruk, in country like this, which is fit only for thipdars and no place for men."

Skruk shook his bullet head. "I have seen her," he said, "and I shall have her if I have to chase her to the shores of Molop Az."

"Our hands are torn by the sharp rock," said another. "Our sandals are almost gone and our feet bleed. We cannot go on. We shall die."

"You may die," said Skruk, "but until then you shall go on. I am Skruk, the chief, and I have spoken."

The others growled resentfully, but when Skruk took up the pursuit again they followed him. Being from a low country they found strenuous exertion in these high altitudes exhausting, it is true, but the actual basis for their disinclination to continue the pursuit was the terror which the dizzy heights inspired in them and the perilous route along which The Red Flower of Zoram was leading them.

From above Jana saw them ascending, and knowing that they were again upon the right trail she stood erect in plain view of them. Her single, soft garment made from the pelt of tarag cubs, whipped about her naked legs, half revealing, half concealing the rounded charms of her girlish figure. The noonday sun shone down upon her light, bronzed skin, glistening from the naked contours of a perfect shoulder and imparting golden glints to her hair that was sometimes a lustrous brown and again a copper bronze. It was piled loosely upon her head and held in place by slender, hollow bones of the dimorphodon, a little long-tailed cousin of the thipdar. The upper ends of these bone pins were ornamented with carving and some of them were colored. A fillet of soft skin ornamented in colors encircled her brow and she wore bracelets and anklets made of the vertebrae of small animals, strung upon leather thongs. These, too, were carved and colored. Upon her feet were stout little sandals, soled with the hide of the mastodon and from the center of her headband rose a single feather. At her hip was a stone knife and in her right hand a light spear.

She stooped and picking up a small fragment of rock hurled it down at Skruk and his companions. "Go back to your swamps, jaloks of the low country," she cried. "The Red Flower of Zoram is not for you," and then she turned and sped away across the pathless granite.

To her left lay Zoram, but there was a mighty chasm between her and the city. Along its rim she made her way, sometimes upon its very verge, but unshaken by the frightful abyss below her. Constantly she sought for a means of descent, since she knew that if she could cross it she might circle back toward Zoram, but the walls rose sheer for two thousand feet offering scarce a handhold in a hundred feet.

As she rounded the shoulder of the peak she saw a vast country stretching away below her—a country that she had never seen before—and she knew that she had crossed the mighty range and was looking on the land that lay beyond. The fissure that she had been following she could see widening below her into a great canyon that led out through foothills to a mighty plain. The slopes of the lower hills were wooded and beyond the plain were forests.

This was a new world to Jana of Zoram, but it held no lure for her; it did not beckon to her for she knew that savage beasts and savage men of the low countries roamed its plains and forests.

To her right rose the mountains she had rounded; to her left was the deep chasm, and behind her were Skruk and his three companions.

For a moment she feared that she was trapped, but after advancing a few yards she saw that the sheer wall of the abyss had given way to a tumbled mass of broken ledges. But whether there were any means of descent, even here, she did not know—she could only hope.

From pausing often to search for a way down into the gorge, Jana had lost precious time and now she became suddenly aware that her pursuers were close behind her. Again she sprang forward, leaping from rock to rock, while they redoubled their speed and stumbled after her in pursuit, positive now that they were about to capture her.

Jana glanced below, and a hundred feet beneath her she saw a tumbled mass of granite that had fallen from above and formed a wide ledge. Just ahead the mountain jutted out forming an overhanging cliff.

She glanced back. Skruk was already in sight. He was stumbling awkwardly along in a clumsy run and breathing heavily, but he was very near and she must choose quickly.

There was but one way—over the edge of the cliff lay temporary escape or certain death. A leather thong, attached a foot below the point of her spear, she fastened around her neck, letting the spear hang down her back, threw herself upon the ground and slid over the edge of the cliff. Perhaps there were handholds; perhaps not. She glanced down. The face of the cliff was rough and not perpendicular, leaning in a little toward the mountain. She felt about with her toes and finally she located a protuberance that would hold her weight. Then she relinquished her hold upon the top of the cliff with one hand and searched about for a crevice in which to insert her fingers, or a projection to which she could cling.

She must work quickly for already the footsteps of the Phelians were sounding above her. She found a hold to which she might cling with scarcely more than the tips of her fingers, but it was something and the horror of the lowland was just above her and only death below.

She relinquished her hold upon the cliff edge with her other hand and lowered herself very slowly down the face of the cliff, searching with her free foot for another support. One foot, two, three she descended, and then attracted by a noise above her she glanced up and saw the hairy face of Skruk just above her.

"Hold my legs," he shouted to his companions, at the same time throwing himself prone at the edge of the cliff, and as they obeyed his command he reached down a long, hairy arm to seize Jana, and the girl was ready to let go all holds and drop to the jagged rocks beneath when Skruk's hand should touch her. Still looking upward she saw the fist of the Phelian but a few inches from her face.

The outstretched fingers of the man brushed the hair of the girl. One of her groping feet found a tiny ledge and she lowered herself from immediate danger of capture. Skruk was furious, but that one glance into the upturned face of the girl so close beneath him only served to add to his determination to possess her. No lengths were too far now to go to achieve his heart's desire, but as he glanced down that frightful escarpment his savage heart was filled with fear for the safety of his prize. It seemed incredible that she had descended as far as she had without falling and she had only commenced the descent. He knew that he and his companions could not follow the trail that she was blazing and he realized, too, that if they menaced her from above she might be urged to a greater haste that would spell her doom.

With these thoughts in his mind Skruk arose to his feet and turned to his companions. "We shall seek an easier way down," he said in a low voice, and then leaning over the cliff edge, he called down to Jana. "You have beaten me, mountain girl," he said. "I go back now to Pheli in the lowland. But I shall return and then I shall take you with me as my mate."

"May the thipdars catch you and tear out your heart before ever you reach Pheli again," cried Jana. But Skruk made no reply and she saw that they were going back the way that they had come, but she did not know that they were merely looking for an easier way into the bottom of the gorge toward which she was descending, or that Skruk's words had been but a ruse to throw her off her guard.

The Red Flower of Zoram, relieved of immediate necessity for haste, picked her way cautiously down the face of the cliff to the first ledge of tumbled granite. Here, by good fortune, she found the egg of a thipdar, which furnished her with both food and drink.

It was a long, slow descent to the bottom of the gorge, but finally the girl accomplished it, and in the meantime Skruk and his companions had found an easier way and had descended into the gorge several miles above her.

For a moment after she reached the bottom Jana was undecided as to what course to pursue. Instinct urged her to turn upward along the gorge in the general direction of Zoram, but her judgment prompted her to descend and skirt the base of the mountain to the left in search of an easier route back across them. And so she came leisurely down toward the valley, while behind her followed the four men from Pheli.

The canyon wall at her left, while constantly lessening in height as she descended, still presented a formidable obstacle, which it seemed wiser to circumvent than to attempt to surmount, and so she continued on downward toward the mouth of the canyon, where it debauched upon a lovely valley.

Never before in all her life had Jana approached the lowland so closely. Never before had she dreamed how lovely the low-land country might be, for she had always been taught that it was a horrid place and no fit abode for the stalwart tribes of the mountains.

The lure of the beauties and the new scenes unfolding before her, coupled with a spirit of exploration which was being born within her, led her downward into the valley much farther than necessity demanded.

Suddenly her attention was attracted by a strange sound coming suddenly from on high—a strange, new note in the dia-pason of her savage world, and glancing upward she finally descried the creature that must be the author of it.

A great thipdar, it appeared to be, moaning dismally far above her head—but what a thipdar! Never in her life had she seen one as large as this.

As she watched she saw another thipdar, much smaller, soaring above it. Suddenly the lesser one swooped upon its intended prey. Faintly she heard sounds of shattering and tearing and then the two combatants plunged earthward. As they did so she saw something separate itself from the mass and as the two creatures, partially supported by the wings of the larger, fell in a great, gliding spiral a most remarkable thing happened to the piece that had broken loose. Something shot out of it and unfolded above it in the air—something that resembled a huge toadstool, and as it did so the swift flight of the falling body was arrested and it floated slowly earthward, swinging back and forth as she had seen a heavy stone do when tied at the end of a buckskin thong.

As the strange thing descended nearer, Jana's eyes went wide in surprise and terror as she recognized the dangling body as that of a man.

Her people had few superstitions, not having advanced suf-ficiently in the direction of civilization to have developed a priesthood, but here was something that could be explained according to no natural logic. She had seen two great, flying reptiles meet in battle, high in air, and out of one of them had come a man. It was incredible, but more than all it was terri-fying. And so The Red Flower of Zoram, reacting in the most natural way, turned and fled.

Back toward the canyon she raced, but she had gone only a short distance when, directly in front of her, she saw Skruk and his three companions.

They, too, had seen the battle in midair and they had seen the thing floating downward toward the ground, and while they had not recognized it for what it was they had been terrified and were themselves upon the point of fleeing when Skruk descried Jana running toward them. Instantly every other consideration was submerged in his desire to have her and growling commands to his terrified henchmen he led them toward the girl.

When Jana discovered them she turned to the right and tried to circle about them, but Skruk sent one to intercept her and when she turned in the opposite direction, the four spread out across her line of retreat so as to effectually bar her escape in that direction.

Choosing any fate rather than that which must follow her capture by Skruk, Jana turned again and fled down the valley and in pursuit leaped the four squat, hairy men of Pheli.

At the instant that Jason Gridley had pulled the rip cord of his parachute a fragment of the broken propeller of his plane had struck him a glancing blow upon the head, and when he regained consciousness he found himself lying upon a bed of soft grasses at the head of a valley, where a canyon, winding out of lofty mountains, opened onto leveler land.

Disgusted by the disastrous end of his futile search for his companions, Gridley arose and removed the parachute harness. He was relieved to discover that he had suffered no more serious injury than a slight abrasion of the skin upon one temple.

His first concern was for his ship and though he knew that it must be a total wreck he hoped against hope that he might at least salvage his rifle and ammunition from it. But even as the thought entered his mind it was forced into the background by a chorus of savage yelps and growls that caused him to turn his eyes quickly to the right. At the summit of a little rise of ground a short distance away he saw four of the ferocious wolf dogs of Pellucidar. As hyaenodons they were known to the paleontologists of the outer crust, and as jaloks to the men of the inner world. As large as full-grown mastiffs they stood there upon their short, powerful legs, their broad, strong jaws parted in angry growls, their snarling lips drawn back to reveal their powerful fangs.

As he discovered them Jason became aware that their attention was not directed upon him—that they seemed not as yet to have discovered him—and as he looked in the direction that they were looking he was astounded to see a girl running swiftly toward them, and at a short distance behind the girl four men, who were apparently pursuing her.

As the vicious growls of the jaloks broke angrily upon the comparative silence of the scene, the girl paused and it was evident that she had not before been aware of the presence of this new menace. She glanced at them and then back at her pursuers.

The hyaenodons advanced toward her at an easy trot. In piteous bewilderment she glanced about her. There was but one way open for escape and then as she turned to flee in that direction her eyes fell upon Jason Gridley, straight ahead in her path of flight and again she hesitated.

To the man came an intuitive understanding of her quandary. Menaced from the rear and upon two sides by known enemies, she was suddenly faced by what might indeed be another, cutting off all hope of retreat.

Acting impulsively and in accordance with the code that dominates his kind, Gridley ran toward the girl, shouting words of encouragement and motioning her to come to him.

Skruk and his companions were closing in upon her from behind and from her right, while upon her left came the jaloks. For just an instant longer, she hesitated and then seemingly determined to place her fate in the hands of an unknown rather than surrender it to the inevitable doom which awaited her either at the hands of the Phelians or the fangs of the jaloks, she turned and sped toward Gridley, and behind her came the four beasts and the four men.

As Gridley ran forward to meet the girl he drew one of his revolvers, a heavy .45 caliber Colt.

The hyaenodons were charging now and the leader was close behind her, and at that instant Jana tripped and fell, and simultaneously Jason reached her side, but so close was the savage beast that when Jason fired the hyaenodon's body fell across the body of the girl.

The shot, a startling sound to which none of them was accustomed, brought the other hyaenodons to a sudden stop, as well as the four men, who were racing rapidly forward under Skruk's command in an effort to save the girl from the beasts.

Quickly rolling the body of the jalok from its intended victim, Jason lifted the girl to her feet and as he did so she snatched her stone knife from its scabbard. Jason Gridley did not know how near he was to death at that instant. To Jana, every man except the men of Zoram was a natural enemy. The first law of nature prompted her to kill lest she be killed, but in the instant before she struck the blade home she saw something in the eyes of this man, something in the expression upon his face that she had never seen in the eyes or face of any man before. As plainly as though it had been spoken in words she understood that this stranger was prompted by solicitousness for her safety; that he was prompted by a desire to befriend rather than to harm her, and though in common with the jaloks and the Phelians she had been terrified by the loud noise and the smoke that had burst from the strange stick in his hand she knew that this had been the means that he had taken to protect her from the jaloks.

Her knife hand dropped to her side, and, as a slow smile lighted the face of the stranger, The Red Flower of Zoram smiled back in response.

They stood as they had when he had lifted her from the ground, his left arm about her shoulders supporting her and he maintained this unconscious gesture of protection as he turned to face the girl's enemies, who, after their first fright, seemed on the point of returning to the attack.

Two of the hyaenodons, however, had transferred their attention to Skruk and his companions, while the third was slinking bare fanged toward Jason and Jana.

The men of Pheli stood ready to receive the charge of the hyaenodons, having taken positions in line, facing their attackers, and at sufficient intervals to permit them properly to wield their clubs. As the beasts charged two of the men hurled their weapons, each singling out one of the fierce carnivores. Skruk hurled his weapon with the greater accuracy, breaking one of the forelegs of the beast attacking him, and as it went down the Phelian standing next to Skruk leaped forward and rained heavy blows upon its skull.

The cudgel aimed at the other beast struck it a glancing blow upon the shoulder, but did not stop it and an instant later it was upon the Phelian whose only defense now was his crude stone knife. But his companion, who had reserved his club for such an emergency, leaped in and swung lustily at the savage brute, while Skruk and the other, having disposed of their adversary, came to the assistance of their fellows.

The savage battle between men and beast went unnoticed by Jason, whose whole attention was occupied by the fourth wolf dog as it moved forward to attack him and his companion.

Jana, fully aware that the attention of each of the men was fully centered upon the attacking beasts, realized that now was the opportune moment to make a break for freedom. She felt the arm of the stranger about her shoulder, but it rested there lightly—so lightly that she might easily disengage herself by a single, quick motion. but there was something in the feel of that arm about her that imparted to her a sense of greater safety than she had felt since she had left the caverns of her people—perhaps the protective instinct which dominated the man subconsciously exerted its natural reaction upon the girl to the end that instead of fleeing she was content to remain, sensing greater safety where she was than elsewhere.

And then the fourth hyaenodon charged, growling, to be met by the roaring bark of the Colt. The creature stumbled and went down, stopped by the force of the heavy charge—but only for an instant—again it was up, maddened by pain, desperate in the face of death. Bloody foam crimsoned its jowls as it leaped for Jason's throat.

Again the Colt spoke, and then the man went down beneath the heavy body of the wolf dog, and at the same instant the Phelians dispatched the second of the beasts which had attacked them.

Jason Gridley was conscious of a great weight upon him as he was borne to the ground and he sought to fend those horrid jaws from his throat by interposing his left forearm, but the jaws never closed and when Gridley struggled from beneath the body of the beast and scrambled to his feet he saw the girl tugging upon the shaft of her crude, stone-tipped spear in an effort to drag it from the body of the jalok.

Whether his last bullet or the spear had dispatched the beast the man did not know, and he was only conscious of gratitude and admiration for the brave act of the slender girl, who had stood her ground at his side, facing the terrible beast without loss of poise or resourcefulness.

The four jaloks lay dead, but Jason Gridley's troubles were by no means over, for scarcely had he arisen after the killing of the second beast when the girl seized him by the arm and pointed toward something behind him.

"They are coming," she said. "They will kill you and take me. Oh, do not let them take me!"

Jason did not understand a word that she had said, but it was evident from her tone of voice and from the expression upon her beautiful face that she was more afraid of the four men approaching them than she had been of the hyaenodons, and as he turned to face them he could not wonder, for the men of Pheli looked quite as brutal as the hyaenodons and there was nothing impressive or magnificent in their appearance as there had been in the mien of the savage carnivores—a fact which is almost universally noticeable when a comparison is made between the human race and the so-called lower orders.

Gridley raised his revolver and leveled it at the leading Phelian, who happened to be another than Skruk. "Beat it!" he said. "Your faces frighten the young lady."

"I am Gluf," said the Phelian. "I kill."

"If I could understand you I might agree with you," replied Jason, "but your exuberant whiskers and your diminutive forehead suggest that you are all wet."

He did not want to kill the man, but he realized that he could not let him approach too closely. But if he had any compunction in the matter of manslaughter, it was evident that the girl did not for she was talking volubly, evidently urging him to some action, and when she realized that he could not understand her she touched his pistol with a brown forefinger and then pointed meaningly at Gluf.

The fellow was now within fifteen paces of them and Jason could see that his companions were starting to circle them. He knew that something must be done immediately and prompted by humanitarian motives he fired his Colt, aiming above the head of the approaching Phelian. The sharp report stopped all four of them, but when they realized that none of them were injured they broke into a torrent of taunts and threats, and Gluf, inspired only by a desire to capture the girl so that they might return to Pheli, resumed his advance, at the same time commencing to swing his club menacingly. Then it was that Jason Gridley regretfully shot, and shot to kill. Gluf stopped in his tracks, stiffened, whirled about and sprawled forward upon his face.

Wheeling upon the others, Gridley fired again, for he realized that those menacing clubs were almost as effective at short range as was his Colt. Another Phelian dropped in his tracks, and then Skruk and his remaining companion turned and fled.

"Well," said Gridley, looking about him at the bodies of the four hyaenodons and the corpses of the two men, "this is a great little country, but I'll be gosh-darned if I see how anyone grows up to enjoy it."

The Red Flower of Zoram stood looking at him admiringly. Everything about this stranger aroused her interest, piqued her curiosity and stimulated her imagination. In no particular was he like any other man she had ever seen. Not one item of his strange apparel corresponded to anything that any other human being of her acquaintance wore. The remarkable weapon, which spat smoke and fire to the accompaniment of a loud roar, left her dazed with awe and admiration; but perhaps the outstanding cause for astonishment, when she gave it thought, was the fact that she was not afraid of this man. Not only was the fear of strangers inherent in her, but from earliest childhood she had been taught to expect only the worst from men who were not of her own tribe and to flee from them upon any and all occasions. Perhaps it was his smile that had disarmed her, or possibly there was something in his friendly, honest eyes that had won her immediate trust and confidence. Whatever the cause, however, the fact remained that The Red Flower of Zoram made no effort to escape from Jason Gridley, who now found himself completely lost in a strange world, which in itself was quite sad enough without having added to it responsibilities for the protection of a strange young woman, who could understand nothing that he said to her and whom, in turn, he could not understand.

8

Jana and Jason

TAR-GASH AND THOAR looked with wonder upon the wreckage of the plane and Tarzan hastily searched it for the body of the pilot. The ape-man experienced at least temporary relief when he discovered that there was no body there, and a moment later he found footprints in the turf upon the opposite side of the plane—the prints of a booted foot which he recognized immediately as having been made by Jason Gridley—and this evidence assured him that the American had not been killed and apparently not even badly injured by the fall. And then he discovered something else which puzzled him exceedingly. Mingling with the footprints of Gridley and evidently made at the same time were those of a small sandaled foot.

A further brief examination revealed the fact that two persons, one of them Gridley and the other apparently a female or a youth of some Pellucidarian tribe, who had accompanied him, had approached the plane after it had crashed, remained in its vicinity for a short time and then returned in the direction from which they had come. With the spoor plain before him there was nothing for Tarzan to do other than to follow it.

The evidence so far suggested that Gridley had been forced to abandon the plane in air and that he had safely made a parachute descent, but where and under what circumstances he had picked up his companion, Tarzan could not even hazard a guess.

He found it difficult to get Thoar away from the airplane, the strange thing having so fired his curiosity and imagination that he must need remain near it and ask a hundred questions concerning it.

With Tar-gash, however, the reaction was entirely different. He had glanced at it with only a faint show of curiosity or interest, and then he had asked one question, "What is it?"

"This is the thing that passed over us and which you said was a flying reptile," replied Tarzan. "I told you at that time that one of my friends was in it. Something happened and the thing fell, but my friend escaped without injury."

"It has no eyes," said Tar-gash. "How could it see to fly?"

"It was not alive," replied Tarzan.

"I heard it growl," said the Sagoth; nor was he ever convinced that the thing was not some strange form of living creature.

They had covered but a short distance along the trail made by Gridley and Jana, after they had left the airplane, when they came upon the carcass of a huge pteranodon. Its head was crushed and battered and almost severed from its body and a splinter of smooth wood projected from its skull—a splinter that Tarzan recognized as a fragment of an airplane propeller—and instantly he knew the cause of Gridley's crash.

Half a mile farther on the three discovered further evidence, some of it quite startling. An opened parachute lay stretched upon the ground where it had fallen and at short distances from it lay the bodies of four hyaenodons and two hairy men.

An examination of the bodies revealed the fact that both of the men and two of the hyaenodons had died from bullet wounds. Everywhere upon the trampled turf appeared the imprints of the small sandals of Jason's companion. It was evident to the keen eyes of Tarzan that two other men, both natives, had taken part in the battle which had been waged here. That they were of the same tribe as the two that had fallen was evidenced by the imprints of their sandals, which were of identical make, while those of Tarzan's companion differed materially from all the others.

As he circled about, searching for further evidence, he saw that the two men who had escaped had run rapidly for some distance toward the mouth of a large canyon, and that, apparently following their retreat, Jason and his companion had set out in search of the plane. Later they had returned to the scene of the battle, and when they had departed they also had gone toward the mountains, but along a line considerably to the right of the trail made by the fleeing natives.

Thoar, too, was much interested in the various tracks that the participants in the battle by the parachute had left, but he said nothing until after Tarzan had completed his investigation.

"There were four men and either a woman or a youth here with my friend," said Tarzan.

"Four of them were low countrymen from Pheli," said Thoar, "and the other was a woman of Zoram."

"How do you know?" asked Tarzan, who was always anxious to add to his store of woodcraft.

"The low-country sandals are never shaped to the foot as closely as are those of the mountain tribes," replied Thoar, "and the soles are much thinner, being made usually of the hides of the thag, which is tough enough for people who do not walk often upon anything but soft grasses or in soggy marshland. The sandals of the mountain tribes are soled with the thick hide of Maj, the cousin of Tandor. If you will look at the spoor you will see that they are not worn at all, while there are holes in the sandals of these dead men of Pheli."

"Are we near Zoram?" asked Tarzan.

"No," replied Thoar. "It lies across the highest range ahead of us."

"When we first met, Thoar, you told me that you were from Zoram."

"Yes, that is my country," replied Thoar.

"Then, perhaps, this woman is someone whom you know?"

"She is my sister," replied Thoar.

Tarzan of the Apes looked at him in surprise. "How do you know?" he demanded.

"I found an imprint where there was no turf, only soft earth, and there the spoor was so distinct that I could recognize the sandals as hers. So familiar with her work am I that I could recognize the stitching alone, where the sole is joined to the upper part of the sandal, and in addition there are the notches, which indicate the tribe. The people of Zoram have three notches in the underside of the sole at the toe of the left sandal."

"What was your sister doing so far from her own country and how is it that she is with my friend?"

"It is quite plain," replied Thoar. "These men of Pheli sought to capture her. One of them wanted her for his mate, but she eluded them and they pursued her across the Mountains of the Thipdars and down into this valley, where she was set upon by jaloks. The man from your country came and killed the jaloks and two of the Phelians and drove the other two away. It is evident that my sister could not escape him, and he captured her."

Tarzan of the Apes smiled. "The spoor does not indicate that she ever made any effort to escape him," he said.

Thoar scratched his head. "That is true," he replied, "and I cannot understand it, for the women of my tribe do not care to mate with the men of other tribes and I know that Jana, my sister, would rather die than mate outside the Mountains of the Thipdars. Many times has she said so and Jana is not given to idle talk."

"My friend would not take her by force," said Tarzan. "If she has gone with him, she has gone with him willingly. And I think that when we find them you will discover that he is simply accompanying her back to Zoram, for he is the sort of man who would not permit a woman to go alone and unprotected."

"We shall see," said Thoar, "but if he has taken Jana against her wishes, he must die."

As Tarzan, Tar-gash, and Thoar followed the spoor of Jason and Jana a disheartened company of men rounded the end of the great Mountains of the Thipdars, fifty miles to the east of them, and entered the Gyor Cors, or great Plains of the Gyors.

The party consisted of ten black warriors and a white man, and, doubtless, never in the history of mankind had eleven men been more completely and hopelessly lost than these.

Muviro and his warriors, than whom no better trackers ever lived, were totally bewildered by their inability even to back-track successfully.

The stampeding of the maddened beasts, from which they had barely escaped with their lives and then only by what appeared nothing short of a miracle, had so obliterated all signs of the party's former spoor that though they were all confident that they had gone but a short distance from the clearing, into which the beasts had been herded by the tarags, they had never again been able to locate the clearing, and now they were wandering hopelessly and, in accordance with Von Horst's plans, keeping as much in the open as possible in the hope that the cruising O-220 might thus discover them, for Von Horst was positive that eventually his companions would undertake a search for them.

Aboard the O-220 the grave fear that had been entertained for the safety of the thirteen missing members of the ship's company had developed into a conviction of disaster when Gridley failed to return within the limit of the time that he might reasonably be able to keep the scout plane in the air.

Then it was that Zuppner had sent Dorf out with another searching party, but at the end of seventy hours they had returned to report absolute failure. They had followed the trail to a clearing where jackals fed upon rotting carrion, but beyond this there was no sign of spoor to suggest in what direction their fellows had wandered.

Going and coming they had been beset by savage beasts and so ruthless and determined had been the attacks of the giant tarags that Dorf reported to Zuppner that he was confident that all of the missing members of the party must by this time have been destroyed by these great cats.

"Until we have proof of that, we must not give up hope," replied Zuppner, "nor may we relinquish our efforts to find them, whether dead or alive, and that we cannot do by remaining here."

There was nothing now to delay the start. While the motors were warming up, the anchor was drawn in and the air expelled from the lower vacuum tanks. As the giant ship rose from the ground Robert Jones jotted down a brief note in a greasy memorandum book: "We sailed from here at noon."

When Skruk and his companion had left the field to the victorious Jason, the latter had returned his six-gun to its holster and faced the girl. "Well," he inquired, "what now?"

She shook her head. "I cannot understand you," she said. "You do not speak the language of gilaks."

Jason scratched his head. "That being the case," he said, "and as it is evident that we are never going to get anywhere on conversation which neither one of us understands, I am going to have a look around for my ship, in the meantime, praying to all the gods that my thirty-thirty and ammunition are safe. It's a cinch that she did not burn for she must have fallen close by and I would have seen the smoke."

Jana listened attentively and shook her head.

"Come on," said Jason, and started off in the direction that he thought the ship might lie.

"No, not that way," exclaimed Jana, and running forward she seized his arm and tried to stop him, pointing back to the tall peaks of the Mountains of the Thipdars, where Zoram lay.

Jason essayed the difficult feat of explaining in a weird sign language of his own invention that he was looking for an airplane that had crashed somewhere in the vicinity, but the conviction soon claimed him that that would be a very difficult thing to accomplish even if the person to whom he was trying to convey the idea knew what an airplane was, and so he ended up by grinning good-naturedly, and, seizing the girl by the hand, gently leading her in the direction he wished to go.

Again that charming smile disarmed The Red Flower of Zoram and though she knew that this stranger was leading her away from the caverns of her people, yet she followed docilely, though her brow was puckered in perplexity as she tried to understand why she was not afraid, or why she was willing to go with this stranger, who evidently was not even a gilak, since he could not speak the language of men.

A half hour's search was rewarded by the discovery of the wreck of the plane, which had suffered far less damage than Jason had expected.

It was evident that in its plunge to earth it must have straightened out and glided to a landing. Of course, it was wrecked beyond repair, even if there had been any facilities for repairs, but it had not burned and Jason recovered his thirty-thirty and all his ammunition.

Jana was intensely interested in the plane and examined every portion of it minutely. Never in her life had she wished so much to ask questions, for never in her life had she seen anything that had so aroused her wonder. And here was the one person in all the world who could answer her questions, but she could not make him understand one of them. For a moment she almost hated him, and then he smiled at her and pressed her hand, and she forgave him and smiled back.

"And now," said Jason, "where do we go from here? As far as I am concerned one place is as good as another."

Being perfectly well aware that he was hopelessly lost, Jason Gridley felt that the only chance he had of being reunited with his companions lay in the possibility that the O-220 might chance to cruise over the very locality where he happened to be, and no matter whither he might wander, whether north or south or east or west, that chance was as slender in one direction as another, and, conversely, equally good. In an hour the O-220 would cover a distance fully as great as he could travel in several days of outer earthly time. And so even if he chanced to be moving in a direction that led away from the ship's first anchorage, he could never go so far that it might not easily and quickly overtake him, if its search should chance to lead it in his direction. Therefore he turned questioningly to the girl, pointing first in one direction, and then in another, while he looked inquiringly at her, attempting thus to convey to her the idea that he was ready and willing to go in any direction she chose, and Jana, sensing his meaning, pointed toward the lofty Mountains of the Thipdars.

"There," she said, "lies Zoram, the land of my people."

"Your logic is unassailable," said Jason, "and I only wish I could understand what you are saying, for I am sure that anyone with such beautiful teeth could never be uninteresting."

Jana did not wait to discuss the matter, but started forthwith for Zoram and beside her walked Jason Gridley of California.

Jana's active mind had been working rapidly and she had come to the conclusion that she could not for long endure the constantly increasing pressure of unsatisfied curiosity. She must find some means of communicating with this interesting stranger and to the accomplishment of this end she could conceive of no better plan than teaching the man her language. But how to commence! Never in her experience or that of her people had the necessity arisen for teaching a language. Previously she had not dreamed of the existence of such a means. If you can feature such a state, which is doubtful, you must concede to this primitive girl of the Stone Age a high degree of intelligence. This was no accidental blowing off of the lid of the teapot upon which might be built a theory. It required, as a matter of fact, a greater reasoning ability. Give a steam engine to a man who had never heard of steam and ask him to make it go—Jana's problem was almost as difficult. But the magnitude of the reward spurred her on, for what will one not do to have one's curiosity satisfied, especially if one happens to be a young and beautiful girl and the object of one's curiosity an exceptionally handsome young man. Skirts may change, but human nature never.

And so The Red Flower of Zoram pointed at herself with a slim, brown forefinger and said, "Jana." She repeated this several times and then she pointed at Jason, raising her eyebrows in interrogation.

"Jason," he said, for there was no misunderstanding her meaning. And so the slow, laborious task began as the two trudged upward toward the foothills of the Mountains of the Thipdars.

There lay before them a long, hard climb to the higher altitudes, but there was water in abundance in the tumbling brooks, dropping down the hillside, and Jana knew the edible plants, and nuts, and fruits which grew in riotous profusion in many a dark, deep ravine, and there was game in plenty to be brought down, when they needed meat, by Jason's thirty-thirty.

As they proceeded in their quest for Zoram, Jason found greater opportunity to study his companion and he came to the conclusion that nature had attained the pinnacle of physical perfection with the production of this little savage. Every line and curve of that lithe, brown body sang of symmetry, for The Red Flower of Zoram was a living poem of beauty. If he had thought that her teeth were beautiful he was forced to admit that they held no advantage in that respect over her eyes, her nose, or any other of her features. And when she fell to with her crude stone knife and helped him skin a kill and prepare the meat for cooking, when he saw the deftness and celerity with which she made fire with the simplest and most primitive of utensils, when he witnessed the almost uncanny certitude with which she located nests of eggs and edible fruit and vegetables, he was conscious that her perfections were not alone physical and he became more than ever anxious to acquire a sufficient understanding of her tongue to be able to communicate with her, though he realized that he might doubtless suffer a rude awakening and disillusionment when, through an understanding of her language, he might be able to judge the limitations of her mind.

When Jana was tired she went beneath a tree, and making a bed of grasses, curled up and fell asleep immediately, and, while she slept, Gridley watched, for the dangers of this primitive land were numerous and constant. Fully as often as he shot for food he shot to protect them from some terrible beast, until the encounters became as prosaic and commonplace as does the constant eluding of death by pedestrians at congested traffic corners in cities of the outer crust.

When Jason felt the need of sleep, Jana watched and sometimes they merely rested without sleeping, usually beneath a tree for there they found the greatest protection from their greatest danger, the fierce and voracious thipdars from which the mountains took their name. These hideous, flying reptiles were a constant menace, but so thoroughly had nature developed a defense against them that the girl could hear their wings at a greater distance than either of them could see the creatures.

Jason had no means for determining how far they had traveled, or how long they had been upon their way, but he was sure that considerable outer earthly time must have elapsed since he had met the girl, when they came to a seemingly insurmountable obstacle, for already he had made considerable progress toward mastering her tongue and they were exchanging short sentences, much to Jana's delight, her merry laughter often marking one of Jason's more flagrant errors in pronunciation or construction.

And now they had come to a deep chasm with overhanging walls that not even Jana could negotiate. To Jason it resembled a stupendous fault that might have been caused by the subsidence of the mountain range for it paralleled the main axis of the range. And if this were true he knew that it might extend for hundreds of miles, effectually barring the way across the mountains by the route they were following.

For a long time Jana sought a means of descent into the crevice. She did not want to turn to the left as that route might lead her eventually back to the canyon that she had descended when pursued by Skruk and his fellows and she well knew how almost unscalable were the perpendicular sides of this terrific gorge. Another thing, perhaps, which decided her against the left-hand route was the possibility that in that direction they might again come in contact with the Phelians, and so she led Jason toward the right and always she searched for a way to the bottom of the rift.

Jason realized that they were consuming a great deal of time in trying to cross, but he became also aware of the fact that time meant nothing in timeless Pellucidar. It was never a factor with which to reckon for the excellent reason that it did not exist, and when he gave the matter thought he was conscious of a mild surprise that he, who had been always a slave of time, so easily and naturally embraced the irresponsible existence of Pellucidar. It was not only the fact that time itself seemed not to matter but that the absence of this greatest of all taskmasters singularly affected one's outlook upon every other consideration of existence. Without time there appeared to be no accountability for one's acts since it is to the future that the slaves of time have learned to look for their reward or

punishment. Where there is no time, there is no future. Jason
Gridley found himself affected much as Tarzan had been in
that the sense of his responsibility for the welfare of his fellows
seemed deadened. What had happened to them had happened
and no act of his could alter it. They were not there with him
and so he could not be of assistance to them, and as it was
difficult to visualize the future beneath an eternal noonday sun
how might one plan ahead for others or for himself?

Jason Gridley gave up the riddle with a shake of his head
and found solace in contemplation of the profile of The Red
Flower of Zoram.

"Why do you look at me so much?" demanded the girl; for
by now they could make themselves understood to one
another.

Jason Gridley flushed slightly and looked quickly away. Her
question had been very abrupt and surprising and for the first
time he realized that he had been looking at her a great deal. He
started to answer, hesitated and stopped. Why *had* he been
looking at her so much? It seemed silly to say that it was
because she was beautiful.

"Why do you not say it, Jason?" she inquired.

"Say what?" he demanded.

"Say the thing that is in your eyes when you look at me," she
replied.

Gridley looked at her in astonishment. No one but an imbecile could have misunderstood her meaning, and Jason Gridley
was no imbecile.

Could it be possible that he had been looking at her *that*
way? Had he gone stark mad that he was even subconsciously
entertaining such thoughts of this little barbarian who seized
her meat in both hands and tore pieces from it with her
flashing, white teeth, who went almost as naked as the beasts of
the field and with all their unconsciousness of modesty? Could
it be that his eyes had told this untutored savage that he was
harboring thoughts of love for her? The artificialities of a thousand years of civilization rose up in horror against such a
thought.

Upon the screen of his memory there was flashed a picture
of the haughty Cynthia Furnois of Hollywood, daughter of the

famous director, Abelard Furnois, né Abe Fink. He recalled Cynthia's meticulous observance of the minutest details of social usages and the studied perfection of her deportment that had sometimes awed him. He saw, too, the aristocratic features of Barbara Green, daughter of old John Green, the Los Angeles realtor, from Texas. It is true that old John was no purist and that his total disregard of the social precedence of forks often shocked the finer sensibilities that Mrs. Green and Barbara had laboriously achieved in the universities of Montmarte and Cocoanut Grove, but Barbara had had two years at Marlborough and knew her suffixes and her hardware.

Of course Cynthia was a rotten little snob, not only on the surface but to the bottom of her shallow, selfish soul, while Barbara's snobbishness, he felt, was purely artificial, the result of mistaking for the genuine the silly artificialities and affectations of the almost celebrities and sudden rich that infest the public places of Hollywood.

But nevertheless these two did, after a fashion, reflect the social environment to which he was accustomed and as he tried to answer Jana's question he could not but picture her seated at dinner with a company made up of such as these. Of course, Jana was a bully companion upon an adventure such as that in which they were engaged, but modern man cannot go adventuring forever in the Stone Age. If his eyes had carried any other message to Jana than that of friendly comradeship he felt sorry, for he realized that in fairness to her, as well as to himself, there could never be anything more than this between them.

As Jason hesitated for a reply, the eyes of The Red Flower of Zoram searched his soul and slowly the half-expectant smile faded from her lips. Perhaps she was a savage little barbarian of the Stone Age, but she was no fool and she was a woman.

Slowly she drew her slender figure erect as she turned away from him and started back along the rim of the rift toward the great gorge through which she had descended from the higher peaks when Skruk and his fellows had been pursuing her.

"Jana," he exclaimed, "don't be angry. Where are you going?"

She stopped and with her haughty little chin in air turned a withering look back upon him across a perfect shoulder. "Go your way, jalok," she said, "and Jana will go hers."

9

To the Thipdar's Nest

HEAVY CLOUDS FORMED about the lofty peaks of the Mountains of the Thipdars—black, angry clouds that rolled down the northern slopes, spreading far to east and west.

"The waters have come again," said Thoar. "They are falling upon Zoram. Soon they will fall here too."

It looked very dark up there above them and presently the clouds swept out across the sky, blotting out the noonday sun.

It was a new landscape upon which Tarzan looked—a sullen, bleak, and forbidding landscape. It was the first time that he had seen Pellucidar in shadow and he did not like it. The effect of the change was strikingly apparent in Thoar and Targash. They seemed depressed, almost fearful. Nor was it man alone that was so strangely affected by the blotting out of the eternal sunlight, for presently from the upper reaches of the mountains the lower animals came, pursuing the sunlight. That they, too, were strangely affected and filled with terror was evidenced by the fact that the carnivores and their prey trotted side by side and that none of them paid any attention to the three men.

"Why do they not attack us, Thoar?" asked Tarzan.

"They know that the water is about to fall," he replied, "and they are afraid of the falling water. They forget their hunger and their quarrels as they seek to escape the common terror."

"Is the danger so great then?" asked the ape-man.

"Not if we remain upon high ground," replied Thoar. "Sometimes the gulleys and ravines fill with water in an instant, but the only danger upon the high land is from the burning spears that are hurled from the black clouds. But if we stay in the open, even these are not dangerous for, as a rule, they are aimed at trees. Do not go beneath a tree while the clouds are hurling their spears of fire."

As the clouds shut off the sunlight, the air became suddenly cold. A raw wind swept down from above and the three men shivered in their nakedness.

"Gather wood," said Tarzan. "We shall build a fire for warmth." And so the three gathered firewood and Tarzan made fire and they sat about it, warming their naked hides; while upon either side of them the brutes passed on their way down toward the sunlight.

The rain came. It did not fall in drops, but in great enveloping blankets that seemed to beat them down and smother them. Inches deep it rolled down the mountainside, filling the depressions and the gulleys, turning the canyons into raging torrents.

The wind lashed the falling water into a blinding maelstrom that the eye could not pierce a dozen feet. Terrified animals stampeded blindly, constituting themselves the greatest menace of the storm. The lightning flashed and the thunder roared, and the beasts progressed from panic to an insanity of fear.

Above the roar of the thunder and the howling of the wind rose the piercing shrieks and screams of the monsters of another day, and in the air above flapped shrieking reptiles fighting toward the sunlight against the pounding wrath of the elements. Giant pteranodons, beaten to the ground, staggered uncertainly upon legs unaccustomed to the task, and through it all the three beast-men huddled at the spot where their fire had been, though not even an ash remained.

It seemed to Tarzan that the storm lasted a great while, but like the others he was inured to the hardships and discomforts of primitive life. Where a civilized man might have railed against fate and cursed the elements, the three beast-men sat in stoic silence, their backs hunched against the storm, for each knew that it would not last forever and each knew that there was nothing he could say or do to lessen its duration or abate its fury.

Had it not been for the example set by Tarzan and Thoar, Tar-gash would have fled toward the sunlight with the other beasts, not that he was more fearful than they, but that he was influenced more by instinct than by reason. But where they stayed, he was content to stay, and so he squatted there with them, in dumb misery, waiting for the sun to come again.

The rain lessened; the howling wind died down; the clouds passed on and the sun burst forth upon a steaming world. The three beast-men arose and shook themselves.

"I am hungry," said Tarzan.

Thoar pointed about them to where lay the bodies of lesser beasts that had been crushed in the mad stampede for safety.

Now even Thoar was compelled to eat his meat raw, for there was no dry wood wherewith to start a fire, but to Tarzan and Tar-gash this was no hardship. As Tarzan ate, the suggestion of a smile smoldered in his eyes. He was recalling a fussy old nobleman with whom he had once dined at a London club and who had almost suffered a stroke of apoplexy because his bird had been slightly underdone.

When the three had filled their bellies, they arose to continue their search for Jana and Jason, only to discover that the torrential rain had effectually erased every vestige of the spoor that they had been following.

"We cannot pick up their trail again," said Thoar, "until we reach the point where they continued on again after the waters ceased to fall. To the left is a deep canyon, whose walls are difficult to scale. In front of us is a fissure, which extends along the base of the mountains for a considerable distance in both directions. But if we go to the right we shall find a place where we can descend into it and cross it. This is the way that they should have gone. Perhaps there we shall pick up their trail again." But though they continued on and crossed the fissure and clambered upward toward the higher peaks, they found no sign that Jana or Jason had come this way.

"Perhaps they reached your country by another route," suggested Tarzan.

"Perhaps," said Thoar. "Let us continue on to Zoram. There is nothing else that we can do. There we can gather the men of my tribe and search the mountains for them."

In the ascent toward the summit Thoar sometimes followed trails that for countless ages the rough pads of the carnivores had followed, or again he led them over trackless wastes of granite, taking such perilous chances along dizzy heights that Tarzan was astonished that any of them came through alive.

Upon a bleak summit they had robbed a thipdar's nest of its eggs and the three were eating when Thoar became suddenly alert and listening. To the ears of the ape-man came faintly a sound that resembled the dismal flapping of distant wings.

"A thipdar," said Thoar, "and there is no shelter for us."

"There are three of us," said Tarzan. "What have we to fear?"

"You do not know them," said Thoar. "They are hard to kill and they are never defeated until they are killed. Their brains are very small. Sometimes when we have cut them open it has been difficult to find the brain at all, and having no brain they have no fear of anything, not even death, for they cannot know what death is. Nor do they seem to be affected much by pain; it merely angers them, making them more terrible. Perhaps we can kill it, but I wish that there were a tree."

"How do you know that it will attack us?" asked Tarzan.

"It is coming in this direction. It cannot help but see us, and whatever living thing they see they attack."

"Have you ever been attacked by one?" asked Tarzan.

"Yes," replied Thoar; "but only when there was no tree or cave. The men of Zoram are not ashamed to admit that they fear the mighty thipdars."

"But if you have killed them in the past, why may we not kill this one?" demanded the ape-man.

"We may," replied Thoar, "but I have never chanced to have an encounter with one, except when there were a number of my tribesmen with me. The lone hunter who goes forth and never returns is our reason for fearing the thipdar. Even when there are many of us to fight them, always there are some killed and many injured."

"It comes," said Tar-gash, pointing.

"It comes," said Thoar, grasping his spear more firmly.

Down to their ears came a sound resembling the escaping of steam through a petcock.

"It has seen us," said Thoar.

Tarzan laid his spear upon the ground at his feet, plucked a handful of arrows from his quiver and fitted one to his bow. Tar-gash swung his club slowly to and fro and growled.

On came the giant reptile, the dismal flapping of its wings punctuated occasionally by a loud and angry hiss. The three men waited, poised, ready, expectant.

There were no preliminaries. The mighty pteranodon dove straight toward them. Tarzan loosed a bolt that drove true to its mark, burying its head in the breast of the pterodactyl. The hiss became a scream of anger and then in rapid succession three more arrows buried themselves in the creature's flesh.

That this was a warmer reception than it had expected was evidenced by the fact that it rose suddenly upward, skimmed above their heads as though to abandon the attack, and then, quite suddenly and with a speed incomprehensible in a creature of its tremendous size, wheeled like a sparrow hawk and dove straight at Tarzan's back.

So quickly did the creature strike that there could be no defense. The ape-man felt sharp talons half buried in his naked flesh and simultaneously he was lifted from the ground.

Thoar raised his spear and Tar-gash swung his cudgel, but neither dared strike for fear of wounding their comrade. And so they were forced to stand there futilely inactive and watch the monster bear Tarzan of the Apes away across the tops of the Mountains of the Thipdars.

In silence they stood watching until the creature passed out of sight beyond the summit of a distant peak, the body of the ape-man still dangling in its talons. Then Tar-gash turned and looked at Thoar.

"Tarzan is dead," said the Sagoth. Thoar of Zoram nodded sadly. Without another word Tar-gash turned and started down toward the valley from which they had ascended. The only bond that had united these two hereditary enemies had parted, and Tar-gash was going his way back to the stamping grounds of his tribe.

For a moment Thoar watched him, and then, with a shrug of his shoulders, he turned his face toward Zoram.

As the pteranodon bore him off across the granite peaks, Tarzan hung limply in its clutches, realizing that if fate held in store for him any hope of escape it could not come in midair and if he were to struggle against his adversary, or seek to battle with it, death upon the jagged rocks below would be the barren reward of success. His one hope lay in retaining consciousness and the power to fight when the creature came to the ground with him. He knew that there were birds of prey that kill their victims by dropping them from great heights, but he hoped that the pteranodons of Pellucidar had never acquired this disconcerting habit.

As he watched the panorama of mountain peaks passing below him, he realized that he was being carried a considerable distance from the spot at which he had been seized; perhaps twenty miles.

The flight at last carried them across a frightful gorge and a short distance beyond the pteranodon circled a lofty granite peak, toward the summit of which it slowly dropped, and there, below him, Tarzan of the Apes saw a nest of small thipdars, eagerly awaiting with wide distended jaws the flesh that their savage parent was bringing to them.

The nest rested upon the summit of a lofty granite spire, the entire area of the summit encompassing but a few square yards, the walls dropping perpendicularly hundreds of feet to the rough granite of the lofty peak the spire surmounted. It was, indeed, a precarious place at which to stage a battle for life.

Cautiously, Tarzan of the Apes drew his keen hunting knife from its sheath. Slowly his left hand crept upward against his body and passed over his left shoulder until his fingers touched the thipdar's leg. Cautiously, his fingers encircled the scaly, birdlike ankle just above the claws.

The reptile was descending slowly toward its nest. The

hideous demons below were screeching and hissing in anticipation. Tarzan's feet were almost in their jaws when he struck
suddenly upward with his blade at the breast of the thipdar.

It was no random thrust. What slender chance for life the
ape-man had depended upon the accuracy and the strength of
that single blow. The giant pteranodon emitted a shrill scream,
stiffened convulsively in midair and, as it collapsed, relaxed its
hold upon its prey, dropping the ape-man into the nest among
the gaping jaws of its frightful brood.

Fortunately for Tarzan there were but three of them and they
were still very young, though their teeth were sharp and their
jaws strong.

Striking quickly to right and left with his blade he scrambled
from the nest with only a few minor cuts and scratches upon
his legs.

Lying partially over the edge of the spire was the body of the
dead thipdar. Tarzan gave it a final shove and watched it as it
fell three hundred feet to the rocks below. Then he turned his
attention to a survey of his surroundings, but almost hopelessly
since the view that he had obtained of the spire while the
thipdar was circling it assured him that there was little or no
likelihood that he could find any means of descent.

The young thipdars were screaming and hissing, but they had
made no move to leave their nest as Tarzan started a close investigation of the granite spire upon the lofty summit of which it
seemed likely that he would terminate his adventurous career.

Lying flat upon his belly he looked over the edge, and thus
moving slowly around the periphery of the lofty aerie he examined the walls of the spire with minute attention to every detail.

Again and again he crept around the edge until he had catalogued within his memory every projection and crevice and
possible handhold that he could see from above.

Several times he returned to one point and then he removed
the coils of his grass rope from about his shoulders and holding
the two ends in one hand, lowered the loop over the edge of the
spire. Carefully he noted the distance that it descended from
the summit and what a pitiful span it seemed—that paltry
twenty-five feet against the three hundred that marked the distance from base to apex.

Releasing one end of the rope, he let that fall to its full length, and when he saw where the lower end touched the granite wall he was satisfied that he could descend at least that far, and below that another twenty-five feet. But it was difficult to measure distances below that point and from there on he must leave everything to chance.

Drawing the rope up again he looped the center of it about a projecting bit of granite, permitting the ends to fall over the edge of the cliff. Then he seized both strands of the rope tightly in one hand and lowered himself over the edge. Twenty feet below was a projection that gave him precarious foothold and a little crevice into which he could insert the fingers of his left hand. Almost directly before his face was the top of a buttress-like projection and below him he knew that there were many more similar to it. It was upon these that he had based his slender hope of success.

Gingerly he pulled upon one strand of the rope with his right hand. So slender was his footing upon the rocky escarpment that he did not dare draw the rope more than a few inches at a time lest the motion throw him off his balance. Little by little he drew it in until the upper end passed around the projection over which the rope had been looped at the summit and fell upon him. And as it descended he held his breath for fear that even this slight weight might topple him to the jagged rocks below.

And now came the slow process of drawing the rope unaided through one hand, fingering it slowly an inch at a time until the center was in his grasp. This he looped over the top of the projection in front of him, seating it as securely as he could, and then he grasped both strands once more in his right hand and was ready to descend another twenty-five feet.

This stage of the descent was the most appalling of all, since the rope was barely seated upon a shelving protuberance from which he was aware it might slip at any instant. And so it was with a sense of unspeakable relief that he again found foothold near the end of the frail strands that were supporting him.

At this point the surface of the spire became much rougher. It was broken by fissures and horizontal cracks that had not been visible from above, with the result that compared with the first fifty feet the descent from here to the base was a miracle of ease, and it was not long before Tarzan stood again squarely upon his two feet and level ground. And now for the first time he had an opportunity to take stock of his injuries.

His legs were scratched and cut by the teeth and talons of the young thipdars, but these wounds were as nothing to those left by the talons of the adult reptile upon his back and shoulders. He could feel the deep wounds, but he could not see them; nor the clotted blood that had dried upon his brown skin.

The wounds pained and his muscles were stiff and sore, but his only fear lay in the possibility of blood poisoning and that did not greatly worry the ape-man, who had been repeatedly torn and mauled by carnivores since childhood.

A brief survey of his position showed him that it would be practically impossible for him to recross the stupendous gorge that yawned between him and the point at which he had been so ruthlessly torn from his companions. And with that discovery came the realization that there was little or no likelihood that the people toward which Tar-gash had been attempting to guide him could be the members of the O-220 expedition. Therefore it seemed useless to attempt the seemingly impossible feat of finding Thoar and Tar-gash again among this maze of stupendous peaks, gorges, and ravines. And so he determined merely to seek a way out of the mountains and back to the forests and plains that held a greater allure for him than did the rough and craggy contours of inhospitable hills. And to the accomplishment of this end he decided to follow the line of least resistance, seeking always the easiest avenues of descent.

Below him, in various directions, he could see the timber-line and toward this he hastened to make his way.

As he descended the way became easier, though on several occasions he was again compelled to resort to his rope to lower himself from one level to another. Then the steep crags gave place to leveler land upon the shoulders of the mighty range and here, where earth could find lodgment, vegetation commenced. Grasses and shrubs, at first, then stunted trees and finally what was almost a forest, and here he came upon a trail.

It was a trail that offered infinite variety. For a while it wound through a forest and then climbed to a ledge of rock that projected from the face of a cliff and overhung a stupendous canyon.

He could not see the trail far ahead for it was continually rounding the shoulders of jutting crags.

As he moved along it, surefooted, silent, alert, Tarzan of the Apes became aware that somewhere ahead of him other feet were treading probably the same trail.

What wind there was was eddying up from the canyon below and carrying the scent spoor of the creature ahead of him as well as his own up toward the mountaintop, so that it was unlikely that either might apprehend the presence of the other by scent; but there was something in the sound of the footsteps that even at a distance assured Tarzan that they were not made by man, and it was evident too that they were going in the same direction as he for they were not growing rapidly more distinct, but very gradually as though he was slowly overhauling the author of them.

The trail was narrow and only occasionally, where it crossed some ravine or shallow gulley, was there a place where one might either descend or ascend from it.

To meet a savage beast upon it, therefore, might prove, to say the least, embarrassing but Tarzan had elected to go this way and he was not in the habit of turning back whatever obstacles in the form of man or beast might bar his way. And, too, he had the advantage over the creature ahead of him whatever it might be, since he was coming upon it from behind and was quite sure that it had no knowledge of his presence, for Tarzan well knew that no creature could move with greater silence than he, when he elected to do so, and now he passed along that trail as noiselessly as the shadow of a shadow.

Curiosity caused him to increase his speed that he might learn the nature of the thing ahead, and as he did so and the sound of its footsteps increased in volume, he knew that he was stalking some heavy, four-footed beast with padded feet—that much he could tell, but beyond that he had no idea of the identity of the creature; nor did the winding trail at any time reveal it to his view. Thus the silent stalker pursued his way until he knew that he was but a short distance behind his quarry when there suddenly broke upon his ears the horrid snarling and growling of an enraged beast just ahead of him.

There was something in the tone of that awful voice that increased the ape-man's curiosity. He guessed from the volume of the sound that it must come from the throat of a tremendous beast, for the very hills seemed to shake to the thunder of its roars.

Guessing that it was attacking or was about to attack some other creature, and spurred, perhaps, entirely by curiosity, Tarzan hastened forward at a brisk trot, and as he rounded the shoulder of a buttressed crag his eyes took in a scene that galvanized him into instant action.

A hundred feet ahead the trail ended at the mouth of a great cave, and in the entrance to the cave stood a boy—a lithe, handsome youth of ten or twelve—while between the boy and Tarzan a huge cave bear was advancing angrily upon the former.

The boy saw Tarzan and at the first glance his eyes lighted with hope, but an instant later, evidently recognizing that the newcomer was not of his own tribe, the expression of hopelessness that had been there before returned to his face, but he stood his ground bravely, his spear and his crude stone knife ready.

The scene before the ape-man told its own story. The bear, returning to its cave, had unexpectedly discovered the youth emerging from it, while the latter, doubtless equally surprised, found himself cornered with no avenue of escape open to him.

By the primitive jungle laws that had guided his youth, Tarzan of the Apes was under no responsibility to assume the dangerous role of savior, but there had always burned within his breast the flame of chivalry, bequeathed him by his English parents, that more often than not found him jeopardizing his own life in the interests of others. This child of a nameless tribe in an unknown world might hold no claim upon the sympathy of a savage beast, or even of savage men who were not of his tribe. And perhaps Tarzan of the Apes would not have admitted that the youth had any claim upon him, yet in reality he exercised a vast power over the ape-man—a power that lay solely in the fact that he was a child and that he was helpless.

One may analyze the deeds of a man of action and speculate upon them, whereas the man himself does not appear to do so at all—he merely acts; and thus it was with Tarzan of the Apes. He saw an emergency confronting him and he was ready to meet it, for since the moment that he had known that there was a beast upon the trail ahead of him he had had his weapons in readiness, years of experience with primitive men and savage beasts having taught him the value of preparedness.

His grass rope was looped in the hollow of his left arm and in the fingers of his left hand were grasped his spear, his bow, and three extra arrows, while a fourth arrow was ready in his right hand.

One glance at the beast ahead of him had convinced him that only by a combination of skill and rare luck could he hope to destroy this titanic monster with the relatively puny weapons with which he was armed, but he might at least divert its attention from the lad and by harassing it draw it away until the boy could find some means of escape. And so it was that within the very instant that his eyes took in the picture his bow twanged and a heavy arrow sank deeply into the back of the bear close to its spine, and at the same time Tarzan voiced a savage cry intended to apprise the beast of an enemy in its rear.

Maddened by the pain and surprised by the voice behind it, the creature evidently associated the two, instantly whirling about on the narrow ledge.

Tarzan's first impression was that in all his life he had never gazed upon such a picture of savage bestial rage as was depicted upon the snarling countenance of the mighty cave bear as its fiery eyes fell upon the author of its hurt.

In quick succession three arrows sank into its chest as it charged, howling, down upon the ape-man.

For an instant longer Tarzan held his ground. Poising his heavy spear he carried his spear hand far back behind his right shoulder, and then with all the force of those giant muscles, backed by the weight of his great body, he launched the weapon.

At the instant that it left his hand the bear was almost upon him and he did not wait to note the effect of his throw, but turned and leaped swiftly down the trail; while close behind him the savage growling and the ponderous footfalls of the carnivore proved the wisdom of his strategy.

He was sure that upon this narrow, rocky ledge, if no obstacle interposed itself, he could outdistance the bear, for only Ara, the lightning, is swifter than Tarzan of the Apes.

There was the possibility that he might meet the bear's mate coming up to their den, and in that event his position would be highly critical, but that, of course, was only a remote possibility and in the meantime he was sure that he had inflicted sufficiently severe wounds upon the great beast to sap its strength and eventually to prove its total undoing. That it possessed an immense reserve of vitality was evidenced by the strength and savagery of its pursuit. The creature seemed tireless and although Tarzan was equally so he found fleeing from an antagonist peculiarly irksome and to a considerable degree obnoxious to his self-esteem. And so he cast about him for some means of terminating the flight and to that end he watched particularly the cliff walls rising above the trail down which he sped, and at last he saw that for which he had hoped—a jutting granite projection protruding from the cliff about twenty-five feet above the trail.

His coiled rope was ready in his left hand, the noose in his right, and as he came within throwing distance of the projection, he unerringly tossed the latter about it. The bear tore down the trail behind him. The ape-man pulled heavily once upon the end of the rope to assure himself that it was safely caught above, and then with the agility of Manu, the monkey, he clambered upward.

10

Only a Man May Go

IT REQUIRED NO Sherlockian instinct to deduce that Jana was angry, and Jason was not so dense as to be unaware of the cause of her displeasure, which he attributed to natural feminine vexation induced by the knowledge that she had been mistaken in assuming that her charms had effected the conquest of his heart. He judged Jana by his own imagined knowledge of feminine psychology. He knew that she was beautiful and he knew that she knew it, too. She had told him of the many men of Zoram who had wanted to take her as their mate, and he had saved her from one suitor, who had pursued her across the terrible Mountains of the Thipdars, putting his life constantly in jeopardy to win her. He felt that it was only natural, therefore, that Jana should place a high valuation upon her charms and believe that any man might fall a victim to their spell, but he saw no reason why she should be angry because she had not succeeded in enthralling him. They had been very happy together. He could not recall when ever before he had been for so long a time in the company of any girl, or so enjoyed the companionship of one of her sex. He was sorry that anything had occurred to mar the even tenor of their friendship and he quickly decided that the manly thing to do was to ignore her tantrum and go on with her as he had before, until she came to her senses. Nor was there anything else that he might do for he certainly could not permit Jana to continue her journey to

Zoram without protection. Of course it was not very nice of her to have called him a jalok, which he knew to be a Pellucidarian epithet of high insult, but he would overlook that for the present and eventually she would relent and ask his forgiveness.

And so he followed her, but he had taken scarcely a dozen steps when she wheeled upon him like a young tiger, whipping her stone knife from its sheath. "I told you to go your way," she cried. "I do not want to see you again. If you follow me I shall kill you."

"I cannot let you go on alone, Jana," he said quietly.

"The Red Flower of Zoram wants no protection from such as you," she replied haughtily.

"We have been such good friends, Jana," he pleaded. "Let us go on together as we have in the past. I cannot help it if—" He hesitated and stopped.

"I do not care that you do not love me," she said. "I hate you. I hate you because your eyes lie. Sometimes lips lie and we are not hurt because we have learned to expect that from lips, but when eyes lie then the heart lies and the whole man is false. I cannot trust you. I do not want your friendship. I want nothing more of you. Go away."

"You do not understand, Jana," he insisted.

"I understand that if you try to follow me I will kill you," she said.

"Then you will have to kill me," he replied, "for I shall follow you. I cannot let you go on alone, no matter whether you hate me or not," and as he ceased speaking he advanced toward her.

Jana stood facing him, her little feet firmly planted, her crude stone dagger grasped in her right hand, her eyes flashing angrily.

His hands at his sides, Jason Gridley walked slowly up to her as though offering his breast as a target for her weapon. The stone blade flashed upward. It poised a moment above her shoulder and then The Red Flower of Zoram turned and fled along the rim of the rift.

She ran very swiftly and was soon far ahead of Jason, who was weighted down by clothes, heavy weapons, and ammunition. He called after her once or twice, begging her to stop, but she did not heed him and he continued doggedly along her trail, making the best time that he could. He felt hurt and angry, but after all the emotion which dominated him was one of regret that their sweet friendship had been thus wantonly blasted.

Slowly the realization was borne in upon him that he had been very happy with Jana and that she had occupied his thoughts almost to the exclusion of every other consideration of the past or future. Even the memory of his lost comrades had been relegated to the hazy oblivion of temporary forgetfulness in the presence of the responsibility which he had assumed for the safe conduct of the girl to her homeland.

"Why, she has made a regular monkey out of me," he mused. "Odysseus never met a more potent Circe. Nor one half so lovely," he added, as he regretfully recalled the charms of the little barbarian.

And what a barbarian she had proven herself—whipping out her stone knife and threatening to kill him. But he could not help but smile when he realized how in the final extremity she had proven herself so wholly feminine. With a sigh he shook his head and plodded on after The Red Flower of Zoram.

Occasionally Jason caught a glimpse of Jana as she crossed a ridge ahead of him and though she did not seem to be traveling as fast as at first, yet he could not gain upon her. His mind was constantly harassed by the fear that she might be attacked by some savage beast and destroyed before he could come to her rescue with his rifle. He knew that sooner or later she would have to stop and rest and then he was hopeful of overtaking her, when he might persuade her to forget her anger and resume their former friendly comradeship.

But it seemed that The Red Flower of Zoram had no intention of resting, though the American had long since reached a stage of fatigue that momentarily threatened to force him to relinquish the pursuit until outraged nature could recuperate. Yet he plodded on doggedly across the rough ground, while the weight of his arms and ammunition seemed to increase until his rifle assumed the ponderous proportions of a field gun. Determined not to give up, he staggered down one hill and struggled up the next, his legs seeming to move mechanically as though they were some detached engine of torture over which he had no control and which were bearing him relentlessly onward, while every fiber of his being cried out for rest.

Added to the physical torture of fatigue, were hunger and thirst and knowing that only thus might time be measured, he was confident that he had covered a great distance since they had last rested and then he topped the summit of a low rise and saw Jana directly ahead of him.

She was standing on the edge of the rift where it opened into a mighty gorge that descended from the mountains and it was evident that she was undecided what course to pursue. The course which she wished to pursue was blocked by the rift and gorge. To her left the way led back down into the valley in a direction opposite to that in which lay Zoram, while to retrace her steps would entail another encounter with Jason.

She was looking over the edge of the precipice, evidently searching for some avenue of descent when she became aware of Jason's approach.

She wheeled upon him angrily. "Go back," she cried, "or I shall jump."

"Please, Jana," he pleaded, "let me go with you. I shall not annoy you. I shall not even speak to you unless you wish it, but let me go with you to protect you from the beasts."

The girl laughed. "You protect me!" she exclaimed, her tone caustic with sarcasm. "You do not even know the dangers which beset the way. Without your strange spear, which spits fire and death, you would be helpless before the attack of even one of the lesser beasts, and in the high Mountains of the Thipdars there are beasts so large and so terrible that they would devour you and your fire spear in a single gulp. Go back to your own people, man of another world; go back to the soft women of which you have told me. Only a man may go where The Red Flower of Zoram goes."

"You half convince me," said Jason with a rueful smile, "that I am only a caterpillar, but nevertheless even a caterpillar must have guts of some sort and so I am going to follow you, Red Flower of Zoram, until some goggle-eyed monstrosity of the Jurassic snatches me from this vale of tears."

"I do not know what you are talking about," snapped Jana;

"but if you follow me you will be killed. Remember what I told you—only a man may go where goes The Red Flower of Zoram," and as though to prove her assertion she turned and slid quickly over the edge of the precipice, disappearing from his view.

Running quickly forward to the edge of the chasm, Jason Gridley looked down and there, a few yards below him, clinging to the perpendicular face of the cliff, Jana was working her way slowly downward. Jason held his breath. It seemed incredible that any creature could find hand- or foothold upon that dizzy escarpment. He shuddered and cold sweat broke out upon him as he watched the girl.

Foot by foot she worked her way downward, while the man, lying upon his belly, his head projecting over the edge of the cliff, watched her in silence. He dared not speak to her for fear of distracting her attention and when, after what seemed an eternity, she reached the bottom, he fell to trembling like a leaf and for the first time realized the extent of the nervous strain he had been undergoing.

"God!" he murmured. "What a magnificent display of nerve and courage and skill!"

The Red Flower of Zoram did not look back or upward once as she resumed her way, following the gorge upward, searching for some point where she might clamber out of it above the rift.

Jason Gridley looked down into the terrible abyss. " 'Only a man may go where goes The Red Flower of Zoram,' " he mused.

He watched the girl until she disappeared behind a mass of fallen rock, where the gorge curved to the right, and he knew that unless he could descend into the gorge she had passed out of his life forever.

"Only a man may go where goes The Red Flower of Zoram!"

Jason Gridley arose to his feet. He readjusted the leather sling upon his rifle so that he could carry the weapon hanging down the center of his back. He slipped the holsters of both of his six-guns to the rear so that they, too, were entirely behind him. He removed his boots and dropped them over the edge of the cliff. Then he lay upon his belly and lowered his body slowly downward, and from a short distance up the gorge two eyes watched him from behind a pile of tumbled granite. There was anger in them at first, then skepticism, then surprise, and then terror.

As gropingly the man sought for some tiny foothold and then lowered himself slowly a few inches at a time the eyes of the girl, wide in horror, never left him for an instant.

"Only a man may go where goes The Red Flower of Zoram!"

Cautiously, Jason Gridley groped for each handhold and foothold—each precarious support from which it seemed that even his breathing might dislodge him. Hunger, thirst, and fatigue were forgotten as he marshaled every faculty to do the bidding of his iron nerve.

Hugging close to the face of the cliff he did not dare turn his head sufficiently to look downward and though it seemed he had clung there, lowering himself inch by inch, for an eternity, yet he had no idea how much farther he had to descend. And so impossible of accomplishment did the task that he had set himself appear that never for an instant did he dare to hope for a successful conclusion. Never for an instant did any new hold impart to him a feeling of security, but each one seemed, if possible, more precarious than its predecessor, and then he reached a point where, grope as he would, he could find no foothold. He could not move to right or left; nor could he ascend. Apparently he had reached the end of his resources, but still he did not give up. Replacing his torn and bleeding feet upon the last, slight hold that they had found, he cautiously sought for new handholds lower down, and when he had found them—mere protuberances of rough granite—he let his feet slip slowly from their support as gradually he lowered his body to its full length, supported only by his fingers, where they clutched at the tiny projections that were his sole support.

As he clung there, desperately searching about with his feet for some slight projection, he reproached himself for not having discarded his heavy weapons and ammunition. And why? Because his life was in jeopardy and he feared to die? No, his only thought was that because of them he would be unable to cling much longer to the cliff and that when his hands slipped from their holds and he was dashed into eternity, his last, slender hope of ever again seeing The Red Flower of Zoram would be gone. It is remarkable, perhaps, that as he clung thus literally upon the brink of eternity, no visions of Cynthia Furnois or Barbara Green impinged themselves upon his consciousness.

He felt his fingers weakening and slipping from their hold. The end came suddenly. The weight of his body dragged one hand loose and instantly the other slipped from the tiny knob it had been clutching, and Jason Gridley dropped downward, perhaps eighteen inches, to the bottom of the cliff.

As he came to a stop, his feet on solid rock, Jason could not readily conceive the good fortune that had befallen him. Almost afraid to look, he glanced downward and then the truth dawned upon him—he had made the descent in safety. His knees sagged beneath him and as he sank to the ground, a girl, watching him from up the gorge, burst into tears.

A short distance below him a spring bubbled from the canyon side, forming a little brooklet which leaped downward in the sunlight toward the bottom of the canyon and the valley, and after he had regained his composure he found his boots and hobbled down to the water. Here he satisfied his thirst and washed his feet, cleansing the cuts as best he could, bandaged them crudely with strips torn from his handkerchief, pulled his boots on once more and started up the canyon after Jana.

Far above, near the summit of the stupendous range, he saw ominous clouds gathering. They were the first clouds that he had seen in Pellucidar, but only for this reason did they seem remarkable or important. That they presaged rain, he could well imagine; but how could he dream of the catastrophic proportions of their menace.

Far ahead of him The Red Flower of Zoram was clambering upward along a precarious trail that gave promise of leading eventually over the rim of the gorge to the upper reaches that she wished to gain. When she had seen Jason's life in imminent jeopardy, she had been filled with terror and remorse, but when he had safely completed the descent her mood changed, and with the perversity of her sex she still sought to elude him.

She had almost gained the summit of the escarpment when the storm broke and with it came a realization that the man behind her was ignorant of the danger which now more surely menaced him than had the descent of the cliff.

Without an instant's hesitation The Red Flower of Zoram turned and fled swiftly down the steep trail she had just so laboriously ascended. She must reach him before the waters reached him. She must guide him to some high place upon the canyon's wall, for she knew that the bottom of this great gorge would soon be a foaming, boiling torrent, spreading from side to side, its waters, perhaps, two hundred feet in depth. Already the water was running deep in the canyon far below her and spilling over the rim above her, racing downward in torrents and cataracts and waterfalls that carried earth and stone with them. Never in her life had Jana witnessed a storm so terrible. The thunder roared and the lightning flashed; the wind howled and the water fell in blinding sheets, and yet constantly menanced by instant death the girl groped her way blindly downward upon her hopeless errand of mercy. How hopeless it was she was soon to see, for the waters in the gorge had risen, she saw them just below her now, nor was the end in sight. Nothing down there could have survived. The man must long since have been washed away.

Jason was dead! The Red Flower of Zoram stood for an instant looking at the rising waters below her. There came to her an urge to throw herself into them. She did not want to live, but something stayed her; perhaps it was the instinct of primeval man, whose whole existence was a battle against death, who knew no other state and might not conceive voluntary surrender to the enemy, and so she turned and fought her way upward as the waters rising below her climbed to overtake her and the waters from above sought to hurl her backward to destruction.

Jason Gridley had witnessed cloudbursts in California and Arizona and he knew how quickly gulleys and ravines may be transformed into raging torrents. He had seen a river a mile wide formed in a few hours in the San Simon Flats, and when he saw the sudden rush of waters in the bottom of the gorge below him and realized that no storm that he had ever previously witnessed could compare in magnitude with this, he lost no time in seeking higher ground; but the sides of the canyon were steep and his upward progress discouragingly slow, as he saw the waters rising rapidly behind him. Yet there was hope, for just ahead and above him he saw a gentle acclivity rising toward the summit of the canyon rim.

As he struggled toward safety the boiling torrent rose and lapped his feet, while from above the torrential rain thundered down upon him, beating him backward so that often for a full minute at a time he could make no headway.

The raging waters that were filling the gorge reached his knees and for an instant he was swept from his footing. Clutching at the ground above him with his hands, he lost his rifle, but as it slid into the turgid waters he clambered swiftly upward and regained momentary safety.

Onward and upward he fought until at last he reached a spot above which he was confident the flood could not reach and there he crouched in the partial shelter of an overhanging granite ledge as Tarzan and Thoar and Tar-gash were crouching in another part of the mountains, waiting in dumb misery for the storm to spend its wrath.

He wondered if Jana had escaped the flood and so much confidence did he have in her masterful ability to cope with the vagaries of savage Pellucidarian life that he harbored few fears for her upon the score of the storm.

In the cold and the dark and the wet he tried to plan for the future. What chance had he to find The Red Flower of Zoram in this savage chaos of stupendous peaks when he did not even know the direction in which her country lay and where there were no roads or trails and where even the few tracks that she might have left must have been wholly obliterated by the torrents of water that had covered the whole surface of the ground?

To stumble blindly on, then, seemed the only course left open to him, since he knew neither the direction of Zoram, other than in a most general way, nor had any idea as to the whereabouts of his fellow members of the O-220 expedition.

At last the rain ceased; the sun burst forth upon a steaming world and beneath the benign influence of its warm rays Jason

felt the cold ashes of hope rekindled within his breast. Revivi-
fied, he took up the search that but now had seemed so
hopeless.

Trying to bear in mind the general direction in which Jana
had told him Zoram lay, he set his face toward what appeared
to be a low saddle between two lofty peaks, which appeared to
surmount the summit of the range. Thirst no longer afflicted
him and the pangs of hunger had become deadened. Nor did it
seem at all likely that he might soon find food since the storm
seemed to have driven all animal life from the higher hills, but
fortune smiled upon him. In a waterworn rocky hollow he
found a nest of eggs that had withstood the onslaught of the
elements. The nature of the creature that had laid them he did
not know; nor whether they were the eggs of fowl or reptile did
he care. They were fresh and they were food and so large were
they that the contents of two of them satisfied his hunger.

A short distance from the spot where he had found them
grew a low stunted tree, and having eaten he carried the three
remaining eggs to this meager protection from the prying eyes
of soaring reptiles and birds of prey. Here he removed his
clothing, hanging it upon the branches of the tree where the
sunlight might dry it, and then he lay down beneath the tree to
sleep, and in the warmth of Pellucidar's eternal noon he found
no discomfort.

How long a time he slept he had no means of estimating, but
when he awoke he was completely rested and refreshed. He
was imbued with a new sense of self-confidence as he arose,
stretching luxuriously, to don his clothes. His stretch half completed, he froze with consternation—his clothes were gone! He
looked hastily about for them or for some sign of the creature
that had purloined them, but never again did he see the one, nor
ever the other.

Upon the ground beneath the tree lay a shirt that, having
fallen, evidently escaped the eye of the marauder. That, his
revolvers and belts of ammunition, which had lain close to him
while he slept, were all that remained to him.

The temperature of Pellucidar is such that clothing is rather
a burden than a necessity, but so accustomed is civilized man
to the strange apparel with which he has encumbered himself

for generations that, bereft of it, his efficiency, self-reliance and resourcefulness are reduced to a plane approximating the vanishing point.

Never in his life had Jason Gridley felt so helpless and futile as he did this instant as he contemplated the necessity which stared him in the face of going forth into this world clothed only in a torn shirt and an ammunition belt. Yet he realized that with the exception of his boots he had lost nothing that was essential either to his comfort or his efficiency, but perhaps he was appalled most by the realization of the effect that this misfortune would have upon the pursuit of the main object of his quest—how could he prosecute the search for The Red Flower of Zoram thus scantily appareled?

Of course The Red Flower had not been overburdened with wearing apparel; yet in her case this seemed no reflection upon her modesty, but the anticipation of finding her was now dampened by a realization of the ridiculousness of the figure he would cut, and already the mere contemplation of such a meeting caused a flush to overspread him.

In his dreams he had sometimes imagined himself walking abroad in some ridiculous state of undress, but now that such a dream had become an actuality he appreciated that in the figment of the subconscious mind he had never fully realized such complete embarrassment and loss of self-confidence as the actuality entailed.

Ruefully he tore his shirt into strips and devised a G-string; then he buckled his ammunition belt around him and stepped forth into the world, an Adam armed with two Colts.

As he proceeded upon his search for Zoram he found that the greatest hardship which the loss of his clothing entailed was the pain and discomfort attendant upon traveling barefoot on soles already lacerated by his descent of the rough granite cliff. This discomfort, however, he eventually partially overcame when with the return of the game to the mountains he was able to shoot a small reptile, from the hide of which he fashioned two crude sandals.

The sun, beating down upon his naked body, had no such effect upon his skin as would the sun of the outer world under like conditions, but it did impart to him a golden bronze color, which gave him a new confidence similar to that which he would have felt had he been able to retrieve his lost apparel, and in this fact he saw what he believed to be the real cause of his first embarrassment at his nakedness—it had been the whiteness of his skin that had made him seem so naked by contrast with other creatures, for this whiteness had suggested softness and weakness, arousing within him a disturbing sensation of inferiority; but now as he took on his heavy coat of tan and his feet became hardened and accustomed to the new conditions, he walked no longer in constant realization of his nakedness.

He slept and ate many times and was conscious, therefore, that considerable outer earthly time had passed since he had been separated from Jana. As yet he had seen no sign of her or any other human being, though he was often menaced by savage beasts and reptiles, but experience had taught him how best to elude these without recourse to his weapons, which he was determined to use only in extreme emergencies for he could not but anticipate with misgivings the time, which must sometime come, when the last of his ammunition would have been exhausted.

He had crossed the summit of the range and found a fairer country beyond. It was still wild and tumbled and rocky, but the vegetation grew more luxuriantly and in many places the mountain slopes were clothed in forests that reached far upward toward the higher peaks. There were more streams and a greater abundance of smaller game, which afforded him relief from any anxiety upon the score of food.

For the purpose of economizing his precious ammunition he had fashioned other weapons; the influence of his association with Jana being reflected in his spear, while to Tarzan of the Apes and the Waziri he owed his crude bow and arrows. Before he had mastered the intricacies of either of his new weapons he might have died of starvation had it not been for his Colts, but eventually he achieved a sufficient degree of adeptness to insure him a full larder at all times.

Jason Gridley had long since given up all hope of finding his ship or his companions and had accepted with what philosophy he could command the future lot from which there seemed no escape, in which he visioned a lifetime spent in Pellucidar, battling with his primitive weapons for survival amongst the savage creatures of the inner world.

Most of all he missed human companionship and he looked forward to the day that he might find a tribe of men with which he could cast his lot. Although he was quite aware from the information that he had gleaned from Jana that it might be extremely difficult, if not impossible, for him to win either the confidence or the friendship of any Pellucidarian tribe whose attitude toward strangers was one of habitual enmity; yet he did not abandon hope and his eyes were always on the alert for a sign of man; nor was he now to have long to wait.

He had lost all sense of direction insofar as the location of Zoram was concerned and was wandering aimlessly from camp to camp in the idle hope that some day he would stumble upon Zoram, when a breeze coming from below brought to his nostrils the acrid scent of smoke. Instantly his whole being was surcharged with excitement, for smoke meant fire and fire meant man.

As he moved cautiously down the mountain in the direction from which the wind was blowing, his eager, searching eyes were presently rewarded by sight of a thin wisp of smoke arising from a canyon just ahead. It was a rocky canyon with precipitous walls, those upon the opposite side from him being lofty, while that which he was approaching was much lower and in many places so broken down by erosion or other natural causes as to give ready ingress to the canyon bottom below.

Creeping stealthily to the rim Jason Gridley peered downward into the canyon. Along the center of its grassy floor tumbled a mountain torrent. Giant trees grew at intervals, lending a parklike appearance to the scene; a similarity which was further accentuated by the gorgeous blooms which starred the sward or blossomed in the trees themselves.

Beside a small fire at the edge of a brook squatted a bronzed warrior, his attention centered upon a fowl which he was roasting above the fire. Jason, watching the warrior, deliberated upon the best method of approaching him, that he might convince him of his friendly intentions and overcome the natural suspicion of strangers that he knew to be inherent in

these savage tribesmen. He had decided that the best plan
would be to walk boldly down to the stranger, his hands empty
of weapons, and he was upon the point of putting his plan into
action when his attention was attracted to the summit of the
cliff upon the opposite side of the narrow canyon.

There had been no sound that had been appreciable to his
ears and the top of the opposite cliff had not been within the
field of his vision while he had been watching the man in
the bottom of the canyon. So what had attracted his attention he
did not know, unless it had been the delicate powers of perception inherent in that mysterious attribute of the mind which we
are sometimes pleased to call a sixth sense.

But be that as it may, his eyes moved directly to a spot upon
the summit of the opposite cliff where stood such a creature as
no living man upon the outer crust had ever looked upon
before—a giant armored dinosaur it was, a huge reptile that
appeared to be between sixty and seventy feet in length,
standing at the rump, which was its highest point, fully twenty-
five feet above the ground. Its relatively small, pointed head
resembled that of a lizard. Along its spine were thin, horny
plates arranged alternately, the largest of which were almost
three feet high and equally as long, but with a thickness of little
more than an inch. The stout tail, which terminated in a long,
horny spine, was equipped with two other such spines upon the
upper side and toward the tip. Each of these spines was about
three feet in length. The creature walked upon four lizardlike
feet, its short, front legs bringing its nose close to the ground,
imparting to it an awkward and ungainly appearance.

It appeared to be watching the man in the canyon, and suddenly, to Jason's amazement, it gathered its gigantic hind legs
beneath it and launched itself straight from the top of the lofty
cliff.

Jason's first thought was that the gigantic creature would be
dashed to pieces upon the ground in the canyon bottom, but to
his vast astonishment he saw that it was not falling but was
gliding swiftly through the air, supported by its huge spinal
plates, which it had dropped to a horizontal position, trans-
forming itself into a gigantic animate glider.

The swish of its passage through the air attracted the

attention of the warrior squatting over his fire. The man leaped to his feet, snatching up his spear as he did so, and simultaneously Jason Gridley sprang over the edge of the cliff and leaped down the rough declivity toward the lone warrior, at the same time whipping both his six-guns from their holsters.

11

The Cavern of Clovi

A S TARZAN SWARMED up the rope the bear, almost upon his heels and running swiftly, squatted upon its haunches to overcome its momentum and came to a stop directly beneath him. And then it was that there occurred one of those unforeseen accidents which no one might have guarded against.

It chanced that the granite projection across which Tarzan had cast his noose was at a single point of knifelike sharpness upon its upper edge, and with the weight of the man dragging down upon it the rope parted where it rested upon this sharp bit of granite, and the Lord of the Jungle was precipitated upon the back of the cave bear.

With such rapidity had these events transpired it is a matter of question as to whether the bear or Tarzan was the more surprised, but primitive creatures who would survive cannot permit surprise to disconcert them. In this instance both of the creatures accepted the happening as though it had been planned and expected.

The bear reared up and shook itself in an effort to dislodge the man-thing from its back, while Tarzan slipped a bronzed arm around the shaggy neck and clung desperately to his hold while he dragged his hunting knife from its sheath. It was a precarious place in which to stage a struggle for life. On one side the cliff rose far above them, and upon the other it dropped away dizzily into the depth of a gloomy gorge, and here the efforts of the cave bear to dislodge its antagonist momentarily bade fair to plunge them both into eternity.

The growls and roars of the quadruped reverberated among the mighty peaks of the Mountains of the Thipdars, but the ape-man battled silently, driving his blade repeatedly into the back of the lunging beast, which was seeking by every means at its command to dislodge him, though ever wary against precipitating itself over the brink into the chasm.

But the battle could not go on forever and at last the blade found the spinal cord. The creature stiffened spasmodically and Tarzan slipped quickly from its back. He found safe footing upon the ledge as the mighty carcass stumbled forward and rolled over the edge to hurtle downward to the gorge's bottom, carrying with it four of Tarzan's arrows and his spear.

The ape-man found his rope lying upon the ledge where it had fallen, and gathering it up he started back along the trail in search of the bow that he had been forced to discard in his flight, as well as to find the boy.

He had taken only a few steps when, upon rounding the shoulder of a crag, he came face to face with the youth. At sight of him the latter stopped, his spear ready, his stone knife loosened in its sheath. He had been carrying Tarzan's bow, but at sight of the ape-man he dropped it at his feet, the better to defend himself in the event that he was attacked by the stranger.

"I am Tarzan of the Apes," said the Lord of the Jungle. "I come as a friend, and not to kill."

"I am Ovan," said the boy. "If you did not come to our country to kill, then you came to steal a mate, and thus it is the duty of every warrior of Clovi to kill you."

"Tarzan seeks no mate," said the ape-man.

"Then why is he in Clovi?" demanded the youth.

"He is lost," replied the ape-man. "Tarzan comes from another world that is beyond Pellucidar. He has become separated from his friends and he cannot find his way back to them. He would be friend with the people of Clovi."

"Why did you attack the bear?" demanded Ovan, suddenly.

"If I had not attacked it it would have killed you," replied the ape-man.

Ovan scratched his head. "It seemed to me," he said presently, "that there could be no other reason. It is what one of the men of my own tribe would have done, but you are not of my tribe. You are an enemy and so I could not understand why you did it. Do you tell me that though I am not of your tribe you would have saved my life?"

"Certainly," replied Tarzan.

Ovan looked long and steadily at the handsome giant standing before him. "I believe you," he said presently, "although I do not understand. I never heard of such a thing before, but I do not know that the men of my tribe will believe. Even after I have told them what you have done for me they may still wish to kill you, for they believe that it is never safe to trust an enemy."

"Where is your village?" asked Tarzan.

"It is not at a great distance," replied Ovan.

"I will go there with you," said Tarzan, "and talk with your chief."

"Very well," said the boy. "You may talk with Avan the chief. He is my father. And if they decide to kill you I shall try to help you, for you saved my life when the ryth would have destroyed me."

"Why were you in the cave?" demanded Tarzan. "It was plainly apparent that it was the den of a wild beast."

"You, too, were upon the same trail," said the boy, "while you chanced to be behind the ryth. It was my misfortune that I was in front of it."

"I did not know where the trail led," said the ape-man.

"Neither did I," said Ovan. "I have never hunted before except in the company of older men, but now I have reached an age when I would be a warrior myself, and so I have come out of the caves of my people to make my first kill alone, for only thus may a man hope to become a warrior. I saw this trail and, though I did not know where it led, I followed it; nor had I been long upon it when I heard the footsteps of the ryth behind me and when I came to the cave and saw that the trail ended there, I knew that I should never again see the caves of my people, that I should never become a warrior. When the great ryth came and saw me standing there he was very angry, but I should have fought him. Perhaps I might have killed him, though I do not believe that that is at all likely.

"And then you came and with this bent stick cast a little spear into the back of the ryth, which so enraged him that he forgot me and turned to pursue you as you knew that he would. They must indeed be brave warriors who come from the land from which you come. Tell me about your country. Where is it? Are your warriors great hunters and is your chief powerful in the land?"

Tarzan tried to explain that his country was not in Pellucidar, but that was beyond Ovan's powers of conception, and so Tarzan turned the conversation from himself to the youth and as they followed a winding trail toward Clovi, Ovan discoursed upon the bravery of the men of his tribe and the beauty of its women.

"Avan, my father, is a great chief," he said, "and the men of my tribe are mighty warriors. Often we battle with the men of Zoram and we have even gone as far as Daroz, which lies beyond Zoram, for always there are more men than women in our tribe and the warriors must seek their mates in Zoram and Daroz. Even now Carb has gone to Zoram with twenty warriors to steal women. The women of Zoram are very beautiful. When I am a little larger I shall go to Zoram and steal a mate."

"How far is it from Clovi to Zoram?" asked Tarzan.

"Some say that it is not so far, and others that it is farther," replied Ovan. "I have heard it said that going to Zoram is much farther than returning inasmuch as the warriors usually eat six times on the journey from Clovi to Zoram, but returning a strong man may make the journey eating only twice and still retain his strength."

"But why should the distance be shorter returning than going?" demanded the ape-man.

"Because when they are returning they are usually pursued by the warriors of Zoram," replied Ovan.

Inwardly Tarzan smiled at the naïveté of Ovan's reasoning, while it again impressed upon him the impossibility of measuring distances or computing time under the anomalous condition obtaining in Pellucidar.

As the two made their way toward Clovi, the boy gradually abandoned his suspicious attitude toward Tarzan and presently seemed to accept him quite as he would have a member of his own tribe. He noticed the wound made by the talons of the thipdar on Tarzan's back and shoulders and when he had wormed the story from his companion he marveled at the courage, resourcefulness, and strength that had won escape for this stranger from what a Pellucidarian would have considered an utterly hopeless situation.

Ovan saw that the wounds were inflamed and realized that they must be causing Tarzan considerable pain and discomfort, and so when first their way led near a brook he insisted upon cleansing them thoroughly, and collecting the leaves of a particular shrub he crushed them and applied the juices to the open wounds.

The pain of the inflammation had been as nothing compared to the acute agony caused by the application thus made by Ovan and yet the boy noticed that not even by the tremor of a single muscle did the stranger evidence the agony that Ovan well knew he was enduring, and once again his admiration for his newfound companion was increased.

"It may hurt," he said, "but it will keep the wounds from rotting and afterward they will heal quickly."

For a short time after they resumed their march the pain continued to be excruciating, but it lessened gradually until it finally disappeared, and thereafter the ape-man felt no discomfort.

The way led to a forest where there were straight, tough, young saplings, and here Tarzan tarried long enough to fashion a new spear and to split and scrape half a dozen additional arrows.

Ovan was much interested in Tarzan's steel-bladed knife and in his bow and arrows, although secretly he looked with contempt upon the latter, which he referred to as little spears for young children. But when they became hungry and Tarzan bowled over a mountain sheep with a single shaft, the lad's contempt was changed to admiration and thereafter he not only evinced great respect for the bow and arrows, but begged to be taught how to make and to use them.

The little Clovian was a lad after the heart of the ape-man and the two became fast friends as they made their way toward the land of Clovi, for Ovan possessed the quiet dignity of the wild beast; nor was he given to that garrulity which is at once the pride and the curse of civilized man—there were no boy orators in the peaceful Pliocene.

"We are almost there," announced Ovan, halting at the brink of a canyon. "Below lie the caves of the Clovi. I hope that Avan, the chief, will receive you as a friend, but that I cannot promise. Perhaps it might be better for you to go your way and not come to the caves of the Clovi. I do not want you to be killed."

"They will not kill me," said Tarzan. "I come as a friend." But in his heart he knew that the chances were that these primitive savages might never accept a stranger among them upon an equal or a friendly footing.

"Come, then," said Ovan, as he started the descent into the canyon. Partway down the trail turned up along the canyon side in the direction of the head of the gorge. It was a level trail here, well kept and much used, with indications that no little engineering skill had entered into its construction. It was by no means the haphazard trail of beasts, but rather the work of intelligent, even though savage and primitive men.

They had proceeded no great distance along the trail when Ovan sounded a low whistle, which, a moment later, was answered from around the bend in the trail ahead, and when the two had passed this turn Tarzan saw before him a wide, natural ledge of rock entirely overhung by beetling cliffs and in the depth of the recess thus formed in the cliffside he saw the dark mouth of a cavern.

Upon the flat surface of the ledge, which comprised some two acres, were congregated fully a hundred men, women and children.

All eyes were turned in their direction as they came into view and on sight of Tarzan the warriors sprang to their feet, seizing spears and knives. The women called their children to them and moved quickly toward the entrance to the cavern.

"Do not fear," cried the boy. "It is only Ovan and his friend, Tarzan."

"We kill," growled some of the warriors.

"Where is Avan the chief?" demanded the boy.

"Here is Avan the chief," announced a deep gruff voice, and Tarzan shifted his gaze to the figure of a stalwart, brawny savage emerging from the mouth of the cavern.

"What have you there, Ovan?" demanded the chief. "If you have brought a prisoner of war, you should have disarmed him first."

"He is no prisoner," replied Ovan. "He is a stranger in Pellucidar and he comes as a friend and not as an enemy."

"He is a stranger," replied Avan, "and you should have killed him. He has learned the way to the caverns of Clovi and if we do not kill him he will return to his people and lead them against us."

"He has no people and he does not know how to return to his own country," said the boy.

"Then he does not speak true words, for that is not possible," said Avan. "There can be no man who does not know the way to his own country. Come! Stand aside, Ovan, while I destroy him."

The lad drew himself stiffly erect in front of Tarzan. "Who would kill the friend of Ovan," he said, "must first kill Ovan."

A tall warrior, standing near the chief, laid his hand upon Avan's arm. "Ovan has always been a good boy," he said. "There is none in Clovi near his age whose words are as full of wisdom as his. If he says that this stranger is his friend and if he does not wish us to kill him, he must have a reason and we should listen to him before we decide to destroy the stranger."

"Very well," said the chief; "perhaps you are right, Ulan. We shall see. Speak, boy, and tell us why we should not kill the stranger."

"Because at the risk of his life he saved mine. Hand-to-hand he fought with a great ryth from which I could not have escaped had it not been for him; nor did he offer to harm me, and what enemy of the Clovi is there, even among the people of Zoram or Daroz who are of our own blood, that would not slay a Clovi youth who was so soon to become a warrior? Not only is he very brave, but he is a great hunter. It would be well for the tribe of Clovi if he came to live with us as a friend."

Avan bowed his head in thought. "When Carb returns we shall call a council and decide what to do," he said. "In the meantime the stranger must remain here as a prisoner."

"I shall not remain as a prisoner," said Tarzan. "I came as a friend and I shall remain as a friend, or I shall not remain at all."

"Let him stay as a friend," said Ulan. "He has marched with Ovan and has not harmed him. Why should we think that he will harm us when we are many and he only one?"

"Perhaps he has come to steal a woman," suggested Avan.

"No," said Ovan, "that is not so. Let him remain and with my life I will guarantee that he will harm no one."

"Let him stay," said some of the other warriors, for Ovan had long been the pet of the tribe so that they were accustomed to humoring him and so unspoiled was he that they still found pleasure in doing so.

"Very well," said Avan. "Let him remain. But Ovan and Ulan shall be responsible for his conduct."

There were only a few of the Clovians who accepted Tarzan without suspicion, and among these was Maral, the mother of Ovan, and Rela, his sister. These two accepted him without question because Ovan had accepted him. Ulan's friendship, too, had been apparent from the first; nor was it without great value, for Ulan, because his intelligence, courage, and ability was a force in the councils of the Clovi.

Tarzan, accustomed to the tribal life of primitive people, took his place naturally among them, paying no attention to those who paid no attention to him, observing scrupulously the ethics of tribal life and conforming to the customs of the Clovi in every detail of his relations with them. He liked to talk with Maral because of her sunny disposition and her marked intelligence. She told him that she was from Zoram, having been captured by Avan when, as a young warrior, he had decided to take a mate. And to her nativity he attributed her great beauty, for it seemed to be an accepted fact among the Clovis that the women of Zoram were the most beautiful of all women.

Ulan he had liked from the first, being naturally attracted to him because he had been the first of the Clovians to champion his cause. In many ways Ulan differed from his fellows. He seemed to have been the first among his people to discover that a brain may be used for purposes other than securing the bare necessities of existence. He had learned to dream and to exercise his brain along pleasant paths that gave entertainment to himself and others—fantastic stories that sometimes amused and sometimes awed his eager audiences; and, too, he was a maker of pictures and these he exhibited to Tarzan with no small measure of pride. Leading the ape-man into the rocky cavern that was the shelter, the storehouse and the citadel of the tribe, he lighted a crude torch which illuminated the walls, revealing the pictures that Ulan had drawn there. Mammoth and saber-tooth and cave bear were depicted, with the red deer, the hyaenodon, and other familiar beasts, and in addition thereto were some with which Tarzan was unfamiliar and one that he had never seen elsewhere than in Pal-ul-don, where it had been known as a gryf. Ulan told him that it was a gyor and that it was found upon the Gyor Cors, or Gyor Plains, which lie at the end of the range of the Mountains of the Thipdars beyond Clovi.

The drawings were in outline and were well executed. The other members of the tribe thought they were very wonderful for Ulan was the first ever to have made them and they could not understand how he did it. Perhaps if he had been a weakling he would have lost caste among them because of this gift, but inasmuch as he was also a noted hunter and warrior his talents but added to his fame and the esteem in which he was held by all.

But though these and a few others were friendly toward him, the majority of the tribe looked upon Tarzan with suspicion, for never within the memory of one of them had a strange warrior entered their village other than as an enemy. They were waiting for the return of Carb and the warriors who had accompanied him, when, the majority of them hoped, the council would sentence the stranger to death.

As they became better acquainted with Tarzan, however, others among them were being constantly won to his cause and this was particularly true when he accompanied them upon their hunts, his skill and his prowess winning their admiration, and his strange weapons which they had at first viewed with contempt, soon commanding their unqualified respect.

And so it was that the longer that Carb remained away the better Tarzan's chances became of being accepted into the tribe upon an equal footing with its other members; a contingency for which he hoped since it would afford him a base from which to prosecute his search for his fellows and allies familiar with the country, whose friendly services he could enlist to aid him in his search.

He was confident that Jason Gridley, if he still lived, was lost somewhere among these stupendous mountains and if he could but find him they might eventually, with the assistance of the Clovians, locate the camp of the O-220.

He had eaten and slept with the Clovi many times and had accompanied them upon several hunts. It had been noon when he arrived and it was still noon, so whether a day or a month had passed he did not know. He was squatting by the cook fire of Maral, talking with her and with Ulan, when from down the gorge there sounded the whistled signal of the Clovians announcing the approach of a friendly party and an instant later a youth rounded the shoulder of the cliff and entered the village.

"It is Tomar," announced Maral. "Perhaps he brings news of Carb."

The youth ran to the center of the ledge upon which the village stood and halted. For a moment he stood there dramatically with upraised hand, commanding silence, and then he spoke. "Carb is returning," he cried. "The victorious warriors of Clovi are returning with the most beautiful woman of Zoram. Great is Carb! Great are the warriors of Clovi!"

Cook fires and the routine occupations of the moment were abandoned as the tribe advanced to await the coming of the victorious war party.

Presently it came into sight, rounding the shoulder of the cliff and filing on to the ledge—twenty warriors led by Carb and among them a girl, her wrists bound behind her back, a rawhide leash around her neck, the free end held by a brawny warrior.

The ape-man's greatest interest lay in Carb, for his position in the tribe, perhaps even his life itself might rest with the decision of this man, whose influence, he had learned, was great in the councils of his people.

Carb was evidently a man of great physical strength; his regular features imparted to him much of the physical beauty that is an attribute of his people, but an otherwise handsome countenance was marred by thin, cruel lips and cold, unsympathetic eyes.

From contemplation of Carb the ape-man's eyes wandered to the face of the prisoner, and there they were arrested by the startling beauty of the girl. Well, indeed, thought Tarzan, might she be acclaimed the most beautiful woman of Zoram, for it was doubtful that there existed many in this world or the outer who might lay claim to greater pulchritude than she.

Avan, the chief, standing in the center of the ledge, received the returning warriors. He looked with favor upon the prize and listened attentively while Carb narrated the more important details of the expedition.

"We shall hold the council at once," announced Avan, "to decide who shall possess the prisoner, and at the same time we may settle another matter that has been awaiting the return of Carb and his warriors."

"What is that?" demanded Carb.

Avan pointed at Tarzan. "There is a stranger who would come into the tribe and be as one of us."

Carb turned his cold eyes in the direction of the ape-man and his face clouded. "Why has he not been destroyed?" he asked. "Let us do away with him at once."

"That is not for you to decide," said Avan, the chief. "The warriors in council alone may say what shall be done."

Carb shrugged. "If the council does not destroy him, I shall kill him myself," he said. "I, Carb, will have no enemy living in the village where I live."

"Let us hold the council at once, then," said Ulan, "for if Carb is greater than the council of the warriors we should know it." There was a note of sarcasm in his voice.

"We have marched for a long time without food or sleep," said Carb. "Let us eat and rest before the council is held, for matters may arise in the council which will demand all of our strength," and he looked pointedly at Ulan.

The other warriors, who had accompanied Carb, also wished to eat and rest before the council was held, and Avan, the chief, acceded to their just demands.

The girl captive had not spoken since she had arrived in the village and she was now turned over to Maral, who was instructed to feed her and permit her to sleep. The bonds were removed from her wrists and she was brought to the cook fire of the chief's mate, where she stood with an expression of haughty disdain upon her beautiful face.

None of the women revealed any inclination to abuse the prisoner—an attitude which rather surprised Tarzan until the reason for it had been explained to him, for he had upon more than one occasion witnessed the cruelties inflicted upon female prisoners by the women of native African tribes into whose hands the poor creatures had fallen.

Maral, in particular, was kind to the girl. "Why should I be otherwise?" she asked when Tarzan commented upon the fact. "Our daughters, or even any one of us, may at any time be captured by the warriors of another tribe, and if it were known that we had been cruel to their women, they would doubtless repay us in kind; nor, aside from this, is there any reason why we should be other than kind to a woman who will live among us for the rest of her life. We are few in numbers and we are constantly together. If we harbored enmities and if we quarreled our lives would be less happy. Since you have been here you have never seen quarreling among the women of Clovi; nor would you if you remained here for the rest of your life. There have been quarrelsome women among us, just as at some time there have been crippled children, but as we destroy the one for the good of the tribe we destroy the others."

She turned to the girl. "Sit down," she said pleasantly.

"There is meat in the pot. Eat, and then you may sleep. Do not be afraid; you are among friends. I, too, am from Zoram."

At that the girl turned her eyes upon the speaker. "You are from Zoram?" she asked. "Then you must have felt as I feel. I want to go back to Zoram. I would rather die than live elsewhere."

"You will get over that," said Maral. "I felt the same way, but when I became acquainted I found that the people of Clovi are much like the people of Zoram. They have been kind to me; they will be kind to you, and you will be happy as I have been. When they have given you a mate you will look upon life very differently."

"I shall not mate with one of them," cried the girl, stamping her sandaled foot. "I am Jana, The Red Flower of Zoram, and I choose my own mate."

Maral shook her head sadly. "Thus spoke I once," she said; "but I have changed, and so will you."

"Not I," said the girl. "I have seen but one man with whom I would mate and I shall never mate with another."

"You are Jana," asked Tarzan, "the sister of Thoar?"

The girl looked at him in surprise, and as though she had noticed him now for the first time her eyes quickly investigated him. "Ah," she said, "you are the stranger whom Carb would destroy?"

"Yes," replied the ape-man.

"What do you know of Thoar, my brother?"

"We hunted together. We were traveling back to Zoram when I became separated from him. We were following the tracks made by you and a man who was with you when a storm came and obliterated them. Your companion was the man who I was seeking."

"What do you know of the man who was with me?" demanded the girl.

"He is my friend," replied Tarzan. "What has become of him?"

"He was caught in a canyon during the storm and he must have been drowned," replied Jana sadly. "You are from his country?"

"Yes."

"How did you know he was with me?" she demanded.

"I recognized his tracks and Thoar recognized yours."

"He was a great warrior," she said, "and a very brave man."

"Are you sure that he is dead?" asked Tarzan.

"I am sure," replied The Red Flower of Zoram.

For a time they were silent, both occupied with thoughts of Jason Gridley. "You were his friend," said Jana. She had moved close to him and had seated herself at his side. Now she leaned still closer. "They are going to kill you," she whispered. "I know the people of these tribes better than you and I know Carb. He will have his way. You were Jason's friend and so was I. If we can escape I can lead the way back to Zoram, and if you are Thoar's friend and mine the people of Zoram will have to accept you."

"Why do you whisper?" asked a gruff voice behind them, and turning they saw Avan, the chief. Without waiting for a reply, he turned to Maral. "Take the woman to the cavern," he said. "She will remain there until the council has decided who shall have her as mate, and in the meantime I will place warriors at the entrance to the cavern to see that she does not escape."

As Maral motioned Jana toward the cavern, the latter arose, and as she did so she cast an appealing glance at Tarzan. The ape-man, who was already upon his feet, looked quickly about him. Perhaps a hundred members of the tribe were scattered about the ledge, while near the opening to the trail which led down the canyon and which afforded the only avenue of escape, fully a dozen warriors loitered. Alone he might have won his way through, but with the girl it would have been impossible. He shook his head and his lips, which were turned away from Avan, formed the word, "Wait," and a moment later The Red Flower of Zoram had entered the dark cavern of the Clovians.

"And as for you, man of another country," said Avan, addressing Tarzan, "until the council has decided upon your fate, you are a prisoner. Go, therefore, into the cavern and remain there until the council of warriors has spoken."

A dozen warriors barred his way to freedom now, but they were lolling idly, expecting no emergency. A bold dash for freedom might carry him beyond them before they could realize that he was attempting escape. He was confident that the voice of the council would be adverse to him and when its decision was announced he would be surrounded by all the warriors of Clovi, alert and ready to prevent his escape. Now, therefore, was the most propitious moment; but Tarzan of the Apes made no break for liberty; instead he turned and strode toward the entrance to the cavern, for The Red Flower of Zoram had appealed to him for aid and he would not desert the sister of Thoar and the friend of Jason.

12

The Phelian Swamp

As JASON GRIDLEY leaped down the canyon side toward the lone warrior who stood facing the attack of the tremendous reptile gliding swiftly through the air from the top of the opposite cliffside, there flashed upon the screen of his recollection the picture of a restoration of a similar extinct reptile and he recognized the creature as a stegosaurus of the Jurassic; but how inadequately had the picture that he had seen carried to his mind the colossal proportions of the creature, or but remotely suggested its terrifying aspect.

Jason saw the lone warrior standing there facing inevitable doom, but in his attitude there was no outward sign of fear. In his right hand he held his puny spear, and in his left his crude stone knife. He would die, but he would give a good account of himself. There was no panic of terror, no futile flight.

The distance between Jason and the stegosaurus was over great for a revolver shot, but the American hoped that he might at least divert the attention of the reptile from its prey and even, perhaps, frighten it away by the unaccustomed sound of the report of the weapon, and so he fired twice in rapid succession as he leaped downward toward the bottom of the canyon. That at least one of the shots struck the reptile was evidenced by the fact that it veered from its course, simultaneously emitting a loud, screaming sound.

Attracted to Jason by the report of the revolver and evidently attributing its hurt to this new enemy, the reptile, using its tail as a rudder and tilting its spine plates up on one side, veered in the direction of the American.

As the two shots shattered the silence of the canyon, the warrior turned his eyes in the direction of the man leaping down the declivity toward him, and then he saw the reptile veer in the direction of the newcomer.

Heredity and training, coupled with experience, had taught this primitive savage that every man's hand was against him, unless that man was a member of his own tribe. Only upon a single occasion in his life had experience controverted these teachings, and so it seemed inconceivable that this stranger, whom he immediately recognized as such, was deliberately risking his life in an effort to succor him; yet there seemed no other explanation, and so the perplexed warrior, instead of seeking to escape now that the attention of the reptile was diverted from him, ran swiftly toward Jason to join forces with him in combatting the attack of the creature.

From the instant that the stegosaurus had leaped from the summit of the cliff, it had hurtled through the air with a speed which seemed entirely out of proportion to its tremendous bulk, so that all that had transpired in the meantime had occupied but a few moments of time, and Jason Gridley found himself facing this onrushing death almost before he had had time to speculate upon the possible results of his venturesome interference.

With wide distended jaws and uttering piercing shrieks, the terrifying creature shot toward him, but now at last it presented an easy target and Jason Gridley was entirely competent to take advantage of the altered situation.

He fired rapidly with both weapons, trying to reach the tiny brain, at the location of which he could only guess and for which his bullets were searching through the roof of the opened mouth. His greatest hope, however, was that the beast could not for long face that terrific fusillade of shots, and in this he was right. The strange and terrifying sound and the pain and shock of the bullets tearing into its skull proved too much for the stegosaurus. Scarcely half a dozen feet from Gridley it swerved upward and passed over his head, receiving two or three bullets in its belly as it did so.

Still shrieking with rage and pain it glided to the ground beyond him.

Almost immediately it turned to renew the attack. This time it came upon its four feet, and Jason saw that it was likely to prove fully as formidable upon the ground as it had been in the air, for considering its tremendous bulk it moved with great agility and speed.

As he stood facing the returning creature, the warrior reached his side.

"Get on that side of him," said the warrior, "and I will attack him on this. Keep out of the way of his tail. Use your spear; you cannot frighten a dyrodor away by making a noise."

Jason Gridley leaped quickly to one side to obey the suggestions of the warrior, smiling inwardly at the naive suggestion of the other that his Colt had been used solely to frighten the creature.

The warrior took his place upon the opposite side of the approaching reptile, but before he had time to cast his spear or Jason to fire again the creature stumbled forward, its nose dug into the ground and it rolled over upon its side, dead.

"It is dead!" said the warrior in a surprised tone. "What could have killed it? Neither one of us has cast a spear."

Jason slipped his Colts into their holsters. "These killed it," he said, tapping them.

"Noises do not kill," said the warrior skeptically. "It is not the bark of the jalok or the growl of the ryth that rends the flesh of man. The hiss of the thipdar kills no one."

"It was not the noise that killed it," said Jason, "but if you will examine its head and especially the roof of its mouth you will see what happened when my weapons spoke."

Following Jason's suggestion the warrior examined the head and mouth of the dyrodor and when he had seen the gaping wounds he looked at Jason with a new respect. "Who are you," he asked, "and what are you doing in the land of Zoram?"

"My God!" exclaimed Jason. "Am I in Zoram?"

"You are."

"And you are one of the men of Zoram?" demanded the American.

"I am; but who are you?"

"Tell me, do you know Jana, the Red Flower of Zoram?" insisted Jason.

"What do you know of The Red Flower of Zoram, stranger?" demanded the other. And then suddenly his eyes widened to a new thought. "Tell me," he cried, "by what name do they call you in the country from which you come?"

"My name is Gridley," replied the American; "Jason Gridley."

"Jason!" exclaimed the other; "yes, Jason Gridley, that is it. Tell me, man, where is The Red Flower of Zoram? What did you do with her?"

"That is what I am asking you," said Jason. "We became separated and I have been searching for her. But what do you know of me?"

"I followed you for a long time," replied the other, "but the waters fell and obliterated your tracks."

"Why did you follow me?" asked Jason.

"I followed because you were with The Red Flower of Zoram," replied the other. "I followed to kill you, but he said you would not harm her; he said that she went with you willingly. Is that true?"

"She came with me willingly for a while," replied Jason, "and then she left me; but I did not harm her."

"Perhaps he was right then," said the warrior. "I shall wait until I find her and if you have not harmed her, I shall not kill you."

"Whom do you mean by 'he'?" asked Jason. "There is no one in Pellucidar who could possibly know anything about me, except Jana."

"Do you not know Tarzan?" asked the warrior.

"Tarzan!" exclaimed Jason. "You have seen Tarzan? He is alive?"

"I saw him. We hunted together and we followed you and Jana, but he is not alive now; he is dead."

"Dead! You are sure that he is dead?"

"Yes, he is dead."

"How did it happen?"

"We were crossing the summit of the mountains when he was seized by a thipdar and carried away."

Tarzan dead! He had feared as much and yet now that he had proof it seemed unbelievable. His mind could scarcely grasp the significance of the words that he had heard as he recalled the strength and vitality of that man of steel. It seemed incredible that that giant frame should cease to pulsate with life; that those mighty muscles no longer rolled beneath the sleek, bronzed hide; that that courageous heart no longer beat.

"You were very fond of him?" asked the warrior, noticing the silence and dejection of the other.

"Yes," said Jason.

"So was I," said the warrior; "but neither Tar-gash nor I could save him, the thipdar struck so swiftly and was gone before we could cast a weapon."

"Who is Tar-gash?" asked Jason.

"A Sagoth—one of the hairy men," replied the warrior. "They live in the forest and are often used as warriors by the Mahars."

"And he was with you and Tarzan?" inquired Jason.

"Yes. They were together when I first saw them, but now Tarzan is dead and Tar-gash has gone back to his own country and I must proceed upon my search for The Red Flower of Zoram. You have saved my life, man from another country, but I do not know that you have not harmed Jana. Perhaps you have slain her. How am I to know? I do not know what I should do."

"I, too, am looking for Jana," said Jason. "Let us look for her together."

"Then if we find her, she shall tell me whether or not I shall kill you," said the warrior.

Jason could not but recall how angry Jana had been with him. She had almost killed him herself. Perhaps she would find it easier to permit this warrior to kill him. Doubtless the man was her sweetheart and if he knew the truth he would need no urging to destroy a rival, but neither by look nor word did he reveal any apprehension as he replied.

"I will go with you," he said, "and if I have harmed The Red Flower of Zoram you may kill me. What is your name?"

"Thoar," replied the warrior.

Jana had spoken of her brother to Jason, but if she had ever mentioned his name, the American had forgotten it, and so he continued to think that Thoar was the sweetheart and possibly the mate of The Red Flower and his reaction to this belief was unpleasant; yet why it should have been he could not have explained. The more he thought of the matter the more certain he was that Thoar was Jana's mate, for who was there who might more naturally desire to kill one who had wronged her. Yes, he was sure that the man was Jana's mate. The thought made him angry for she had certainly led him to believe that she was not mated. That was just like a woman, he meditated; they were all flirts; they would make a fool of a man merely to pass an idle hour, but she had not made a fool of him. He had not fallen victim to her lures, that is why she had been so angry—her vanity had been piqued—and being a very primitive young person the first thought that had come to her mind had been to kill him. What a little devil she was to try to get him to make love to her when she already had a mate, and thus Jason almost succeeded in working himself into a rage until his sense of humor came to his rescue; yet even though he smiled, way down deep within him something hurt and he wondered why.

"Where did you last see Jana?" asked Thoar. "We can return there and try and locate her tracks."

"I do not know that I can explain," replied Jason. "It is very difficult for me to locate myself or anything else where there are no points of compass."

"We can start together at the point where we found your tracks with Jana's," said Thoar.

"Perhaps that will not be necessary if you are familiar with the country on the other side of the range," said Jason. "Returning toward the mountains from the spot where I first saw Jana, there was a tremendous gorge upon our left. It was toward this gorge that the two men of the four that had been pursuing her ran after I had killed two of their number. Jana tried to find a way to the summit, far to the right of this gorge, but our path was blocked by a deep rift which paralleled the base of the mountains, so that she was compelled to turn back again toward the gorge, into which she descended. The last I saw of her she was going up the gorge, so that if you know where this gorge lies it will not be necessary for us to go all the way back to the point at which I first met her."

"I know the gorge," said Thoar, "and if the two Phelians entered it it is possible that they captured her. We will search in the direction of the gorge then and if we do not find any trace of her, we shall drop down to the country of the Phelians in the lowland."

Through a maze of jagged peaks Thoar led the way. To him time meant nothing; to Jason Gridley it was little more than a memory. When they found food they ate; when they were tired they slept, and always just ahead there were perilous crags to skirt and stupendous cliffs to scale. To the American it would have seemed incredible that a girl ever could find her way here had he not had occasion to follow where The Red Flower of Zoram led.

Occasionally they were forced to take a lower route which led into the forests that climbed higher along the slopes of the mountains, and here they found more game and with Thoar's assistance Jason fashioned a garment from the hide of a mountain goat. It was at best but a sketchy garment; yet it sufficed for the purpose for which it was intended and left his arms and legs free. Nor was it long before he realized its advantages and wondered why civilized man of the outer crust should so encumber himself with useless clothing, when the demands of temperature did not require it.

As Jason became better acquainted with Thoar he found his regard for him changing from suspicion to admiration, and finally to a genuine liking for the savage Pellucidarian, in spite of the fact that this sentiment was tinged with a feeling that, while not positive animosity, was yet akin to it. It was difficult for Jason to fathom the sentiment which seemed to animate him. There could be no rivalry between him and this primitive warrior and yet Jason's whole demeanor and attitude toward Thoar was such as might be scrupulously observed by any honorable man toward an honorable opponent or rival.

They seldom, if ever, spoke of Jana; yet thoughts of her were uppermost in the mind of each of them. Jason often found himself reviewing every detail of his association with her; every little characteristic gesture and expression was indelibly imprinted upon his memory, as were the contours of her perfect figure and the radiant loveliness of her face. Not even the bitter words with which she had parted with him could erase the memory of her joyous comradeship. Never before in his life had he missed the companionship of any woman. At times he tried to crowd her from his thoughts by recalling incidents of his friendship with Cynthia Furnois or Barbara Green, but the vision of The Red Flower of Zoram remained persistently in the foreground, while that of Cynthia and Barbara always faded gradually into forgetfulness.

This state of mental subjugation to the personality of an untutored savage, however beautiful, annoyed his ego and he tried to escape it by dwelling upon the sorrow entailed by the death of Tarzan; but somehow he never could convince himself that Tarzan was dead. It was one of those things that it was simply impossible to conceive.

Failing in this, he would seek to occupy his mind with conjectures concerning the fate of Von Horst, Muviro, and the Waziri warriors, or upon what was transpiring aboard the great dirigible in search of which his eyes were often scanning the cloudless Pellucidarian sky. But travel where it would, even to his remote Tarzana hills in far-off California, it would always return to hover around the girlish figure of The Red Flower of Zoram.

Thoar, upon his part, found in the American a companion after his own heart—a dependable man of quiet ways, always ready to assume his share of the burden and responsibilities of the savage trail they trod.

So the two came at last to the rim of the great gorge and though they followed it up and down for a great distance in each direction they found no trace of Jana, nor any sign that she had passed that way.

"We shall go down to the lowlands," said Thoar, "to the country that is called Pheli and even though we may not find her, we shall avenge her."

The idea of primitive justice suggested by Thoar's decision aroused no opposing question of ethics in the mind of the civilized American; in fact, it seemed quite the most natural thing in the world that he and Thoar should constitute themselves a court of justice as well as the instrument of its punishment, for thus easily does man slough off the thin veneer of civilization, which alone differentiates him from his primitive ancestors.

Thus a gap of perhaps a hundred thousand years which yawned between Thoar of Zoram, and Jason Gridley of Tarzana was closed. Imbued with the same hatred, they descended the slopes of the Mountains of the Thipdars toward the land of Pheli, and the heart of each was hot with the lust to kill. No greedy munitions manufacturer was needed here to start a war.

Down through stately forests and across rolling foothills went Thoar and Jason toward the land of Pheli. The country teemed with game of all descriptions and their way was beset by fierce carnivores, by stupid, irritable herbivores of ponderous weight and short tempers, or by gigantic reptiles beneath whose charging feet the earth trembled. It was by the exercise of the superior intelligence of man combined with a considerable share of luck that they passed unscathed to the swampland where Pheli lies. Here the world seemed dedicated to the reptilia. They swarmed in countless thousands and in all sizes and infinite varieties. Aquatic and amphibious, carnivorous and herbivorous, they hissed and screamed and fought and devoured one another constantly, so that Jason wondered in what intervals they found the time to propagate their kind and he marveled that the herbivores among them could exist at all. A terrific orgy of extermination seemed to constitute the entire existence of a large proportion of the species and yet the tremendous size of many of them, including several varieties of the herbivores, furnished ample evidence that considerable numbers of them lived to a great age, for unlike mammals, reptiles never cease to grow while they are living.

The swamp, in which Thoar believed the villages of the Phelians were to be found, supported a tremendous forest of gigantic trees and so interlaced were their branches that oftentimes the two men found it expedient to travel among them rather than upon the treacherous, boggy ground. Here, too, the reptiles were smaller, though scarcely less numerous. Among these, however, there were exceptions, and those which caused them the greatest anxiety were snakes of such titanic proportions that when he first encountered one Jason could not believe the testimony of his own eyes. They came upon the creature suddenly as it was in the act of swallowing a trachodon that was almost as large as an elephant. The huge herbivorous dinosaur was still alive and battling bravely to extricate itself from the jaws of the serpent, but not even its giant strength nor its terrific armament of teeth, which included a reserve supply of over four hundred in the lower jaw alone, availed it in its unequal struggle with the colossal creature that was slowly swallowing it alive.

Perhaps it was their diminutive size as much as their brains or luck that saved the two men from the jaws of these horrid creatures. Or, again, it may have been the dense stupidity of the reptiles themselves, which made it comparatively easy for the men to elude them.

Here in this dismal swamp of horrors not even the giant tarags or the equally ferocious lions and leopards of Pellucidar dared venture, and how man existed there it was beyond the power of Jason to conceive. In fact he doubted that the Phelians or any other race of men made their homes here.

"Men could not exist in such a place," he said to Thoar. "Pheli must lie elsewhere."

"No," said his companion, "members of my tribe have come down here more than once in the memory of man to avenge the stealing of a woman and the stories that they have brought back have familiarized us all with the conditions existing in the land of Pheli. This is indeed it."

"You may be right," said Jason, "but, like these snakes that we have seen, I shall have to see the villages of the Phelians before I will believe that they exist here and even then I won't know whether to believe it or not."

"It will not be long now," said Thoar, "before you shall see the Phelians in their own village."

"What makes you think so?" asked Jason.

"Look down below you and you will see what I have been searching for," replied Thoar, pointing.

Jason did as he was bid and discovered a small stream meandering through the swamp. "I see nothing but a brook," he said.

"That is what I have been searching for," replied Thoar. "All of my people who have been here say that Phelians live upon the banks of a river that runs through the swamp. In places the land is high and upon these hills the Phelians build their homes. They do not live in caverns as do we, but they make houses of great trees so strong that not even the largest reptiles can break into them."

"But why should anyone choose to live in such a place?" demanded the American.

"To eat and to breed in comparative peace and contentment," replied Thoar. "The Phelians, unlike the mountain people, are not a race of warriors. They do not like to fight and so they have hidden their villages away in this swamp where no man would care to come and thus they are practically free from human enemies. Also, here, meat abounds in such quantities that food lies always at their doors. For them then the conditions are ideal and here, more than elsewhere in Pellucidar, may they find contentment."

As they advanced now they exercised the greatest caution, knowing that any moment they might come within sight of a Phelian village. Nor was it long before Thoar halted and drew back behind the bole of a tree through which they were passing, then he pointed forward. Jason, looking, saw a bare hill before them, just a portion of which was visible through the trees. It was evident that the hill had been cleared by man, for many stumps remained. Within the range of his vision was but a single house, if such it might be called.

It was constructed of logs, a foot or two in diameter. Three or four of these logs, placed horizontally and lying one upon the other, formed the wall that was presented to Jason's view. The other side wall paralleled it at a distance of five or six feet, and across the top of the upper logs were laid sections of smaller trees, about six inches in diameter, and placed not more than a foot apart. These supported the roof, which consisted of several logs, a little longer than the logs constituting the walls. The roof logs were laid close together, the interstices being filled with mud. The front of the building was formed by shorter logs set upright in the ground, a single small aperture being left to form a doorway. But the most noticeable feature of Phelian architecture consisted of long pointed stakes, which protruded diagonally from the ground at an angle of about forty-five degrees, pointing outward from the base of the walls entirely around the building at intervals of about eighteen inches. The stakes themselves were six or eight inches in diameter and about ten feet long, being sharpened at the upper end, and forming a barrier against which few creatures, however brainless they might be, would venture to hurl themselves.

Drawing closer the two men had a better view of the village, which contained upon that side of the hill they were approaching and upon the top four buildings similar to that which they had first discovered. Close about the base of the hill grew the dense forest, but the hill itself had been entirely denuded of vegetation so that nothing, either large or small, could approach the habitation of the Phelians without being discovered.

No one was in sight about the village, but that did not deceive Thoar, who guessed that anything which transpired upon the hillside would be witnessed by many eyes peering through the openings between the wall logs from the dim interiors of the long buildings, beneath whose low ceilings Phelians must spend their lives either squatting or lying down, since there was not sufficient headroom to permit an adult to stand erect.

"Well," said Jason, "here we are. Now, what are we going to do?"

Thoar looked longingly at Jason's two Colts. "You have refused to use those for fear of wasting the deaths which they spit from their blue mouths," he said, "but with one of those we might soon find Jana if she was here or quickly avenge her if she is not."

"Come on then," said Jason. "I would sacrifice more than my ammunition for The Red Flower of Zoram." As he spoke he descended from the tree and started toward the nearest Phelian dwelling. Close behind him was Thoar and neither saw the eyes that watched them from among the trees that grew thickly upon the river side of the hill—cruel eyes that gleamed from whiskered faces.

13

The Horibs

A VAN, CHIEF OF the Clovi, had placed warriors before the entrance to the cavern and as Tarzan approached it to enter they halted him.

"Where are you going?" demanded one.

"Into the cavern," replied Tarzan.

"Why?" asked the warrior.

"I wish to sleep," replied the ape-man. "I have entered often before and no one has ever stopped me."

"Avan has issued orders that no strangers are to enter or leave the cavern until after the council of the warriors," exclaimed the guard.

At this juncture Avan approached. "Let him enter," he said. "I sent him hither, but do not let him come out again."

Without a word of comment or question the Lord of the Jungle passed into the interior of the gloomy cavern of Clovi. It was several moments before his eyes became accustomed to the subdued light within and permitted him to take account of his surroundings.

That portion of the cavern which was visible and with which he was familiar was of considerable extent. He could see the walls on either side, and, very vaguely, a portion of the rear wall, but adjoining that was utter darkness, suggesting that the cavern extended farther into the mountainside. Against the walls upon pallets of dry grasses covered with hide lay many warriors and a few women and children, almost all of whom were wrapped in slumber. In the greater light near the entrance a group squatted engaged in whispered conversation as, silently, he moved about the cavern searching for the girl from Zoram. It was she who recognized him first, attracting his attention by a low whistle.

"You have a plan of escape?" she asked as Tarzan seated himself upon a skin beside her.

"No," he said, "all that we may do is to await developments and take advantage of any opportunity that may present itself."

"I should think that it would be easy for you to escape," said the girl; "they do not treat you as a prisoner; you go about among them freely and they have permitted you to retain your weapons."

"I am a prisoner now," he replied. "Avan just instructed the warriors at the entrance not to permit me to leave here until after the council of warriors had decided my fate."

"Your future does not look very bright then," said Jana, "and as for me I already know my fate, but they shall not have me, Carb nor any other!"

They talked together in low tones with many periods of long silence, but when Jana turned the conversation upon the world from which Jason had come, the silences were few and far between. She would not let Tarzan rest, but plied him with questions, the answers to many of which were far beyond her powers to understand. Steam and electricity and all the countless activities of civilized existence which are dependent upon them were utterly beyond her powers of comprehension, as were the heavenly bodies or musical instruments or books, and yet despite what appeared to be the darkest depth of ignorance, to the very bottom of which she had plumbed, she was intelligent and when she spoke of those things pertaining to her own world with which she was familiar, she was both interesting and entertaining.

Presently a warrior near them opened his eyes, sat up and stretched. He looked about him and then he arose to his feet. He walked around the apartment awakening the other warriors.

"Awaken," he said to each, "and attend the council of the warriors."

When he approached Tarzan and Jana he recognized the former and stopped to glare down at him.

"What are you doing here?" he demanded.

Tarzan arose and faced the Clovian warrior, but he did not reply to the other's question.

"Answer me," growled Carb. "Why are you here?"

"You are not the chief," said Tarzan. "Go and ask your question of women and children."

Carb sputtered angrily. "Go!" said Tarzan, pointing toward the exit. For an instant the Clovian hesitated, then he continued on around the apartment, awakening the remaining warriors.

"Now he will see that you are killed," said the girl.

"He had determined on that before," replied Tarzan. "We are no worse off than we were."

Now they lapsed into silence, each waiting for the doom that was to be pronounced upon them. They knew that outside upon the ledge the warriors were sitting in a great circle and that there would be much talking and boasting and argument before any decision was reached, most of it unnecessary, for that has been the way with men who make laws from time immemorial, a great advantage, however, lying with our modern lawmakers in that they know more words than the first ape-men.

As Tarzan and Jana waited a youth entered the cavern. He

bore a torch in the light of which he searched about the interior. Presently he discovered Tarzan and came swiftly toward him. It was Ovan.

"The council has reached its decision," he said. "They will kill you and the girl goes to Carb."

Tarzan of the Apes rose to his feet. "Come," he said to Jana, "now is as good a time as any. If we can cross the ledge and reach the trail only a swift warrior can overtake us. And if you are my friend," he continued, turning to Ovan, "and you have said that you are, you will remain silent and give us our chance."

"I am your friend," replied the youth; "that is why I am here, but you would never live to cross the ledge to the trail, there are too many warriors and they are all prepared. They know that you are armed and they expect that you will try to escape."

"There is no other way," said Tarzan.

"There is another way," replied the boy, "and I have come to show it to you."

"Where?" asked Jana.

"Follow me," replied Ovan, and he started back into the remote recesses of the cavern, which were fitfully illumined by his flickering torch, while behind him followed Jana and the ape-man.

The walls of the cavern narrowed, the floor rose steeply ahead of them, so that in places it was only with considerable difficulty that they ascended in the semidarkness. At last Ovan halted and held his torch high above his head, revealing a small, natural chamber, at the far end of which there was a dark fissure.

"In that dark hole," he said, "lies a trail that leads to the summit of the mountains. Only the chief and the chief's first son ever know of this trail. If my father learns that I have shown it to you, he will have to kill me, but he shall never know for when next they find me I shall be asleep upon a skin in the cavern far below. The trail is steep and rough, but it is the only way. Go now. This is the return I make you for having saved my life." With that he dashed the torch to the floor, leaving them in utter darkness. He did not speak again, but

Tarzan heard the soft falls of his sandaled feet groping their way back down toward the cavern of the Clovi.

The ape-man reached out through the darkness and found Jana's hand. Carefully he led her through the stygian darkness toward the mouth of the fissure. Feeling his way step-by-step, groping forward with his free hand, the ape-man finally discovered the entrance to the trail.

Clambering upward over broken masses of jagged granite through utter darkness, it seemed to the two fugitives that they made no progress whatever. If time could be measured by muscular effort and physical discomfort, the two might have guessed that they passed an eternity in this black fissure, but at length the darkness lessened and they knew that they were approaching the opening in the summit of the mountains; nor was it long thereafter before they emerged into the brilliant light of the noonday sun.

"And now," said Tarzan, "in which direction lies Zoram?"

The girl pointed. "But we cannot reach it by going back that way," she said, "for every trail will be guarded by Carb and his fellows. Do not think that they will let us escape so easily. Perhaps in searching for us they may even find the fissure and follow us here."

"This is your world," said Tarzan. "You are more familiar with it than I. What, then, do you suggest?"

"We should descend the mountains, going directly away from Clovi," replied Jana, "for it is in the mountains that they will look for us. When we have reached the lowland we can turn back along the foot of the range until we are below Zoram, but not until then should we come back to the mountains."

The descent of the mountains was slow because neither of them was familiar with this part of the range. Oftentimes, their way barred by yawning chasms, they were compelled to retrace their steps to find another way around. They ate many times and slept thrice and thus only could Tarzan guess that they had consumed considerable time in the descent, but what was time to them?

During the descent Tarzan had caught glimpses of a vast plain, stretching away as far as the eye could reach. The last stage of their descent was down a long, winding canyon, and when, at last, they came to its mouth they found themselves upon the edge of the plain that Tarzan had seen. It was almost treeless and from where he stood it looked as level as a lake.

"This is the Gyor Cors," said Jana, "and may we not have the bad fortune to meet a Gyor."

"And what is a Gyor?" asked Tarzan.

"Oh, it is a terrible creature," replied Jana. "I have never seen one, but some of the warriors of Zoram have been to the Gyor Cors and they have seen them. They are twice the size of a tandor and their length is more than that of four tall men, lying upon the ground. They have a curved beak and three great horns, two above their eyes and one above their nose. Standing upright at the back of their heads is a great collar of bony substance covered with thick, horny hide, which protects them from the horns of their fellows and spears of men. They do not eat flesh, but they are irritable and short tempered, charging every creature that they see and thus keeping the Gyor Cors for their own use."

"Theirs is a vast domain," said Tarzan, letting his eyes sweep the illimitable expanse of pasture land that rolled on and on, curving slowly upward into the distant haze, "and your description of them suggests that they have few enemies who would care to dispute their dominion."

"Only the Horibs," replied Jana. "They hunt them for their flesh and hide."

"What are Horibs?" asked Tarzan.

The girl shuddered. "The snake people," she whispered in an awed tone.

"Snake people," repeated Tarzan, "and what are they?"

"Let us not speak of them. They are horrible. They are worse than the Gyors. Their blood is cold and men say that they have no hearts, for they do not possess any of the characteristics that men admire, knowing not friendship or sympathy or love."

Along the bottom of the canyon through which they had descended a mountain torrent had cut a deep gorge, the sides of which were so precipitous that they found it expedient to follow the stream down into the plain in order to discover an easier crossing, since the stream lay between them and Zoram.

They had proceeded for about a mile below the mouth of the

canyon; around them were low, rolling hills which gradually merged with the plain below; here and there were scattered clumps of trees; to their knees grew the gently waving grasses that rendered the Gyor Cors a paradise for the huge herbivorous dinosaurs. The noonday sun shone down upon a scene of peace and quiet, yet Tarzan of the Apes was restless. The apparent absence of animal life seemed almost uncanny to one familiar with the usual teeming activity of Pellucidar; yet the ape-man knew that there were creatures about and it was the strange and unfamiliar scent spoors carried to his nostrils that aroused within him a foreboding of ill omen. Familiar odors had no such effect upon him, but here were scents that he could not place, strangely disagreeable in the nostrils of man. They suggested the scent spoor of Histah the snake, but they were not his.

For Jana's sake Tarzan wished that they might quickly find a crossing and ascend again to the higher levels on their journey to Zoram, for there the creatures would be well known to them, and the dangers which they portended familiar dangers with which they were prepared to cope, but the vertical banks of the raging torrent as yet offered no means of descent and now they saw that the appearance of flatness which distance had imparted to the great Gyor Cors was deceptive, since it was cut by ravines and broken by depressions, some of which were of considerable extent and depth. Presently a lateral ravine, opening into the now comparatively shallow gorge of the river, necessitated a detour which took them directly away from Zoram. They had proceeded for about a mile in this direction when they discovered a crossing and as they emerged upon the opposite side the girl touched Tarzan's arm and pointed. The thing that she saw he had seen simultaneously.

"A Gyor," whispered the girl. "Let us lie down and hide in this tall grass."

"He has not seen us yet," said Tarzan, "and he may not come in this direction."

No description of the beast looming tremendously before them could convey an adequate impression of its titanic proportions or its frightful mien. At the first glance Tarzan was impressed by its remarkable likeness to the Gryfs of

Pal-ul-don. It had the two large horns above the eyes, a medial horn on the nose, a horny beak and a great, horny hood or transverse crest over the neck, and its coloration was similar but more subdued, the predominant note being a slaty gray with yellowish belly and face. The blue bands around the eyes were less well marked and the red of the hood and the bony protuberances along the spine were less brilliant than in the Gryf. That it was herbivorous, a fact that he had learned from Jana, convinced him that he was looking upon an almost unaltered type of the gigantic triceratop that had, with its fellow dinosaurs, ruled the ancient Jurassic world.

Jana had thrown herself prone among the grasses and was urging Tarzan to do likewise. Crouching low, his eyes just above the grasses, Tarzan watched the huge dinosaur.

"I think he has caught our scent," he said. "He is standing with his head up, looking about him; now he is trotting around in a circle. He is very light on his feet for a beast of such enormous size. There, he has caught a scent, but it is not ours; the wind is not in the right direction. There is something approaching from our left, but it is still at a considerable distance. I can just hear it, a faint suggestion of something moving. The Gyor is looking in that direction now. Whatever is coming is coming swiftly. I can tell by the rapidly increasing volume of sound, and there are more than one—there are many. He is moving forward now to investigate, but he will pass at a considerable distance to our left." Tarzan watched the Gyor and listened to the sound coming from the, as yet, invisible creatures that were approaching. "Whatever is approaching is coming along the bottom of the ravine we just crossed," he whispered. "They will pass directly behind us."

Jana remained hiding low in the grasses. She did not wish to tempt fate by revealing even the top of her head to attract the attention of the Gyor. "Perhaps we had better try to crawl away while his attention is attracted elsewhere," she suggested.

"They are coming out of the ravine," whispered Tarzan. "They are coming up over the edge—a number of men—but in the name of God what is it that they are riding?"

Jana raised her eyes above the level of the grasses and looked in the direction that Tarzan was gazing. She shuddered.

"They are not men," she said; "they are the Horibs and the things upon the backs of which they ride are Gorobors. If they see us we are lost. Nothing in the world can escape the Gorobors, for there is nothing in all Pellucidar so swift as they. Lie still. Our only chance is that they may not discover us."

At sight of the Horibs, the Gyor emitted a terrific bellow that shook the ground and, lowering his head, he charged straight for them. Fully fifty of the Horibs on their horrid mounts had emerged from the ravine. Tarzan could see that the riders were armed with long lances—pitiful and inadequate weapons, he thought, with which to face an enraged triceratop. But it soon became apparent that the Horibs did not intend to meet that charge head-on. Wheeling to their right they formed in single file behind their leader and then for the first time Tarzan had an exhibition of the phenomenal speed of the huge lizards upon which they were mounted, which is comparable only to the lightninglike rapidity of a tiny desert lizard known as a swift.

Following tactics similar to those of the plains Indians of western America, the Horibs were circling their prey. The bellowing Gyor, aroused to a frenzy of rage, charged first in one direction and then another, but the Gorobors darted from his path so swiftly that he never could overtake them. Panting and blowing, he presently came to bay and then the Horibs drew their circle closer, whirling dizzily about him, while Tarzan watched the amazing scene, wondering by what means they might ever hope to dispatch the ten tons of incarnate fury that wheeled first this way and then that at the center of their circle.

Presently a Horib darted in close to the Gyor at such speed that the mount and the rider were little more than a blur. The Gyor wheeled to meet him, head down, the three terrible horns set to impale him, and then two other Horibs darted in from the rear upon either side.

As swiftly as they had darted in all three wheeled and were out again, part of the racing circle, but in the sides of the Gyor they had left two lances deeply imbedded. The fury of the wounded triceratop transcended any of his previous demonstrations. His bellowing became a hoarse, coughing scream as once again he lowered his head and charged.

This time he did not turn and charge in another direction as he had in the past, but kept on in a straight line, possibly in the hope of breaking through the encircling Horibs, and to his dismay the ape-man saw that he and Jana were directly in the path of the charging beast. If the Horibs did not turn him, they were lost.

A dozen of the reptile-men darted in upon the rear of the Gyor. A dozen more lances sank deeply into its body, proving sufficient to turn him in an effort to avenge himself upon those who had inflicted these new hurts.

This charge had carried the Gyor within fifty feet of Tarzan and Jana. It had given the ape-man an uncomfortable moment, but its results were almost equally disastrous for it brought the circling Horibs close to their position.

The Gyor stood now with lowered head, breathing heavily and bleeding from more than a dozen wounds. A Horib now rode slowly toward him, approaching him directly from in front. The attention of the triceratop was centered wholly upon this single adversary as two more moved toward him diagonally from the rear, one on either side, but in such a manner that they were concealed from his view by the great transverse crest encircling his neck behind the horns and eyes. The three approached thus to within about fifty feet of the brute and then those in the rear darted forward simultaneously at terrific speed, leaning well forward upon their mounts, their lances lowered. At the same instant each struck heavily upon either side of the Gyor, driving their spears far in. So close did they come to their prey that their mounts struck the shoulders of the Gyor as they turned and darted out again.

For an instant the great creature stood reeling in its tracks and then it slumped forward heavily and rolled over upon its side—the final lances had pierced its heart.

Tarzan was glad that it was over as he had momentarily feared discovery by the circling Horibs and he was congratulating himself upon their good fortune when the entire band of snake-men wheeled their mounts and raced swiftly in the direction of their hiding place. Once more they formed their circle, but this time Tarzan and Jana were at its center. Evidently the Horibs had seen them, but had temporarily ignored them until after they had dispatched the Gyor.

"We shall have to fight," said Tarzan, and as concealment was no longer possible he arose to his feet.

"Yes," said Jana, arising to stand beside him. "We shall have to fight, but the end will be the same. There are fifty of them and we are but two."

Tarzan fitted an arrow to his bow. The Horibs were circling slowly about them inspecting their new prey. Finally they came closer and halted their mounts, facing the two.

Now for the first time Tarzan was able to obtain a good view of the snake-men and their equally hideous mounts. The conformation of the Horibs was almost identical to man insofar as the torso and extremities were concerned. Their three-toed feet and five-toed hands were those of reptiles. The head and face resembled a snake, but pointed ears and two short horns gave a grotesque appearance that was at the same time hideous. The arms were better proportioned than the legs, which were quite shapeless. The entire body was covered with scales, although those upon the hands, feet, and face were so minute as to give the impression of bare skin, a resemblance which was further emphasized by the fact that these portions of the body were a much lighter color, approximating the shiny dead whiteness of a snake's belly. They wore a single apronlike garment fashioned from a piece of very heavy hide, apparently that of some gigantic reptile. This garment was really a piece of armor, its sole purpose being, as Tarzan later learned, to cover the soft, white bellies of the Horibs. Upon the breast of each garment was a strange device—an eight-pronged cross with a circle in the center. Around his waist each Horib wore a leather belt, which supported a scabbard in which was inserted a bone knife. About each wrist and above each elbow was a band or bracelet. These completed their apparel and ornaments. In addition to his knife each Horib carried a long lance shod with bone. They sat on their grotesque mounts with their toes locked behind the elbows of the Gorobors, anomodont reptiles of the Triassic, known to paleontologists as Pareiasuri. Many of these creatures measured ten feet in length, though they stood low upon squat and powerful legs.

As Tarzan gazed in fascination upon the Horibs, whose "blood ran cold and who had no hearts," he realized that he might be gazing upon one of the vagaries of evolution or possibly upon a replica of some form that had once existed upon the outer crust and that had blazed the trail that some, to us, unknown creature must have blazed from the age of reptiles to the age of man. Nor did it seem to him, after reflection, any more remarkable that a manlike reptile might evolve from reptiles than that birds should have done so or, as scientific discoveries are now demonstrating, mammals must have.

These thoughts passed quickly, almost instantaneously, through his mind as the Horibs sat there with their beady, lidless eyes fastened upon them, but if Tarzan had been astounded by the appearance of these creatures the emotion thus aroused was nothing compared with the shock he received when one of them spoke, addressing him in the common language of the gilaks of Pellucidar.

"You cannot escape," he said. "Lay down your weapons."

14

Through the Dark Forest

JASON GRIDLEY RAN swiftly up the hill toward the Phelian village in which he hoped to find The Red Flower of Zoram and at his side was Thoar, ready with spear and knife to rescue or avenge his sister, while behind them, concealed by the underbrush that grew beneath the trees along the river's bank, a company of swarthy, bearded men watched the two.

To Thoar's surprise no defending warriors rushed from the building they were approaching, nor did any sound come from the interior. "Be careful," he cautioned Jason, "we may be running into a trap," and the American, profiting by the advice of his companion, advanced more cautiously. To the very entrance of the building they came and as yet no opposition to their advance had manifested itself.

Jason stopped and looked through the low doorway, then, stooping, he entered with Thoar at his heels.

"There is no one here," said Jason; "the building is deserted."

"Better luck in the next one then," said Thoar; but there was no one in the next building, nor in the next, nor in any of the buildings of the Phelian village.

"They have all gone," said Jason.

"Yes," replied Thoar, "but they will return. Let us go down among the trees at the riverside and wait for them there in hiding."

Unconscious of danger, the two walked down the hillside and entered the underbrush that grew luxuriantly beneath the trees. They followed a narrow trail, worn by Phelian sandals.

Scarcely had the foliage closed about them when a dozen men sprang upon them and bore them to the ground. In an instant they were disarmed and their wrists bound behind their backs; then they were jerked roughly to their feet and Jason Gridley's eyes went wide as they got the first glimpse of his captors.

"Well, for Pete's sake!" he exclaimed. "I have learned to look with comparative composure upon woolly rhinoceroses, mammoths, trachodons, pterodactyls, and dinosaurs, but I never expected to see Captain Kidd, Lafitte, and Sir Henry Morgan in the heart of Pellucidar."

In his surprise he reverted to his native tongue, which, of course, none of the others understood.

"What language is that?" demanded one of their captors. "Who are you and from what country do you come?"

"That is good old American, from the U.S.A.," replied Jason; "but who the devil are you and why have you captured us?" and then turning to Thoar, "These are not the Phelians, are they?"

"No," replied Thoar. "These are strange men, such as I have never before seen."

"We know who you are," said one of the bearded men. "We know the country from which you come. Do not try to deceive us."

"Very well, then, if you know, turn me loose, for you must know that we haven't a war on with anyone."

"Your country is always at war with Korsar," replied the speaker. "You are a Sarian. I know it by the weapons that you carry. The moment I saw them, I knew that you were from distant Sari. The Cid will be glad to have you and so will Bulf. Perhaps," he added, turning to one of his fellows, "this is Tanar, himself. Did you see him when he was a prisoner in Korsar?"

"No, I was away upon a cruise," replied the other. "I did not see him, but if this is indeed he we shall be well rewarded."

"We might as well return to the ship now," said the first speaker. "There is no use waiting any longer for these flat-footed natives with but one chance in a thousand of finding a good-looking woman among them."

"They told us farther down the river that these people sometimes captured women from Zoram. Perhaps it would be well to wait."

"No," said the other, "I should like well enough to see one of these women from Zoram that I have heard of all my life, but the natives will not return as long as we are in the vicinity. We have been gone from the ship too long now and if I know the captain, he will be wanting to slit a few throats by the time we get back."

Moored to a tree along the shore and guarded by five other Korsars was a ship's longboat, but of a style that was reminiscent of Jason's boyhood reading as were the bearded men with their bizarre costumes, their great pistols and cutlasses and their ancient arquebuses.

The prisoners were bundled into the boat, the Korsars entered and the craft was pushed off into the stream, which here was narrow and swift.

As the current bore them rapidly along Jason had an opportunity to examine his captors. They were as villainous a looking crew as he had ever imagined outside of fiction and were more typically piratical than the fiercest pirates of his imagination. What with earrings and, in some instances, nose rings of gold, with the gay handkerchiefs bound about their heads and body sashes around their waists, they would have presented a gorgeous and colorful picture at a distance sufficiently great to transform their dirt and patches into a pleasing texture.

Although in the story of Tanar of Pellucidar that Jason had received by radio from Perry, he had become familiar with the appearance and nature of the Korsars, yet he now realized that heretofore he had accepted them more as he had accepted the pirates of history and of his boyhood reading—as fictionary or, at best, legendary—and not men of flesh and bone such as he saw before him, their mouths filled with oaths and coarse jokes, the grime and filth of reality marking them as real human beings.

In these savage Korsars, their boat, their apparel, and their ancient firearms, Jason saw conclusive proof of their descent from men of the outer crust and realized how they must have carried to the mind of David Innes an overwhelming conviction of the existence of a polar opening leading from Pellucidar to the outer world.

While Thoar was disheartened by the fate that had thrown them into the hands of these strange people, Jason was not at all sure but that it might prove a stroke of fortune for himself, as from the conversation and comments that he had heard since their capture it seemed reasonable to assume that they were to be taken to Korsar, the city in which David Innes was confined and which was, therefore, the first goal of their expedition to effect the rescue of the Emperor of Pellucidar.

That he would arrive there alone and a prisoner were not in themselves causes for rejoicing; yet, on the whole, he would be no worse off than to remain wandering aimlessly through a country filled with unknown dangers without the faintest shadow of a hope of ever being able to locate his fellows. Now, at least, he was almost certain of being transported to a place that they also were attempting to reach and thus the chances of a reunion were so much the greater.

The stream down which they floated wound through a swampy forest, crossing numerous lagoons that sometimes were of a size that raised them to the dignity of lakes. Everywhere the waters and the banks teemed with reptilian life, suggesting to Jason Gridley that he was reviewing a scene such as might have been enacted in a Mesozoic paradise countless ages before upon the outer crust. So numerous and oftentimes so colossal and belligerent were the savage reptiles that the descent of the river became a running fight, during which the Korsars were constantly upon the alert and frequently were compelled to discharge their arquebuses in defense of their lives. More often than not the noise of the weapons frightened off the attacking reptiles, but occasionally one would persist in its attack until it had been killed; nor was the possibility ever remote that in one of these encounters some fierce and brainless saurian might demolish their craft and with its fellows devour the crew.

Jason and Thoar had been placed in the middle of the boat, where they squatted upon the bottom, their wrists still secured behind their backs. Close to Jason was a Korsar whose fellows addressed him as Lajo. There was something about this fellow that attracted Jason's particular attention. Perhaps it was his more open countenance or a less savage and profane demeanor. He had not joined the others in the coarse jokes that were directed against their captives; in fact, he paid little attention to anything other than the business of defending the boat against the attacking monsters.

There seemed to be no one in command of the party, all matters being discussed among them and in this way a decision arrived at; yet Jason had noticed that the others listened attentively when Lajo spoke, which was seldom, though always intelligently and to the point. Guided by the result of these observations he selected Lajo as the most logical Korsar through whom to make a request. At the first opportunity, therefore, he attracted the man's attention.

"What do you want?" asked Lajo.

"Who is in command here?" asked Jason.

"No one," replied the Korsar. "Our officer was killed on the way up. Why do you ask?"

"I want the bonds removed from our wrists," replied Jason. "We cannot escape. We are unarmed and outnumbered and, therefore, cannot harm you; while in the event that the boat is destroyed or capsized by any of these reptiles we shall be helpless with our wrists tied behind our backs."

Lajo drew his knife.

"What are you going to do?" asked one of the other Korsars who had been listening to the conversation.

"I am going to cut their bonds," replied Lajo. "There is nothing to be gained by keeping them bound."

"Who are you to say that their bonds shall be cut?" demanded the other belligerently.

"Who are you to say that they shall not?" returned Lajo quietly, moving toward the prisoners.

"I'll show you who I am," shouted the other, whipping out his knife and advancing toward Lajo.

There was no hesitation. Like a panther Lajo swung upon his adversary, striking up the other's knife-hand with his left forearm and at the same time plunging his villainous-looking blade to the hilt in the other's breast. Voicing a single blood-curdling scream the man sank lifeless to the bottom of the boat. Lajo wrenched his knife from the corpse, wiped it upon his adversary's shirt and quietly cut the bonds that confined the wrists of Thoar and Jason. The other Korsars looked on, apparently unmoved by the killing of their fellow, except for a coarse joke or two at the expense of the dead man and a grunt of approbation for Lajo's act.

The killer removed the weapons from the body of the dead man and cast them aft out of reach of the prisoners, then he motioned to the corpse. "Throw it overboard," he commanded, addressing Jason and Thoar.

"Wait," cried another member of the crew. "I want his boots."

"His sash is mine," cried another, and presently half a dozen of them were quarreling over the belongings of the corpse like a pack of dogs over a bone. Lajo took no part in this altercation and presently the few wretched belongings that had served to cover the nakedness of the dead man were torn from his corpse and divided among them by the simple expedient of permitting the stronger to take what they could; then Jason and Thoar eased the naked body over the side, where it was immediately seized upon by voracious denizens of the river.

Interminable, to an unknown destination, seemed the journey to Jason. They ate and slept many times and still the river wound through the endless swamp. The luxuriant vegetation and flowering blooms which lined the banks long since had ceased to interest, their persistent monotony making them almost hateful to the eyes.

Jason could not but wonder at the superhuman efforts that must have been necessary to row this large, heavy boat upstream in the face of all the terrific assaults which must have been launched upon it by the reptilian hordes that contested every mile of the downward journey.

But presently the landscape changed, the river widened and the low swamp gave way to rolling hills. The forests, which still lined the banks, were freer from underbrush, suggesting that they might be the feeding grounds of droves of herbivorous animals, a theory that was soon substantiated by sight of grazing herds, among which Jason recognized red deer, bison, bos and several other species of herbivorous animals. The forest upon the right bank was open and sunny and with its grazing herds presented a cheerful aspect of warmth and life, but the forest upon the left bank was dark and gloomy. The foliage of the trees, which grew to tremendous proportions, was so dense as practically to shut out the sunlight, the space between the boles giving the impression of long, dark aisles, gloomy and forbidding.

There were fewer reptiles in the stream here, but the Korsars appeared unusually nervous and apprehensive of danger after they entered this stretch of the river. Previously they had been drifting with the current, using but a single oar, scull fashion, from the stern to keep the nose of the boat pointed downstream, but now they manned the oars, pressing Jason and Thoar into service to row with the others. Loaded arquebuses lay beside the oarsmen, while in the bow and stern armed men were constantly upon watch. They paid little attention to the right bank of the river, but toward the dark and gloomy left bank they directed their nervous, watchful gaze. Jason wondered what it was that they feared, but he had no opportunity to inquire and there was no respite from the rowing, at least not for him or Thoar, though the Korsars alternated between watching and rowing.

Between oars and current they were making excellent progress, though whether they were close to the end of the danger zone or not, Jason had no means of knowing any more than he could guess the nature of the menace which must certainly threaten them if aught could be judged by the attitude of the Korsars.

The two prisoners were upon the verge of exhaustion when Lajo noticed their condition and relieved them from the oars. How long they had been rowing, Jason could not determine, although he knew that while no one had either eaten or slept, since they had entered this stretch of the river, the time must have been considerable. The distance they had come he estimated roughly at something over a hundred miles, and he and Thoar had been continuously at the oars during the entire period, without food or sleep, but they had barely thrown themselves to the bottom of the boat when a cry, vibrant with excitement, arose from the bow. "There they are!" shouted the man, and instantly all was excitement aboard the boat.

"Keep to the oars!" shouted Lajo. "Our best chance is to run through them."

Although almost too spent with fatigue to find interest even in impending death, Jason dragged himself to a sitting position that raised his eyes above the level of the gunwales of the boat. At first he could not even vaguely classify the horde of creatures swimming out upon the bosom of the placid river with the evident intention of intercepting them, but presently he saw that they were manlike creatures riding upon the backs of hideous reptiles. They bore long lances and their scaly mounts sped through the waters at incredible speed. As the boat approached them he saw that the creatures were not men, though they had the forms of men, but were grotesque and horrid reptiles with the heads of lizards to whose naturally frightful mein, pointed ears and short horns added a certain horrid grotesquery.

"My God!" he exclaimed. "What are they?"

Thoar, who had also dragged himself to a sitting posture, shuddered. "They are the Horibs," he said. "It is better to die than to fall into their clutches."

Carried downward by the current and urged on by the long sweeps and its own terrific momentum, the heavy boat shot straight toward the hideous horde. The distance separating them was rapidly closing; the boat was almost upon the leading Horib when an arquebus in the bow spoke. Its loud report broke the menacing silence that had overhung the river like a pall. Directly in front of the boat's prow the horde of Horibs separated and a moment later they were racing along on either side of the craft. Arquebuses were belching smoke and fire, scattering the bits of iron and pebbles with which they were loaded among the hissing enemy, but for every Horib that fell there were two to take its place.

Now they withdrew to a little distance, but with apparently no effort whatever their reptilian mounts kept pace with the boat and then, one after another on either side, a rider would dart in and cast his lance; nor apparently ever did one miss its mark. So deadly was their aim that the Korsars were compelled to abandon their oars and drop down into the bottom of the boat, raising themselves above the gunwales only long enough to fire their arquebuses, when they would again drop down into concealment to reload. But even these tactics could not preserve them for long, since the Horibs, darting in still closer to the side of the boat, could reach over the edge and lance the inmates. Straight to the muzzles of the arquebuses they came, apparently entirely devoid of any conception of fear; great holes were blown entirely through the bodies of some, others were decapitated,while more than a score lost a hand or an arm, yet still they came.

Presently one succeeded in casting the noose of a long leather rope over a cleat upon the gunwale and instantly several of the Horibs seized it and headed their mounts toward the river's bank.

Practically exhausted and without weapons to defend themselves, Jason and Thoar had remained lying upon the bottom of the boat almost past caring what fate befell them. Half covered by the corpses of the Korsars that had fallen, they lay in a pool of blood. About them arquebuses still roared amid screams and curses, and above all rose the shrill, hissing screech that seemed to be the war cry of the Horibs.

The boat was dragged to shore and the rope made fast about the bole of a tree, though three times the Korsars had cut the line and three times the Horibs had been forced to replace it.

There was only a handful of the crew who had not been killed or wounded when the Horibs left their mounts and swarmed over the gunwales to fall upon their prey. Cutlasses, knives, and arquebuses did their deadly work, but still the slimy snake-men came, crawling over the bodies of their dead to fall upon the survivors until the latter were practically buried by greater numbers.

When the battle was over there were but three Korsars who had escaped death or serious wounds—Lajo was one of them. The Horibs bound their wrists and took them ashore, after which they started unloading the dead and wounded from the boat, killing the more seriously wounded with their knives. Coming at last upon Jason and Thoar and finding them unwounded, they bound them as they had the living Korsars and placed them with the other prisoners on the shore.

The battle over, the prisoners secured, the Horibs now fell upon the corpses of the dead, nor did they rest until they had devoured them all, while Jason and his fellow prisoners sat nauseated with horror during the grizzly feast. Even the Korsars, cruel and heartless as they were, shuddered at the sight.

"Why do you suppose they are saving us?" asked Jason.

Lajo shook his head. "I do not know," he said.

"Doubtless to feed us to their women and children," said Thoar. "They say that they keep their human prisoners and fatten them."

"You know what they are? You have seen them before?" Lajo asked Thoar.

"Yes, I know what they are," said Thoar, "but these are the first that I have ever seen. They are the Horibs, the snake people. They dwell between the Rela Am and the Gyor Cors."

As Jason watched the Horibs at their grizzly feast, he became suddenly conscious of a remarkable change that was taking place in their appearance. When he had first seen them and all during the battle they had been of a ghastly bluish color, the hands, feet, and faces being several shades paler than the balance of the body, but as they settled down to their gory repast this hue gradually faded to be replaced by a reddish tinge, which varied in intensity in different individuals, the faces and extremities of a few of whom became almost crimson as the feast progressed.

If the appearance and bloodthirsty ferocity of the creatures appalled him, he was no less startled when he first heard them converse in the common language of the men of Pellucidar.

The general conformation of the creatures, their weapons, which consisted of long lances and stone knives, the apronlike apparel which they wore and the evident attempt at ornamentation as exemplified by the insignia upon the breasts of their garments and the armlets which they wore, all tended toward establishing a suggestion of humanity that was at once grotesque and horrible, but when to these other attributes was added human speech the likeness to man created an impression that was indescribably repulsive.

So powerful was the fascination that the creatures aroused in the mind of Jason that he could divert neither his thoughts nor his eyes from them. He noticed that while the majority of them were about six feet in height, there were many much smaller, ranging downward to about four feet, while there was one tremendous individual that must have been fully nine feet tall; yet all were proportioned identically and the difference in height did not have the appearance of being at all related to a difference in age, except that the scales upon the largest of them were considerably thicker and coarser. Later, however, he was to learn that differences in size predicated differences in age, the growth of these creatures being governed by the same law which governs the growth of reptiles, which, unlike mammals, continue to grow throughout the entire duration of their lives.

When they had gorged themselves upon the flesh of the Korsars, the Horibs lay down, but whether to sleep or not Jason never knew since their lidless eyes remained constantly staring. And now a new phenomenon occurred. Gradually the reddish tinge faded from their bodies to be replaced by a dull brownish gray, which harmonized with the ground upon which they lay.

Exhausted by his long tour at the oars and by the horrors that he had witnessed, Jason gradually drifted off into deep slumber, which was troubled by hideous dreams in which he saw Jana in the clutches of a Horib. The creature was attempting to devour The Red Flower of Zoram, while Jason struggled with the bonds that secured him.

He was awakened by a sharp pain in his shoulder and opening his eyes he saw one of the homosaurians, as he had mentally dubbed them, standing over him, prodding him with the point of his sharp lance. "Make less noise," said the creature, and Jason realized that he must have been raving in his sleep.

The other Horibs were rising from the ground, voicing strange whistling hisses, and presently from the waters of the river and from the surrounding aisles of the gloomy forest their hideous mounts came trooping in answer to the summons.

"Stand up!" said the Horib who had awakened Jason. "I am going to remove your bonds," he continued. "You cannot escape. If you try to you will be killed. Follow me," he then commanded after he had removed the thongs which secured Jason's wrists.

Jason accompanied the creature into the midst of the herd of periosauri that was milling about, snapping and hissing, along the shore of the river.

Although the Gorobors all looked alike to Jason, it was evident that the Horibs differentiated between individuals among them for he who was leading Jason threaded his way through the mass of slimy bodies until he reached the side of a particular individual.

"Get up," he said, motioning Jason to mount the creature. "Sit well forward on its neck."

It was with a sensation of the utmost disgust that Jason vaulted onto the back of the Gorobor. The feel of its cold, clammy, rough hide against his naked legs sent a chilly shudder up his spine. The reptile-man mounted behind him and presently the entire company was on the march, each of the other prisoners being mounted in front of a Horib.

Into the gloomy forest the strange cavalcade marched, down dark, winding corridors overhung with dense vegetation, much of which was of a dead pale cast through lack of sunlight. A clammy chill, unusual in Pellucidar, pervaded the atmosphere and a feeling of depression weighed heavily upon all the prisoners.

"What are you going to do with us?" asked Jason after they had proceeded in silence for some distance.

"You will be fed upon eggs until you are fit to be eaten by the females and the little ones," replied the Horib. "They tire of fish and Gyor flesh. It is not often that we get as much gilak meat as we have just had."

Jason relapsed into silence, discovering that, as far as he was concerned, the Horib was conversationally a total loss and for long after the horror of the creature's reply weighed upon his mind. It was not that he feared death; it was the idea of being fattened for slaughter that was peculiarly abhorrent.

As they rode between the never-ending trees he tried to speculate as to the origin of these gruesome creatures. It seemed to him that they might constitute a supreme effort upon the part of Nature to reach a higher goal by a less devious route than that which evolution had pursued upon the outer crust from the age of reptiles upward to the age of man.

During the march Jason caught occasional glimpses of Thoar and the other prisoners, though he had no opportunity to exchange words with them, and after what seemed an interminable period of time the cavalcade emerged from the forest into the sunlight and Jason saw in the distance the shimmering blue waters of an inland lake. As they approached its shores he discerned throngs of Horibs, some swimming or lolling in the waters of the lake, while others lay or squatted upon the muddy bank. As the company arrived among them they showed only a cold, reptilian interest in the returning warriors, though some of the females and young evinced a suggestive interest in the prisoners.

The adult females differed but slightly from the males. Aside from the fact that they were hornless and went naked, Jason could discover no other distinguishing feature. He saw no signs of a village, nor any indication of arts or crafts other than those necessary to produce their crude weapons and the simple apronlike armor that the warriors wore to protect the soft skin of their bellies.

The prisoners were now dragged from their mounts and herded together by several of the warriors, who conducted them along the edge of the lake toward a slightly higher bank.

On the way they passed a number of females laying eggs, which they deposited in the soft, warm mud just above the waterline, covering them lightly with mud, afterward pushing a slender stake into the ground at the spot to mark the nest. All along the shore at this point were hundreds of such stakes and farther on Jason saw several tiny Horibs, evidently but just hatched, wriggling upward out of the mud. No one paid the slightest attention to them as they stumbled and reeled about trying to accustom themselves to the use of their limbs, upon all four of which they went at first, like tiny, grotesque lizards.

Arrived at the higher bank the warrior in charge of Thoar, who was in the lead, suddenly clapped his hand over the prisoner's mouth, pinching Thoar's nose tightly between his thumb and first finger, and, without other preliminaries, dove head foremost into the waters of the lake carrying his victim with him.

Jason was horrified as he saw his friend and companion disappear beneath the muddy waters, which, after a moment of violent agitation, settled down again, leaving only an ever-widening circular ripple to mark the spot where the two had disappeared. An instant later another Horib dove in with Lajo and in rapid succession the other two Korsars shared a similar fate.

With a superhuman effort Jason sought to tear himself free from the clutches of his captor, but the cold, clammy hands held him tightly. One of them was suddenly clapped over his mouth and nose and an instant later he felt the warm waters of the lake close about him.

Still struggling to free himself he was conscious that the Horib was carrying him swiftly beneath the surface. Presently he felt slimy mud beneath him, along which his body was being dragged. His lungs cried out in tortured agony for air, his senses reeled and momentarily all went black before him, though no blacker than the stygian darkness of the hole into which he was being dragged, and then the hand was removed from his mouth and nose; mechanically his lungs gasped for air and as consciousness slowly returned Jason realized that he was not drowned, but that he was lying upon a bed of mud inhaling air and not water.

Total darkness surrounded him; he felt a clammy body scrape against his, and then another and another. There was a sound of splashing, gurgling water and then silence—the silence of the tomb.

15

Prisoners

STANDING UPON THE edge of the great Gyor plains surrounded by armed creatures, who had but just demonstrated their ability to destroy one of the most powerful and ferocious creatures that evolution has ever succeeded in producing, Tarzan of the Apes was yet loath to lay down his weapons as he had been instructed and surrender, without resistance, to an unknown fate.

"What do you intend to do with us?" he demanded of the Horib who had ordered him to lay down his weapons.

"We shall take you to our village where you will be well fed," replied the creature. "You cannot escape us; no one escapes the Horibs."

The ape-man hesitated. The Red Flower of Zoram moved closer to his side. "Let us go with them," she whispered. "We cannot escape them now; there are too many of them. Possibly if we go with them we shall find an opportunity later."

Tarzan nodded and then he turned to the Horib. "We are ready," he said.

Mounted upon the necks of Gorobors, each in front of a Horib warrior, they were carried across a corner of the Gyor Cors to the same gloomy forest through which Jason and Thoar had been taken, though they entered it from a different direction.

Rising at the east end of the Mountains of the Thipdars, a river flows in a southeasterly direction entering upon its course the gloomy forest of the Horibs, through which it runs down to the Rela Am, or River of Darkness. It was near the confluence of these two rivers that the Korsars had been attacked by the Horibs and it was along the upper reaches of the same river that Tarzan and Jana were being conducted downstream toward the village of the lizard-men.

The lake of the Horibs lies at a considerable distance from the eastern end of the mountains of the Thipdars, perhaps five hundred miles, and where there is no time and distances are measured by food and sleep it makes little difference whether places are separated by five miles or five hundred. One man might travel a thousand miles without mishap, while another, in attempting to go one mile, might be killed, in which event the one mile would be much farther than the thousand miles, for, in fact, it would have proved an interminable distance to him who had essayed it in this instance.

As Tarzan and Jana rode through the dismal forest, hundreds of miles away Jason Gridley drew himself to a sitting position in such utter darkness that he could almost feel it. "God!" he exclaimed.

"Who spoke?" asked a voice out of the darkness, and Jason recognized the voice as Thoar's.

"It is I, Jason," replied Gridley.

"Where are we?" demanded another voice. It was Lajo.

"It is dark. I wish they had killed us," said a fourth voice.

"Don't worry," said a fifth, "we shall be killed soon enough."

"We are all here," said Jason. "I thought we were all done for when I saw them drag you into the water one by one."

"Where are we?" demanded one of the Korsars. "What sort of hole is this into which they have put us?"

"In the world from which I come," said Jason, "there are huge reptiles, called crocodiles, who build such nests or retreats in the banks of rivers, just above the waterline, but the only entrance leads down below the waters of the river. It is such a hole as that into which we have been dragged."

"Why can't we swim out again?" asked Thoar.

"Perhaps we could," replied Jason, "but they would see us and bring us back again."

"Are we going to lie here in the mud and wait to be slaughtered?" demanded Lajo.

"No," said Jason; "but let us work out a reasonable plan of escape. It will gain us nothing to act rashly."

For some time the men sat in silence, which was finally broken by the American. "Do you think we are alone here?" he asked in a low tone. "I have listened carefully, but I have heard no sound other than our own breathing."

"Nor I," said Thoar.

"Come closer then," said Jason, and the five men groped through the darkness and arranged themselves in a circle, where they squatted leaning forward till their heads touched. "I have a plan," continued Jason. "When they were bringing us here I noticed that the forest grew close to the lake at this point. If we can make a tunnel into the forest, we may be able to escape."

"Which way is the forest?" asked Lajo.

"That is something that we can only guess at," replied Jason. "We may guess wrong, but we must take the chance. But I think that it is reasonable to assume that the direction of the forest is directly opposite the entrance through which we were carried into this hole."

"Let us start digging at once," exclaimed one of the Korsars.

"Wait until I locate the entrance," said Thoar.

He crawled away upon his hands and knees, groping through the darkness and the mud. Presently he announced that he had found the opening, and from the direction of his voice the others knew where to start digging.

All were filled with enthusiasm, for success seemed almost within the range of possibility, but now they were confronted with the problem of the disposal of the dirt which they excavated from their tunnel. Jason instructed Lajo to remain at the point where they intended excavating and then had the others crawl in different directions in an effort to estimate the size of the chamber in which they were confined. Each man was to crawl in a straight line in the direction assigned him and count the number of times that his knees touched the ground before he came to the end of the cavern.

By this means they discovered that the cave was long and narrow and, if they were correct in the directions they had assumed, it ran parallel to the lakeshore. For twenty feet it extended in one direction and for over fifty in the other.

It was finally decided that they should distribute the earth equally over the floor of the chamber for a while and then carry it to the farther end, piling it against the farther wall uniformly so as not to attract unnecessary attention in the event that any of the Horibs visited them.

Digging with their fingers was slow and laborious work, but they kept steadily at it, taking turns about. The man at work would push the dirt behind him and the others would gather it up and distribute it, so that at no time was there a fresh pile of earth upon the ground to attract attention should a Horib come. Horibs did come; they brought food, but the men could hear the splash of their bodies in the water as they dove into the lake to reach the tunnel leading to the cave and being thus warned they grouped themselves in front of the entrance to their tunnel effectually hiding it from view. The Horibs who came into the chamber at no time gave any suggestion of suspicion that all was not right. While it was apparent that they could see in the dark it was also quite evident that they could not discern things clearly and thus the greatest fear that their plot might be discovered was at least partially removed.

After considerable effort they had succeeded in excavating a tunnel some three feet in diameter and about ten feet long when Jason, who was excavating at the time, unearthed a large shell, which greatly facilitated the process of excavation. From then on their advance was more rapid, yet it seemed to them all that it was an endless job; nor was there any telling at what moment the Horibs would come to take them for the feast.

It was Jason's wish to get well within the forest before turning their course upward toward the surface, but to be certain of this he knew that they must first encounter roots of trees and pass beyond them, which might necessitate a detour and delay; yet to come up prematurely would be to nullify all that they had accomplished so far and to put a definite end to all hope of escape.

And while the five men dug beneath the ground in the dark hole that was stretching slowly out beneath the dismal forest of the Horibs a great ship rode majestically high in air above the northern slopes of the Mountains of the Thipdars.

"They never passed this way," said Zuppner. "Nothing short of a mountain goat could cross this range."

"I quite agree with you, sir," said Hines. "We might as well search in some other direction now."

"God!" exclaimed Zuppner, "if I only knew in what direction to search."

Hines shook his head. "One direction is as good as another, sir," he said.

"I suppose so," said Zuppner, and, obeying his light touch upon the helm, the nose of the great dirigible swung to port. Following an easterly course she paralleled the Mountains of the Thipdars and sailed out over the Gyor Cors. A slight turn of the wheel would have carried her to the southeast, across the dismal forest through whose gloomy corridors Tarzan and Jana were being borne to a horrible fate. But Captain Zuppner did not know and so the O-220 continued on toward the east, while the Lord of the Jungle and The Red Flower of Zoram rode silently toward their doom.

From almost the moment that they had entered the forest Tarzan had known that he might escape. It would have been the work of but an instant to have leaped from the back of the Gorobor upon which he was riding to one of the lower branches of the forest, some of which barely grazed their heads as they passed beneath, and once in the trees he knew that no

Horib nor any Gorobor could catch him, but he could not desert Jana; nor could he acquaint her with his plans for they were never sufficiently close together for him to whisper to her unheard by the Horibs. But even had he been able to lay the whole thing before her, he doubted her ability to reach the safety of the trees before the Horibs recaptured her.

If he could but get near enough to take hold of her, he was confident that he could effect a safe escape for both of them and so he rode on in silence, hoping against hope that the opportunity he so desired would eventually develop.

They had reached the upper end of the lake and were skirting its western shore and, from remarks dropped by the Horibs in their conversations, which were far from numerous, the ape-man guessed that they were almost at their destination, and still escape seemed as remote as ever.

Chafing with impatience Tarzan was on the point of making a sudden break for liberty, trusting that the unexpectedness of his act would confuse the lizard-men for just the few seconds that would be necessary for him to throw Jana to his shoulder and swing to the lower terrace that beckoned invitingly from above.

The nerves and muscles of Tarzan of the Apes are trained to absolute obedience to his will; they are never surprised into any revelation of emotion, nor are they often permitted to reveal what is passing in the mind of the ape-man when he is in the presence of strangers or enemies, but now, for once, they were almost shocked into revealing the astonishment that filled him as a vagrant breeze carried to his nostrils a scent spoor that he had never thought to know again.

The Horibs were moving almost directly upwind so that Tarzan knew that the authors of the familiar odors that he had sensed were somewhere ahead of them. He thought quickly now, but not without weighing carefully the plan that had leaped to his mind the instant that that familiar scent spoor had impinged upon his nostrils. His major consideration was for the safety of the girl, but in order to rescue her he must protect himself. He felt that it would be impossible for them both to escape simultaneously, but there was another way now—a way which seemed to offer excellent possibilities for success.

Behind him, upon the Gorobor, and so close that their bodies
touched, sat a huge Horib. In one hand he carried a lance, but
the other hand was free. Tarzan must move so quickly that
the fellow could not touch him with his free hand before he
was out of reach. To do this would require agility of an almost
superhuman nature, but there are few creatures who can
compare in this respect with the ape-man. Low above them
swung the branches of the dismal forest; Tarzan waited,
watching for the opportunity he sought. Presently he saw it—
a sturdy branch with ample headroom above it—a doorway
in the ceiling of somber foliage. He leaned forward, his
hands resting lightly upon the neck of the Gorobor. They were
almost beneath the branch he had selected when he sprang
lightly to his feet and almost in the same movement sprang
upward into the tree. So quickly had he accomplished the feat
that he was gone before the Horib that had been guarding him
realized it. When he did it was too late—the prisoner had gone.
With others, who had seen the escape, he raised a cry of
warning to those ahead, but neither by sight nor sound could
they locate the fugitive, for Tarzan traveled through the upper
terrace and all the foliage beneath hid him from the eyes of his
enemies.

Jana, who had been riding a little in the rear of Tarzan, saw
his escape and her heart sank, for in the presence of the Horibs
The Red Flower of Zoram had come as near to experiencing
fear as she ever had in her life. She had derived a certain sense
of comfort from the presence of Tarzan and now that he was
gone, she felt very much alone. She did not blame him for
escaping when he had the opportunity, but she was sure in her
own heart that Jason would not thus have deserted her.

Following the scent spoor that was his only guide, Tarzan of
the Apes moved rapidly through the trees. At first he climbed
high to the upper terraces and here he found a new world—a
world of sunlight and luxuriant foliage, peopled by strange
birds of gorgeous plumage which darted swiftly hither and
thither. There were flying reptiles, too, and great gaudy moths.
Snakes coiled upon many a branch and because they were of
varieties unknown to him, he did not know whether they constituted a real menace or not. It was at once a beautiful and a

repulsive world, but the feature of it which attracted him most was its silence, for its denizens seemed to be voiceless. The presence of the snakes and the dense foliage rendered it an unsatisfactory world for one who wished to travel swiftly and so the ape-man dropped to a lower level, and here he found the forest more open and the scent spoor clearer in his nostrils.

Not once had he doubted the origin of that scent, although it seemed preposterously unbelievable that he should discover it here in this gloomy wood in vast Pellucidar.

He was moving very rapidly for he wished, if possible, to reach his destination ahead of the Horibs. He hoped that his escape might delay the lizard-men and this was, in fact, the case, for they had halted immediately while a number of them had climbed into the trees searching for Tarzan. There was little in their almost expressionless faces to denote their anger, but the sickly bluish cast which overspread their scales denoted their mounting rage at the ease with which this gilak prisoner had escaped them, and when, finally, thwarted in their search, they resumed their interrupted march, they were in a particularly ugly mood.

Far ahead of them now Tarzan of the Apes dropped to the lower terraces. Strong in his nostrils was the scent spoor he had been following, telling him in a language more dependable than words that he had but little farther to go to find those he sought, and a moment later he dropped down into one of the gloomy aisles of the forest, dropping as from heaven into the astonished view of ten stalwart warriors.

For an instant they stood looking at him in wide-eyed amazement and then they ran forward and threw themselves upon their knees about him, kissing his hands as they shed tears of happiness. "Oh, Bwana, Bwana," they cried; "it is indeed you! Mulungu has been good to his children; he has given their Big Bwana back to them alive."

"And now I have work for you, my children," said Tarzan; "the snake people are coming and with them is a girl whom they have captured. I thank God that you are armed with rifles and I hope that you have plenty of ammunition."

"We have saved it, Bwana, using our spears and our arrows whenever we could."

"Good," said Tarzan; "we shall need it now. How far are we from the ship?"

"I do not know," said Muviro.

"You do not know?" repeated Tarzan.

"No, Bwana, we are lost. We have been lost for a long while," replied the chief of the Waziri.

"What were you doing away from the ship alone?" demanded Tarzan.

"We were sent out with Gridley and Von Horst to search for you, Bwana."

"Where are they?" asked Tarzan.

"A long time ago, I do not know how long, we became separated from Gridley and never saw him again. At that time it was savage beasts that separated us, but how Von Horst became separated from us we do not know. We had found a cave and had gone into it to sleep; when we awoke Von Horst was gone; we never saw him again."

"They are coming!" warned Tarzan.

"I hear them, Bwana," replied Muviro.

"Have you seen them—the snake people?" asked Tarzan.

"No, Bwana, we have seen no people for a long time; only beasts—terrible beasts."

"You are going to see some terrible men now," Tarzan warned them; "but do not be frightened by their appearance. Your bullets will bring them down."

"When, Bwana, have you seen a Waziri frightened?" asked Muviro proudly.

The ape-man smiled. "One of you let me take his rifle," he said, "and then spread out through the forest. I do not know exactly where they will pass, but the moment that any of you makes contact with them commence shooting and shoot to kill, remembering, however, that the girl rides in front of one of them. Be careful that you do not harm her."

He had scarcely ceased speaking when the first of the Horibs rode into view. Tarzan and the Waziri made no effort to seek concealment and at sight of them the leading Horib gave voice to a shrill cry of pleasure. Then a rifle spoke and the leading Horib writhed convulsively and toppled sideways to the ground. The others in the lead, depending upon the swiftness of their mounts, darted quickly toward the Waziri and the tall, white giant who led them, but swifter than the Gorobors were the bullets of the outer world. As fast as Tarzan and the Waziri could fire the Horibs fell. Never before had they known defeat. They blazed blue with rage, which faded to a muddy gray when the bullets found their hearts and they rolled dead upon the ground.

So swiftly did the Gorobors move and so rapidly did Tarzan and the Waziri fire that the engagement was decided within a few minutes of its inception, and now the remaining Horibs, discovering that they could not hope to overcome and capture gilaks armed with these strange weapons that hit them more swiftly than they could hurl their lances, turned and scattered in an effort to pass around the enemy and continue on their way.

As yet Tarzan had not caught a glimpse of Jana, though he knew that she must be there somewhere in the rear of the remaining Horibs, and then he saw her as she flashed by in the distance, borne swiftly upon the back of a fleet Gorobor. What appeared to be the only chance to save her now was to shoot down the swift beast upon which she was being borne away. Tarzan swung his rifle to his shoulder and at the same instant a riderless Gorobor struck him in the back and sent him sprawling upon the ground. By the time he had regained his feet, Jana and her captor were out of sight, hidden by the boles of intervening trees.

Milling near the Waziri were a number of terrified, riderless Gorobors. It was from this number that the fellow had broken who had knocked Tarzan down. The beasts seemed to be lost without the guidance of their masters, but when they saw one of their number start in pursuit of the Horibs who had ridden away, the others followed and in their mad rush these savage beasts constituted as great a menace as the Horibs themselves.

Muviro and his warriors leaped nimbly behind the boles of large trees to escape them, but to the mind of the ape-man they carried a new hope, offering as they did the only means whereby he might overtake the Horib who was bearing away The Red Flower of Zoram, and then, to the horror and astonishment of the Waziri, Tarzan leaped to the back of one of the great lizards as it scuttled abreast of him. Locking his toes beneath its elbows, as he had seen the Horibs do, he was carried swiftly in the mad rush of the creature to overtake its fellows and its masters. No need to urge it on, if he had known what means to employ to do so, for probably still terrified and excited by the battle it darted with incredible swiftness among the boles of the gray trees, outstripping its fellows and leaving them behind.

Presently, just ahead of him, Tarzan saw the Horib who was bearing Jana away and he saw, too, that he would soon overtake him, but so swiftly was his own mount running that it seemed quite likely that he would be carried past Jana without being able to accomplish anything toward her rescue, and with this thought came the realization that he must stop the Horib's mount.

There was just an instant in which to decide and act, but in that instant he raised his rifle and fired. Perhaps it was a wonderful bit of marksmanship, or perhaps it was just luck, but the bullet struck the Gorobor in the spine and a moment later its hind legs collapsed and it rolled over on its side, pitching Jana and the Horib heavily to the ground. Simultaneously Tarzan's mount swept by and the ape-man, risking a bad fall, slipped from its back to go tumbling head over heels against the carcass of the Horib's mount.

Leaping to his feet, he faced the lizard-man and as he did so the ground gave way beneath him and he dropped suddenly into a hole, almost to his armpits. As he was struggling to extricate himself something seized him by the ankles and dragged him downward—cold fingers that clung relentlessly to him dragging him into a dark, subterranean hole.

16

Escape

THE O-220 CRUISED slowly above the Gyor Cors, watchful eyes scanning the ground below, but the only living things they saw were huge dinosaurs. Disturbed by the motors of the dirigible, the great beasts trotted angrily about in circles and occasionally an individual, sighting the ship above him, would gallop after it, bellowing angrily, or again one might charge the elliptical shadow that moved along the ground directly beneath the O-220.

"Sweet-tempered little fellows," remarked Lieutenant Hines, who had been watching them from a messroom port.

"Jes' which *am* dem bad dreams, Lieutenant?" asked Robert Jones.

"Triceratops," replied the officer.

"Ah'll try most anything once, suh, but not dem babies," replied Robert.

Unknown to the bewildered navigating officer, the ship was taking a southeasterly course. Far away, on its port side, loomed a range of mountains, hazily visible in the upcurving distance, and now a river cut the plain—a river that came down from the distant mountains—and this they followed, knowing that men lost in a strange country are prone to follow the course of a river, if they are so fortunate as to find one.

They had followed the river for some distance when Lieutenant Dorf telephoned down from the observation cabin.

"There is a considerable body of water ahead, sir," he reported to Captain Zuppner. "From its appearance I should say that we might be approaching the shore of a large ocean."

All eyes were now strained ahead and presently a large body of water became visible to all on board. The ship cruised slowly up and down the coast for a short distance, and as it had been some time since they had had fresh water or fresh meat, Zuppner decided to land and make camp, selecting a spot just north of the river they had been following, where it emptied into the sea. And as the great ship settled gently to rest upon a rolling, grassy meadow, Robert Jones made an entry in his little black diary.

"Arrived here at noon."

While the great ship settled down beside the shore of the silent Pellucidarian sea, Jason Gridley and his companions, hundreds of miles to the west, pushed their tunnel upward toward the surface of the ground. Jason was in front, laboriously pushing the earth backward a few handfuls at a time to those behind him. They were working frantically now because the length of the tunnel already was so great that it was with difficulty that they could return to the cavern in time to forestall discovery when they heard Horibs approaching.

As Jason scraped away at the earth above him, there broke suddenly upon his ears what sounded like the muffled reverberation of rifle shots. He could not believe that they were such, and yet what else could they be? For so long had he been separated from his fellows that it seemed impossible that any freak of circumstance had brought them to this gloomy corner of Pellucidar, and though hope ran high yet he cast this idea from his mind, substituting for it a more natural conclusion—that the shots had come from the arquebuses of Korsars, who had come up from the ship that Lajo had told him was anchored somewhere below in the Rela Am. Doubtless the captain had sent an expedition in search of the missing members of his crew, but even the prospects of falling again into the hands of the fierce Korsars appeared a heavenly one by comparison to the fate with which they were confronted.

Now Jason redoubled his efforts, working frantically to drive his narrow shaft upward toward the surface. The sound of the shots, which had lasted but a few minutes, had ceased, to be followed by the rapidly approaching thunder of many feet, as though heavy animals were racing in his direction. He heard them passing almost directly overhead and they seemed so close that he was positive he must be near the surface of the ground. Another shot sounded almost directly above him; he heard the thud of a heavy body and the earth about him shook to the impact of its fall. Jason's excitement had arisen to the highest pitch when suddenly the earth gave way above him and something dropped into the shaft upon his head.

His mind long imbued with the fear that their plan for escape would be discovered by the Horibs, Jason reacted instinctively to the urge of self-preservation, the best chance for the accomplishment of which seemed to be to drag the discoverer of their secret out of sight as quickly as possible, and with this end in view he backed quickly into the tunnel, dragging the interloper with him, and to a certain point this was not difficult, but it so happened that Tarzan had clung to his rifle. The rifle chanced to strike the ground in a horizontal position, as the ape-man was dragged into the tunnel, and the muzzle and butt lodged upon opposite sides of the opening, thus forming a rigid bar across the mouth of the aperture, to which the ape-man clung as Jason dragged frantically upon his ankles, and then slowly the steel thews of the Jungle Lord tensed and as he drew himself upward, he drew Jason Gridley with him. Strain and struggle as he would, the American could not overcome the steady pull of those giant thews. Slowly, irresistibly, he was dragged into the shaft and upward toward the surface of the ground.

By this time, of course, he knew that the creature to which he clung was no Horib, for his fingers were closed upon the smooth skin of a human being, and not upon the scaly hide of a lizard-man, but yet he felt that he must not let the fellow escape.

The Horib, who had been expecting Tarzan's attack, had seen him disappear mysteriously into the ground; nor did he wait to investigate the miracle, but seizing Jana by the wrist he hurried after his fellows, dragging the struggling girl with him.

The two were just disappearing among the boles of the trees

down a gloomy aisle of the somber forest when Tarzan, emerging from the shaft, caught a single fleeting glimpse of them. It was almost the growl of an enraged beast that escaped his lips as he realized that this last calamity might have definitely precluded the possibility of effecting the girl's rescue. Chafing at the restraint of the clutching fingers clinging desperately to his ankles, the ape-man kicked violently in an effort to dislodge them and with such good effect that he sent Jason tumbling back into his tunnel, while he leaped to the solid ground and freedom to spring into pursuit of the Horib and The Red Flower of Zoram.

Calling back to his companions to hurry after him, Jason clambered swiftly to the surface of the ground just in time to see a half-naked bronzed giant before he disappeared from view behind the bole of a large tree, but that single glimpse awakened familiar memories and his heart leaped within him at the suggestion it implied. But how could it be? Had not Thoar seen the Lord of the Jungle carried to his doom? Whether the man was Tarzan or not was of less import than the reason for his haste. Was he escaping or pursuing? But in either event something seemed to tell Jason Gridley that he should not lose sight of him; at least he was not a Horib, and if not a Horib, then he must be an enemy of the lizard-men. So rapidly had events transpired that Jason was confused in his own mind as to the proper course to pursue; yet something seemed to urge him not to lose sight of the stranger and acting upon this impulse, he followed at a brisk run.

Through the dark wood ran Tarzan of the Apes, guided only by the delicate and subtle aroma that was the scent spoor of The Red Flower of Zoram and which would have been perceptible to no other human nostrils than those of the Lord of the Jungle. Strong in his nostrils, also, was the sickening scent of the Horibs and fearful lest he come upon them unexpectedly in numbers, he swung lightly into the trees and, with undiminished speed, raced in the direction of his quarry; nor was it long before he saw them beneath him—a single Horib dragging the still-struggling Jana.

There was no hesitation, there was no diminution in his speed as he launched himself like a living projectile straight for the ugly back of the Horib. With such force he struck the creature that it was half stunned as he bore it to the ground. A sinewy arm encircled its neck as Tarzan arose dragging the creature up with him. Turning quickly and bending forward, Tarzan swung the body over his head and hurled it violently to the ground, still retaining his hold about its neck. Again and again he whipped the mighty body over his head and dashed it to the gray earth, while the girl, wide-eyed with astonishment at this exhibition of Herculean strength, looked on.

At last, satisfied that the creature was dead or stunned, Tarzan released it. Quickly he appropriated its stone knife and picked up its fallen lance, then he turned to Jana. "Come," he said, "there is but one safe place for us," and lifting her to his shoulder he leaped to the low-hanging branch of a nearby tree. "Here, at least," he said, "you will be safe from Horibs, for I doubt if any Gorobor can follow us here."

"I always thought that there were no warriors like the warriors of Zoram," said Jana, "but that was before I had known you and Jason"; nor could she, as Tarzan well knew, have voiced a more sincere appreciation of what he had done for her, for to the primitive woman there are no men like her own men. "I wish," she continued sadly after a pause, "that Jason had lived. He was a great man and a mighty warrior, but above all he was a kind man. The men of Zoram are never cruel to their women, but they are not always thoughtful and considerate. Jason seemed always to think of my comfort before everything except my safety."

"You were very fond of him, were you not?" asked Tarzan.

The Red Flower of Zoram did not answer. There were tears in her eyes and in her throat so that she could only nod her head.

Once in the trees, Tarzan had lowered Jana to her feet, presently discovering that she could travel quite without assistance, as might have been expected of one who could leap lightly from crag to crag upon the dizzy slopes of Thipdars' heights. They moved without haste back to the point where they had last seen Muviro, and his Waziri warriors, but as the way took them downwind Tarzan could not hope to pick up the scent spoor of his henchmen and so his ears were constantly upon the alert for any slightest sound that might reveal their whereabouts. Presently they were rewarded by the sound of footsteps hurrying through the forest toward them.

The ape-man drew the girl behind the bole of a large tree and waited, silent, motionless, for all footfalls are not the footfalls of friends.

They had waited for but a moment when there came into view upon the ground below them an almost naked man clothed in a bit of filthy goatskin, which was almost undistinguishable as such beneath a coating of mud, while the original color of his skin was hidden beneath a similar covering. A great mass of tousled black hair surmounted his head. He was quite the filthiest-appearing creature that Tarzan had ever looked upon, but he was evidently no Horib and he was unarmed. What he was doing there alone in the grim forest, the ape-man could not imagine, so he dropped to the ground immediately in front of the surprised wayfarer.

At sight of the ape-man, the other stopped, his eyes wide with astonishment and incredulity. "Tarzan!" he exclaimed. "My God, it is really you. You are not dead. Thank God you are not dead."

It was an instant before the ape-man could recognize the speaker, but not so the girl hiding in the tree above. The instant that she had heard his voice she had known him.

A slow smile overspread the features of the Lord of the Jungle. "Gridley!" he exclaimed. "Jason Gridley! Jana told me that you were dead."

"Jana!" exclaimed Jason. "You know her? You have seen her? Where is she?"

"She is here with me," replied Tarzan.

The Red Flower of Zoram had slipped to the ground upon the opposite side of the tree and now she stepped from behind its trunk.

"Jana!" cried Jason, coming eagerly toward her.

The girl drew herself to her full height and turned a shoulder toward him. "Jalok!" she cried contemptuously. "Must I tell you again to keep away from The Red Flower of Zoram?"

Jason halted in his tracks, his arms dropped limply to his sides, his attitude one of utter dejection.

Tarzan looked silently on, his brows momentarily revealing his perplexity; but it was not his way to interfere in affairs that were wholly the concern of others. "Come," he said, "we must find the Waziri."

Suddenly loud voices just ahead apprised them of the presence of other men and in the babel of excited voices Tarzan recognized the tones of his Waziri. Hurrying forward the three came upon a scene that was momentarily ludicrous, but which might soon have developed into tragedy had they not arrived in time.

Ten Waziri warriors armed with rifles had surrounded Thoar and the three Korsars and each party was jabbering volubly in a language unknown to the other.

The Pellucidarians, never before having seen human beings of the rich, deep, black color of the Waziri and assuming that all strangers were enemies, apprehended only the worst and were about to make a concerted effort to escape their captors, while Muviro, believing that these men might have some sinister connection with the disappearance of his master, was determined to hold and question them; nor would he have hesitated to kill them had they resisted him. It was, therefore, a relief to both parties when Tarzan, Jason, and Jana appeared, and the Waziri saw their Big Bwana greet one of their captives with every indication of friendship.

Thoar was even more surprised to find Tarzan alive than Jason had been, and when he saw Jana the natural reserve which ordinarily marked his bearing was dissipated by the joy and relief which he felt in finding her safe and well; nor any less surprised and happy was Jana as she rushed forward and threw herself into her brother's arms.

His breast filled with emotion such as he had never experienced before, Jason Gridley stood apart, a silent witness of this loving reunion, and then, probably for the first time, there came to him an acute realization of the fact that the sentiment which he entertained for this little barbarian was nothing less than love.

It galled him even to admit it to himself and he felt that he was contemptible to harbor jealousy of Thoar, not only because Thoar was his friend, but because he was only a primitive savage, while he, Jason Gridley, was the product of ages of culture and civilization.

Thoar, Lajo, and the other two Korsars were naturally delighted when they found that the strange warriors whom they had looked upon as enemies were suddenly transformed into friends and allies, and when they heard the story of the battle with the Horibs they knew that the greatest danger which threatened them was now greatly minimized because of the presence of these warriors armed with death-dealing weapons that made the ancient arquebuses of the Korsars appear as inadequate as slingshots, and that escape from this horrible country was as good as accomplished.

Resting after their recent exertion, each party briefly narrated the recent adventures that had befallen them and attempts were made to formulate plans for the future, but here difficulties arose. Thoar wished to return to Zoram with Jana. Tarzan, Jason, and the Waziri desired only to find the other members of their expedition; while Lajo and his two fellows were principally concerned with getting back to their ship.

Tarzan and Jason, realizing that it might not be expedient to acquaint the Korsars with the real purpose of their presence in Pellucidar and finding that the men were familiar with the story of Tanar, gave them to believe that they were merely searching for Sari in order to pay a friendly visit to Tanar and his people.

"Sari is a long way," said Lajo. "He who would go to Sari from here must sleep over a hundred times upon the journey, which would take him across the Korsar Az and then through strange countries filled with enemies, even as far as The Land of Awful Shadow. Maybe one would never reach it."

"Is there no way overland?" asked Tarzan.

"Yes," replied Lajo, "and if we were at Korsar, I might direct you, but that, too, would be a terrible journey, for no man knows what savage tribes and beasts beset the long marches that must lie between Korsar and Sari."

"And if we went to Korsar," said Jason, "we could not hope to be received as friends. Is this not true, Lajo?"

The Korsar nodded. "No," he said. "You would not be received as friends."

"Nevertheless," said Tarzan to Jason, "I believe that if we

are ever to find the O-220 again our best chance is to look for it in the vicinity of Korsar."

Jason nodded in acquiescence. "But that will not accord with Thoar's plans," he said, "for, if I understand it correctly, we are much nearer to Zoram now than we are to Korsar and if we decide to go to Korsar, our route will lead directly away from Zoram. But unless we accompany them with the Waziri, I doubt if Thoar and Jana could live to reach Zoram if they returned by the route that he and I have followed since we left the Mountains of the Thipdars."

Tarzan turned to Thoar. "If you will come with us, we can return you very quickly to Zoram if we find our ship. If we do not find it within a reasonable time, we will accompany you back to Zoram. In either event you would have a very much better chance of reaching your own country than you would if you and Jana set out alone from here."

"We will accompany you, then," said Thoar, and then his brow clouded as some thought seemed suddenly to seize upon his mind. He looked for a moment at Jason, and then he turned to Jana. "I had almost forgotten," he said. "Before we can go with these people as friends, I must know if this man offered you any injury or harm while you were with him. If he did, I must kill him."

Jana did not look at Jason as she replied. "You need not kill him," she said. "Had that been necessary The Red Flower of Zoram would have done it herself."

"Very well," said Thoar, "I am glad because he is my friend. Now we may all go together."

"Our boat is probably in the river where the Horibs left it after they captured us," said Lajo. "If it is we can soon drop down to our ship, which is anchored in the lower waters of the Rela Am."

"And be taken prisoners by your people," said Jason. "No, Lajo, the tables are turned now and if you go with us, it is you who will be the prisoners."

The Korsar shrugged. "I do not care," he said. "We will doubtless get a hundred lashes apiece when the captain finds that we have been unsuccessful, that we have brought back nothing and that he has lost an officer and many members of his crew."

It was finally decided that they would return to the Rela Am and look for the longboat of the Korsars. If they found it they would float down in search of the ship, when they would at least make an effort to persuade the captain to receive them as friends and transport them to the vicinity of Korsar.

On the march back to the Rela Am they were not molested by the Horibs, who had evidently discovered that they had met their masters in the Waziri. During the march Jason made it a point to keep as far away from Jana as possible. The very sight of her reminded him of his hopeless and humiliating infatuation, and to be very near her constituted a form of refined agony which he could not endure. Her contempt, which she made no effort to conceal, galled him bitterly, though it was no greater than his own self-contempt when he realized that in spite of every reason that he had to dislike her, he still loved her—loved her more than he had thought it was possible for him to love any woman.

The American was glad when a glimpse of the broad waters of the Rela Am ahead of them marked the end of this stage of their journey, which his own unhappy thoughts, combined with the depressing influence of the gloomy forest, had transformed into one of the saddest periods of his life.

To the relief of all, the boat was found still moored where the Horibs had left it; nor did it take them long to embark and push out upon the waters of the River of Darkness.

The river widened as they floated down toward the sea until it became possible to step a mast and set sail, after which their progress was still more rapid. Though the way was often beset by dangers in the form of angry and voracious saurians, the rifles of the Waziri proved adequate protection when other means of defense had failed.

The river became very wide so that but for the current they might have considered it an arm of the sea and at Lajo's direction they kept well in toward the left bank, near which, he said, the ship was anchored. Dimly visible in the distance was the opposite shore, but only so because the surface of Pellucidar curved upward. At the same distance upon the outer crust, it would have been hidden by the curvature of the earth.

As they neared the sea it became evident that Lajo and the two other Korsars were much concerned because they had not sighted their ship.

"We have passed the anchorage," said Lajo at last. "That wooded hill, which we just passed, was directly opposite the spot where the ship lay. I cannot be mistaken because I noted it particularly and impressed it upon my memory as a landmark against the time when we should return from our expedition up the river."

"He has sailed away and left us," growled one of the Korsars, applying a vile epithet to the captain of the departed ship.

Continuing on down to the ocean they sighted a large island directly off the mouth of the river, which Lajo told them afforded good hunting with plenty of fresh water and as they were in need of meat they landed there and made camp. It was an ideal spot inasmuch as that part of the island at which they had touched seemed to be peculiarly free from the more dangerous forms of carnivorous mammals and reptiles; nor did they see any sign of the presence of man. Game, therefore, was abundant.

Discussing their plans for the future, it was finally decided that they would push on toward Korsar in the longboat, for Lajo assured them that it lay upon the coast of the same landmass that loomed plainly from their island refuge. "What lies in that direction," he said, pointing south, "I do not know, but there lies Korsar, upon this same coast," and he pointed in a direction a little east of north. "Otherwise I am not familiar with this sea, or with this part of Pellucidar, since never before has an expedition come as far as the Rela Am."

In preparation for the long cruise to Korsar, great quantities of meat were cut into strips and dried in the sun, or smoked over slow fires, after which it was packed away in bladders that had been carefully cleaned and dried. These were stowed in the boat together with other bladders filled with fresh water, for, although it was their intention to hug the coast on the way to Korsar, it might not always be expedient to land for water or food and there was always the possibility that a storm arising they might be blown out to sea.

At length, all preparations having been made, the strangely assorted company embarked upon their hazardous journey toward distant Korsar.

Jana had worked with the others preparing the provisions and the containers and though she had upon several occasions worked side by side with Jason, she had never relaxed toward him; nor appeared to admit that she was cognizant of his presence.

"Can't we be friends, Jana?" he asked once. "I think we would both be very much happier if we were."

"I am as happy as I can be," she replied lightly, "until Thoar takes me back to Zoram."

17

Reunited

AS FAVORABLE WINDS carried the longboat and its company up the sunlit sea, the O-220, following the same route, made occasional wide circles inland upon what Zuppner now considered an almost hopeless quest for the missing members of the expedition, and not only was he hopeless upon this score, but he also shared the unvoiced hopelessness of the balance of the company with regard to the likelihood of their ever being able to find the polar opening and return again to the outer world. With them, he knew that even their tremendous reserve of fuel and oil would not last indefinitely and if they were unable to find the polar opening, while they still had sufficient in reserve to carry them back to civilization, they must resign themselves to remaining in Pellucidar for the rest of their lives.

Lieutenant Hines finally broached this subject and the two officers, after summoning Lieutenant Dorf to their conference, decided that before their fuel was entirely exhausted they would try to locate some district where they might be reasonably free from attacks by savage tribesmen, or the even more dangerous menace of the mighty carnivores of Pellucidar.

While the remaining officers of the O-220 pondered the serious problems that confronted them, the great ship moved serenely through the warm Pellucidarian sunlight and the members of the crew went quietly and efficiently about their various duties.

Robert Jones of Alabama, however, was distressed. He seemed never to be able to accustom himself to the changed conditions of Pellucidar. He often mumbled to himself, shaking his head vehemently, and frequently he wound a battered alarm clock or took it down from the hook upon which it hung and held it to his ear.

Below the ship there unrolled a panorama of lovely seacoast, indented by many beautiful bays and inlets. There were rolling hills and plains and forests and winding rivers blue as turquoise. It was a scene to inspire the loftiest sentiments in the lowliest heart nor was it without its effect upon the members of the ship's company, which included many adventurous spirits, who would experience no regret should it develop that they must remain forever in this, to them, enchanted land. But there were others who had left loved ones at home and these were already beginning to discuss the possibilities and the probabilities of the future. With few exceptions, they were keen and intelligent men and fully as cognizant of the possible plight of the O-220 as was its commander, but they had been chosen carefully and there was not one who waivered even momentarily in loyalty to Zuppner, for they well knew that whatever fate was to be theirs, he would share it with them and, too, they had confidence that if any man could extricate them from their predicament, it was he. And so the great ship rode its majestic

way between the sun and earth and each part, whether
mechanical or human, functioned perfectly.

The captain and his lieutenant discussed the future as
Robert Jones laboriously ascended the climbing shaft to the
walking-way upon the ship's back, a hundred and fifty feet
above his galley. He did not come entirely out of the climbing
shaft onto the walking-way, but merely looked about the blue
heaven and when his gaze had completed the circle, he hesitated a moment and then looked straight up, where, directly
overhead, hung the eternal noonday sun of Pellucidar.

Robert Jones blinked his eyes and retreated into the shaft,
closing the hatch after him. Muttering to himself, he descended
carefully to the galley, crossed it, took the clock off its hook
and, walking to an open port, threw it overboard.

To the occupants of the longboat dancing over the blue
waves, without means of determining either time or distance,
the constant expectation of nearing their journey's end lessened the monotony as did the oft recurring attacks of the
frightful denizens of this Mesozoic sea. To the highly civilized
American the utter timelessness of Pellucidarian existence
brought a more marked nervous reaction than to the others. To
a lesser degree Tarzan felt it, while the Waziri were only
slightly conscious of the anomalous conditions. Upon the Pellucidarians, accustomed to no other state, it had no effect whatever. It was apparent when Tarzan and Jason discussed the
matter with them that they had practically no conception of the
meaning of time.

But time did elapse, leagues of ocean passed beneath them
and conditions changed.

As they moved along the coast their course changed; though
without instruments or heavenly bodies to guide them they
were not aware of it. For a while they had moved northeast and
then, for a long distance, to the east, where the coast curved
gradually until they were running due north.

Instinct told the Korsars that they had come about three
quarters of the distance from the island where they had out-
fitted to their destination. A land breeze was blowing stiffly
and they were tacking briskly up the coast at a good clip. Lajo
was standing erect in the bow apparently sniffing the air, as

might a hunting dog searching out a scent spoor. Presently he turned to Tarzan.

"We had better put in to the coast," he said. "We are in for a stiff blow." But it was too late, the wind and the sea mounted to such proportions that finally they had to abandon the attempt and turn and flee before the storm. There was no rain nor lightning, for there were no clouds—just a terrific wind that rose to hurricane violence and stupendous sea that threatened momentarily to engulf them.

The Waziri were frankly terrified, for the sea was not their element. The mountain girl and her brother seemed awed, but if they felt fear they gave no outward indication of it. Tarzan and Jason were convinced that the boat could not live and the latter made his way to where Jana sat huddled upon a thwart. The howling of the wind made speech almost impossible, but he bent low placing his lips close to her ear.

"Jana," he said, "it is impossible for this small boat to ride out such a storm. We are going to die, but before we die, whether you hate me or not, I am going to tell you that I love you," and then before she could reply, before she could humiliate him further, he turned away and moved forward to where he had been before.

He knew that he had done wrong; he knew that he had no right to tell Thoar's sweetheart that he loved her; it had been an act of disloyalty and yet a force greater than loyalty, greater than pride, had compelled him to speak those words—he could not die with them unspoken. Perhaps it had been a little easier because he could not help but have noticed the seemingly platonic relationship which existed between Thoar and Jana and being unable to picture Jana as platonic in love, he had assumed that Thoar did not appreciate her. He was always kind to her and always pleasant, but he had never been quite as thoughtful of her as Jason thought that he should have been. He felt that perhaps it was one of the strange inflections of Pellucidarian character, but it was difficult to know either Jana or Thoar and also to believe that, for they were evidently quite as normal human beings as was he, and though they had much of the natural primitive reserve and dignity that civilized man now merely affects; yet it seemed unlikely that either one of them could have been for so long a time in close association without inadvertently, at least, having given some indication of their love. "Why," mused Jason, "they might be brother and sister from the way they act."

By some miracle of fate the boat lived through the storm, but when the wind diminished and the seas went down there were only tumbling waters to be seen on every hand; nor any sign of land.

"Now that we have lost the coast, Lajo, how are we going to set our course for Korsar?" asked Tarzan.

"It will not be easy," replied Lajo. "The only guide that we have is the wind. We are well out on the Korsar Az and I know from which direction the wind usually blows. By keeping always on the same tack we shall eventually reach land and probably not far from Korsar."

"What is that?" asked Jana, pointing, and all eyes turned in the direction that she indicated.

"It is a sail," said Lajo presently. "We are saved."

"But suppose the ship is manned by unfriendly people?" asked Jason.

"It is not," said Lajo. "It is manned by Korsars, for no other ships sail the Korsar Az."

"There is another," exclaimed Jana. "There are many of them."

"Come about and run for it," said Tarzan; "perhaps they have not seen us yet."

"Why should we try to escape?" asked Lajo.

"Because we have not enough men to fight them," replied Tarzan. "They may not be your enemies, but they will be ours."

Lajo did as he was bid, nor had he any alternative since the Korsars aboard were only three unarmed men, while there were ten Waziri with rifles.

All eyes watched the sails in the distance and it soon became apparent that they were coming closer, for the longboat, with its small sail, was far from fast. Little by little the distance between them and the ships decreased until it was evident that they were being pursued by a considerable fleet.

"Those are no Korsars," said Lajo. "I have never seen ships like those before."

The longboat wallowed through the sea making the best headway that it could, but the pursuing ships, stringing out as far as the eye could reach until their numbers presented the appearance of a vast armada, continued to close up rapidly upon it.

The leading ship was now closing up so swiftly upon them that the occupants of the longboat had an excellent view of it. It was short and broad of beam with rather a high bow. It had two sails and in addition was propelled by oars, which protruded through ports along each side, there being some fifty oars all told. Above the line of oars, over the sides of the ship, were hung the shields of the warriors.

"Lord!" exclaimed Jason to Tarzan; "Pellucidar not only boasts Spanish pirates, but vikings as well, for if those are not viking ships they certainly are an adaptation of them."

"Slightly modernized, however," remarked the Lord of the Jungle. "There is a gun mounted on a small deck built in the bow."

"So there is," exclaimed Jason, "and I think we had better come about. There is a fellow up there turning it on us now."

Presently another man appeared upon the elevated bow deck of the enemy. "Heave to," he cried, "or I'll blow you out of the water."

"Who are you?" demanded Jason.

"I am Ja of Anoroc," replied the man, "and this is the fleet of David I, Emperor of Pellucidar."

"Come about," said Tarzan to Lajo.

"Someone in this boat must have been born on Sunday," exclaimed Jason. "I never knew there was so much good luck in the world."

"Who are you?" demanded Ja as the longboat came slowly about.

"We are friends," replied Tarzan.

"The Emperor of Pellucidar can have no friends upon the Korsar Az," replied Ja.

"If Abner Perry is with you, we can prove that you are wrong," replied Jason.

"Abner Perry is not with us," said Ja; "but what do you know of him?"

By this time the two boats were alongside and the bronzed Mezop warriors of Ja's crew were gazing down curiously upon the occupants of the boat.

"This is Jason Gridley," said Tarzan to Ja, indicating the American. "Perhaps you have heard Abner Perry speak of him. He organized an expedition in the outer world to come here to rescue David Innes from the dungeons of the Korsars."

The three Korsars of the longboat made Ja suspicious, but when a full explanation had been made and especially when he had examined the rifles of the Waziri, he became convinced of the truth of their statements and welcomed them warmly aboard his ship, about which were now gathered a considerable number of the armada. When word was passed among them that two of the strangers were friends from the outer world who had come to assist in the rescue of David Innes, a number of the captains of other ships came aboard Ja's flagship to greet Tarzan and Jason. Among these captains were Dacor the Strong One, brother of Dian the Beautiful, Empress of Pellucidar; Kolk, son of Goork, who is chief of the Thurians; and Tanar, son of Ghak, the Hairy One, King of Sari.

From these Tarzan and Jason learned that this fleet was on its way to effect the rescue of David. It had been building for a great while, so long that they had forgotten how many times they had eaten and slept since the first keel was laid, and then they had had to find a way into the Korsar Az from the Lural Az, where the ships were built upon the island of Anoroc.

"Far down the Sojar Az beyond the Land of Awful Shadow we found a passage that led to the Korsar Az. The Thurians had heard of it and while the fleet was building they sent warriors out to see if it was true and they found the passage and soon we shall be before the city of Korsar."

"How did you expect to rescue David with only a dozen men?" asked Tanar.

"We are not all here," said Tarzan. "We became separated from our companions and have been unable to find them. However, there were not very many men in our expedition. We depended upon other means than manpower to effect the rescue of your Emperor."

At this moment a great cry arose from one of the ships. The excitement rose and spread. The warriors were all looking into the air and pointing. Already some of them were elevating the muzzles of their cannons and all were preparing their rifles, and as Tarzan and Jason looked up they saw the O-220 far above them.

The dirigible had evidently discovered the fleet and was descending toward it in a wide spiral.

"Now I *know* someone was born on Sunday," said Jason. "That is our ship. Those are our friends," he added, turning to Ja.

All that transpired on board the flagship passed quickly from ship to ship until every member of the armada knew that the great thing hovering above them was no gigantic flying reptile, but a ship of the air in which were friends of Abner Perry and their beloved Emperor, David I.

Slowly the great ship settled toward the surface of the sea and as it did so Jason Gridley borrowed a spear from one of the warriors and tied Lajo's head handkerchief to its tip. With this improvised flag he signaled, "O-220 ahoy! This is the war fleet of David I, Emperor of Pellucidar, commanded by Ja of Anoroc; Lord Greystoke, ten Waziri, and Jason Gridley aboard."

A moment later a gun boomed from the rear turret of the O-220, marking the beginning of the first international salute of twenty-one guns that had ever reverberated beneath the eternal sun of Pellucidar, and when the significance of it was explained to Ja he returned the salute with the bow gun of his flagship.

The dirigible dropped lower until it was within speaking distance of the flagship.

"Are you all well aboard?" asked Tarzan.

"Yes," came back the reassuring reply in Zuppner's booming tone.

"Is Von Horst with you?" asked Jason.

"No," replied Zuppner.

"Then he alone is missing," said Jason sadly.

"Can you drop a sling and take us aboard?" asked Tarzan.

Zuppner maneuvered the dirigible to within fifty feet of the deck of Ja's flagship, a sling was lowered and one after another the members of the party were taken on board the O-220, the Waziri first and then Jana and Thoar, followed by Jason and Tarzan, the three Korsars being left prisoners with Ja with the understanding that they were to be treated humanely.

Before Tarzan left the deck of the flagship he told Ja that if he would proceed toward Korsar, the dirigible would keep in touch with him and in the meantime they would be perfecting plans for the rescue of David Innes.

As Thoar and Jana were hoisted aboard the O-220, they were filled with a boundless amazement. To them such a creation as the giant dirigible was inconceivable. As Jana expressed it afterward: "I knew that I was dreaming, but yet at the same time I knew that I could not dream about such a thing as this because no such thing existed."

Jason introduced Jana and Thoar to Zuppner and Hines, but Lieutenant Dorf did not come to the cabin until after Tarzan had boarded the ship, and it was the latter who introduced them to Dorf.

He presented Lieutenant Dorf to Jana and then, indicating Thoar, "This is Thoar, the brother of The Red Flower of Zoram."

As those words broke upon the ears of Jason Gridley he reacted almost as to the shock of a physical blow. He was glad that no one chanced to be looking at him at the time and instantly he regained his composure, but it left him with a distinct feeling of injury. They had all known it and none of them had told him. He was almost angry at them until it occurred to him that they had all probably assumed that he had known it too, and yet try as he would he could not quite forgive Jana. But, really, what difference did it make, for, whether sister or mate of Thoar or another, he knew that The Red Flower of Zoram was not for him. She had made that definitely clear in her attitude toward him, which had convinced him even more definitely than had her bitter words.

The reunited officers of the expedition had much to discuss and many reminiscences to narrate as the O-220 followed above the slowly moving fleet. It was a happy reunion, clouded only by the absence of Von Horst.

As the dirigible moved slowly above the waters of the Korsar Az, Zuppner dropped occasionally to within speaking distance of Ja of Anoroc, and when the distant coast of Korsar was sighted a sling was lowered and Ja was taken aboard the O-220, where plans for the rescue of David were discussed, and when they were perfected Ja was returned to his ship, and Lajo and the two other Korsars were taken aboard the dirigible.

The three prisoners were filled with awe and consternation as Jason and Tarzan personally conducted them throughout the giant craft. They were shown the armament, which was carefully explained to them, special stress being laid upon the destructive power of the bombs which the O-220 carried.

"One of these," said Jason to Lajo, "would blow The Cid's palace a thousand feet into the air and, as you see, we have many of them. We could destroy all of Korsar and all the Korsar ships."

While Ja's fleet was still a considerable distance off the coast, the O-220 raced ahead at full speed toward Korsar, for the plan which they had evolved was such that, if successful, David's release would be effected without the shedding of blood—a plan which was especially desirable since if it was necessary to attack Korsar either from the sea or the air, the Emperor's life would be placed in jeopardy from the bombs and cannons of his friends, as well as from a possible spirit of vengeance which might animate The Cid.

As the dirigible glided almost silently over the city of Korsar, the streets and courtyards filled with people staring upward in awestruck wonder.

Three thousand feet above the city the ship stopped and Tarzan sent for the three Korsar prisoners.

"As you know," he said to them, "we are in a position to destroy Korsar. You have seen the great fleet coming to the rescue of the Emperor of Pellucidar. You know that every warrior manning those ships is armed with a weapon far more effective than your best; even with their knives and spears and their bows and arrows they might take Korsar without their rifles, but they have the rifles and they have better ammunition than yours and in each ship of the fleet cannons are mounted. Alone the fleet could reduce Korsar, but in addition to the fleet there is this airship. Your shots could never reach it as it sailed back and forth above Korsar, dropping bombs upon the city. Do you think, Lajo, that we can take Korsar?"

"I know it," replied the Korsar.

"Very well," said Tarzan. "I am going to send you with a message to The Cid. Will you tell him the truth?"

"I will," replied Lajo.

"The message is simple," continued Tarzan. "You may tell him that we have come to effect the release of the Emperor of Pellucidar. You may explain to him the means that we have to enforce our demands, and then you may say to him that if he will place the Emperor upon a ship and take him out to our fleet and deliver him unharmed to Ja of Anoroc, we will return to Sari without firing a shot. Do you understand?"

"I do," said Lajo.

"Very well, then," said Tarzan. He turned to Dorf. "Lieutenant, will you take him now?" he asked.

Dorf approached with a bundle in his hand. "Slip into this," he said.

"What is it?" asked Lajo.

"It is a parachute," said Dorf.

"What is that?" demanded Lajo.

"Here," said Dorf, "put your arms through here." A moment later he had the parachute adjusted upon the Korsar.

"Now," said Jason, "a great distinction is going to be conferred upon you—you are going to make the first parachute jump that has ever been witnessed in Pellucidar."

"I don't understand what you mean," said Lajo.

"You will presently," said Jason. "You are going to take Lord Greystoke's message to The Cid."

"But you will have to bring the ship down to the ground before I can," objected Lajo.

"On the contrary we are going to stay right where we are," said Jason; "you are going to jump overboard."

"What?" exclaimed Lajo. "You are going to kill me?"

"No," said Jason with a laugh. "Listen carefully to what I tell you and you will land safely. You have seen some wonderful things on board this ship so you must have some conception of what we of the outer world can do. Now you are going to have a demonstration of another very wonderful invention and you may take my word for it that no harm will befall you if you do precisely as I tell you to. Here is an iron ring," and he touched the ring opposite Lajo's left breast; "take hold of it with your right hand. After you jump from the ship, pull it; give it a good jerk and you will float down to the ground as lightly as a feather."

"I will be killed," objected Lajo.

"If you are a coward," said Jason, "perhaps one of these other men is braver than you. I tell you that you will not be hurt."

"I am not afraid," said Lajo. "I will jump."

"Tell The Cid," said Tarzan, "that if we do not presently see a ship sail out alone to meet the fleet, we shall start dropping bombs upon the city."

Dorf led Lajo to a door in the cabin and flung it open. The man hesitated.

"Do not forget to jerk the ring," said Dorf, and at the same time he gave Lajo a violent push that sent him headlong through the doorway and a moment later the watchers in the cabin saw the white folds of the parachute streaming in the air. They saw it open and they knew that the message of Tarzan would be delivered to The Cid.

What went on in the city below we may not know, but presently a great crowd was seen to move from the palace down toward the river, where the ships were anchored, and a little later one of the ships weighed anchor and as it drifted slowly with the current its sails were set and presently it was moving directly out to sea toward the fleet from Sari.

The O-220 followed above it and Ja's flagship moved forward to meet it, and thus David Innes, Emperor of Pellucidar, was returned to his people.

As the Korsar ship turned back to port the dirigible dropped low above the flagship of the Sarian fleet and greetings were exchanged between David and his rescuers—men from another world whom he had never seen.

The Emperor was half starved and very thin and weak from

his long period of confinement, but otherwise he had been unharmed, and great was the rejoicing aboard the ships of Sari as they turned back to cross the Korsar Az toward their own land.

Tarzan was afraid to accompany the fleet back to Sari for fear that their rapidly diminishing store of fuel would not be sufficient to complete the trip and carry them back to the outer world. He followed the fleet only long enough to obtain from David explicit directions for reaching the polar opening from the city of Korsar.

"We have another errand to fulfill first," said Jason to Tarzan. "We must return Thoar and Jana to Zoram."

"Yes," said the ape-man, "and drop these two Korsars off near their city. I have thought of all that and we shall have fuel enough for that purpose."

"I am not going to return with you," said Jason. "I wish to be put aboard Ja's flagship."

"What?" exclaimed Tarzan. "You are going to remain here?"

"This expedition was undertaken at my suggestion. I feel responsible for the life and safety of every man in it and I shall never return to the outer world while the fate of Lieutenant Von Horst remains a mystery."

"But how can you find Von Horst if you go back to Sari with the fleet?" asked Tarzan.

"I shall ask David Innes to equip an expedition to go in search of him," replied Jason, "and with such an expedition made up of native Pellucidarians I shall stand a very much better chance of finding him than we would in the O-220."

"I quite agree with you," said Tarzan, "and if you are un-alterably determined to carry out your project, we will lower you to Ja's ship immediately."

As the O-220 dropped toward Ja's flagship and signaled it to heave to, Jason gathered what belongings he wished to take with him, including rifles and revolvers and plenty of ammunition. These were lowered first to Ja's ship, while Jason bid farewell to his companions of the expedition.

"Good-bye, Jana," he said, after he had shaken hands with the others.

The girl made no reply, but instead turned to her brother.

"Good-bye, Thoar," she said.

"Good-bye?" he asked. "What do you mean?"

"I am going to Sari with the man I love," replied The Red Flower of Zoram.

TARZAN THE INVINCIBLE

Contents

1

Little Nkima

I AM NO historian, no chronicler of facts, and, furthermore, I hold a very definite conviction that there are certain subjects which fiction writers should leave alone, foremost among which are politics and religion. However, it seems to me not unethical to pirate an idea occasionally from one or the other, provided that the subject be handled in such a way as to impart a definite impression of fictionizing.

Had the story that I am about to tell you broken in the newspapers of two certain European powers, it might have precipitated another and a more terrible world war. But with that I am not particularly concerned. What interests me is that it is a good story that is particularly well adapted to my requirements through the fact that Tarzan of the Apes was intimately connected with many of its most thrilling episodes.

I am not going to bore you with dry political history, so do not tax your intellect needlessly by attempting to decode such fictitious names as I may use in describing certain people and places, which, it seems to me, to the best interest of peace and disarmament, should remain incognito.

Take the story simply as another Tarzan story, in which, it is hoped, you will find entertainment and relaxation. If you find food for thought in it, so much the better.

Doubtless, very few of you saw, and still fewer will remember having seen, a news dispatch that appeared inconspicuously in the papers some time since, reporting a rumor that French Colonial troops stationed in Somaliland, on the northeast coast of Africa, had invaded an Italian African colony. Back of that news item is a story of conspiracy, intrigue, adventure, and love—a story of scoundrels and of fools, of brave men, of beautiful women, a story of the beasts of the forest and the jungle.

If there were few who saw the newspaper account of the invasion of Italian Somaliland upon the northeast coast of Africa, it is equally a fact that none of you saw a harrowing incident that occurred in the interior some time previous to this affair. That it could possibly have any connection whatsoever with European international intrigue, or with the fate of nations, seems not even remotely possible, for it was only a very little monkey fleeing through the treetops and screaming in terror. It was little Nkima, and pursuing him was a large, rude monkey—a much larger monkey than little Nkima.

Fortunately for the peace of Europe and the world, the speed of the pursuer was in no sense proportionate to his unpleasant disposition, and so Nkima escaped him; but for long after the larger monkey had given up the chase, the smaller one continued to flee through the treetops, screeching at the top of his shrill little voice, for terror and flight were the two major activities of little Nkima.

Perhaps it was fatigue, but more likely it was a caterpillar or a bird's nest that eventually terminated Nkima's flight and left him scolding and chattering upon a swaying bough, far above the floor of the jungle.

The world into which little Nkima had been born seemed a very terrible world, indeed, and he spent most of his waking hours scolding about it, in which respect he was quite as human as he was simian. It seemed to little Nkima that the world was populated with large, fierce creatures that liked monkey meat. There were Numa, the lion, and Sheeta, the panther, and Histah, the snake—a triumvirate that rendered unsafe his entire world from the loftiest treetop to the ground. And then there were the great apes, and the lesser apes, and the baboons, and countless species of monkeys, all of which God had made larger than He had made little Nkima, and all of which seemed to harbor a grudge against him.

Take, for example, the rude creature which had just been pursuing him. Little Nkima had done nothing more than throw a stick at him while he was asleep in the crotch of a tree, and just for that he had pursued little Nkima with unquestionable homicidal intent—I use the word without purposing any reflection upon Nkima. It had never occurred to Nkima, as it never seems to occur to some people, that, like beauty, a sense of humor may sometimes be fatal.

Brooding upon the injustices of life, little Nkima was very sad. But there was another and more poignant cause of sadness that depressed his little heart. Many, many moons ago his master had gone away and left him. True, he had left him in a nice, comfortable home with kind people who fed him, but little Nkima missed the great Tarmangani, whose naked shoulder was the one harbor of refuge from which he could with perfect impunity hurl insults at the world. For a long time now little Nkima had braved the dangers of the forest and the jungle in search of his beloved Tarzan.

Because hearts are measured by content of love and loyalty, rather than by diameters in inches, the heart of little Nkima was very large—so large that the average human being could hide his own heart and himself, as well, behind it—and for a long time it had been just one great ache in his diminutive breast. But fortunately for the little Manu his mind was so ordered that it might easily be distracted even from a great sorrow. A butterfly or a luscious grub might suddenly claim his attention from the depths of brooding, which was well, since otherwise he might have grieved himself to death.

And now, therefore, as his melancholy thoughts returned to contemplation of his loss, their trend was suddenly altered by the shifting of a jungle breeze that brought to his keen ears a sound that was not primarily of the jungle sounds that were a part of his hereditary instincts. It was a discord. And what is it that brings discord into the jungle as well as into every elsewhere that it enters? Man. It was the voices of men that Nkima heard.

Silently the little monkey glided through the trees into the direction from which the sounds had come; and presently, as the sounds grew louder, there came also that which was the definite, final proof of the identity of the noisemakers, as far as Nkima, or, for that matter, any other of the jungle folk, might be concerned—the scent spoor.

You have seen a dog, perhaps your own dog, half recognize you by sight; but was he ever entirely satisfied until the evidence of his eyes had been tested and approved by his sensitive nostrils?

And so it was with Nkima. His ears had suggested the presence of men, and now his nostrils definitely assured him that men were near. He did not think of them as men, but as great apes. There were Gomangani, Great Black Apes, Negroes, among them. This his nose told him. And there were Tarmangani, also. These, which to Nkima would be Great White Apes, were white men.

Eagerly his nostrils sought for the familiar scent spoor of his beloved Tarzan, but it was not there—that he knew even before he came within sight of the strangers.

The camp upon which Nkima presently looked down from a nearby tree was well established. It had evidently been there for a matter of days and might be expected to remain still longer. It was no overnight affair. There were the tents of the white men and the beyts of Arabs neatly arranged with almost military precision and behind these the shelters of the Negroes, lightly constructed of such materials as Nature had provided upon the spot.

Within the open front of an Arab beyt sat several white burnoosed Beduins drinking their inevitable coffee; in the shade of a great tree before another tent four white men were engrossed in a game of cards; among the native shelters a group of stalwart Galla warriors were playing at minkala. There were blacks of other tribes too—men of East Africa and of Central Africa, with a sprinkling of West Coast Negroes.

It might have puzzled an experienced African traveler or hunter to catalog this motley aggregation of races and colors. There were far too many blacks to justify a belief that all were porters, for with all the impedimenta of the camp ready for transportation there would have been but a small fraction of a load for each of them, even after more than enough had been included among the askari, who do not carry any loads beside their rifles and ammunition.

Then, too, there were more rifles than would have been needed to protect even a larger party. There seemed, indeed, to be a rifle for every man. But these were minor details which made no impression upon Nkima. All that impressed him was the fact that here were many strange Tarmangani and Gomangani in the country of his master; and as all strangers were, to Nkima, enemies, he was perturbed. Now more than ever he wished that he might find Tarzan.

A swarthy, turbaned East Indian sat cross-legged upon the ground before a tent, apparently sunk in meditation; but could one have seen his dark, sensuous eyes, he would have discovered that their gaze was far from introspective—they were bent constantly upon another tent that stood a little apart from its fellows—and when a girl emerged from this tent, Raghunath Jafar arose and approached her. He smiled an oily smile as he spoke to her, but the girl did not smile as she replied. She spoke civilly, but she did not pause, continuing her way toward the four men at cards.

As she approached their table they looked up; and upon the face of each was reflected some pleasurable emotion, but whether it was the same in each, the masks that we call faces, and which are trained to conceal our true thoughts, did not divulge. Evident it was, however, that the girl was popular.

"Hello, Zora!" cried a large, smooth-faced fellow. "Have a good nap?"

"Yes, Comrade," replied the girl; "but I am tired of napping. This inactivity is getting on my nerves."

"Mine, too," agreed the man.

"How much longer will you wait for the American, Comrade Zveri?" asked Raghunath Jafar.

The big man shrugged. "I need him," he replied. "We might easily carry on without him, but for the moral effect upon the world of having a rich and highborn American identified actively with the affair it is worth waiting."

"Are you quite sure of this gringo, Zveri?" asked a swarthy

young Mexican sitting next to the big, smooth-faced man, who was evidently the leader of the expedition.

"I met him in New York and again in San Francisco," replied Zveri. "He has been very carefully checked and favorably recommended."

"I am always suspicious of these fellows who owe everything they have to capitalism," declared Romero. "It is in their blood—at heart they hate the proletariat, just as we hate them."

"This fellow is different, Miguel," insisted Zveri. "He has been won over so completely that he would betray his own father for the good of the cause—and already he is betraying his country."

A slight, involuntary sneer, that passed unnoticed by the others, curled the lip of Zora Drinov as she heard this description of the remaining member of the party, who had not yet reached the rendezvous.

Miguel Romero, the Mexican, was still unconvinced. "I have no use for gringos of any sort," he said.

Zveri shrugged his heavy shoulders. "Our personal animosities are of no importance," he said, "as against the interests of the workers of the world. When Colt arrives we must accept him as one of us; nor must we forget that however much we may detest America and Americans nothing of any moment may be accomplished in the world of today without them and their filthy wealth."

"Wealth ground out of the blood and sweat of the working class," growled Romero.

"Exactly," agreed Raghunath Jafar, "but how appropriate that this same wealth should be used to undermine and overthrow capitalistic America and bring the workers eventually into their own."

"That is precisely the way I feel about it," said Zveri. "I would rather use American gold in furthering the cause than any other—and after that British."

"But what do the puny resources of this single American mean to us?" demanded Zora. "A mere nothing compared to what America is already pouring into Soviet Russia. What is his treason compared with the treason of those others who are already doing more to hasten the day of world communism than the Third Internationale itself—it is nothing, not a drop in the bucket."

"What do you mean, Zora?" asked Miguel.

"I mean the bankers, and manufacturers, and engineers of America, who are selling their own country and the world to us in the hope of adding more gold to their already bursting coffers. One of their most pious and lauded citizens is building great factories for us in Russia, where we may turn out tractors and tanks; their manufacturers are vying with one another to furnish us with engines for countless thousands of airplanes; their engineers are selling us their brains and their skill to build a great modern manufacturing city, in which ammunitions and engines of war may be produced. These are the traitors, these are the men who are hastening the day when Moscow shall dictate the policies of our world."

"You speak as though you regretted it," said a dry voice at her shoulder.

The girl turned quickly. "Oh, is it you, Sheykh Abu Batn?" she said, as she recognized the swart Arab who had strolled over from his coffee. "Our own good fortune does not blind me to the perfidiousness of the enemy, nor cause me to admire treason in anyone, even though I profit by it."

"Does that include me?" demanded Romero, suspiciously.

Zora laughed. "You know better than that, Miguel," she said. "You are of the working class—you are loyal to the workers of your own country—but these others are of the capitalistic class; their government is a capitalistic government that is so opposed to our beliefs that it has never recognized our government; yet, in their greed, these swine are selling out their own kind and their own country for a few more rotten dollars. I loathe them."

Zveri laughed. "You are a good Red, Zora," he cried; "you hate the enemy as much when he helps us as when he hinders."

"But hating and talking accomplish so little," said the girl. "I wish we might do something. Sitting here in idleness seems so futile."

"And what would you have us do?" demanded Zveri, good-naturedly.

"We might at least make a try for the gold of Opar," she

said. "If Kitembo is right, there should be enough there to finance a dozen expeditions such as you are planning, and we do not need this American—what do they call them, cake eaters?—to assist us in that venture."

"I have been thinking along similar lines," said Raghunath Jafar.

Zveri scowled. "Perhaps some of the rest of you would like to run this expedition," he said, crustily. "I know what I am doing and I don't have to discuss all my plans with anyone. When I have orders to give, I'll give them. Kitembo has already received his, and preparations have been under way for several days for the expedition to Opar."

"The rest of us are as much interested and are risking as much as you, Zveri," snapped Romero. "We were to work together—not as master and slaves."

"You'll soon learn that I am master," snarled Zveri in an ugly tone.

"Yes," sneered Romero, "the czar was master, too, and Obregon. You know what happened to them?"

Zveri leaped to his feet and whipped out a revolver, but as he leveled it at Romero the girl struck his arm up and stepped between them. "Are you mad, Zveri?" she cried.

"Do not interfere, Zora; this is my affair and it might as well be settled now as later. I am chief here and I am not going to have any traitors in my camp. Stand aside."

"No!" said the girl with finality. "Miguel was wrong and so were you, but to shed blood—our own blood—now would utterly ruin any chance we have of success. It would sow the seed of fear and suspicion and cost us the respect of the blacks, for they would know that there was dissension among us. Furthermore, Miguel is not armed; to shoot him would be cowardly murder that would lose you the respect of every decent man in the expedition." She had spoken rapidly in Russian, a language that was understood by only Zveri and herself, of those who were present; then she turned again to Miguel and addressed him in English. "You were wrong, Miguel," she said gently. "There must be one responsible head, and Comrade Zveri was chosen for the responsibility. He regrets that he acted hastily. Tell him that you are sorry for what you said, and then the two of you shake hands and let us all forget the matter."

For an instant Romero hesitated; then he extended his hand toward Zveri. "I am sorry," he said.

The Russian took the proffered hand in his and bowed stiffly. "Let us forget it, Comrade," he said; but the scowl was still upon his face, though no darker than that which clouded the Mexican's.

Little Nkima yawned and swung by his tail from a branch far overhead. His curiosity concerning these enemies was sated. They no longer afforded him entertainment, but he knew that his master should know about their presence; and that thought, entering his little head, recalled his sorrow and his great yearning for Tarzan, to the end that he was again imbued with a grim determination to continue his search for the ape-man. Perhaps in half an hour some trivial occurrence might again distract his attention, but for the moment it was his life work. Swinging through the forest, little Nkima held the fate of Europe in his pink palm, but he did not know it.

The afternoon was waning. In the distance a lion roared. An instinctive shiver ran up Nkima's spine. In reality, however, he was not much afraid, knowing, as he did, that no lion could reach him in the treetops.

A young man marching near the head of a safari cocked his head and listened. "Not so very far away, Tony," he said.

"No, sir; much too close," replied the Filipino.

"You'll have to learn to cut out that 'sir' stuff, Tony, before we join the others," admonished the young man.

The Filipino grinned. "All right, Comrade," he assented. "I got so used calling everybody 'sir' it hard for me to change."

"I'm afraid you're not a very good Red then, Tony."

"Oh, yes I am," insisted the Filipino emphatically. "Why else am I here? You think I like come this Godforsaken country full of lion, ant, snake, fly, mosquito just for the walk? No, I come lay down my life for Philippine independence."

"That's noble of you all right, Tony," said the other gravely; "but just how is it going to make the Philippines free?"

Antonio Mori scratched his head. "I don't know," he admitted; "but it make trouble for America."

High among the treetops a little monkey crossed their path. For a moment he paused and watched them; then he resumed his journey in the opposite direction.

A half hour later the lion roared again, and so disconcertingly close and unexpected rose the voice of thunder from the jungle beneath him that little Nkima nearly fell out of the tree through which he was passing. With a scream of terror he scampered as high aloft as he could go and there he sat, scolding angrily.

The lion, a magnificent full-maned male, stepped into the open beneath the tree in which the trembling Nkima clung. Once again he raised his mighty voice until the ground itself trembled to the great, rolling volume of his challenge. Nkima looked down upon him and suddenly ceased to scold. Instead he leaped about excitedly, chattering and grimacing. Numa, the lion, looked up; and then a strange thing occurred. The monkey ceased its chattering and voiced a low, peculiar sound. The eyes of the lion, that had been glaring balefully upward, took on a new and almost gentle expression. He arched his back and rubbed his side luxuriously against the bole of the tree, and from those savage jaws came a soft, purring sound. Then little Nkima dropped quickly downward through the foliage of the tree, gave a final nimble leap, and alighted upon the thick mane of the king of beasts.

2

The Hindu

WITH THE COMING of a new day came a new activity to the camp of the conspirators. Now were the Bedaùwy drinking no coffee in the múk'aad; the cards of the whites were put away and the Galla warriors played no longer at minkala.

Zveri sat behind his folding camp table directing his aides and with the assistance of Zora and Raghunath Jafar issued ammunition to the file of armed men marching past them. Miguel Romero and the two remaining whites were supervising the distribution of loads among the porters. Savage black Kitembo moved constantly among his men, hastening laggards from belated breakfast fires and forming those who had received their ammunition into companies. Abu Batn, the sheik, squatted aloof with his sun-bitten warriors. They, always ready, watched with contempt the disorderly preparations of their companions.

"How many are you leaving to guard the camp?" asked Zora.

"You and Comrade Jafar will remain in charge here," replied Zveri. "Your boys and ten askaris also will remain as camp guard."

"That will be plenty," replied the girl. "There is no danger."

"No," agreed Zveri, "not now, but if that Tarzan were here it would be different. I took pains to assure myself as to that before I chose this region for our base camp, and I have learned that he has been absent for a great while—went on some fool dirigible expedition that has never been heard from. It is almost certain that he is dead."

When the last of the blacks had received his issue of ammunition, Kitembo assembled his tribesmen at a little distance from the rest of the expedition and harangued them in a low voice. They were Basembos, and Kitembo, their chief, spoke to them in the dialect of their people.

Kitembo hated all whites. The British had occupied the land that had been the home of his people since before the memory of man; and because Kitembo, hereditary chief, had been irreconcilable to the domination of the invaders they had deposed him, elevating a puppet to the chieftaincy.

To Kitembo, the chief—savage, cruel, and treacherous—all whites were anathema, but he saw in his connection with Zveri an opportunity to be avenged upon the British; and so he had gathered about him many of his tribesmen and enlisted in the expedition that Zveri promised him would rid the land forever of the British and restore Kitembo to even greater power and glory than had formerly been the lot of Basembo chiefs.

It was not, however, always easy for Kitembo to hold the interest of his people in this undertaking. The British had greatly undermined his power and influence, so that warriors, who formerly might have been as subservient to his will as slaves, now dared openly to question his authority. There had been no demur so long as the expedition entailed no greater hardships than short marches, pleasant camps, and plenty of food, with West Coast blacks, and members of other tribes less warlike than the Basembos, to act as porters, carry the loads, and do all of the heavy work; but now, with fighting looming ahead, some of his people had desired to know just what they were going to get out of it, having, apparently, little stomach for risking their hides for the gratification of the ambitions or hatreds of either the white Zveri or the black Kitembo.

It was for the purpose of mollifying these malcontents that Kitembo was now haranguing his warriors, promising them loot on the one hand and ruthless punishment on the other as a choice between obedience and mutiny. Some of the rewards he dangled before their imaginations might have caused Zveri and

the other white members of the expedition considerable pertur-
bation could they have understood the Basembo dialect; but
perhaps a greater argument for obedience to his commands
was the genuine fear that most of his followers still entertained
for their pitiless chieftain.

Among the other blacks of the expedition were outlaw
members of several tribes and a considerable number of porters
hired in the ordinary manner to accompany what was officially
described as a scientific expedition.

Abu Batn and his warriors were animated to temporary loyalty to Zveri by two motives—a lust for loot and hatred for all
Nasrâny as represented by the British influence in Egypt and
out into the desert, which they considered their hereditary
domain.

The members of other races accompanying Zveri were
assumed to be motivated by noble, humanitarian aspirations;
but it was, nevertheless, true that their leader spoke to them
more often of the acquisition of personal riches and power than
of the advancement of the brotherhood of man or the rights of
the proletariat.

It was, then, such a loosely knit, but nonetheless formidable
expedition, that set forth this lovely morning upon the sack of
the treasure vaults of mysterious Opar.

As Zora Drinov watched them depart, her beautiful, in-
scrutable eyes remained fixed steadfastly upon the person of
Peter Zveri until he had disappeared from view along the river
trail that led into the dark forest.

Was it a maid watching in trepidation the departure of her
lover upon a mission fraught with danger, or—

"Perhaps he will not return," said an oily voice at her
shoulder.

The girl turned her head to look into the half-closed eyes of
Raghunath Jafar. "He will return, Comrade," she said. "Peter
Zveri always returns to me."

"You are very sure of him," said the man, with a leer.

"It is written," replied the girl as she started to move toward
her tent.

"Wait," said Jafar.

She stopped and turned toward him. "What do you want?" she asked.

"You," he replied. "What do you see in that uncouth swine, Zora? What does he know of love or beauty? I can appreciate you, beautiful flower of the morning. With me you may attain the transcendent bliss of perfect love, for I am an adept in the cult of love. A beast like Zveri would only degrade you."

The sickening disgust that the girl felt she hid from the eyes of the man, for she realized that the expedition might be gone for days and that during that time she and Jafar would be practically alone together, except for a handful of savage black warriors whose attitude toward a matter of this nature between an alien woman and an alien man she could not anticipate; but she was nonetheless determined to put a definite end to his advances.

"You are playing with death, Jafar," she said quietly. "I am here upon no mission of love, and if Zveri should learn of what you have said to me he would kill you. Do not speak to me again on this subject."

"It will not be necessary," replied the Hindu, enigmatically. His half-closed eyes were fixed steadily upon those of the girl. For perhaps less than half a minute the two stood thus, while there crept through Zora Drinov a sense of growing weakness, a realization of approaching capitulation. She fought against it, pitting her will against that of the man. Suddenly she tore her eyes from his. She had won, but victory left her weak and trembling as might be one who had but just experienced a stubbornly contested physical encounter. Turning quickly away, she moved swiftly toward her tent, not daring to look back for fear that she might again encounter those twin pools of vicious and malignant power that were the eyes of Raghunath Jafar; and so she did not see the oily smile of satisfaction that twisted the sensuous lips of the Hindu, nor did she hear his whispered repetition—"It will not be necessary."

As the expedition wound along the trail that leads to the foot of the barrier cliffs that hem the lower frontier of the arid plateau beyond which stand the ancient ruins that are Opar,

Wayne Colt, far to the west, pushed on toward the base camp of the conspirators. To the south, a little monkey rode upon the back of a great lion, shrilling insults now with perfect impunity at every jungle creature that crossed their path; while, with equal contempt for all lesser creatures, the mighty carnivore strode haughtily downwind, secure in the knowledge of his unquestioned might. A herd of antelope, grazing in his path, caught the acrid scent of the cat and moved nervously about; but when he came within sight of them they trotted only a short distance to one side, making a path for him; and, while he was still in sight, they resumed their feeding, for Numa, the lion, had fed well and the herbivores knew, as creatures of the wild know many things that are beyond the dull sensibilities of man, and felt no fear of Numa with a full belly.

To others, yet far off, came the scent of the lion; and they, too, moved nervously, though their fear was less than had been the first fear of the antelopes. These others were the great apes of the tribe of To-yat, whose mighty bulls had little cause to fear even Numa himself, though their shes and their balus might well tremble.

As the cat approached, the Mangani became more restless and more irritable. To-yat, the king ape, beat his breast and bared his great fighting fangs. Ga-yat, his powerful shoulders hunched, moved to the edge of the herd nearest the approaching danger. Zu-tho thumped a warning menace with his calloused feet. The shes called their balus to them, and many took to the lower branches of the larger trees or sought positions close to an arborial avenue of escape.

It was at this moment that an almost naked white man dropped from the dense foliage of a tree and alighted in their midst. Taut nerves and short tempers snapped. Roaring and snarling, the herd rushed upon the rash and hated man-thing. The king ape was in the lead.

"To-yat has a short memory," said the man in the tongue of the Mangani.

For an instant the ape paused, surprised perhaps to hear the language of his kind issuing from the lips of a man-thing. "I am To-yat!" he growled. "I kill."

"I am Tarzan," replied the man, "mighty hunter, mighty fighter. I come in peace."

"Kill! Kill!" roared To-yat, and the other great bulls advanced, bare-fanged, menacingly.

"Zu-tho! Ga-yat!" snapped the man, "it is I, Tarzan of the Apes"; but the bulls were nervous and frightened now, for the scent of Numa was strong in their nostrils, and the shock of Tarzan's sudden appearance had plunged them into a panic.

"Kill! Kill!" they bellowed, though as yet they did not charge, but advanced slowly, working themselves into the necessary frenzy of rage that would terminate in a sudden, blood-mad rush that no living creature might withstand and which would leave naught but torn and bloody fragments of the object of their wrath.

And then a shrill scream broke from the lips of a great, hairy mother with a tiny balu on her back. "Numa!" she shrieked, and, turning, fled into the safety of the foliage of a nearby tree.

Instantly the shes and balus remaining upon the ground took to the trees. The bulls turned their attention for a moment from the man to the new menace. What they saw upset what little equanimity remained to them. Advancing straight toward them, his round, yellow-green eyes blazing in ferocity, was a mighty, yellow lion; and upon his back perched a little monkey, screaming insults at them. The sight was too much for the apes of To-yat, and the king was the first to break before it. With a roar, the ferocity of which may have salved his self-esteem, he leaped for the nearest tree; and instantly the others broke and fled, leaving the white giant to face the angry lion alone.

With blazing eyes the king of beasts advanced upon the man, his head lowered and flattened, his tail extended, the brush flicking. The man spoke a single word in a low tone that might have carried but a few yards. Instantly the head of the lion came up, the horrid glare died in his eyes; and at the same instant the little monkey, voicing a shrill scream of recognition and delight, leaped over Numa's head and in three prodigious bounds was upon the shoulder of the man, his little arms encircling the bronzed neck.

"Little Nkima!" whispered Tarzan, the soft cheek of the monkey pressed against his own.

The lion strode majestically forward. He sniffed the bare legs of the man, rubbed his head against his side and lay down at his feet.

"Jad-bal-ja!" greeted the ape man.

The great apes of the tribe of To-yat watched from the safety of the trees. Their panic and their anger had subsided. "It is Tarzan," said Zu-tho.

"Yes, it is Tarzan," echoed Ga-yat.

To-yat grumbled. He did not like Tarzan, but he feared him; and now, with this new evidence of the power of the great Tarmangani, he feared him even more.

For a time Tarzan listened to the glib chattering of little Nkima. He learned of the strange Tarmangani and the many Gomangani warriors who had invaded the domain of the Lord of the Jungle.

The great apes moved restlessly in the trees, wishing to descend; but they feared Numa, and the great bulls were too heavy to travel in safety upon the high-flung leafy trails along which the lesser apes might pass with safety, and so could not depart until Numa had gone.

"Go away!" cried To-yat, the king. "Go away, and leave the Mangani in peace."

"We are going," replied the ape-man, "but you need not fear either Tarzan or the Golden Lion. We are your friends. I have told Jad-bal-ja that he is never to harm you. You may descend."

"We shall stay in the trees until he has gone," said To-yat; "he might forget."

"You are afraid," said Tarzan contemptuously. "Zu-tho or Ga-yat would not be afraid."

"Zu-tho is afraid of nothing," boasted that great bull.

Without a word Ga-yat climbed ponderously from the tree in which he had taken refuge and, if not with marked enthusiasm, at least with slight hesitation, advanced toward Tarzan and Jad-bal-ja, the Golden Lion. His fellows eyed him intently, momentarily expecting to see him charged and mauled by the yellow-eyed destroyer that lay at Tarzan's feet watching every move of the shaggy bull. The Lord of the Jungle also watched great Numa, for none knew better than he that a lion, however accustomed to obey his master, is still a lion. The years of their companionship, since Jad-bal-ja had been a little, spotted, fluffy ball, had never given him reason to doubt the loyalty of the carnivore, though there had been times when he had found it both difficult and dangerous to thwart some of the beast's more ferocious hereditary instincts.

Ga-yat approached, while little Nkima scolded and chattered from the safety of his master's shoulder; and the lion, blinking lazily, finally looked away. The danger, if there had been any, was over—it is the fixed, intent gaze of the lion that bodes ill.

Tarzan advanced and laid a friendly hand upon the shoulder of the ape. "This is Ga-yat," he said addressing Jad-bal-ja, "friend of Tarzan; do not harm him." He did not speak in any language of man. Perhaps the medium of communication that he used might not properly be called a language at all, but the lion and the great ape and the little Manu understood him.

"Tell the Mangani that Tarzan is the friend of little Nkima," shrilled the monkey. "He must not harm little Nkima."

"It is as Nkima has said," the ape-man assured Ga-yat.

"The friends of Tarzan are the friends of Ga-yat," replied the great ape.

"It is well," said Tarzan, "and now I go. Tell To-yat and the others what we have said and tell them also that there are strange men in this country which is Tarzan's. Let them watch them, but do not let the men see them, for these are bad men, perhaps, who carry the thunder sticks that hurl death with smoke and fire and a great noise. Tarzan goes now to see why these men are in his country."

Zora Drinov had avoided Jafar since the departure of the expedition to Opar. Scarcely had she left her tent, feigning a headache as an excuse, nor had the Hindu made any attempt to invade her privacy. Thus passed the first day. Upon the morning of the second Jafar summoned the head man of the askaris that had been left to guard them and to procure meat.

"Today," said Raghunath Jafar, "would be a good day to

hunt. The signs are propitious. Go, therefore, into the forest, taking all your men, and do not return until the sun is low in the west. If you do this there will be presents for you, besides all the meat you can eat from the carcasses of your kills. Do you understand?"

"Yes, Bwana," replied the black.

"Take with you the boy of the woman. He will not be needed here. My boy will remain to cook for us."

"Perhaps he will not come," suggested the Negro.

"You are many, he is only one; but do not let the woman know that you are taking him."

"What are the presents?" demanded the head man.

"A piece of cloth and cartridges," replied Jafar.

"And the curved sword that you carry when we are on the march."

"No," said Jafar.

"This is not a good day to hunt," replied the black, turning away.

"Two pieces of cloth and fifty cartridges," suggested Jafar.

"And the curved sword," and thus, after much haggling, the bargain was made.

The head man gathered his askaris and bade them prepare for the hunt, saying that the brown bwana had so ordered, but he said nothing about any presents. When they were ready, he dispatched one to summon the white woman's servant.

"You are to accompany us on the hunt," he said to the boy.

"Who said so?" demanded Wamala.

"The brown bwana," replied Kahiya, the head man.

Wamala laughed. "I take my orders from my mistress—not from the brown bwana."

Kahiya leaped upon him and clapped a rough palm across his mouth as two of his men seized Wamala upon either side. "You take your orders from Kahiya," he said. Hunting spears were pressed against the boy's trembling body. "Will you go upon the hunt with us?" demanded Kahiya.

"I go," replied Wamala. "I did but joke."

As Zveri led his expedition toward Opar, Wayne Colt, impatient to join the main body of the conspirators, urged his men to greater speed in their search for the camp. The principal conspirators had entered Africa at different points that they might not arouse too much attention by their numbers. Pursuant to this plan Colt had landed on the west coast and had traveled inland a short distance by train to railhead, from which point he had had a long and arduous journey on foot; so that now, with his destination almost in sight, he was anxious to put a period to this part of his adventure. Then, too, he was curious to meet the other principals in this hazardous undertaking, Peter Zveri being the only one with whom he was acquainted.

The young American was not unmindful of the great risks he was inviting in affiliating himself with an expedition which aimed at the peace of Europe and at the ultimate control of a large section of Northeastern Africa through the disaffection by propaganda of large and warlike native tribes, especially in view of the fact that much of their operation must be carried on within British territory, where British power was considerably more than a mere gesture. But, being young and enthusiastic, however misguided, these contingencies did not weigh heavily upon his spirits, which, far from being depressed, were upon the contrary eager and restless for action.

The tedium of the journey from the coast had been unrelieved by pleasurable or adequate companionship, since the childish mentality of Tony could not rise above a muddy conception of Philippine independence and a consideration of the fine clothes he was going to buy when, by some vaguely visualized economic process, he was to obtain his share of the Ford and Rockefeller fortunes.

However, notwithstanding Tony's mental shortcomings, Colt was genuinely fond of the youth and as between the companionship of the Filipino or Zveri, he would have chosen the former, his brief acquaintance with the Russian in New York and San Francisco having convinced him that as a playfellow he left everything to be desired; nor had he any reason to anticipate that he would find any more congenial associates among the conspirators.

Plodding doggedly onward, Colt was only vaguely aware of the now familiar sights and sounds of the jungle, both of which by this time, it must be admitted, had considerably palled upon him. Even had he taken particular note of the latter, it is to be doubted that his untrained ear would have caught the persistent chatter of a little monkey that followed in the trees behind him; nor would this have particularly impressed him, unless he had been able to know that this particular little monkey rode upon the shoulder of a bronzed Apollo of the forest, who moved silently in his wake along a leafy highway of the lower terraces.

Tarzan had guessed that perhaps this white man, upon whose trail he had come unexpectedly, was making his way toward the main camp of the party of strangers for which the Lord of the Jungle was searching; and so, with the persistence and patience of the savage stalker of the jungle, he followed Wayne Colt; while little Nkima, riding upon his shoulder, berated his master for not immediately destroying the Tarmangani and all his party, for little Nkima was a bloodthirsty soul when the spilling of blood was to be accomplished by someone else.

And while Colt impatiently urged his men to greater speed and Tarzan followed and Nkima scolded, Raghunath Jafar approached the tent of Zora Drinov. As his figure darkened the entrance, casting a shadow across the book she was reading, the girl looked up from the cot upon which she was lying.

The Hindu smiled his oily, ingratiating smile. "I came to see if your headache was better," he said.

"Thank you, no," said the girl coldly; "but perhaps with undisturbed rest I may be better soon."

Ignoring the suggestion, Jafar entered the tent and seated himself in a camp chair. "I find it lonely," he said, "since the others have gone. Do you not also?"

"No," replied Zora. "I am quite content to be alone and resting."

"Your headache developed very suddenly," said Jafar. "A short time ago you seemed quite well and animated."

The girl made no reply. She was wondering what had become of her boy, Wamala, and why he had disregarded her explicit instructions to permit no one to disturb her. Perhaps Raghunath Jafar read her thoughts, for to East Indians are often attributed uncanny powers, however little warranted such a belief may be. However that may be, his next words suggested the possibility.

"Wamala has gone hunting with the askaris," he said.

"I gave him no such permission," said Zora.

"I took the liberty of doing so," said Jafar.

"You had no right," said the girl angrily, sitting up upon the edge of her cot. "You have presumed altogether too far, Comrade Jafar."

"Wait a moment, my dear," said the Hindu soothingly. "Let us not quarrel. As you know, I love you and love does not find confirmation in crowds. Perhaps I have presumed, but it was only for the purpose of giving me an opportunity to plead my cause without interruption; and then, too, as you know, all is fair in love and war."

"Then we may consider this as war," said the girl, "for it certainly is not love, either upon your side or upon mine. There is another word to describe what animates you, Comrade Jafar, and that which animates me now is loathing. I could not abide you if you were the last man on earth, and when Zveri returns, I promise you that there shall be an accounting."

"Long before Zveri returns I shall have taught you to love me," said the Hindu, passionately. He arose and came toward her. The girl leaped to her feet, looking about quickly for a weapon of defense. Her cartridge belt and revolver hung over the chair in which Jafar had been sitting, and her rifle was upon the opposite side of the tent.

"You are quite unarmed," said the Hindu; "I took particular note of that when I entered the tent. Nor will it do you any good to call for help; for there is no one in camp but you, and me, and my boy and he knows that, if he values his life, he is not to come here unless I call him."

"You are a beast," said the girl.

"Why not be reasonable, Zora?" demanded Jafar. "It would not harm you any to be kind to me, and it will make it very much easier for you. Zveri need know nothing of it, and once we are back in civilization again, if you still feel that you do not wish to remain with me I shall not try to hold you; but I am sure that I can teach you to love me and that we shall be very happy together."

"Get out!" ordered the girl. There was neither fear nor hysteria in her voice. It was very calm and level and controlled. To a man not entirely blinded by passion, that might have meant something—it might have meant a grim determination to carry self-defense to the very length of death—but Raghunath Jafar saw only the woman of his desire, and stepping quickly forward he seized her.

Zora Drinov was young and lithe and strong, yet she was no match for the burly Hindu, whose layers of greasy fat belied the great physical strength beneath them. She tried to wrench herself free and escape from the tent, but he held her and dragged her back. Then she turned upon him in a fury and struck him repeatedly in the face, but he only enveloped her more closely in his embrace and bore her backward upon the cot.

3

Out of the Grave

WAYNE COLT'S GUIDE, who had been slightly in advance of the American, stopped suddenly and looked back with a broad smile. Then he pointed ahead. "The camp, Bwana!" he exclaimed triumphantly.

"Thank the Lord!" exclaimed Colt with a sigh of relief.

"It is deserted," said the guide.

"It does look that way, doesn't it?" agreed Colt. "Let's have a look around," and, followed by his men, he moved in among the tents. His tired porters threw down their loads and, with the askaris, sprawled at full length beneath the shade of the trees, while Colt, followed by Tony, commenced an investigation of the camp.

Almost immediately the young American's attention was attracted by the violent shaking of one of the tents. "There is someone or something in there," he said to Tony, as he walked briskly toward the entrance.

The sight within that met his eyes brought a sharp ejaculation to his lips—a man and woman struggling upon the ground, the former choking the bare throat of his victim while the girl struck feebly at his face with clenched fists.

So engrossed was Jafar in his unsuccessful attempt to subdue the girl that he was unaware of Colt's presence until a heavy hand fell upon his shoulder and he was jerked violently aside.

Consumed by maniacal fury, he leaped to his feet and struck at the American only to be met with a blow that sent him reeling backward. Again he charged and again he was struck heavily upon the face. This time he went to the ground, and as he staggered to his feet, Colt seized him, wheeled him around and hurtled him through the entrance of the tent, accelerating his departure with a well-timed kick. "If he tries to come back, Tony, shoot him," he snapped at the Filipino, and then turned to assist the girl to her feet. Half carrying her, he laid her on the cot and then, finding water in a bucket, bathed her forehead, her throat, and her wrists.

Outside the tent Raghunath Jafar saw the porters and the askaris lying in the shade of a tree. He also saw Antonio Mori with a determined scowl upon his face and a revolver in his hand, and with an angry imprecation he turned and made his way toward his own tent, his face livid with anger and murder in his heart.

Presently Zora Drinov opened her eyes and looked up into the solicitous face of Wayne Colt, bending over her.

From the leafy seclusion of a tree above the camp, Tarzan of the Apes overlooked the scene below. A single, whispered syllable had silenced Nkima's scolding. Tarzan had noted the violent shaking of the tent that had attracted Colt's attention, and he had seen the precipitate ejection of the Hindu from its interior and the menacing attitude of the Filipino preventing Jafar's return to the conflict. These matters were of little interest to the ape-man. The quarrelings and defections of these people did not even arouse his curiosity. What he wished to learn was the reason for their presence here, and for the purpose of obtaining this information he had two plans. One was to keep them under constant surveillance until their acts divulged that which he wished to know. The other was to determine definitely the head of the expedition and then to enter the camp and demand the information he desired. But this he would not do until he had obtained sufficient information to give him an advantage. What was going on within the tent he did not know, nor did he care.

For several seconds after she opened her eyes Zora Drinov gazed intently into those of the man bent upon her. "You must be the American," she said finally.

"I am Wayne Colt," he replied, "and I take it from the fact that you guessed my identity that this is Comrade Zveri's camp."

She nodded. "You came just in time, Comrade Colt," she said.

"Thank God for that," he said.

"There is no God," she reminded him.

Colt flushed. "We are creatures of heredity and habit," he explained.

Zora Drinov smiled. "That is true," she said, "but it is our business to break a great many bad habits not only for ourselves, but for the entire world."

Since he had laid her upon the cot, Colt had been quietly appraising the girl. He had not known that there was a white woman in Zveri's camp, but had he it is certain that he would not have anticipated one at all like this girl. He would rather have visualized a female agitator capable of accompanying a band of men to the heart of Africa as a coarse and unkempt peasant woman of middle age; but this girl, from her head of glorious, wavy hair to her small well-shaped foot, suggested the antithesis of a peasant origin and, far from being unkempt, was as trig and smart as it were possible for a woman to be under such circumstances and, in addition, she was young and beautiful.

"Comrade Zveri is absent from camp?" he asked.

"Yes, he is away on a short expedition."

"And there is no one to introduce us to one another?" he asked, with a smile.

"Oh, pardon me," she said. "I am Zora Drinov."

"I had not anticipated such a pleasant surprise," said Colt. "I expected to find nothing but uninteresting men like myself. And who was the fellow I interrupted?"

"That was Raghunath Jafar, a Hindu."

"He is one of us?" asked Colt.

"Yes," replied the girl, "but not for long—not after Peter Zveri returns."

"You mean—?"

"I mean that Peter will kill him."

Colt shrugged. "It is what he deserves," he said. "Perhaps I should have done it."

"No," said the girl, "leave that for Peter."

"Were you left alone here in this camp without any protection?" demanded Colt.

"No. Peter left my boy and ten askaris, but in some way Jafar got them all out of camp."

"You will be safe now," he said. "I shall see to that until Comrade Zveri returns. I am going now to make my camp, and I shall send two of my askaris to stand guard before your tent."

"That is good of you," she said, "but I think now that you are here it will not be necessary."

"I shall do it anyway," he said. "I shall feel safer."

"And when you have made camp, will you come and have supper with me?" she asked, and then, "Oh, I forgot, Jafar has sent my boy away, too. There is no one to cook for me."

"Then, perhaps, you will dine with me," he said. "My boy is a fairly good cook."

"I shall be delighted, Comrade Colt," she replied.

As the American left the tent, Zora Drinov lay back upon the cot with half-closed eyes. How different the man had been from what she had expected. Recalling his features, and especially his eyes, she found it difficult to believe that such a man could be a traitor to his father or to his country, but then, she realized, many a man has turned against his own for a principle. With her own people it was different. They had never had a chance. They had always been ground beneath the heel of one tyrant or another. What they were doing they believed implicitly to be for their own and for their country's good. Among those of them who were motivated by honest conviction there could not fairly be brought any charge of treason, and yet, Russian though she was to the core, she could not help but look with contempt upon the citizens of other countries who turned against their governments to aid the ambitions of a foreign power. We may be willing to profit by the act of foreign mercenaries and traitors, but we cannot admire them.

As Colt crossed from Zora's tent to where his men lay to give the necessary instructions for the making of his camp, Raghunath Jafar watched him from the interior of his own tent. A malignant scowl clouded the countenance of the Hindu, and hatred smoldered in his eyes.

Tarzan, watching from above, saw the young American issuing instructions to his men. The personality of this young stranger had impressed Tarzan favorably. He liked him as well as he could like any stranger, for deeply ingrained in the fiber of the ape-man was the wild beast suspicion of all strangers and especially of all white strangers. As he watched him now nothing else within the range of his vision escaped him. It was thus that he saw Raghunath Jafar emerge from his tent, carrying a rifle. Only Tarzan and little Nkima saw this, and only Tarzan placed any sinister interpretation upon it.

Raghunath Jafar walked directly away from camp and entered the jungle. Swinging silently through the trees, Tarzan of the Apes followed him. Jafar made a half circle of the camp just within the concealing verdure of the jungle, and then he halted. From where he stood the entire camp was visible to him, but his own position was concealed by foliage.

Colt was watching the disposition of his loads and the pitching of his tent. His men were busy with the various duties assigned to them by their headman. They were tired and there was little talking. For the most part they worked in silence, and an unusual quiet pervaded the scene—a quiet that was suddenly and unexpectedly shattered by an anguished scream and the report of a rifle, blending so closely that it was impossible to say which had preceded the other. A bullet whizzed by Colt's head and nipped the lobe off the ear of one of his men standing behind him. Instantly the peaceful activities of the camp were supplanted by pandemonium. For a moment there was a difference of opinion as to the direction from which the shot and the scream had come, and then Colt saw a wisp of smoke rising from the jungle just beyond the edge of camp.

"There it is," he said, and started toward the point.

The headman of the askaris stopped him. "Do not go, Bwana," he said. "Perhaps it is an enemy. Let us fire into the jungle first."

"No," said Colt, "we will investigate first. Take some of your men in from the right, and I'll take the rest in from the left. We'll work around slowly through the jungle until we meet."

"Yes, Bwana," said the headman, and calling his men he gave the necessary instructions.

No sound of flight or any suggestion of a living presence greeted the two parties as they entered the jungle; nor had they discovered any signs of a marauder when, a few moments later, they made contact with one another. They were now formed in a half circle that bent back into the jungle and, at a word from Colt, they advanced toward the camp.

It was Colt who found Raghunath Jafar lying dead just at the edge of camp. His right hand grasped his rifle. Protruding from his heart was the shaft of a sturdy arrow.

The Negroes gathering around the corpse looked at one another questioningly and then back into the jungle and up into the trees. One of them examined the arrow. "It is not like any arrow I have ever seen," he said. "It was not made by the hand of man."

Immediately the blacks were filled with superstitious fears. "The shot was meant for the bwana," said one; "therefore the demon who shot the arrow is a friend of our bwana. We need not be afraid."

This explanation satisfied the blacks, but it did not satisfy

Wayne Colt. He was puzzling over it as he walked back into camp, after giving orders that the Hindu be buried.

Zora Drinov was standing in the entrance to her tent, and as she saw him she came to meet him. "What was it?" she asked. "What happened?"

"Comrade Zveri will not kill Raghunath Jafar," he said.

"Why?" she asked.

"Because Raghunath Jafar is already dead."

"Who could have shot the arrow?" she asked, after he had told her of the manner of the Hindu's death.

"I haven't the remotest idea," he admitted. "It is an absolute mystery, but it means that the camp is being watched and that we must be very careful not to go into the jungle alone. The men believe that the arrow was fired to save me from an assassin's bullet; and while it is entirely possible that Jafar may have been intending to kill me, I believe that if I had gone into the jungle alone instead of him it would have been I that would be lying out there dead now. Have you been bothered at all by natives since you made camp here, or have you had any unpleasant experiences with them at all?"

"We have not seen a native since we entered this camp. We have often commented upon the fact that the country seems to be entirely deserted and uninhabited, notwithstanding the fact that it is filled with game."

"This thing may help to account for the fact that it is uninhabited," suggested Colt, "or rather apparently uninhabited. We may have unintentionally invaded the country of some unusually ferocious tribe that takes this means of acquainting newcomers with the fact that they are persona non grata."

"You say one of our men was wounded?" asked Zora.

"Nothing serious. He just had his ear nicked a little."

"Was he near you?"

"He was standing right behind me," replied Colt.

"I think there is no doubt that Jafar meant to kill you," said Zora.

"Perhaps," said Colt, "but he did not succeed. He did not even kill my appetite; and if I can succeed in calming the excitement of my boy, we shall have supper presently."

From a distance Tarzan and Nkima watched the burial of Raghunath Jafar and a little later saw the return of Kahiya and his askaris with Zora's boy Wamala, who had been sent out of camp by Jafar.

"Where," said Tarzan to Nkima, "are all the many Tarmangani and Gomangani that you told me were in this camp?"

"They have taken their thundersticks and gone away," replied the little Manu. "They are hunting for Nkima."

Tarzan of the Apes smiled one of his rare smiles. "We shall have to hunt them down and find out what they are about, Nkima," he said.

"But it grows dark in the jungle soon," pleaded Nkima, "and then will Sabor, and Sheeta, and Numa, and Histah be abroad, and they, too, search for little Nkima."

Darkness had fallen before Colt's boy announced supper, and in the meantime Tarzan, changing his plans, had returned to the trees above the camp. He was convinced that there was something irregular in the aims of the expedition whose base he had discovered. He knew from the size of the camp that it had contained many men. Where they had gone and for what purpose were matters that he must ascertain. Feeling that this expedition, whatever its purpose, might naturally be a principal topic of conversation in the camp, he sought a point of vantage wherefrom he might overhear the conversations that passed between the two white members of the party beneath him; and so it was that as Zora Drinov and Wayne Colt seated themselves at the supper table, Tarzan of the Apes crouched amid the foliage of a great tree just above them.

"You have passed through a rather trying ordeal today," said Colt, "but you do not appear to be any the worse for it. I should think that your nerves would be shaken."

"I have passed through too much already in my life, Comrade Colt, to have any nerves left at all," replied the girl.

"I suppose so," said Colt. "You must have passed through the revolution in Russia."

"I was only a little girl at the time," she explained, "but I remember it quite distinctly."

Colt was gazing at her intently. "From your appearance,"

he ventured, "I imagine that you were not by birth of the proletariat."

"My father was a laborer. He died in exile under the Tzarist regime. That was how I learned to hate everything monarchistic and capitalistic. And when I was offered this opportunity to join Comrade Zveri, I saw another field in which to encompass my revenge, while at the same time advancing the interests of my class throughout the world."

"When I last saw Zveri in the United States," said Colt, "he evidently had not formulated the plans he is now carrying out, as he never mentioned any expedition of this sort. When I received orders to join him here, none of the details was imparted to me; and so I am rather in the dark as to what his purpose is."

"It is only for good soldiers to obey," the girl reminded him.

"Yes, I know that," agreed Colt, "but at the same time even a poor soldier may act more intelligently sometimes if he knows the objective."

"The general plan, of course, is no secret to any of us here," said Zora, "and I shall betray no confidence in explaining it to you. It is a part of a larger plan to embroil the capitalistic powers in wars and revolutions to such an extent that they will be helpless to unite against us.

"Our emissaries have been laboring for a long time toward the culmination of the revolution in India that will distract the attention and the armed forces of Great Britain. We are not succeeding so well in Mexico as we had planned, but there is still hope, while our prospects in the Philippines are very bright. The conditions in China you well know. She is absolutely helpless, and we have hope that with our assistance she will eventually constitute a real menace to Japan. Italy is a very dangerous enemy, and it is largely for the purpose of embroiling her in war with France that we are here."

"But just how can that be accomplished in Africa?" asked Colt.

"Comrade Zveri believes that it will be simple," said the girl. "The suspicion and jealousy that exist between France and Italy are well known; their race for naval supremacy amounts almost to a scandal. At the first overt act of either against the other, war might easily result, and a war between Italy and France would embroil all of Europe."

"But just how can Zveri, operating in the wilds of Africa, embroil Italy and France in war?" demanded the American.

"There is now in Rome a delegation of French and Italian Reds engaged in this very business. The poor men know only a part of the plan and, unfortunately for them, it will be necessary to martyr them in the cause for the advancement of our world plan. They have been furnished with papers outlining a plan for the invasion of Italian Somaliland by French troops. At the proper time one of Comrade Zveri's secret agents in Rome will reveal the plot to the Fascist government; and almost simultaneously a considerable number of our own blacks, disguised in the uniforms of French native troops, led by the white men of our expedition, uniformed as French officers, will invade Italian Somaliland.

"In the meantime our agents are carrying on in Egypt and Abyssinia and among the native tribes of North Africa, and already we have definite assurance that with the attention of France and Italy distracted by war and Great Britain embarrassed by a revolution in India the natives of North Africa will arise in what will amount almost to a holy war for the purpose of throwing off the yoke of foreign domination and the establishment of autonomous soviet states throughout the entire area."

"A daring and stupendous undertaking," exclaimed Colt, "but one that will require enormous resources in money as well as men."

"It is Comrade Zveri's pet scheme," said the girl. "I do not know, of course, all the details of his organization and backing; but I do know that while he is already well financed for the initial operations, he is depending to a considerable extent upon this district for furnishing most of the necessary gold to carry on the tremendous operations that will be necessary to insure final success."

"Then I am afraid he is foredoomed to failure," said Colt, "for he surely cannot find enough wealth in this savage country to carry on any such stupendous program."

"Comrade Zveri believes to the contrary," said Zora; "in

fact, the expedition that he is now engaged upon is for the purpose of obtaining the treasure he seeks."

Above them, in the darkness, the silent figure of the ape-man lay stretched at ease upon a great branch, his keen ears absorbing all that passed between them, while curled in sleep upon his bronzed back lay little Nkima, entirely oblivious of the fact that he might have listened to words well calculated to shake the foundations of organized government throughout the world.

"And where," demanded Colt, "if it is no secret, does Comrade Zveri expect to find such a great store of gold?"

"In the famous treasure vaults of Opar," replied the girl. "You certainly must have heard of them."

"Yes," answered Colt, "but I never considered them other than purely legendary. The folklore of the entire world is filled with these mythical treasure vaults."

"But Opar is no myth," replied Zora.

If the startling information divulged to him affected Tarzan, it induced no outward manifestation. Listening in silence imperturbably, trained to the utmost refinement of self-control, he might have been part and parcel of the great branch upon which he lay, or of the shadowy foliage which hid him from view.

For a time Colt sat in silence, contemplating the stupendous possibilities of the plan that he had just heard unfolded. It seemed to him little short of the dream of a madman, and he did not believe that it had the slightest chance for success. What he did realize was the jeopardy in which it placed the members of the expedition, for he believed that there would be no escape for any of them once Great Britain, France and Italy were apprised of their activities; and, without conscious volition, his fears seemed centered upon the safety of the girl. He knew the type of people with whom he was working and so he knew that it would be dangerous to voice a doubt as to the practicability of the plan, for scarcely without exception the agitators whom he had met had fallen naturally into two separate categories, the impractical visionary, who believed everything that he wanted to believe, and the shrewd knave, actuated by motives of avarice, who hoped to profit either in power or riches by any change that he might be instrumental in bringing about in the established order of things. It seemed horrible that a young and beautiful girl should have been enticed into such a desperate situation. She seemed far too intelligent to be merely a brainless tool, and even his brief association with her made it most difficult for him to believe that she was a knave.

"The undertaking is certainly fraught with grave dangers," he said, "and as it is primarily a job for men I cannot understand why you were permitted to face the dangers and hardships that must of necessity be entailed by the carrying out of such a perilous campaign."

"The life of a woman is of no more value than that of a man," she declared, "and I was needed. There is always a great deal of important and confidential clerical work to be done which Comrade Zveri can entrust only to one in whom he has implicit confidence. He reposes such trust in me and, in addition, I am a trained typist and stenographer. Those reasons in themselves are sufficient to explain why I am here, but another very important one is that I desire to be with Comrade Zveri."

In the girl's words Colt saw the admission of a romance; but to his American mind this was all the greater reason why the girl should not have been brought along, for he could not conceive of a man exposing the girl he loved to such dangers.

Above them Tarzan of the Apes moved silently. First he reached over his shoulder and lifted little Nkima from his back. Nkima would have objected, but the veriest shadow of a whisper silenced him. The ape-man had various methods of dealing with enemies—methods that he had learned and practiced long before he had been cognizant of the fact that he was not an ape. Long before he had ever seen another white man he had terrorized the Gomangani, the black men of the forest and the jungle, and had learned that a long step toward defeating an enemy may be taken by first demoralizing its morale. He knew now that these people were not only the invaders of his own domain and, therefore, his own personal enemies, but that they threatened the peace of Great Britain, which was dear to him, and of the rest of the civilized world, with which, at least,

Tarzan had no quarrels. It is true that he held civilization in general in considerable contempt, but in even greater contempt he held those who interfered with the rights of others or with the established order of jungle or city.

As Tarzan left the tree in which he had been hiding, the two below him were no more aware of his departure than they had been of his presence. Colt found himself attempting to fathom the mystery of love. He knew Zveri, and it appeared inconceivable to him that a girl of Zora Drinov's type could be attracted by a man of Zveri's stamp. Of course, it was none of his affair, but it bothered him nevertheless because it seemed to constitute a reflection upon the girl and to lower her in his estimation. He was disappointed in her, and Colt did not like to be disappointed in people to whom he had been attracted.

"You knew Comrade Zveri in America, did you not?" asked Zora.

"Yes," replied Colt.

"What do you think of him?" she demanded.

"I found him a very forceful character," replied Colt. "I believe him to be a man who would carry on to a conclusion anything that he attempted. No better man could have been chosen for this mission."

If the girl had hoped to surprise Colt into an expression of personal regard or dislike for Zveri, she had failed, but if such was the fact she was too wise to pursue the subject further. She realized that she was dealing with a man from whom she would get little information that he did not wish her to have; but on the other hand a man who might easily wrest information from others, for he was that type which seemed to invite confidences, suggesting as he did, in his attitude, his speech, and his manner a sterling uprightness of character that could not conceivably abuse a trust. She rather liked this upstanding young American, and the more she saw of him the more difficult she found it to believe that he had turned traitor to his family, his friends, and his country. However, she knew that many honorable men had sacrificed everything to a conviction and, perhaps, he was one of these. She hoped that this was the explanation.

Their conversation drifted to various subjects—to their lives and experiences in their native lands—to the happenings that had befallen them since they had entered Africa, and, finally, to the experiences of the day. And while they talked, Tarzan of the Apes returned to the tree above them, but this time he did not come alone.

"I wonder if we shall ever know," she said, "who killed Jafar."

"It is a mystery that is not lessened by the fact that none of the askaris could recognize the type of arrow with which he was slain, though that, of course, might be accounted for by the fact that none of them are of this district."

"It has considerably shaken the nerves of the men," said Zora, "and I sincerely hope that nothing similar occurs again. I have found that it does not take much to upset these natives, and while most of them are brave in the face of known dangers, they are apt to be entirely demoralized by anything bordering on the supernatural."

"I think they felt better when they got the Hindu planted underground," said Colt, "though some of them were not at all sure that he might not return anyway."

"There is not much chance of that," rejoined the girl, laughing.

She had scarcely ceased speaking when the branches above them rustled, and a heavy body plunged downward to the table-top between them, crushing the flimsy piece of furniture to earth.

The two sprang to their feet, Colt whipping out his revolver and the girl stifling a cry as she stepped back. Colt felt the hairs rise upon his head and gooseflesh form upon his arms and back, for there between them lay the dead body of Raghunath Jafar upon its back, the dead eyes rolled backward staring up into the night.

4

Into the Lion's Den

NKIMA WAS ANGRY. He had been awakened from the depth of a sound sleep, which was bad enough, but now his master had set out upon such foolish errands through the darkness of the night that mingled with Nkima's scoldings were the whimperings of fear, for in every shadow he saw Sheeta, the panther, lurking and in each gnarled limb of the forest the likeness of Histah, the snake. While Tarzan had remained in the vicinity of the camp, Nkima had not been particularly perturbed, and when he had returned to the tree with his burden the little Manu was sure that he was going to remain there for the rest of the night; but instead he had departed immediately and now was swinging through the black forest with an evident fixity of purpose that boded ill for either rest or safety for little Nkima during the remainder of the night.

Whereas Zveri and his party had started slowly along winding jungle trails, Tarzan moved almost in an air line through the jungle toward his destination, which was the same as that of Zveri. The result was that before Zveri reached the almost perpendicular crag which formed the last and greatest natural barrier to the forbidden valley of Opar, Tarzan and Nkima had disappeared beyond the summit and were crossing the desolate valley, upon the far side of which loomed the great walls and lofty spires and turrets of ancient Opar. In the bright light of the African sun, domes and minarets shone red and gold above the city; and once again the ape-man experienced the same feeling that had impressed him upon the occasion, now years gone, when his eyes had first alighted upon the splendid panorama of mystery that had unfolded before them.

No evidence of ruin was apparent at this great distance. Once again, in imagination, he beheld a city of magnificent beauty, its streets and temples thronged with people; and once again his mind toyed with the mystery of the city's origin, when back somewhere in the dim vista of antiquity a race of rich and powerful people had conceived and built this enduring monument to a vanished civilization. It was possible to conceive that Opar might have existed when a glorious civilization flourished upon the great continent of Atlantis, which, sinking beneath the waves of the ocean, left this lost colony to death and decay.

That its few inhabitants were direct descendants of its once powerful builders seemed not unlikely in view of the rites and ceremonies of the ancient religion which they practiced, as well as by the fact that by scarcely any other hypothesis could the presence of a white-skinned people be accounted for in this remote inaccessible African vastness.

The peculiar laws of heredity, which seemed operative in Opar as in no other portion of the world, suggested an origin differing materially from that of other men; for it is a peculiar fact that the men of Opar bear little or no resemblance to the females of their kind. The former are short, heavyset, hairy, almost apelike in their conformation and appearance, while the women are slender, smooth skinned, and often beautiful. There were certain physical and mental attributes of the men that had suggested to Tarzan the possibility that at some time in the past the colonists had, either by choice or necessity, interbred with the great apes of the district; and he also was aware that owing to the scarcity of victims for the human sacrifice, which their rigid worship demanded, it was common practice among them to use for this purpose either males or females who deviated considerably from the standard time had established for each sex, with the result that through the laws of natural selection an overwhelming majority of the males would be grotesque and the females normal and beautiful.

It was with such reveries that the mind of the ape-man was occupied as he crossed the desolate valley of Opar, which lay shimmering in the bright sunlight that was relieved only by the shade of an occasional gnarled and stunted tree. Ahead of him and to his right was the small rocky hillock, upon the summit of which was located the outer entrance to the treasure vaults of Opar. But with this he was not now interested, his sole object being to forewarn La of the approach of the invaders that she might prepare her defense.

It had been long since Tarzan had visited Opar; but upon that last occasion, when he had restored La to her loyal people and reestablished her supremacy following the defeat of the forces of Cadj, the high priest, and the death of the latter beneath the fangs and talons of Jad-bal-ja, he had carried away with him for the first time a conviction of the friendliness of all of the people of Opar. He had for years known that La was secretly his friend, but her savage, grotesque retainers always heretofore had feared and hated him; and so it was now that he approached Opar as one might approach any citadel of one's friends, without stealth and without any doubt but that he would be received in friendship.

Nkima, however, was not so sure. The gloomy ruins terrified him. He scolded and pleaded, but all to no avail; and at last terror overcame his love and loyalty so that, as they were approaching the outer wall, which loomed high above them, he leaped from his master's shoulder and scampered away from the ruins that confronted him, for deep in his little heart was an abiding fear of strange and unfamiliar places, that not even his confidence in Tarzan could overcome.

Nkima's keen eyes had noted the rocky hillock which they had passed a short time before, and to the summit of this he scampered as a comparatively safe haven from which to await the return of his master from Opar.

As Tarzan approached the narrow fissure which alone gave entrance through the massive outer walls of Opar, he was conscious, as he had been years before on the occasion of his first approach to the city, of unseen eyes upon him, and at any moment he expected to hear a greeting when the watchers recognized him.

Without hesitation, however, and with no apprehensiveness, Tarzan entered the narrow cleft and descended a flight of concrete steps that led to the winding passage through the thick outer wall. The narrow court, beyond which loomed the inner wall, was silent and deserted; nor was the silence broken as he crossed it to another narrow passage which led through it; at the end of this he came to a broad avenue, upon the opposite side of which stood the crumbling ruins of the great temple of Opar.

In silence and solitude he entered the frowning portal, flanked by its rows of stately pillars, from the capitals of which grotesque birds glared down upon him as they had stared through all the countless ages since forgotten hands had carved them from the solid rock of the monoliths. On through the temple toward the inner courtyard, where he knew the activities of the city were carried on, Tarzan made his way in silence. Perhaps another man would have given notice of his coming, voicing a greeting to apprise them of his approach; but Tarzan of the Apes in many respects is less man than beast. He goes the silent way of most beasts, wasting no breath in useless mouthing. He had not sought to approach Opar stealthily, and he knew that he had not arrived unseen. Why a greeting was delayed he did not know, unless it was that, after carrying word of his coming to La, they were waiting for her instructions.

Through the main corridor Tarzan made his way, noting again the tables of gold with their ancient and long undeciphered hieroglyphics. Through the chamber of the seven golden pillars he passed and across the golden floor of an adjoining room, and still only silence and emptiness, yet with vague suggestions of figures moving in the galleries that overlooked the apartment through which he was passing; and then at last he came to a heavy door beyond which he was sure he would find either priests or priestesses of this great temple of the Flaming God. Fearlessly he pushed it open and stepped across the threshold, and in the same instant a knotted club descended heavily upon his head, felling him senseless to the floor.

Instantly he was surrounded by a score of gnarled and knotted men; their matted beards fell low upon their hairy chests as they rolled forward upon their short, crooked legs. They chattered in low, growling gutturals as they bound their victim's wrists and ankles with stout thongs, and then they lifted him and carried him along other corridors and through the crumbling glories of magnificent apartments to a great tiled room, at one end of which a young woman sat upon a massive throne, resting upon a dais a few feet above the level of the floor.

Standing beside the girl upon the throne was another of the gnarled and knotted men. Upon his arms and legs were bands of gold and about his throat many necklaces. Upon the floor beneath these two was a gathering of men and women— the priests and priestesses of the Flaming God of Opar.

Tarzan's captors carried their victim to the foot of the throne and tossed his body upon the tile floor. Almost simultaneously the ape-man regained consciousness and, opening his eyes, looked about him.

"Is it he?" demanded the girl upon the throne.

One of Tarzan's captors saw that he had regained consciousness and with the help of others dragged him roughly to his feet.

"It is he, Oah," exclaimed the man at her side.

An expression of venomous hatred convulsed the face of the woman. "God has been good to His high priestess," she said. "I have prayed for this day to come as I prayed for the other, and as the other came so has this."

Tarzan looked quickly from the woman to the man at her side. "What is the meaning of this, Dooth?" he demanded. "Where is La? Where is your high priestess?"

The girl rose angrily from her throne. "Know, man of the outer world, that I am high priestess. I, Oah, am high priestess of the Flaming God."

Tarzan ignored her. "Where is La?" he demanded again of Dooth.

Oah flew into a frenzy of rage. "She is dead!" she screamed, advancing to the edge of the dais as though to leap upon Tarzan, the jeweled handle of her sacrificial knife gleaming in the sunlight, which poured through a great aperture where a portion of the ancient roof of the throne room had fallen in. "She is dead!" she repeated. "Dead as you will be when next we honor the Flaming God with the lifeblood of a man. La was weak. She loved you, and thus she betrayed her God, who had chosen you for sacrifice. But Oah is strong—strong with the hate she has nursed in her breast since Tarzan and La stole the throne of Opar from her. Take him away!" she screamed to his captors, "and let me not see him again until I behold him bound to the altar in the court of sacrifice."

They cut the bonds now that secured Tarzan's ankles so that he might walk; but even though his wrists were tied behind him it was evident that they still held him in great fear, for they put ropes about his neck and his arms and led him as man might lead a lion. Down into the familiar darkness of the pits of Opar they led him, lighting the way with torches; and when finally they had brought him to the dungeon in which he was to be confined it was some time before they could muster sufficient courage to cut the bonds that held his wrists, and even then they did not do so until they had again bound his ankles securely so that they might escape from the chamber and bolt the door before he could release his feet and pursue them. Thus greatly had the prowess of Tarzan impressed itself upon the brains of the crooked priests of Opar.

Tarzan had been in the dungeons of Opar before and, before, he had escaped; and so he set to work immediately seeking for a means of escape from his present predicament, for he knew that the chances were that Oah would not long delay the moment for which she had prayed—the instant when she should plunge the gleaming sacrificial knife into his breast. Quickly removing the thongs from his ankles, Tarzan groped his way carefully along the walls of his cell until he had made a complete circuit of it; then, similarly, he examined the floor. He discovered that he was in a rectangular chamber about ten feet long and eight wide and that by standing upon his tiptoes he could just reach the ceiling. The only opening was the door through which he had entered, in which an aperture, protected by iron bars, gave the cell its only ventilation but, as it opened upon a dark corridor, admitted no light. Tarzan examined the bolts and the hinges of the door, but they were, as he had conjectured, too substantial to be forced; and then, for the first time, he saw that a priest sat on guard in the corridor without, thus putting a definite end to any thoughts of surreptitious escape.

For three days and nights priests relieved each other at intervals; but upon the morning of the fourth day Tarzan discovered that the corridor was empty, and once again he turned his attention actively to thoughts of escape.

It had so happened that at the time of Tarzan's capture his hunting knife had been hidden by the tail of the leopard skin that formed his loincloth; and, in their excitement, the ignorant, half-human priests of Opar had overlooked it when they took his other weapons away from him. Doubly thankful was Tarzan for his good fortune, since, for sentimental reasons, he cherished the hunting knife of his long-dead sire—the knife that had started him upon the upward path to ascendancy over the beasts of the jungle that day, long gone, when, more by accident than intent, he had plunged it into the heart of Bolgani, the gorilla. But for more practical reasons it was, indeed, a gift from the gods, since it afforded him not only a weapon of defense, but an instrument wherewith he might seek to make good his escape.

Years before had Tarzan of the Apes escaped from the pits of Opar, and so he well knew the construction of their massive walls. Granite blocks of various sizes, hand hewn to fit with perfection, were laid in courses without mortar, the one wall that he had passed through having been fifteen feet in thickness. Fortune had favored him upon that occasion in that he had been placed in a cell which, unknown to the present inhabitants of Opar, had a secret entrance, the opening of which was closed by a single layer of loosely laid courses that the ape-man had been able to remove without great effort.

Naturally he sought for a similar condition in the cell in which he now found himself, but his search was not crowned with success. No single stone could be budged from its place, anchored as each was by the tremendous weight of the temple walls they supported; and so, perforce, he turned his attention toward the door.

He knew that there were few locks in Opar since the present degraded inhabitants of the city had not developed sufficient ingenuity either to repair old ones or construct new. Those locks that he had seen were ponderous affairs opened by huge keys and were, he guessed, of an antiquity that reached back to the days of Atlantis; but, for the most part, heavy bolts and bars secured such doors as might be fastened at all, and he guessed that it was such a crude contrivance that barred his way to freedom.

Groping his way to the door, he examined the small opening that let in air. It was about shoulder high and perhaps ten inches square and was equipped with four vertical iron bars half an inch square, set an inch and a half apart—too close to permit him to insert his hands between them, but this fact did not entirely discourage the ape-man. Perhaps there was another way.

His steel-thewed fingers closed upon the center of one of the bars. With his left hand he clung to another, and bracing one knee high against the door he slowly flexed his right elbow. Rolling like plastic steel, the muscles of his forearm and his biceps swelled, until gradually the bar bent inward toward him. The ape-man smiled as he took a new grip upon the iron bar. Then he surged backward with all his weight and all the strength of that mighty arm, and the bar bent to a wide U as he wrenched it from its sockets. He tried to insert his arm through the new opening, but it still was too small. A moment later another bar was torn away, and now, his arm through the aperture to its full length, he groped for the bar or bolts that held him prisoner.

At the fullest extent to which he could reach his fingertips downward against the door, he just touched the top of the bar, which was a timber about three inches in thickness. Its other dimensions, however, he was unable to ascertain, or whether it would release by raising one end or must be drawn back through keepers. It was most tantalizing! To have freedom almost within one's grasp and yet to be denied it was maddening.

Withdrawing his arm from the aperture, he removed his hunting knife from his scabbard and, again reaching outward, pressed the point of the blade into the wood of the bar. At first he tried lifting the bar by this means, but his knife point only pulled out of the wood. Next, he attempted to move the bar backward in a horizontal plane, and in this he was successful. Though the distance that he moved it in one effort was small, he was satisfied, for he knew that patience would win its reward. Never more than a quarter of an inch, sometimes only a sixteenth of an inch at a time, Tarzan slowly worked the bar backward. He worked methodically and carefully, never hurrying, never affected by nervous anxiety, although he never knew at what moment a savage warrior priest of Opar might make his rounds; and at last his efforts were rewarded, and the door swung upon its hinges.

Stepping quickly out, Tarzan shot the bar behind him and, knowing no other avenue of escape, turned back up the corridor along which his captors had conducted him to his prison cell. Faintly in the distance he discerned a lessening darkness, and toward this he moved upon silent feet. As the light increased slightly, he saw that the corridor was about ten feet wide and that at irregular intervals it was pierced by doors, all of which were closed and secured by bolts or bars.

A hundred yards from the cell in which he had been incarcerated he crossed a transversed corridor, and here he paused an instant to investigate with palpitating nostrils and keen eyes and ears. In neither direction could he discern any light, but faint sounds came to his ears indicating that life existed somewhere behind the doors along this corridor, and his nostrils were assailed by a medley of scents—the sweet aroma of incense, the odor of human bodies, and the acrid scent of carnivores; but there was nothing there to attract his further investigation, so he continued on his way along the corridor toward the rapidly increasing lights ahead.

He had advanced but a short distance when his keen ears detected the sound of approaching footsteps. Here was no place to risk discovery. Slowly he fell back toward the transverse corridor, seeking to take concealment there until the danger had passed; but it was already closer than he had imagined, and an instant later half a dozen priests of Opar turned into the corridor from one just ahead of him. They saw him instantly and halted, peering through the gloom.

"It is the ape-man," said one. "He has escaped," and with their knotted cudgels and their wicked knives they advanced upon him.

That they came slowly evidenced the respect in which they held his prowess, but still they came; and Tarzan fell back, for even he, armed only with a knife, was no match for six of these savage half-men with their heavy cudgels. As he retreated, a plan formed quickly in his alert mind, and when he reached the transverse corridor he backed slowly into it. Knowing that now that he was hidden from them they would come very slowly, fearing that he might be lying in wait for them, he turned and ran swiftly along the corridor. He passed several doors, not because he was looking for any door in particular, but because he knew that the more difficult it was for them to find him the greater his chances of eluding them; but at last he paused before one secured by a huge wooden bar. Quickly he raised it, opened the door and stepped within just as the leader of the priests came into view at the intersection of the corridor.

The instant that Tarzan stepped into the dark and gloomy chamber beyond he knew that he had made a fatal blunder. Strong in his nostrils was the acrid scent of Numa, the lion; the silence of the pit was shattered by a savage roar; in the dark background he saw two yellow-green eyes flaming with hate, and then the lion charged.

5

Before the Walls of Opar

PETER ZVERI ESTABLISHED his camp on the edge of the forest at the foot of the barrier cliff that guards the desolate valley of Opar. Here he left his porters and a few askaris as guards and then, with his fighting men, guided by Kitembo, commenced the arduous climb to the summit.

None of them had ever come this way before, not even Kitembo, though he had known the exact location of Opar from one who had seen it; and so when the first view of the distant city broke upon them they were filled with awe, and vague questionings arose in the primitive minds of the black men.

It was a silent party that filed across the dusty plain toward Opar; nor were the blacks the only members of the expedition to be assailed with doubt, for in their black tents on distant deserts the Arabs had imbibed with the milk of their mothers the fear of jân and ghrôl and had heard, too, of the fabled city of Nimmr, which it was not well for men to approach. With such thoughts and forebodings were the minds of the men filled as they approached the towering ruins of the ancient Atlantian city.

From the top of the great boulder that guards the outer entrance to the treasure vaults of Opar a little monkey watched the progress of the expedition across the valley. He was a very much distraught little monkey, for in his heart he knew that his

master should be warned of the coming of these many Gomangani and Tarmangani with their thundersticks; but fear of the
forbidding ruins gave him pause, and so he danced about upon
the top of the rock, chattering and scolding. The warriors of
Peter Zveri marched right past and never paid any attention to
him; and as they marched, other eyes were upon them, peering
from out of the foliage of the trees that grew rank among the
ruins.

If any member of the party saw a little monkey scampering
quickly past upon their right, or saw him clamber up the ruined
outer wall of Opar, he doubtless gave the matter no thought; for
his mind, like the minds of all his fellows, was occupied by
speculation as to what lay within that gloomy pile.

Kitembo did not know the location of the treasure vaults
of Opar. He had but agreed to guide Zveri to the city, but,
like Zveri, he entertained no doubt but that it would be easy to
discover the vaults if they were unable to wring its location
from any of the inhabitants of the city. Surprised, indeed,
would they have been had they known that no living Oparian
knew either of the location of the treasure vaults or of their
existence and that, among all living men, only Tarzan and
some of his Waziri warriors knew their location or how to
reach them.

"The place is nothing but a deserted ruin," said Zveri to one
of his white companions.

"It is an ominous-looking place though," replied the other,
"and it has already had its effect upon the men."

Zveri shrugged. "This might frighten them at night, but not
in broad daylight; they are certainly not that yellow."

They were close to the ruined outer wall now, which
frowned down upon them menacingly, and here they halted
while several searched for an opening. Abu Batn was the first
to find it—the narrow crevice with the flight of concrete steps
leading upward. "Here is a way through, Comrade," he called
to Zveri.

"Take some of your men with you and reconnoiter," ordered
Zveri.

Abu Batn summoned a half dozen of his black men, who
advanced with evident reluctance.

Gathering the skirt of his thôb about him, the sheik entered the crevice, and at the same instant a piercing screech broke from the interior of the ruined city—a long-drawn, high-pitched shriek that ended in a series of low moans. The Bedaùwy halted. The blacks froze in terrified rigidity.

"Go on!" yelled Zveri. "A scream can't kill you!"

"Wullah!" exclaimed one of the Arabs; "but jân can."

"Get out of there, then!" cried Zveri angrily. "If you damned cowards are afraid to go, I'll go in myself."

There was no argument. The Arabs stepped aside. And then a little monkey, screaming with terror, appeared upon the top of the wall from the inside of the city. His sudden and noisy appearance brought every eye to bear upon him. They saw him turn an affrighted glance backward over his shoulder and then, with a loud scream, leap far out to the ground below. It scarcely seemed that he could survive the jump, yet it barely sufficed to interrupt his flight, for he was on his way again in an instant as, with prodigious leaps and bounds, he fled screaming out across the barren plains.

It was the last straw. The shaken nerves of the superstitious blacks gave way to the sudden strain; and almost with one accord they turned and fled the dismal city, while close upon their heels were Abu Batn and his desert warriors in swift and undignified retreat.

Peter Zveri and his three white companions, finding themselves suddenly deserted, looked at one another questioningly. "The dirty cowards!" exclaimed Zveri angrily. "You go back, Mike, and see if you can rally them. We are going on in, now that we are here."

Michael Dorsky, only too glad of any assignment that took him farther away from Opar, started at a brisk run after the fleeing warriors, while Zveri turned once more into the fissure with Miguel Romero and Paul Ivitch at his heels.

The three men passed through the outer wall and entered the courtyard, across which they saw the lofty inner wall rising before them. Romero was the first to find the opening that led to the city proper and, calling to his fellows, he stepped boldly into the narrow passage. Then once again the hideous scream shattered the brooding silence of the ancient temple.

The three men halted. Zveri wiped the perspiration from his brow. "I think we have gone as far as we can alone," he said. "Perhaps we had all better go back and rally the men. There is no sense in doing anything foolhardy." Miguel Romero threw him a contemptuous sneer, but Ivitch assured Zveri that the suggestion met with his entire approval.

The two men crossed the court quickly without waiting to see whether the Mexican followed them or not and were soon once again outside the city.

"Where is Miguel?" asked Ivitch.

Zveri looked around. "Romero!" he shouted in a loud voice, but there was no reply.

"It must have got him," said Ivitch with a shudder.

"Small loss," grumbled Zveri.

But whatever the thing was that Ivitch feared, it had not, as yet, gotten the young Mexican, who, after watching his companions' precipitate flight, had continued on through the opening in the inner wall determined to have at least one look at the interior of the ancient city of Opar that he had traveled so far to see and of the fabulous wealth of which he had been dreaming for weeks.

Before his eyes spread a magnificent panorama of stately ruins, before which the young and impressionable Latin-American stood spellbound; and then once again the eerie wail rose from the interior of a great building before him, but if he was frightened Romero gave no evidence of it. Perhaps he grasped his rifle a little more tightly; perhaps he loosened his revolver in his holster, but he did not retreat. He was awed by the stately grandeur of the scene before him, where age and ruin seemed only to enhance its pristine magnificence.

A movement within the temple caught his attention. He saw a figure emerge from somewhere, the figure of a gnarled and knotted man that rolled on short crooked legs; and then another and another came until there were fully a hundred of the savage creatures approaching slowly toward him. He saw their knotted bludgeons and their knives, and he realized that here was a menace more effective than an unearthly scream.

With a shrug he backed into the passageway. "I cannot fight

an army single-handed," he muttered. Slowly he crossed the outer court, passed through the first great wall and stood again upon the plain outside the city. In the distance he saw the dust of the fleeing expedition and, with a grin, he started in pursuit, swinging along at an easy walk as he puffed upon a cigarette. From the top of the rocky hill at his left a little monkey saw him pass—a little monkey, which still trembled from fright, but whose terrified screams had become only low, pitiful moans. It had been a hard day for little Nkima.

So rapid had been the retreat of the expedition that Zveri, with Dorsky and Ivitch, did not overtake the main party until the greater part of it was already descending the barrier cliffs; nor could any threats or promises stay the retreat, which ended only when camp was reached.

Immediately Zveri called Abu Batn, together with Dorsky and Ivitch, into council. The affair had been Zveri's first reverse, and it was a serious one inasmuch as he had relied heavily upon the inexhaustible store of gold to be found in the treasure vaults of Opar. First, he berated Abu Batn, Kitembo, their ancestors and all their followers for cowardice; but all that he accomplished was to arouse the anger and resentment of these two.

"We came with you to fight the white men, not demons and ghosts," said Kitembo. "I am not afraid. I would go into the city, but my men will not accompany me and I cannot fight the enemy alone."

"Nor I," said Abu Batn, a sullen scowl still further darkening his swart countenance.

"I know," sneered Zveri, "you are both brave men, but you are much better runners than you are fighters. Look at us. We were not afraid. We went in and we were not harmed."

"Where is Comrade Romero?" demanded Abu Batn.

"Well, perhaps, he is lost," admitted Zveri. "What do you expect? To win a battle without losing a man?"

"There was no battle," said Kitembo, "and the man who went farthest into the accursed city did not return."

Dorsky looked up suddenly. "There he is now!" he exclaimed, and as all eyes turned up the trail toward Opar, they saw Miguel Romero strolling jauntily into camp.

"Greetings, my brave comrades!" he cried to them. "I am glad to find you alive. I feared that you might all succumb to heart failure."

Sullen silence greeted his raillery, and no one spoke until he had approached and seated himself near them.

"What detained you?" demanded Zveri presently.

"I wanted to see what was beyond the inner wall," replied the Mexican.

"And you saw?" asked Abu Batn.

"I saw magnificent buildings in splendid ruin," replied Romero, "a dead and moldering city of the dead past."

"And what else?" asked Kitembo.

"I saw a company of strange warriors, short heavy men on crooked legs, with long powerful arms and hairy bodies. They came out of a great building that might have been a temple. There were too many of them for me. I could not fight them alone, so I came away."

"Did they have weapons?" asked Zveri.

"Clubs and knives," replied Romero.

"You see," exclaimed Zveri, "just a band of savages armed with clubs. We could take the city without the loss of a man."

"What did they look like?" demanded Kitembo. "Describe them to me," and when Romero had done so, with careful attention to details, Kitembo shook his head. "It is as I thought," he said. "They are not men; they are demons."

"Men or demons, we are going back there and take their city," said Zveri angrily. "We must have the gold of Opar."

"You may go, white man," returned Kitembo, "but you will go alone. I know my men, and I tell you that they will not follow you there. Lead us against white men, or brown men, or black men, and we will follow you. But we will not follow you against demons and ghosts."

"And you, Abu Batn?" demanded Zveri.

"I have talked with my men on the return from the city, and they tell me that they will not go back there. They will not fight the jân and ghrôl. They heard the voice of the jin warning them away, and they are afraid."

Zveri stormed and threatened and cajoled, but all to no

effect. Neither the Aarab sheik nor the African chief could be moved.

"There is still a way," said Romero.

"And what is that?" asked Zveri.

"When the gringo comes and the Filipino, there will be six of us who are neither Aarabs nor Africans. We six can take Opar." Paul Ivitch made a wry face, and Zveri cleared his throat.

"If we are killed," said the latter, "our whole plan is wrecked. There will be no one left to carry on."

Romero shrugged. "It was only a suggestion," he said, "but, of course, if you are afraid—"

"I am not afraid," stormed Zveri, "but neither am I a fool."

An ill-concealed sneer curved Romero's lips. "I am going to eat," he said, and, rising, he left them.

The day following his advent into the camp of his fellow conspirators, Wayne Colt wrote a long message in cipher and dispatched it to the Coast by one of his boys. From her tent Zora Drinov had seen the message given to the boy. She had seen him place it in the end of a forked stick and start off upon his long journey. Shortly after, Colt joined her in the shade of a great tree beside her tent.

"You sent a message this morning, Comrade Colt," she said.

He looked up at her quickly. "Yes," he replied.

"Perhaps you should know that only Comrade Zveri is permitted to send messages from the expedition," she told him.

"I did not know," he said. "It was merely in relation to some funds that were to have been awaiting me when I reached the Coast. They were not there. I sent the boy back after them."

"Oh," she said, and then their conversation drifted to other topics.

That afternoon he took his rifle and went out to look for game and Zora went with him, and that evening they had supper together again, but this time she was the hostess. And so the days passed until an excited native aroused the camp one day with an announcement that the expedition was returning. No words were necessary to apprise those who had been left behind that victory had not perched upon the banner of their little army. Failure was clearly written upon the faces of the leaders. Zveri greeted Zora and Colt, introducing the latter to his companions, and when Tony had been similarly presented the returning warriors threw themselves down upon cots or upon the ground to rest.

That night, as they gathered around the supper table, each party narrated the adventures that had befallen them since the expedition had left camp. Colt and Zora were thrilled by the stories of weird Opar, but no less mysterious was their tale of the death of Raghunath Jafar and his burial and uncanny resurrection.

"Not one of the boys would touch the body after that," said Zora. "Tony and Comrade Colt had to bury him themselves."

"I hope you made a good job of it this time," said Miguel.

"He hasn't come back again," rejoined Colt with a grin.

"Who could have dug him up in the first place?" demanded Zveri.

"None of the boys certainly," said Zora. "They were all too much frightened by the peculiar circumstances surrounding his death."

"It must have been the same creature that killed him," suggested Colt, "and whoever or whatever it was must have been possessed of almost superhuman strength to carry that heavy corpse into a tree and drop it upon us."

"The most uncanny feature of it to me," said Zora, "is the fact that it was accomplished in absolute silence. I'll swear that not even a leaf rustled until just before the body hurtled down upon our table."

"It could have been only a man," said Zveri.

"Unquestionably," said Colt, "but what a man!"

As the company broke up later, repairing to their various tents, Zveri detained Zora with a gesture. "I want to talk to you a minute, Zora," he said, and the girl sank back into the chair she had just quitted. "What do you think of this American? You have had a good opportunity to size him up."

"He seems to be all right. He is a very likable fellow," replied the girl.

"He said or did nothing, then, that might arouse your suspicion?" demanded Zveri.

"No," said Zora, "nothing at all."

"You two have been alone here together for a number of days," continued Zveri. "Did he treat you with perfect respect?"

"He was certainly much more respectful than your friend, Raghunath Jafar."

"Don't mention that dog to me," said Zveri. "I wish that I had been here to kill him myself."

"I told him that you would when you got back, but someone beat you to it."

They were silent for several moments. It was evident that Zveri was trying to frame into words something that was upon his mind. At last he spoke. "Colt is a very prepossessing young man. See that you don't fall in love with him, Zora."

"And why not?" she demanded. "I have given my mind and my strength and my talent to the cause and, perhaps, most of my heart. But there is a corner of it that is mine to do with as I wish."

"You mean to say that you are in love with him?" demanded Zveri.

"Certainly not. Nothing of the kind. Such an idea had not entered my head. I just want you to know, Peter, that in matters of this kind you may not dictate to me."

"Listen, Zora. You know perfectly well that I love you, and what is more, I am going to have you. I get what I go after."

"Don't bore me, Peter. I have no time for anything so foolish as love now. When we are well through with this undertaking, perhaps I shall take the time to give it a little thought."

"I want you to give it a lot of thought right now, Zora," he insisted. "There are some details in relation to this expedition that I have not told you. I have not divulged them to anyone, but I am going to tell you now because I love you and you are going to become my wife. There is more at stake in this for us than you dream. After all the thought and all the risks and all the hardships, I do not intend to surrender all of the power and the wealth that I shall have gained to anyone."

"You mean not even to the cause?" she asked.

"I mean not even to the cause, except that I shall use them both for the cause."

"Then what do you intend? I do not understand you," she said.

"I intend to make myself Emperor of Africa," he declared, "and I intend to make you my empress."

"Peter!" she cried. "Are you crazy?"

"Yes, I am crazy for power, for riches, and for you."

"You can never do it, Peter. You know how far-reaching are the tentacles of the power we serve. If you fail it, if you turn traitor, those tentacles will reach you and drag you down to destruction."

"When I win my goal, my power will be as great as theirs, and then I may defy them."

"But how about these others with us, who are serving loyally the cause which they think you represent? They will tear you to pieces, Peter."

The man laughed. "You do not know them, Zora. They are all alike. All men and women are alike. If I offered to make them grand dukes and give them each a palace and a harem, they would slit their own mothers' throats to obtain such a prize."

The girl arose. "I am astounded, Peter. I thought that you, at least, were sincere."

He arose quickly and grasped her by the arm. "Listen, Zora," he hissed in her ear, "I love you, and because I love you I have put my life in your hands. But understand this, if you betray me, no matter how well I love you, I shall kill you. Do not forget that."

"You did not have to tell me that, Peter. I was perfectly well aware of it."

"And you will not betray me?" he demanded.

"I never betray a friend, Peter," she said.

The next morning Zveri was engaged in working out the details of a second expedition to Opar based upon Romero's suggestions. It was decided that this time they would call for volunteers; and as the Europeans, the two Americans, and the Filipino had already indicated their willingness to take part in the adventure, it remained now only to seek to enlist the services of some of the blacks and Arabs, and for this purpose Zveri summoned the entire company to a palaver. Here he explained just what they purposed doing. He stressed the fact that Comrade Romero had seen the inhabitants of the city and that they were only members of a race of stunted savages, armed only with sticks. Eloquently he explained how easily they might be overcome with rifles.

Practically the entire party was willing to go as far as the walls of Opar; but there were only ten warriors who would agree to enter the city with the white men, and all of these were from the askaris who had been left behind to guard camp and from those who had accompanied Colt from the Coast, none of whom had been subjected to the terrors of Opar. Not one of those who had heard the weird screams issuing from the ruins would agree to enter the city, and it was admitted among the whites that it was not at all unlikely that their ten volunteers might suddenly develop a change of heart when at last they stood before the frowning portals of Opar and heard the weird warning cry from its defenders.

Several days were spent in making careful preparations for the new expedition, but at last the final detail was completed; and early one morning Zveri and his followers set out once more upon the trail to Opar.

Zora Drinov had wished to accompany them, but as Zveri was expecting messages from a number of his various agents throughout Northern Africa, it had been necessary to leave her behind. Abu Batn and his warrors were left to guard the camp, and these, with a few black servants, were all who did not accompany the expedition.

Since the failure of the first expedition and the fiasco at the gates of Opar, the relations of Abu Batn and Zveri had been strained. The sheik and his warriors, smarting under the charges of cowardice, had kept more to themselves than formerly; and though they would not volunteer to enter the city of Opar, they still resented the affront of their selection to remain behind as camp guards; and so it was that as the others departed, the Aarabs sat in the múk'aad of their sheik's beyt es-sh'ar, whispering over their thick coffee, their swart scowling faces half hidden by their thorrîbs.

They did not deign even to glance at their departing comrades, but the eyes of Abu Batn were fixed upon the slender figure of Zora Drinov as the sheik sat in silent meditation.

6

Betrayed

THE HEART OF little Nkima had been torn by conflicting emotions, as from the vantage point of the summit of the rocky hillock he had watched the departure of Miguel Romero from the city of Opar. Seeing these brave Tarmangani, armed with death-dealing thundersticks, driven away from the ruins, he was convinced that something terrible must have befallen his master within the grim recesses of that crumbling pile. His loyal heart prompted him to return and investigate, but Nkima was only a very little Manu—a little Manu who was very much afraid; and though he started twice again toward Opar, he could not muster his courage to the sticking point; and at last, whimpering pitifully, he turned back across the plains toward the grim forest, where, at least, the dangers were familiar ones.

The door of the gloomy chamber which Tarzan had entered swung inward, and his hands were still upon it as the menacing roar of the lion apprised him of the danger of his situation. Agile and quick is Numa, the lion, but with even greater celerity functioned the mind and muscles of Tarzan of the Apes. In the instant that the lion sprang toward him a picture of the whole scene flashed to the mind of the ape-man. He saw the gnarled priests of Opar advancing along the corridor in pursuit of him. He saw the heavy door that swung inward. He saw the charging lion, and he pieced these various factors together to create a situation far more to his advantage than they normally presented. Drawing the door quickly inward, he stepped behind it as the lion charged, with the result that the beast, either carried forward by his own momentum or sensing escape, sprang into the corridor full in the faces of the advancing priests, and at the same instant Tarzan closed the door behind him.

Just what happened in the corridor without he could not see, but from the growls and screams that receded quickly into the distance he was able to draw a picture that brought a quiet smile to his lips; and an instant later a piercing shriek of agony and terror announced the fate of at least one of the fleeing Oparians.

Realizing that he would gain nothing by remaining where he was, Tarzan decided to leave the cell and seek a way out of the labyrinthine mazes of the pits beneath Opar. He knew that the lion upon its prey would doubtless bar his passage along the route he had been following when his escape had been interrupted by the priests and though, as a last resort, he might face Numa, he was of no mind to invite such an unnecessary risk; but when he sought to open the heavy door he found that he could not budge it, and in an instant he realized what had happened and that he was now in prison once again in the dungeons of Opar.

The bar that secured this particular door was not of the sliding type but, working upon a pin at the inner end, dropped into heavy wrought-iron keepers bolted to the door itself and to its frame. When he had entered, he had raised the bar, which had dropped into place of its own weight when the door slammed to, imprisoning him as effectually as though the work had been done by the hand of man.

The darkness of the corridor without was less intense than that of the passage upon which his former cell had been located; and though not enough light entered the cell to illuminate its interior, there was sufficient to show him the nature of the ventilating opening in the door, which he found to consist of a number of small round holes, none of which was of sufficient diameter to permit him to pass his hand through in an attempt to raise the bar.

As Tarzan stood in momentary contemplation of his new predicament, the sound of stealthy movement came to him from the black recesses at the rear of the cell. He wheeled quickly, drawing his hunting knife from its sheath. He did not have to ask himself what the author of this sound might be, for he knew that the only other living creature that might have occupied this cell with its former inmate was another lion. Why it had not joined in the attack upon him, he could not guess, but that it would eventually seize him was a foregone conclusion. Perhaps even now it was preparing to sneak up on him. He wished that his eyes might penetrate the darkness, for if he could see the lion as it charged he might be better prepared to meet it. In the past he had met the charges of other lions, but always before he had been able to see their swift spring and to elude the sweep of their mighty talons as they reared upon their hind legs to seize him. Now it would be different, and for once in his life, Tarzan of the Apes felt death was inescapable. He knew that his time had come.

He was not afraid. He simply knew that he did not wish to die and that the price at which he would sell his life would cost his antagonist dearly. In silence he waited. Again he heard that faint, yet ominous sound. The foul air of the cell reeked with the stench of the carnivores. From somewhere in a distant corridor he heard the growling of a lion at its kill; and then a voice broke the silence.

"Who are you?" it asked. It was the voice of a woman, and it came from the back of the cell in which the ape-man was imprisoned.

"Where are you?" demanded Tarzan.

"I am here at the back of the cell," replied the woman.

"Where is the lion?"

"He went out when you opened the door," she replied.

"Yes, I know," said Tarzan, "but the other one. Where is he?"

"There is no other one. There was but one lion here and it is gone. Ah, now I know you!" she exclaimed. "I know the voice. It is Tarzan of the Apes."

"La!" exclaimed the ape-man, advancing quickly across the cell. "How could you be here with the lion and still live?"

"I am in an adjoining cell that is separated from this one by a door made of iron bars," replied La. Tarzan heard metal hinges creak. "It is not locked," she said. "It was not necessary to lock it, for it opens into this other cell where the lion was."

Groping forward through the dark, the two advanced until their hands touched one another.

La pressed close to the man. She was trembling. "I have been afraid," she said, "but I shall not be afraid now."

"I shall not be of much help to you," said Tarzan. "I also am a prisoner."

"I know it," replied La, "but I always feel safe when you are near."

"Tell me what has happened," demanded Tarzan. "How is it that Oah is posing as high priestess and you a prisoner in your own dungeons?"

"I forgave Oah her former treason when she conspired with Cadj to wrest my power from me," explained La, "but she could not exist without intrigue and duplicity. To further her ambitions, she made love to Dooth, who has been high priest since Jad-bal-ja killed Cadj. They spread stories about me through the city; and as my people have never forgiven me for my friendship for you, they succeeded in winning enough to their cause to overthrow and imprison me. All the ideas were Oah's, for Dooth and the other priests, as you well know, are stupid beasts. It was Oah's idea to imprison me thus with a lion for company, merely to make my suffering more terrible, until the time should come when she might prevail upon the priests to offer me in sacrifice to the Flaming God. In that she has had some difficulty, I know, as those who have brought my food have told me."

"How could they bring food to you here?" asked Tarzan. "No one could pass through the outer cell while the lion was there."

"There is another opening in the lion's cell, that leads into a low, narrow corridor into which they can drop meat from above. Thus they would entice the lion from this outer cell, after which they would lower a gate of iron bars across the opening of the small corridor into which he went, and while he was thus imprisoned they brought my food to me. But they did not feed him much. He was always hungry and often growling and pawing at the bars of my cell. Perhaps Oah hoped that some day he would batter them down."

"Where does this other corridor, in which they fed the lion, lead?" asked Tarzan.

"I do not know," replied La, "but I imagine that it is only a blind tunnel built in ancient times for this very purpose."

"We must have a look at it," said Tarzan. "It may offer a means of escape."

"Why not escape through the door by which you entered?" asked La; and when the ape-man had explained why this was impossible, she pointed out the location of the entrance to the small tunnel.

"We must get out of here as quickly as possible, if it is possible at all," said Tarzan, "for if they are able to capture the lion, they will certainly return him to this cell."

"They will capture him," said La. "There is no question as to that."

"Then I had better hurry and make my investigation of the tunnel, for it might prove embarrassing were they to return him to the cell while I was in the tunnel, if it proved to be a blind one."

"I will listen at the outer door while you investigate," offered La. "Make haste."

Groping his way toward the section of the wall that La had indicated, Tarzan found a heavy grating of iron closing an aperture leading into a low and narrow corridor. Lifting the barrier, Tarzan entered and with his hands extended before him moved forward in a crouching position, since the low ceiling would not permit him to stand erect. He had progressed but a short distance when he discovered that the corridor made an abrupt right-angle turn to the left, and beyond the turn he saw at a short distance a faint luminosity. Moving quickly forward, he came to the end of the corridor, at the bottom of a vertical shaft, the interior of which was illuminated by subdued daylight. The shaft was constructed of the usual rough-hewn granite of the foundation walls of the city, but here set with no great nicety or precision, giving the interior of the shaft a rough and uneven surface.

As Tarzan was examining it, he heard La's voice coming along the tunnel from the cell in which he had left her. Her tone was one of excitement, and her message one that presaged a situation wrought with extreme danger to them both.

"Make haste, Tarzan. They are returning with the lion!"

The ape-man hurried quickly back to the mouth of the tunnel.

"Quick!" he cried to La, as he raised the gate that had fallen behind him after he had passed through.

"In there?" she demanded in an affrighted voice.

"It is our only chance of escape," replied the ape-man.

Without another word La crowded into the corridor beside him. Tarzan lowered the grating and, with La following closely behind him, returned to the opening leading into the shaft. Without a word, he lifted La in his arms and raised her as high as he could, nor did she need to be told what to do. With little difficulty she found both hand- and footholds upon the rough surface of the interior of the shaft, and with Tarzan just below her, assisting and steadying her, she made her way slowly aloft.

The shaft led directly upward into a room in the tower, which overlooked the entire city of Opar; and here, concealed by the crumbling walls, they paused to formulate their plans.

They both knew that their greatest danger lay in discovery by one of the numerous monkeys infesting the ruins of Opar, with which the inhabitants of the city are able to converse. Tarzan was anxious to be away from Opar that he might thwart the plans of the white men who had invaded his domain. But first he wished to bring about the downfall of La's enemies and reinstate her upon the throne of Opar, or if that should prove impossible, to insure the safety of her flight.

As he viewed her now in the light of day he was struck again by the matchlessness of her deathless beauty that neither time, nor care, nor danger seemed capable of dimming, and he wondered what he should do with her; where he could take her; where this savage priestess of the Flaming God could find a place in all the world, outside the walls of Opar, with the environments of which she would harmonize. And as he pondered, he was forced to admit to himself that no such place existed. La was of Opar, a savage queen born to rule a race of savage half-men. As well introduce a tigress to the salons of civilization as La of Opar. Two or three thousand years earlier she might have been a Cleopatra or a Sheba, but today she could be only La of Opar.

For some time they had sat in silence, the beautiful eyes of the high priestess resting upon the profile of the forest god. "Tarzan!" she said.

The man looked up. "What is it, La?" he asked.

"I still love you, Tarzan," she said in a low voice.

A troubled expression came into the eyes of the ape-man. "Let us not speak of that."

"I like to speak of it," she murmured. "It gives me sorrow, but it is a sweet sorrow—the only sweetness that has ever come into my life."

Tarzan extended a bronzed hand and laid it upon her slender, tapering fingers. "You have always possessed my heart, La," he said, "up to the point of love. If my affection goes no further than this, it is through no fault of mine nor yours."

La laughed. "It is certainly through no fault of mine, Tarzan," she said, "but I know that such things are not ordered by ourselves. Love is a gift of the gods. Sometimes it is awarded as a recompense; sometimes as a punishment. For me it has been a punishment, perhaps, but I would not have it otherwise. I had nurtured it in my breast since first I met you; and without that love, however hopeless it may be, I should not care to live."

Tarzan made no reply, and the two relapsed into silence, waiting for night to fall that they might descend into the city unobserved. Tarzan's alert mind was occupied with plans for reinstating La upon her throne, and presently they fell to discussing these.

"Just before the Flaming God goes to his rest at night," said

La, "the priests and the priestesses all gather in the throne room. There they will be tonight before the throne upon which Oah will be seated. Then may we descend to the city."

"And then what?" asked Tarzan.

"If we can kill Oah in the throne room," said La, "and Dooth at the same time, they would have no leaders; and without leaders they are lost."

"I cannot kill a woman," said Tarzan.

"I can," returned La, "and you can attend to Dooth. You certainly would not object to killing him?"

"If he attacked, I would kill him," said Tarzan, "but not otherwise. Tarzan of the Apes kills only in self-defense and for food, or when there is no other way to thwart an enemy."

In the floor of the ancient room in which they were waiting were two openings; one was the mouth of the shaft through which they had ascended from the dungeons, the other opened into a similar but larger shaft, to the bottom of which ran a long wooden ladder set in the masonry of its sides. It was this shaft which offered them a means of escape from the tower, and as Tarzan sat with his eyes resting idly upon the opening, an unpleasant thought suddenly obtruded itself upon his consciousness.

He turned toward La. "We had forgotten," he said, "that whoever casts the meat down the shaft to the lion must ascend by this other shaft. We may not be as safe from detection here as we had hoped."

"They do not feed the lion very often," said La, "not every day."

"When did they feed him last?" asked Tarzan.

"I do not recall," said La. "Time drags so heavily in the darkness of the cell that I lost count of days."

"S-st!" cautioned Tarzan. "Someone is ascending now."

Silently the ape-man arose and crossed the floor to the opening, where he crouched upon the side opposite the ladder. La moved stealthily to his side, so that the ascending man, whose back would be toward them, as he emerged from the shaft, would not see them. Slowly the man ascended. They could hear his shuffling progress coming nearer and nearer to the top. He did not climb as the apelike priests of Opar are wont to climb. Tarzan thought perhaps he was carrying a load either of such weight or cumbersomeness as to retard his progress, but when finally his head came into view the ape-man saw that he was an old man, which accounted for his lack of agility; and then powerful fingers closed about the throat of the unsuspecting Oparian, and he was lifted bodily out of the shaft.

"Silence!" said the ape-man. "Do as you are told and you will not be harmed."

La had snatched a knife from the girdle of their victim, and now Tarzan forced him to the floor of the room and slightly released his hold upon the fellow's throat, turning him around so that he faced them.

An expression of incredulity and surprise crossed the face of the old priest as his eyes fell upon La.

"Darus!" exclaimed La.

"All honor to the Flaming God who has ordered your escape!" exclaimed the priest.

La turned to Tarzan. "You need not fear Darus," she said; "he will not betray us. Of all the priests of Opar, there never lived one more loyal to his queen."

"That is right," said the old man, shaking his head.

"Are there many more loyal to the high priestess, La?" demanded Tarzan.

"Yes, very many," replied Darus, "but they are afraid. Oah is a she-devil and Dooth is a fool. Between the two of them there is no longer either safety or happiness in Opar."

"How many are there whom you absolutely know may be depended upon?" demanded La.

"Oh, very many," replied Darus.

"Gather them in the throne room tonight then, Darus; and as the Flaming God goes to his couch, be ready to strike at the enemies of La, your priestess."

"You will be there?" asked Darus.

"I shall be there," replied La. "This, your dagger, shall be the signal. When you see La of Opar plunge it into the breast of Oah, the false priestess, fall upon those who are the enemies of La."

"It shall be done, just as you say," Darus assured her, "and now I must throw this meat to the lion and be gone."

Slowly the old priest descended the ladder, gibbering and muttering to himself, after he had cast a few bones and scraps of meat into the other shaft to the lion.

"You are quite sure you can trust him, La?" demanded Tarzan.

"Absolutely," replied the girl. "Darus would die for me, and I know that he hates Oah and Dooth."

The slow remaining hours of the afternoon dragged on, the sun was low in the west, and now the two must take their greatest risk, that of descending into the city while it was still light and making their way to the throne room, although the risk was greatly minimized by the fact that the inhabitants of the city were all supposed to be congregated in the throne room at this time, performing the age-old rite with which they speeded the Flaming God to his night of rest. Without interruption they descended to the base of the tower, crossed the courtyard and entered the temple. Here, through devious and roundabout passages, La led the way to a small doorway that opened into the throne room at the back of the dais upon which the throne stood. Here she paused, listening to the services being conducted within the great chamber, waiting for the cue that would bring them to a point when all within the room, except the high priestess, were prostrated with their faces pressed against the floor.

When that instant arrived, La swung open the door and leaped silently upon the dais behind the throne in which her victim sat. Close behind her came Tarzan, and in that first instant both realized that they had been betrayed, for the dais was swarming with priests ready to seize them.

Already one had caught La by an arm, but before he could drag her away Tarzan sprang upon him, seized him by the neck and jerked his head backward so suddenly and with such force that the sound of his snapping vertebra could be heard across the room. Then he raised the body high above his head and cast it into the faces of the priests charging upon him. As they staggered back, he seized La and swung her into the corridor along which they had approached the throne room.

It was useless to stand and fight, for he knew that even though he might hold his own for a while, they must eventually overcome him and that once they laid their hands upon La they would tear her limb from limb.

Down the corridor behind them came the yelling horde of priests, and in their wake, screaming for the blood of her victim, was Oah.

"Make for the outer walls by the shortest route, La," directed Tarzan, and the girl sped on winged feet, leading him through the labyrinthine corridors of the ruin, until they broke suddenly into the chamber of the seven pillars of gold, and then Tarzan knew the way.

No longer needing his guide, and realizing that the priests were overtaking them, being fleeter of foot than La, he swept the girl into his arms and sped through the echoing chambers of the temple toward the inner wall. Through that, across the courtyard and through the outer wall they passed, and still the priests pursued, urged on by screaming Oah. Out across the deserted valley they fled; and now the priests were losing ground for their short, crooked legs could not compete with the speed of Tarzan's clean-limbed stride, even though he was burdened by the weight of La.

The sudden darkness of the near tropics that follows the setting of the sun soon obliterated the pursuers from their sight; and a short time thereafter the sounds of pursuit ceased, and Tarzan knew that the chase had been abandoned, for the men of Opar have no love for the darkness of the outer world.

Then Tarzan paused and lowered La to the ground; but as he did so her soft arms encircled his neck and she pressed close to him, her cheek against his breast, and burst into tears.

"Do not cry, La," he said. "We shall come again to Opar, and when we do you shall be seated upon your throne again."

"I am not crying for that," she replied.

"Then why do you cry?" he asked.

"I am crying for joy," she said, "joy that perhaps I shall be alone with you now for a long time."

In pity, Tarzan pressed her to him for a moment, and then they set off once more toward the barrier cliff.

That night they slept in a great tree in the forest at the foot of the cliff, after Tarzan had constructed a rude couch for La between two branches, while he settled himself in a crotch of the tree a few feet below her.

It was dawn when Tarzan awoke. The sky was overcast, and he sensed an approaching storm. No food had passed his lips for many hours, and he knew that La had not eaten since the morning of the previous day. Food, therefore, was a prime essential and he must find it and return to La before the storm broke. Since it was meat that he craved, he knew that he must be able to make fire and cook it before La could eat it, though he himself still preferred it raw. He looked into La's cot and saw that she was still asleep. Knowing that she must be exhausted from all that she had passed through the previous day, he let her sleep on; and swinging to a nearby tree, he set out upon his search for food.

As he moved upwind through the middle terrace, every faculty of his delicately attuned senses was alert. Like the lion, Tarzan particularly relished the flesh of Pacco, the zebra, but either Bara, the antelope, or Horta, the boar, would have proved an acceptable substitute; but the forest seemed to be deserted by every member of the herds he sought. Only the scent spoor of the great cats assailed his nostrils, mingled with the lesser and more human odor of Manu, the monkey. Time means little to a hunting beast. It meant little to Tarzan, who, having set out in search of meat, would return only when he had found meat.

When La awakened, it was some time before she could place her surroundings; but when she did, a slow smile of happiness and contentment parted her lovely lips, revealing an even row of perfect teeth. She sighed, and then she whispered the name of the man she loved. "Tarzan!" she called.

There was no reply. Again she spoke his name, but this time louder, and again the only answer was silence. Slightly troubled, she arose upon an elbow and leaned over the side of her sleeping couch. The tree beneath her was empty.

She thought, correctly, that perhaps he had gone to hunt, but still she was troubled by his absence, and the longer she waited the more troubled she became. She knew that he did not love her and that she must be a burden to him. She knew, too, that he was as much a wild beast as the lions of the forest and that the same desire for freedom, which animated them, must animate him. Perhaps he had been unable to withstand the temptation longer and while she slept, he had left her.

There was not a great deal in the training or ethics of La of Opar that could have found exception to such conduct, for the life of her people was a life of ruthless selfishness and cruelty. They entertained few of the finer sensibilities of civilized man, or the great nobility of character that marked so many of the wild beasts. Her love for Tarzan had been the only soft spot in La's savage life, and realizing that she would think nothing of deserting a creature she did not love, she was fair enough to cast no reproaches upon Tarzan for having done the thing that she might have done, nor to her mind did it accord illy with her conception of his nobility of character.

As she descended to the ground, she sought to determine some plan of action for the future, and in this moment of her loneliness and depression she saw no alternative but to return to Opar, and so it was toward the city of her birth that she turned her steps; but she had not gone far before she realized the danger and futility of this plan, which could but lead to certain death while Oah and Dooth ruled in Opar. She felt bitterly toward Darus, who she believed had betrayed her; and accepting his treason as an index of what she might expect from others whom she had believed to be friendly to her, she realized the utter hopelessness of regaining the throne of Opar without outside help. La had no happy life to which she might look forward; but the will to live was yet strong within her, the result more, perhaps, of the courageousness of her spirit than of any fear of death, which, to her, was but another word for defeat.

She paused in the trail that she had reached a short distance from the tree in which she had spent the night; and there, with almost nothing to guide her, she sought to determine in what direction she should break a new trail into the future, for wherever she went, other than back to Opar, it would be a new trail, leading among peoples and experiences as foreign to her as though she had suddenly stepped from another planet, or from the long-lost continent of her progenitors.

It occurred to her that perhaps there might be other people in this strange world as generous and chivalrous as Tarzan. At least in this direction there lay hope. In Opar there was none, and so she turned back away from Opar; and above her black clouds rolled and billowed as the storm king marshaled his forces, and behind her a tawny beast with gleaming eyes slunk through the underbrush beside the trail that she followed.

7

In Futile Search

TARZAN OF THE Apes, ranging far in search of food, caught at length the welcome scent of Horta, the boar. The man paused and, with a deep and silent inhalation, filled his lungs with air until his great bronzed chest expanded to the full. Already he was tasting the fruits of victory. The red blood coursed through his veins, as every fiber of his being reacted to the exhilaration of the moment—the keen delight of the hunting beast that has scented its quarry. And then swiftly and silently he sped in the direction of his prey.

Presently he came upon it, a young tusker, powerful and agile, his wicked tusks gleaming as he tore bark from a young tree. The ape-man was poised just above him, concealed by the foliage of a great tree.

A vivid flash of lightning broke from the billowing black clouds above. Thunder crashed and boomed. The storm broke, and at the same instant the man launched himself downward upon the back of the unsuspecting boar, in one hand the hunting knife of his long-dead sire.

The weight of the man's body crushed the boar to the earth, and before it could struggle to its feet again, the keen blade had severed its jugular. Its lifeblood gushing from the wound, the boar sought to rise and turn to fight; but the steel thews of the ape-man dragged it down, and an instant later, with a last convulsive shudder, Horta died.

Leaping to his feet, Tarzan placed a foot upon the carcass of his kill and, raising his face to the heavens, gave voice to the victory cry of the bull-ape.

Faintly to the ears of marching men came the hideous scream. The blacks in the party halted, wide-eyed.

"What the devil was that?" demanded Zveri.

"It sounded like a panther," said Colt.

"That was no panther," said Kitembo. "It was the cry of a bull-ape who has made a kill, or—"

"Or what?" demanded Zveri.

Kitembo looked fearfully in the direction from which the sound had come. "Let us get away from here," he said.

Again the lightning flashed and the thunder crashed, and as the torrential rain deluged them, the party staggered on in the direction of the barrier cliffs of Opar.

Cold and wet, La of Opar crouched beneath a great tree that only partially protected her almost naked body from the fury of the storm, and in the dense underbrush a few yards from her a tawny carnivore lay with unblinking eyes fixed steadily upon her.

The storm, titanic in its brief fury, passed on, leaving the deep-worn trail a tiny torrent of muddy water; and La, thoroughly chilled, hastened onward in an effort to woo new warmth to her chilled body.

She knew that trails must lead somewhere, and in her heart she hoped that this one would lead to the country of Tarzan. If she could live there, seeing him occasionally, she would be content. Even knowing that he was near her would be better than nothing. Of course she had no conception of the immensity of the world she trod. A knowledge of even the extent of the forest that surrounded her would have appalled her. In her imagination she visualized a small world, dotted with the remains of ruined cities like Opar, in which dwelt creatures like those she had known; gnarled and knotted men like the priests of Opar, white men like Tarzan, black men such as she had seen, and great shaggy gorillas like Bolgani, who had ruled in the Valley of the Palace of Diamonds.

And thinking these thoughts, she came at last to a clearing into which the unbroken rays of the warm sun poured without interruption. Near the center of the clearing was a small boulder; and toward this she made her way with the intention of basking in the warm rays of the sun until she should be thoroughly dried and warmed, for the dripping foliage of the forest had kept her wet and cold even after the rain had ceased.

As she seated herself she saw a movement at the edge of the clearing ahead of her, and an instant later a great leopard bounded into view. The beast paused at sight of the woman, evidently as much surprised as she; and then, apparently realizing the defenselessness of this unexpected prey, the creature crouched and with twitching tail slowly wormed itself forward.

La rose and drew from her girdle the knife that she had taken from Darus. She knew that flight was futile. In a few bounds the great beast could overtake her, and even had there been a tree that she could have reached before she was overtaken, it would have proven no sanctuary from a leopard. Defense, too, she knew to be futile, but surrender without battle was not within the fiber of La of Opar.

The metal discs, elaborately wrought by the hands of some long-dead goldsmith of ancient Opar, rose and fell above her firm breasts as her heart beat, perhaps a bit more rapidly, beneath them. On came the leopard. She knew that in an instant he would charge; and then of a sudden he rose to his feet, his back arched, his mouth grinning in a fearful snarl; and simultaneously a tawny streak whizzed by her from behind, and she saw a great lion leap upon her would-be destroyer.

At the last instant, but too late, the leopard had turned to flee; and the lion seized him by the back of the neck, and with his jaws and one great paw he twisted the head back until the spine snapped. Then, almost contemptuously, he cast the body from him and turned toward the girl.

In an instant La realized what had happened. The lion had been stalking her, and seeing another about to seize his prey, he had leaped to battle in defense. She had been saved, but only to fall victim immediately to another and more terrible beast.

The lion stood looking at her. She wondered why he did not charge and claim his prey. She did not know that within that little brain the scent of the woman had aroused the memory of another day, when Tarzan had lain bound upon the sacrificial altar of Opar with Jad-bal-ja, the golden lion, standing guard above him. A woman had come—this same woman—and Tarzan, his master, had told him not to harm her, and she had approached and cut the bonds that secured him.

This Jad-bal-ja remembered, and he remembered, too, that he was not to harm this woman; and if he was not to harm her, then nothing must harm her. For this reason he had killed Sheeta, the leopard.

But all this, La of Opar did not know, for she had not recognized Jad-bal-ja. She merely wondered how much longer it would be; and when the lion came closer she steeled herself, for still she meant to fight; yet there was something in his attitude that she could not understand. He was not charging; he was merely walking toward her, and when he was a couple of yards from her he half turned away and lay down and yawned.

For what seemed an eternity to the girl she stood there watching him. He paid no attention to her. Could it be that, sure of his prey and not yet hungry, he merely waited until he was quite ready to make his kill? The idea was horrible, and even La's iron nerves commenced to weaken beneath the strain.

She knew that she could not escape, and so better instant death than this suspense. She determined, therefore, to end the matter quickly and to discover once and for all whether the lion considered her already his prey or would permit her to depart.

Gathering all the forces of self-control that she possessed, she placed the point of her dagger to her heart and walked boldly past the lion. Should he attack her, she would end the agony instantly by plunging the blade into her heart.

Jad-bal-ja did not move, but with lazy, half-closed eyes he watched the woman cross the clearing and disappear beyond the turn of the trail that wound its way back into the jungle.

All that day La moved on with grim determination, looking always for a ruined city like Opar, astonished by the immensity of the forest, appalled by its loneliness. Surely, she thought, she must soon come to the country of Tarzan. She found fruits and tubers to allay her hunger, and as the trail descended a valley in which a river ran, she did not want for water. But night came again, and still no sight of man or city. Once again she crept into a tree to sleep, but this time there was no Tarzan of the Apes to fashion a couch for her or to watch over her safety.

After Tarzan had slain the boar, he cut off the hindquarters and started back to the tree in which he had left La. The storm made his progress much slower than it otherwise would have been, but notwithstanding this he realized long before he reached his destination that his hunting had taken him much farther afield than he had imagined.

When at last he reached the tree and found that La was not there, he was slightly disconcerted, but thinking that perhaps she had descended to stretch her limbs after the storm, he called her name aloud several times. Receiving no answer, he became genuinely apprehensive for her safety and, dropping to the ground, sought some sign of her spoor. It so happened that beneath the tree her footprints were still visible, not having been entirely obliterated by the rain. He saw that they led back in the direction of Opar, so that, although he lost them when they reached the trail, in which water still was running, he was nonetheless confident that he knew her intended destination; and so he set off in the direction of the barrier cliff.

It was not difficult for him to account for her absence and for the fact that she was returning to Opar, and he reproached himself for his thoughtlessness in having left her for so long a time without first telling her of his purpose. He guessed, rightly, that she had imagined herself deserted and had turned back to the only home she knew, to the only place in the world where La of Opar might hope to find friends; but that she would find them even there Tarzan doubted, and he was determined that she must not go back until she could do so with a force of warriors sufficiently great to insure the overthrow of her enemies.

It had been Tarzan's plan first to thwart the scheme of the party whose camp he had discovered in his dominion and then to return with La to the country of his Waziri, where he would gather a sufficient body of those redoubtable warriors to insure the safety and success of La's return to Opar. Never communicative, he had neglected to explain his purposes to La; and this he now regretted, since he was quite certain that had he done so she would not have felt it necessary to have attempted to return alone to Opar.

But he was not much concerned with the outcome since he was confident that he could overtake her long before she reached the city; and, inured as he was to the dangers of the forest and the jungle, he minimized their importance, as we do those which confront us daily in the ordinary course of our seemingly humdrum existence, where death threatens us quite as constantly as it does the denizens of the jungle.

At any moment expecting to catch sight of her whom he sought, Tarzan traversed the back trail to the foot of the rocky escarpment that guards the plain of Opar; and now he commenced to have his doubts, for it did not seem possible that La could have covered so great a distance in so short a time. He scaled the cliff and came out upon the summit of the flat mountain that overlooked distant Opar. Here only a light rain had fallen, the storm having followed the course of the valley below, and plain in the trail were the footprints of himself and La where they had passed down from Opar the night before; but nowhere was there any sign of spoor to indicate that the girl had returned, nor, as he looked out across the valley, was there any moving thing in sight.

What had become of her? Where could she have gone? In the great forest that spread below him there were countless trails. Somewhere below, her spoor must be plain in the freshly wet earth, but he realized that even for him it might prove a long and difficult task to pick it up again.

As he turned back rather sorrowfully to descend the barrier cliff, his attention was attracted by a movement at the edge of the forest below. Dropping to his belly behind a low bush, Tarzan watched the spot to which his attention had been attracted; and as he did so the head of a column of men debouched from the forest and moved toward the foot of the cliff.

Tarzan had known nothing of what had transpired upon the occasion of Zveri's first expedition to Opar, which had occurred while he had been incarcerated in the cell beneath the city. The apparent mysterious disappearance of the party that he had known to have been marching on Opar had mystified him; but here it was again, and where it had been in the meantime was of no moment.

Tarzan wished that he had his bow and arrow, which the Oparians had taken from him and which he had not had an opportunity to replace since he had escaped. But if he did not have them, there were other ways of annoying the invaders. From his position he watched them approach the cliff and commence the ascent.

Tarzan selected a large boulder, many of which were strewn about the flat top of the mountain, and when the leaders of the party were about halfway to the summit and the others were strung out below them, the ape-man pushed the rock over the edge of the cliff just above them. In its descent it just grazed Zveri, struck a protuberance beyond him, bounded over Colt's head, and carried two of Kitembo's warriors to death at the base of the escarpment.

The ascent stopped instantly. Several of the blacks who had accompanied the first expedition started a hasty retreat; and utter disorganization and rout faced the expedition, whose nerves had become more and more sensitive the nearer that they approached Opar.

"Stop the damn cowards!" shouted Zveri to Dorsky and

Ivitch, who were bringing up the rear. "Who will volunteer to go over the top and investigate?"

"I'll go," said Romero.

"And I'll go with him," offered Colt.

"Who else?" demanded Zveri; but no one else volunteered, and already the Mexican and the American were climbing upward.

"Cover our advance with a few rifles," Colt shouted back to Zveri. "That ought to keep them away from the edge."

Zveri issued instructions to several of the askaris who had not joined in the retreat; and when their rifles commenced popping, it put new heart into those who had started to flee, and presently Dorsky and Ivitch had rallied the men and the ascent was resumed.

Perfectly well aware that he might not stop the advance single-handed, Tarzan had withdrawn quickly along the edge of the cliff to a spot where tumbled masses of granite offered concealment and where he knew that there existed a precipitous trail to the bottom of the cliff. Here he could remain and watch, or, if necessary, make a hasty retreat. He saw Romero and Colt reach the summit and immediately recognized the latter as the man he had seen in the base camp of the invaders. He had previously been impressed by the appearance of the young American, and now he acknowledged his unquestioned bravery and that of his companion in leading a party over the summit of the cliff in the face of an unknown danger.

Romero and Colt looked quickly about them, but there was no enemy in sight, and this word they passed back to the ascending company.

From his point of vantage Tarzan watched the expedition surmount the summit of the cliff and start on its march toward Opar. He believed that they would never find the treasure vaults; and now that La was not in the city, he was not concerned with the fate of those who had turned against her. Upon the bare and inhospitable Oparian plain, or in the city itself, they could accomplish little in furthering the objects of the expedition he had overheard Zora Drinov explaining to Colt. He knew that eventually they must return to their base camp, and in the meantime he would prosecute his search for La; and so as Zveri led his expedition once again toward Opar, Tarzan of the Apes slipped over the edge of the barrier cliff and descended swiftly to the forest below.

Just inside the forest and upon the bank of the river was an admirable campsite; and having noticed that the expedition was accompanied by no porters, Tarzan naturally assumed that they had established a temporary camp within striking distance of the city, and it occurred to him that in this camp he might find La a prisoner.

As he had expected, he found the camp located upon the spot where, upon other occasions, he had camped with his Waziri warriors. An old thorn boma that had encircled it for years had been repaired by the newcomers, and within it a number of rude shelters had been erected, while in the center stood the tents of the white men. Porters were dozing in the shade of the trees; a single askari made a pretense of standing guard, while his fellows lolled at their ease, their rifles at their sides; but nowhere could he see La of Opar.

He moved downwind from the camp, hoping to catch her scent spoor if she was a prisoner there, but so strong was the smell of smoke and the body odors of the blacks that he could not be sure but that these drowned La's scent. He decided, therefore, to wait until darkness had fallen when he might make a more careful investigation, and he was further prompted to this decision by the sight of weapons, which he sorely needed. All of the warriors were armed with rifles, but some, clinging through force of ancient habit to the weapons of their ancestors, carried also bows and arrows, and in addition there were many spears.

As a few mouthfuls of the raw flesh of Horta had constituted the only food that had passed Tarzan's lips for almost two days, he was ravenously hungry. With the discovery that La had disappeared, he had cached the hindquarter of the boar in the tree in which they had spent the night and set out upon his fruitless search for her; so now, while he waited for darkness, he hunted again, and this time Bara, the antelope, fell a victim to his prowess, nor did he leave the carcass of his kill until he had satisfied his hunger. Then he lay up in a nearby tree and slept.

The anger of Abu Batn against Zveri was rooted deeply in his inherent racial antipathy for Europeans and their religion, and its growth was stimulated by the aspersions which the Russian had cast upon the courage of the Aarab and his followers.

"Dog of a Nasrâny!" ejaculated the sheik. "He called us cowards, we Bedaùwy, and he left us here like old men and boys to guard the camp and the woman."

"He is but an instrument of Allah," said one of the Aarabs, "in the great cause that will rid Africa of all Nasrâny."

"Wellah-billah!" ejaculated Abu Batn. "What proof have we that these people will do as they promise? I would rather have my freedom on the desert and what wealth I can gather by myself than to lie longer in the same camp with these Nasrâny pigs."

"There is no good in them," muttered another.

"I have looked upon their woman," said the sheik, "and I find her good. I know a city where she would bring many pieces of gold."

"In the trunk of the chief Nasrâny there are many pieces of gold and silver," said one of the men. "His boy told that to a Galla, who repeated it to me."

"The plunder of the camp is rich besides," suggested a swarthy warrior.

"If we do this thing, perhaps the great cause will be lost," suggested he who had first answered the sheik.

"It is the cause of the Nasrâny," said Abu Batn, "and it is only for profit. Is not the huge pig always reminding us of the money, and the women, and the power that we shall have when we have thrown out the English? Man is moved only by his greed. Let us take our profits in advance and be gone."

Wamala was preparing the evening meal for his mistress. "Before, you were left with the brown bwana," he said, "and he was no good; nor do I like any better the sheykh Abu Batn. He is no good. I wish that Bwana Colt were here."

"So do I," said Zora. "It seems to me that the Aarabs have

been sullen and surly ever since the expedition returned from Opar."

"They have sat all day in the tent of their chief talking together," said Wamala, "and often Abu Batn looked at you."

"That is your imagination, Wamala," replied the girl. "He would not dare to harm me."

"Who would have thought that the brown bwana would have dared to?" Wamala reminded her.

"Hush, Wamala, the first thing you know you will have me frightened," said Zora, and then suddenly, "Look, Wamala! Who is that?"

The black boy turned his eyes in the direction toward which his mistress was looking. At the edge of the camp stood a figure that might have wrung an exclamation of surprise from a Stoic. A beautiful woman stood there regarding them intently. She had halted just at the edge of camp—an almost naked woman whose gorgeous beauty was her first and most striking characteristic. Two golden discs covered her firm breasts, and a narrow stomacher of gold and precious stones encircled her hips, supporting in front and behind a broad strip of soft leather, studded with gold and jewels, which formed the pattern of a pedestal on the summit of which was seated a grotesque bird. Her feet were shod in sandals that were covered with mud, as were her shapely legs upward to above her knees. A mass of wavy hair, shot with golden bronze lights by the rays of the setting sun, half surrounded an oval face, and from beneath narrow penciled brows fearless gray eyes regarded them.

Some of the Aarabs had caught sight of her, too, and they were coming forward now toward her. She looked quickly from Zora and Wamala toward the others. Then the European girl arose quickly and approached her that she might reach her before the Arabs did; and as she came near the stranger with outstretched hands, Zora smiled. La of Opar came quickly to meet her as though sensing in the smile of the other an index to the friendly intent of this stranger.

"Who are you," asked Zora, "and what are you doing here alone in the jungle?"

La shook her head and replied in a language that Zora did not understand.

Zora Drinov was an accomplished linguist but she exhausted every language in her repertoire, including a few phrases from various Bantu dialects, and still found no means of communicating with the stranger, whose beautiful face and figure but added to the interest of the tantalizing enigma she presented to pique the curiosity of the Russian girl.

The Aarabs addressed her in their own tongue and Wamala in the dialect of his tribe, but all to no avail. Then Zora put an arm about her and led her toward her tent; and there, by means of signs, La of Opar indicated that she would bathe. Wamala was directed to prepare a tub in Zora's tent, and by the time supper was prepared the stranger reappeared, washed and refreshed.

As Zora Drinov seated herself opposite her strange guest, she was impressed with the belief that never before had she looked upon so beautiful a woman, and she marveled that one who must have felt so utterly out of place in her surroundings should still retain a poise that suggested the majestic bearing of a queen rather than of a stranger ill at ease.

By signs and gestures, Zora sought to converse with her guest until even the regal La found herself laughing; and then La tried it too until Zora knew that her guest had been threatened with clubs and knives and driven from her home, that she had walked a long way, that either a lion or a leopard had attacked her and that she was very tired.

When supper was over, Wamala prepared another cot for La in the tent with Zora, for something in the faces of the Aarabs had made the European girl fear for the safety of her beautiful guest.

"You must sleep outside the tent door tonight, Wamala," she said. "Here is an extra pistol."

In his goat-hair beyt Abu Batn, the sheik, talked long into the night with the principal men of his tribe. "The new one," he said, "will bring a price such as has never been paid before."

Tarzan awoke and glanced upward through the foliage at the stars. He saw that the night was half gone, and he arose and stretched himself. He ate again sparingly of the flesh of Bara and slipped silently into the shadows of the night.

The camp at the foot of the barrier cliff slept. A single askari kept guard and tended the beast fire. From a tree at the edge of the camp two eyes watched him, and when he was looking away a figure dropped silently into the shadows. Behind the huts of the porters it crept, pausing occasionally to test the air with dilated nostrils. It came at last, among the shadows, to the tents of the Europeans, and one by one it ripped a hole in each rear wall and entered. It was Tarzan searching for La, but he did not find her and, disappointed, he turned to another matter.

Making a half circuit of the camp, moving sometimes only inch by inch as he wormed himself along on his belly, lest the askari upon guard might see him, he made his way to the shelters of the other askaris, and there he selected a bow and arrows, and a stout spear, but even yet he was not done.

For a long time he crouched waiting—waiting until the askari by the fire should turn in a certain direction.

Presently the sentry arose and threw some dry wood upon the fire, after which he walked toward the shelter of his fellows to awaken the man who was to relieve him. It was this moment for which Tarzan had been waiting. The path of the askari brought him close to where Tarzan lay in hiding. The man approached and passed, and in the same instant Tarzan leaped to his feet and sprang upon the unsuspecting black. A strong arm encircled the fellow from behind and swung him to a broad, bronzed shoulder. As Tarzan had anticipated, a scream of terror burst from the man's lips, awakening his fellows; and then he was borne swiftly through the shadows of the camp away from the beast fire as, with his prey struggling futilely in his grasp, the ape-man leaped the thorn boma and disappeared into the black jungle beyond.

So sudden and violent was the attack, so complete the man's surprise, that he had loosened his grasp upon his rifle in an effort to clutch his antagonist as he was thrown lightly to the shoulder of his captor.

His screams, echoing through the forest, brought his terrified companions from their shelters in time to see an indistinct form leap the boma and vanish into the darkness. They stood temporarily paralyzed by fright, listening to the diminishing cries of their comrade. Presently these ceased as suddenly as they had commenced. Then the head man found his voice.

"Simba!" he said.

"It was not Simba," declared another. "It ran high upon two legs, like a man I saw it."

Presently from the dark jungle came a hideous, long-drawn cry. "That is the voice of neither man nor lion," said the head man.

"It is a demon," whispered another, and then they huddled about the fire, throwing dry wood upon it until its blaze had crackled high into the air.

In the darkness of the jungle Tarzan paused and laid aside his spear and bow, possession of which had permitted him to use but one hand in his abduction of the sentry. Now the fingers of his free hand closed upon the throat of his victim, putting a sudden period to his screams. Only for an instant did Tarzan choke the man; and when he relaxed his grasp upon the fellow's throat, the black made no further outcry, fearing to invite again the ungentle grip of those steel fingers. Quickly Tarzan jerked the fellow to his feet, relieved him of his knife and, grasping him by his thick wool, pushed him ahead of him into the jungle, after stooping to retrieve his spear and bow. It was then that he voiced the victory cry of the bull-ape, for the value of the effect that it would have not only upon his victim, but upon his fellows in the camp behind them.

Tarzan had no intention of harming the fellow. His quarrel was not with the innocent black tools of the white men; and, while he would not have hesitated to take the life of the black had it been necessary, he knew them well enough to know that he might effect his purpose with them as well without bloodshed as with it.

The whites could not accomplish anything without their black allies, and if Tarzan could successfully undermine the morale of the latter, the schemes of their masters would be as effectually thwarted as though he had destroyed them, since he was confident that they would not remain in a district where they were constantly reminded of the presence of a malign, supernatural enemy. Furthermore, this policy accorded better with Tarzan's grim sense of humor and, therefore, amused him, which the taking of life never did.

For an hour he marched his victim ahead of him in an utter silence, which he knew would have its effect upon the nerves of the black man. Finally he halted him, stripped his remaining clothing from him, and taking the fellow's loincloth bound his wrists and ankles together loosely. Then, appropriating his cartridge belt and other belongings, Tarzan left him, knowing that the black would soon free himself from his bonds; yet, believing that he had made his escape, would remain for life convinced that he had narrowly eluded a terrible fate.

Satisfied with his night's work, Tarzan returned to the tree in which he had cached the carcass of Bara, ate once more and lay up in sleep until morning, when he again took up his search for La, seeking trace of her up the valley beyond the barrier cliff of Opar, in the general direction that her spoor had indicated she had gone, though, as a matter of fact, she had gone in precisely the opposite direction, down the valley.

NIGHT WAS FALLING when a frightened little monkey took
refuge in a treetop. For days he had been wandering
through the jungle, seeking in his little mind a solution for
his problem during those occasional intervals that he could
concentrate his mental forces upon it. But in an instant
he might forget it to go swinging and scampering through
the trees, or again a sudden terror would drive it from his
consciousness, as one or another of the hereditary menaces
to his existence appeared within the range of his perceptive
faculties.

While his grief lasted, it was real and poignant, and tears
welled in the eyes of little Nkima as he thought of his absent
master. Lurking always within him upon the borderland of
conviction was the thought that he must obtain succor for
Tarzan. In some way he must fetch aid to his master. The great
black Gomangani warriors, who were also the servants of
Tarzan, were many darknesses away, but yet it was in the general direction of the country of the Waziri that he drifted. Time
was in no sense the essence of the solution of this or any other
problem in the mind of Nkima. He had seen Tarzan enter Opar
alive. He had not seen him destroyed, nor had he seen him
come out of the city; and, therefore, by the standards of his
logic Tarzan must still be alive and in the city, but because the
city was filled with enemies Tarzan must be in danger. As con-

ditions were they would remain. He could not readily visualize any change that he did not actually witness, and so, whether he found and fetched the Waziri today or tomorrow would have little effect upon the result. They would go to Opar and kill Tarzan's enemies, and then little Nkima would have his master once more, and he would not have to be afraid of Sheeta, or Sabor, or Histah.

Night fell, and in the forest Nkima heard a gentle tapping. He aroused himself and listened intently. The tapping grew in volume until it rolled and moved through the jungle. Its source was at no great distance, and as Nkima became aware of this, his excitement grew.

The moon was well up in the heavens, but the shadows of the jungle were dense. Nkima was upon the horns of a dilemma, between his desire to go to the place from which the drumming emanated and his fear of the dangers that might lie along the way; but at length the urge prevailed over his terror, and keeping well up in the relatively greater safety of the treetops, he swung quickly in the direction from which the sound was coming to halt at last, above a little natural clearing that was roughly circular in shape.

Below him, in the moonlight, he witnessed a scene that he had spied upon before, for here the great apes of To-yat were engaged in the death dance of the Dum-Dum. In the center of the amphitheater was one of those remarkable earthen drums, which from time immemorial primitive man has heard, but which few have seen. Before the drum were seated two old shes, who beat upon its resounding surface with short sticks. There was a rough rhythmic cadence to their beating, and to it, in a savage circle, danced the bulls; while encircling them in a thin outer line, the females and the young squatted upon their haunches, enthralled spectators of the savage scene. Close beside the drum lay the dead body of Shetta, the leopard, to celebrate whose killing the Dum-Dum had been organized.

Presently the dancing bulls would rush in upon the body and beat it with heavy sticks and, leaping out again, resume their dance. When the hunt, and the attack, and the death had been depicted at length, they would cast away their bludgeons and with bared fangs leap upon the carcass, tearing and rending it as they fought among themselves for large pieces or choice morsels.

Now Nkima and his kind are noted neither for their tact nor judgment. One wiser than little Nkima would have remained silent until the dance and the feast were over and until a new day had come and the great bulls of the tribe of To-yat had recovered from the hysterical frenzy that the drum and the dancing always induced within them. But little Nkima was only a monkey. What he wanted, he wanted immediately, not being endowed with that mental poise which results in patience, and so he swung by his tail from an overhanging branch and scolded at the top of his voice in an effort to attract the attention of the great apes below.

"To-yat! Ga-yat! Zu-tho!" he cried. "Tarzan is in danger! Come with Nkima and save Tarzan!"

A great bull stopped in the midst of the dancing and looked up. "Go away, Manu," he growled. "Go away or we kill!" But little Nkima thought that they could not catch him, and so he continued to swing from the branch and yell and scream at them until finally To-yat sent a young ape, who was not too heavy, to clamber into the upper branches of the tree, to catch little Nkima and kill him.

Here was an emergency which Nkima had not foreseen. Like many people, he had believed that everyone would be as interested in what interested him as he; and when he had first heard the booming of the drums of the Dum-Dum, he thought that the moment the apes learned of Tarzan's peril they would set out upon the trail to Opar.

Now, however, he knew differently, and as the real menace of his mistake became painfully apparent with the leaping of a young ape into the tree below him, little Nkima emitted a loud shriek of terror and fled through the night; nor did he pause until, panting and exhausted, he had put a good mile between himself and the tribe of To-yat.

When La of Opar awoke in the tent of Zora Drinov she looked about her, taking in the unfamiliar objects that surrounded her, and presently her gaze rested upon the face of her sleeping hostess. These, indeed, she thought, must be the people of Tarzan, for had they not treated her with kindness and courtesy? They had offered her no harm and had fed her and given her shelter. A new thought crossed her mind now and her brows contracted, as did the pupils of her eyes into which there came a sudden, savage light. Perhaps this woman was Tarzan's mate. La of Opar grasped the hilt of Darus' knife where it lay ready beside her. But then, as suddenly as it had come, the mood passed, for in her heart she knew that she could not return evil for good, nor could she harm whom Tarzan loved, and when Zora opened her eyes La greeted her with a smile.

If the European girl was a cause for astonishment to La, she herself filled the other with profoundest wonder and mystification. Her scant, yet rich and gorgeous apparel harked back to an ancient age, and the gleaming whiteness of her skin seemed as much out of place in the heart of an African jungle as did her trappings in the twentieth century. Here was a mystery that nothing in the past experience of Zora Drinov could assist in solving. How she wished that she could converse with her, but all that she could do was to smile back at the beautiful creature regarding her so intently.

La, accustomed as she had been to being waited upon all her life by the lesser priestesses of Opar, was surprised by the facility with which Zora Drinov attended to her own needs as she rose to bathe and dress, the only service she received being in the form of a pail of hot water that Wamala fetched and poured into her folding tub; yet though La had never before been expected to lift a hand in the making of her toilet, she was far from helpless, and perhaps she found pleasure in the new experience of doing for herself.

Unlike the customs of the men of Opar, those of its women required scrupulous bodily cleanliness, so that in the past much of La's time had been devoted to her toilet, to the care of her nails, and her teeth, and her hair, and to the massaging of her body with aromatic unguents—customs, handed down from a cultured civilization of antiquity, to take on in ruined Opar the significance of religious rites.

By the time the two girls were ready for breakfast, Wamala was prepared to serve it; and as they sat outside the tent beneath the shade of a tree, eating the coarse fare of the camp, Zora noted unwonted activity about the beyts of the Aarabs, but she gave the matter little thought, as they had upon other occasions moved their tents from one part of the camp to another.

Breakfast over, Zora took down her rifle, wiped out the bore and oiled the breech mechanism, for today she was going out after fresh meat, the Aarabs having refused to hunt. La watched her with evident interest and later saw her depart with Wamala and two of the black porters; but she did not attempt to accompany her since, although she had looked for it, she had received no sign to do so.

Ibn Dammuk was the son of a sheik of the same tribe as Abu Batn, and upon this expedition he was the latter's righthand man. With the fold of his thôb drawn across the lower part of his face, leaving only his eyes exposed, he had been watching the two girls from a distance. He saw Zora Drinov quit the camp with a gun-bearer and two porters and knew that she had gone to hunt.

For some time after she had departed he sat in silence with two companions. Then he arose and sauntered across the camp toward La of Opar, where she sat buried in reverie in a camp chair before Zora's tent. As the three men approached, La eyed them with level gaze, her natural suspicion of strangers aroused in her breast. As they came closer and their features became distinct, she felt a sudden distrust of them. They were crafty, malign-looking men, not at all like Tarzan, and instinctively she distrusted them.

They halted before her and Ibn Dammuk, the son of a sheik, addressed her. His voice was soft and oily, but it did not deceive her.

La eyed him haughtily. She did not understand him and she did not wish to, for the message that she read in his eyes disgusted her. She shook her head to signify that she did not understand and turned away to indicate that the interview was terminated, but Ibn Dammuk stepped closer and laid a hand familiarly upon her naked shoulder.

Her eyes flaming with anger, La leaped to her feet, one hand moving swiftly to the hilt of her dagger. Ibn Dammuk stepped back, but one of his men leaped forward to seize her.

Misguided fool! Like a tigress she was upon him; and before his friends could intervene, the sharp blade of the knife of Darus, the priest of the Flaming God, had sunk thrice into his breast, and with a gasping scream he had slumped to the ground dead.

With flaming eyes and bloody knife, the high priestess of Opar stood above her kill, while Abu Batn and the other Aarabs, attracted by the death cry of the stricken man, ran hurriedly toward the little group.

"Stand back!" cried La. "Lay no profaning hand upon the person of the high priestess of the Flaming God."

They did not understand her words, but they understood her flashing eyes and her dripping blade. Jabbering volubly, they gathered around her, but at a safe distance. "What means this, Ibn Dammuk?" demanded Abu Batn.

"Dogman did but touch her, and she flew at him like el adrea, lord of the broad head."

"A lioness she may be," said Abu Batn, "but she must not be harmed."

"Wullah!" exclaimed Ibn Dammuk, "but she must be tamed."

"Her taming we may leave to him who will pay many pieces of gold for her," replied the sheik. "It is necessary only for us to cage her. Surround her, my children, and take the knife from her. Make her wrists secure behind her back, and by the time the other returns we shall have struck camp and be ready to depart."

A dozen brawny men leaped upon La simultaneously. "Do not harm her! Do not harm her!" screamed Abu Batn, as, fighting like a lioness indeed, La sought to defend herself. Slashing right and left with her dagger, she drew blood more than once before they overpowered her; nor did they accomplish it before another Aarab fell with a pierced heart, but at length they succeeded in wrenching the blade from her and securing her wrists.

Leaving two warriors to guard her, Abu Batn turned his attention to gathering up the few black servants that remained in camp. These he forced to prepare loads of such of the camp equipment and provisions as he required. While this work was going on under Ibn Dammuk's supervision, the sheik ransacked the tents of the Europeans, giving special attention to those of Zora Drinov and Zveri, where he expected to find the gold that the leader of the expedition was reputed to have in large quantities; nor was he entirely disappointed since he found in Zora's tent a box containing a considerable amount of money, though by no means the great quantity that he had expected, a fact which was due to the foresight of Zveri, who had personally buried the bulk of his funds beneath the floor of his tent.

Zora met with unexpected success in her hunting, for within a little more than an hour of her departure from camp she had come upon antelope, and two quick shots had dropped as many members of the herd. She waited while the porters skinned and dressed them and then returned leisurely toward camp. Her mind was occupied to some extent with the disquieting attitude of the Aarabs, but she was not at all prepared for the reception that she met when she approached camp about noon.

She was walking in advance, immediately followed by Wamala, who was carrying both of her rifles, while behind them were the porters, staggering under their heavy loads. Just as she was about to enter the clearing, Aarabs leaped from the underbrush on either side of the trail. Two of them seized Wamala and wrenched the rifles from his grasp, while others laid heavy hands upon Zora. She tried to free herself from them and draw her revolver, but the attack had taken her so by surprise that before she could accomplish anything in defense, she was overpowered and her hands bound at her back.

"What is the meaning of this?" she demanded. "Where is Abu Batn, the sheykh?"

The men laughed at her. "You shall see him presently," said one. "He has another guest whom he is entertaining, so he could not come to meet you," at which they all laughed again.

As she stepped into the clearing where she could obtain

an unobstructed view of the camp, she was astounded by what she saw. Every tent had been struck. The Aarabs were leaning on their rifles ready to march, each of them burdened with a small pack, while the few black men, who had been left in camp, were lined up before heavy loads. All the rest of the paraphernalia of the camp, which Abu Batn had not men enough to transport, was heaped in a pile in the center of the clearing, and even as she looked she saw men setting torches to it.

As she was led across the clearing toward the waiting Aarabs, she saw her erstwhile guest between two warriors, her wrists confined by thongs even as her own. Near her, scowling malevolently, was Abu Batn.

"Why have you done this thing, Abu Batn?" demanded Zora.

"Allah was wroth that we should betray our land to the Nas-rány," said the sheik. "We have seen the light, and we are going back to our own people."

"What do you intend to do with this woman and with me?" asked Zora.

"We shall take you with us for a little way," replied Abu Batn. "I know a kind man who is very rich, who will give you both a good home."

"You mean that you are going to sell us to some black sultan?" demanded the girl.

The sheik shrugged. "I would not put it that way," he said. "Rather let us say that I am making a present to a great and good friend and saving you and this other woman from certain death in the jungle should we depart without you."

"Abu Batn, you are a hypocrite and a traitor," cried Zora, her voice vibrant with contempt.

"The Nasrány like to call names," said the sheik with a sneer. "Perhaps if the pig, Zveri, had not called us names, this would not have happened."

"So this is your revenge," asked Zora, "because he reproached you for your cowardice at Opar?"

"Enough!" snapped Abu Batn. "Come, my children, let us be gone."

As the flames licked at the edges of the great pile of provisions and equipment that the Aarabs were forced to leave behind, the deserters started upon their march toward the west.

The girls marched near the head of the column, the feet of the Aarabs and the carriers behind them totally obliterating their spoor from the motley record of the trail. They might have found some comfort in their straits had they been able to converse with one another; but La could understand no one and Zora found no pleasure in speaking to the Aarabs, while Wamala and the other blacks were so far toward the rear of the column that she could not have communicated with them had she cared to.

To pass the time away, Zora conceived the idea of teaching her companion in misery some European language, and because in the original party there had been more who were familiar with English than any other tongue, she selected that language for her experiment.

She began by pointing to herself and saying "woman" and then to La and repeating the same word, after which she pointed to several of the Arabs in succession and said "man" in each instance. It was evident that La understood her purpose immediately, for she entered into the spirit of it with eagerness and alacrity, repeating the two words again and again, each time indicating either a man or a woman.

Next the European girl again pointed to herself and said "Zora." For a moment La was perplexed, and then she smiled and nodded.

"Zora," she said, pointing to her companion, and then, swiftly, she touched her own breast with a slender forefinger and said, "La."

And this was the beginning. Each hour La learned new words, all nouns at first, that described each familiar object that appeared oftenest to their view. She learned with remarkable celerity, evidencing an alert and intelligent mind and a retentive memory, for once she learned a word she never forgot it. Her pronunciation was not always perfect, for she had a decidedly foreign accent that was like nothing Zora Drinov ever had heard before, and so altogether captivating that the teacher never tired of hearing her pupil recite.

As the march progressed, Zora realized that there was little likelihood that they would be mistreated by their captors, it being evident to her that the sheik was impressed with the belief that the better the condition in which they could be presented to their prospective purchaser the more handsome the return that Abu Batn might hope to receive.

Their route lay to the northwest through a section of the Galla country of Abyssinia, and from scraps of conversation Zora overheard she learned that Abu Batn and his followers were apprehensive of danger during this portion of the journey. And well they may have been, since for ages the Arabs have conducted raids in Galla territory for the purpose of capturing slaves, and among the Negroes with them was a Galla slave that Abu Batn had brought with him from his desert home.

After the first day the prisoners had been allowed the freedom of their hands, but always Aarab guards surrounded them, though there seemed little likelihood that an unarmed girl would take the risk of escaping into the jungle, where she would be surrounded by the dangers of wild beasts or almost certain starvation. However, could Abu Batn have read their thoughts, he might have been astonished to learn that in the mind of each was a determination to escape to any fate rather than to march docilely on to an end that the European girl was fully conscious of and which La of Opar unquestionably surmised in part.

La's education was progressing nicely by the time the party approached the border of the Galla country, but in the meantime both girls had become aware of a new menace threatening La of Opar. Ibn Dammuk marched often beside her, and in his eyes, when he looked at her, was a message that needed no words to convey. But when Abu Batn was near, Ibn Dammuk ignored the fair prisoner, and this caused Zora the most apprehension, for it convinced her that the wily Ibn was but biding his time until he might find conditions favorable to the carrying out of some scheme that he already had decided upon, nor did Zora harbor any doubts as to the general purpose of his plan.

At the edge of the Galla country they were halted by a river in flood. They could not go north into Abyssinia proper, and they dared not go south, where they might naturally have expected pursuit to follow. So perforce they were compelled to wait where they were.

And while they waited Ibn Dammuk struck.

9

In the Death Cell of Opar

ONCE AGAIN PETER Zveri stood before the walls of Opar, and once again the courage of his black soldiers was dissipated by the weird cries of the inmates of the city of mystery. The ten warriors, who had not been to Opar before and who had volunteered to enter the city, halted trembling as the first of the blood-curdling screams rose, shrill and piercing, from the forbidding ruins.

Miguel Romero once more led the invaders, and directly behind him was Wayne Colt. According to the plan the blacks were to have followed closely behind these two, with the rest of the whites bringing up the rear, where they might rally and encourage the Negroes, or if necessary, force them on at the points of their pistols. But the blacks would not even enter the opening of the outer wall, so demoralized were they by the uncanny warning screams which their superstitious minds attributed to malignant demons, against which there could be no defense and whose animosity meant almost certain death for those who disregarded their wishes.

"In with you, you dirty cowards!" cried Zveri, menacing the

blacks with his revolver in an effort to force them into the opening.

One of the warriors raised his rifle threateningly. "Put away your weapon, white man," he said. "We will fight men, but we will not fight the spirits of the dead."

"Lay off, Peter," said Dorsky. "You will have the whole bunch on us in a minute and we shall all be killed."

Zveri lowered his pistol and commenced to plead with the warriors, promising them rewards that amounted to riches to them if they would accompany the whites into the city; but the volunteers were obdurate—nothing could induce them to venture into Opar.

Seeing failure once again imminent and with a mind already obsessed by the belief that the treasures of Opar would make him fabulously wealthy and insure the success of his secret scheme of empire, Zveri determined to follow Romero and Colt with the remainder of his aides, which consisted only of Dorsky, Ivitch, and the Filipino boy. "Come on," he said, "we will have to make a try at it alone, if these yellow dogs won't help us."

By the time the four men had passed through the outer wall, Romero and Colt were already out of sight beyond the inner wall. Once again the warning scream broke menacingly upon the brooding silence of the ruined city.

"God!" ejaculated Ivitch. "What do you suppose it could be?"

"Shut up," exclaimed Zveri irritably. "Stop thinking about it, or you'll go yellow like those damn blacks."

Slowly they crossed the court toward the inner wall, nor was there much enthusiasm manifest among them other than for an evident desire in the breast of each to permit one of the others the glory of leading the advance. Tony had reached the opening when a bedlam of noise from the opposite side of the wall burst upon their ears—a hideous chorus of war cries, mingled with the sound of rushing feet. There was a shot, and then another and another.

Tony turned to see if his companions were following him. They had halted and were standing with blanched faces, listening.

Then Ivitch turned. "To hell with the gold!" he said, and started back toward the outer wall at a run.

"Come back, you lousy cur," cried Zveri, and took after him with Dorsky at his heels. Tony hesitated for a moment and then scurried in pursuit, nor did any of them halt until they were beyond the outer wall. There Zveri overtook Ivitch and seized him by the shoulder. "I ought to kill you," he cried in a trembling voice.

"You were as glad to get out of there as I was," growled Ivitch. "What was the sense of going in there? We should only have been killed like Colt and Romero. There were too many of them. Didn't you hear them?"

"I think Ivitch is right," said Dorsky. "It's all right to be brave, but we have got to remember the cause—if we are killed everything is lost."

"But the gold!" exclaimed Zveri. "Think of the gold!"

"Gold is no good to dead men," Dorsky reminded him.

"How about our comrades?" asked Tony. "Are we to leave them to be killed?"

"To hell with the Mexican," said Zveri, "and as for the American I think his funds will still be available as long as we can keep the news of his death from getting back to the Coast."

"You are not even going to try to rescue them?" asked Tony.

"I cannot do it alone," said Zveri.

"I will go with you," said Tony.

"Little good two of us can accomplish," mumbled Zveri, and then in one of his sudden rages, he advanced menacingly upon the Filipino, his great figure towering above that of the other.

"Who do you think you are anyway?" he demanded. "I am in command here. When I want your advice I'll ask for it."

When Romero and Colt passed through the inner wall, that part of the interior of the temple which they could see appeared deserted, and yet they were conscious of movement in the darker recesses and the apertures of the ruined galleries that looked down into the courtway.

Colt glanced back. "Shall we wait for the others?" he asked.

Romero shrugged. "I think we are going to have this glory all to ourselves, comrade," he said with a grin.

Colt smiled back at him. "Then let's get on with the business," he said. "I don't see anything very terrifying yet."

"There is something in there though," said Romero. "I've seen things moving."

"So have I," said Colt.

With their rifles ready, they advanced boldly into the temple; but they had not gone far when, from shadowy archways and from numerous gloomy doorways there rushed a horde of horrid men, and the silence of the ancient city was shattered by hideous war cries.

Colt was in advance and now he kept on moving forward, firing a shot above the heads of the grotesque warrior priests of Opar. Romero saw a number of the enemy running along the side of the great room which they had entered, with the evident intention of cutting off their retreat. He swung about and fired, but not over their heads. Realizing the gravity of their position, he shot to kill, and now Colt did the same, with the result that the screams of a couple of wounded men mingled now with the war cries of their fellows.

Romero was forced to drop back a few steps to prevent the Oparians from surrounding him. He shot rapidly now and succeeded in checking the advance around their flank. A quick glance at Colt showed him standing his ground, and at the same instant he saw a hurled club strike the American on the head. The man dropped like a log, and instantly his body was covered by the terrible little men of Opar.

Miguel Romero realized that his companion was lost, and even if not now already dead, he, single-handed, could accomplish nothing toward his rescue. If he escaped with his own life he would be fortunate, and so, keeping up a steady fire, he fell back toward the aperture in the inner wall.

Having captured one of the invaders, seeing the other falling back, and fearing to risk further the devastating fire of the terrifying weapon in the hand of their single antagonist, the Oparians hesitated.

Romero passed through the inner wall, turned, and ran swiftly to the outer and a moment later had joined his companions upon the plain.

"Where is Colt?" demanded Zveri.

"They knocked him out with a club and captured him," said Romero. "He is probably dead by this time."

"And you deserted him?" asked Zveri.

The Mexican turned upon his chief in fury. "You ask me that?" he demanded. "You turned pale and ran even before you saw the enemy. If you fellows had backed us up Colt might not have been lost, but to let us go in there alone the two of us didn't have a Chinaman's chance with that bunch of wild men. And you accuse me of cowardice?"

"I didn't do anything of the kind," said Zveri sullenly. "I never said you were a coward."

"You meant to imply it though," snapped Romero, "but let me tell you, Zveri, that you can't get away with that with me or anyone else who has been to Opar with you."

From behind the walls rose a savage cry of victory; and while it still rumbled through the tarnished halls of Opar, Zveri turned dejectedly away from the city. "It's no use," he said. "I can't capture Opar alone. We are returning to camp."

The little priests, swarming over Colt, stripped him of his weapons and secured his hands behind his back. He was still unconscious, and so they lifted him to the shoulder of one of their fellows and bore him away into the interior of the temple.

When Colt regained consciousness he found himself lying on the floor of a large chamber. It was the throne room of the temple of Opar, where he had been fetched that Oah, the high priestess, might see the prisoner.

Perceiving that their captive had regained consciousness, his guards jerked him roughly to his feet and pushed him forward toward the foot of the dais upon which stood Oah's throne.

The effect of the picture bursting suddenly upon him imparted to Colt the definite impression that he was the victim of an hallucination or a dream. The outer chamber of the ruin, in which he had fallen, had given no suggestion of the size and semibarbaric magnificence of this great chamber, the grandeur of which was scarcely dimmed by the ruin of ages.

He saw before him, upon an ornate throne, a young woman of exceptional physical beauty, surrounded by the semi-barbaric grandeur of an ancient civilization. Grotesque and hairy men and beautiful maidens formed her entourage. Her eyes, resting upon him, were cold and cruel; her mien haughty and contemptuous. A squat warrior, more apelike in his conformation than human, was addressing her in a language unfamiliar to the American.

When he had finished, the girl rose from the throne and, drawing a long knife from her girdle, raised it high above her head as she spoke rapidly and almost fiercely, her eyes fixed upon the prisoner.

From among a group of priestesses at the right of Oah's throne, a girl, just come into womanhood, regarded the prisoner through half-closed eyes, and beneath the golden plates that confined her smooth, white breasts, the heart of Nao palpitated to the thoughts that contemplation of this strange warrior engendered within her.

When Oah had finished speaking, Colt was led away, quite ignorant of the fact that he had been listening to the sentence of death imposed upon him by the high priestess of the Flaming God. His guards conducted him to a cell just within the entrance of a tunnel leading from the sacrificial court to the pits beneath the city, and because it was not entirely below ground, fresh air and light had access to it through a window and the grated bars of its doorway. Here the escort left him, after removing the bonds from his wrists.

Through the small window in his cell Wayne Colt looked out upon the inner court of the Temple of the Sun at Opar. He saw the surrounding galleries rising tier upon tier to the summit of a lofty wall. He saw the stone altar standing in the center of the court, and the brown stains upon it and upon the pavement at its foot told him what the unintelligible words of Oah had been unable to convey. For an instant he felt his heart sink within his breast, and a shudder passed through his frame as he contemplated his inability to escape the fate which confronted him. There could be no mistaking the purpose of that altar when viewed in connection with the grinning skulls of former human sacrifices which stared through eyeless sockets upon him from their niches in the surrounding walls.

Fascinated by the horror of his situation, he stood staring at the altar and skulls, but presently he gained control of himself and shook the terror from him, yet the hopelessness of his situation continued to depress him. His thoughts turned to his companion. He wondered what Romero's fate had been. There, indeed, had been a brave and gallant comrade, in fact the only member of the party who had impressed Colt favorably, or in whose society he had found pleasure. The others had seemed either ignorant fanatics or avaricious opportunists, while the manner and speech of the Mexican had stamped him as a lighthearted soldier of fortune, who might gayly offer his life in any cause which momentarily seized his fancy with an eye more singly for excitement and adventure than for any serious purpose. He did not know, of course, that Zveri and the others had deserted him; but he was confident that Romero had not before his cause had become utterly hopeless, or until the Mexican himself had been killed or captured.

In lonely contemplation of his predicament, Colt spent the rest of the long afternoon. Darkness fell, and still there came no sign from his captors. He wondered if they intended leaving him there without food or water, or if, perchance, the ceremony that was to see him offered in sacrifice upon that grim, brown-stained altar was scheduled to commence so soon that they felt it unnecessary to minister to his physical needs.

He had lain down upon the hard cementlike surface of the cell floor and was trying to find momentary relief in sleep, when his attention was attracted by the shadow of a sound coming from the courtyard where the altar stood. As he listened he was positive that someone was approaching, and rising quietly he went to the window and looked out. In the shadowy darkness of the night, relieved only by the faint light of distant stars, he saw something moving across the courtyard toward his cell, but whether man or beast he could not distinguish; and then, from somewhere high up among the lofty ruins, there pealed out upon the silent night the long-drawn scream, which seemed now to the American as much a part of the mysterious city of Opar as the crumbling ruins themselves.

* * *

It was a sullen and discouraged party that made its way back to the camp at the edge of the forest below the barrier cliffs of Opar, and when they arrived it was to find only further disorganization and discouragement.

No time was lost in narrating to the members of the returning expedition the story of the sentry who had been carried off into the jungle at night by a demon, from whom the man had managed to escape before being devoured. Still fresh in their minds was the uncanny affair of the death of Raghunath Jafar, nor were the nerves of those who had been before the walls of Opar inclined to be at all steadied by that experience, so that it was a nervous company that bivouacked that night beneath the dark trees at the edge of the gloomy forest and, with sighs of relief, witnessed the coming of dawn.

Later, after they had taken up the march toward the base camp, the spirit of the blacks gradually returned to normal and presently the tension under which they had been laboring for days was relieved by song and laughter, but the whites were gloomy and sullen. Zveri and Romero did not speak to one another, while Ivitch, like all weak characters, nursed a grievance against everyone because of his own display of cowardice during the fiasco at Opar.

From the interior of a hollow tree in which he had been hiding, little Nkima saw the column pass; and after it was safely by he emerged from his retreat and, dancing up and down upon a limb of the tree, shouted dire threats after them and called them many names.

Tarzan of the Apes lay stretched upon his belly upon the back of Tantor, the elephant, his elbows upon the broad head, his chin resting in his cupped hands. Futile had been his search for the spoor of La of Opar. Had the Earth opened and swallowed her she could not more effectually have disappeared.

Today Tarzan had come upon Tantor and, as had been his custom from childhood, he had tarried for that silent communion with the sagacious old patriarch of the forest, which seemed always to impart to the man something of the beast's great strength of character and poise. There was an atmosphere of restful stability about Tantor that filled the ape-man with a peace and tranquility that he found restful; and Tantor, upon his part, welcomed the companionship of the Lord of the Jungle, whom, alone, of all two-legged creatures, he viewed with friendship and affection.

The beasts of the jungle acknowledge no master, least of all the cruel tyrant that drives civilized man throughout his headlong race from the cradle to the grave—Time, the master of countless millions of slaves. Time, the measurable aspect of duration, was measureless to Tarzan and Tantor. Of all the vast resources that Nature had placed at their disposal, she had been most profligate with Time, since she had awarded to each all that he could use during his lifetime, no matter how extravagant of it he might be. So great was the supply of it that it could not be wasted, since there was always more, even up to the moment of death, after which it ceased, with all things, to be essential to the individual. Tantor and Tarzan, therefore, were wasting no time as they communed together in silent meditation; but though Time and space go on forever, whether in curves or straight lines, all other things must end; and so the quiet and the peace that the two friends were enjoying were suddenly shattered by the excited screams of a diminutive monkey in the foliage of a great tree above them.

It was Nkima. He had found his Tarzan, and his relief and joy aroused the jungle to the limit of his small, shrill voice. Lazily Tarzan rolled over and looked up at the jabbering simian above him; and then Nkima, satisfied now beyond peradventure of a doubt that this was, indeed, his master, launched himself downward to alight upon the bronzed body of the ape-man. Slender, hairy little arms went around Tarzan's neck as Nkima hugged close to this haven of refuge which imparted to him those brief moments in his life when he might enjoy the raptures of a temporary superiority complex. Upon Tarzan's shoulder he felt almost fearless and could, with impunity, insult the entire world.

"Where have you been, Nkima?" asked Tarzan.

"Looking for Tarzan," replied the monkey.

"What have you seen since I left you at the walls of Opar?" demanded the ape-man.

"I have seen many things. I have seen the great Mangani dancing in the moonlight around the dead body of Sheeta. I have seen the enemies of Tarzan marching through the forest. I have seen Histah, gorging himself on the carcass of Bara."

"Have you seen a Tarmangani she?" demanded Tarzan.

"No," replied Nkima. "There were no shes among the Gomangani and Tarmangani enemies of Tarzan. Only bulls, and they marched back toward the place where Nkima first saw them."

"When was this?" asked Tarzan.

"Kudu had climbed into the heavens but a short distance out of the darkness when Nkima saw the enemies of Tarzan marching back to the place were he first saw them."

"Perhaps we had better see what they are up to," said the ape-man. He slapped Tantor affectionately with his open palm in farewell, leaped to his feet and swung nimbly into the overhanging branches of a tree; while far away Zveri and his party plodded through the jungle toward their base camp.

Tarzan of the Apes follows no earthbound trails where the density of the forest offers him the freedom of leafy highways, and thus he moves from point to point with a speed that has often been disconcerting to his enemies.

Now he moved in an almost direct line so that he overtook the expedition as it made camp for the night. As he watched them from behind a leafy screen of high-flung foliage, he noticed, though with no surprise, that they were not burdened with any treasure from Opar.

As the success and happiness of jungle dwellers, nay, even life itself, is largely dependent upon their powers of observation, Tarzan had developed his to a high degree of perfection. At his first encounter with this party he had made himself familiar with the faces, physiques, and carriages of all of its principals and of many of its humble warriors and porters, with the result that he was immediately aware that Colt was no longer with the expedition. Experience permitted Tarzan to draw a rather accurate picture of what had happened at Opar and of the probable fate of the missing man.

Years ago he had seen his own courageous Waziri turn and flee upon the occasion of their first experience of the weird warning screams from the ruined city, and he could easily guess that Colt, attempting to lead the invaders into the city, had been deserted and found either death or capture within the gloomy interior. This, however, did not greatly concern Tarzan. While he had been rather drawn toward Colt by that tenuous and invisible power known as personality, he still considered him as one of his enemies, and if he were either dead or captured Tarzan's cause was advanced by that much.

From Tarzan's shoulder Nkima looked down upon the camp, but he kept silent as Tarzan had instructed him to do. Nkima saw many things that he would have liked to have possessed, and particularly he coveted a red calico shirt worn by one of the askaris. This, he thought, was very grand, indeed, being set off as it was by the unrelieved nakedness of the majority of the blacks. Nkima wished that his master would descend and slay them all, but particularly the man with the red shirt; for, at heart, Nkima was bloodthirsty, which made it fortunate for the peace of the jungle that he had not been born a gorilla. But Tarzan's mind was not set upon carnage. He had other means for thwarting the activities of these strangers. During the day he had made a kill, and now he withdrew to a safe distance from the camp and satisfied his hunger, while Nkima searched for birds' eggs, fruit, and insects.

And so night fell and when it had enveloped the jungle in impenetrable darkness, relieved only by the beast fires of the camp, Tarzan returned to a tree where he could overlook the activities of the bivouacked expedition. He watched them in silence for a long time, and then suddenly he raised his voice in a long scream that perfectly mimicked the hideous warning cry of Opar's defenders.

The effect upon the camp was instantaneous. Conversation, singing, and laughter ceased. For a moment the men sat as in a paralysis of terror. Then, seizing their weapons, they came closer to the fire.

With the shadow of a smile upon his lips, Tarzan melted away into the jungle.

10

The Love of a Priestess

IBN DAMMUK HAD bided his time and now, in the camp by the swollen river at the edge of the Galla country, he at last found the opportunity he had so long awaited. The surveillance over the two prisoners had somewhat relaxed, due largely to the belief entertained by Abu Batn that the women would not dare to invite the perils of the jungle by attempting to escape from captors who were, at the same time, their protectors from even greater dangers. He had, however, reckoned without a just estimation of the courage and resourcefulness of his two captives, who, had he but known it, were constantly awaiting the first opportunity for escape. It was this fact, as well, that played into the hands of Ibn Dammuk.

With great cunning he enlisted the services of one of the blacks who had been forced to accompany them from the base camp and who was virtually a prisoner. By promising him his liberty Ibn Dammuk had easily gained the man's acquiescence in the plan that he had evolved.

A separate tent had been pitched for the two women, and before it sat a single sentry, whose presence Abu Batn considered more than sufficient for this purpose, which was, perhaps, even more to protect the women from his own followers than to prevent a very remotely possible attempt at escape.

This night, which Ibn Dammuk had chosen for his villainy, was one for which he had been waiting, since it found upon duty before the tent of the captives one of his own men, a member of his own tribe, who was bound by laws of hereditary loyalty to serve and obey him. In the forest, just beyond the camp, waited Ibn Dammuk, with two more of his own tribesmen, four slaves that they had brought from the desert, and the black porter who was to win his liberty by this night's work.

The interior of the tent that had been pitched for Zora and La was illuminated by a paper lantern, in which a candle burned dimly; and in this subdued light the two sat talking in La's newly acquired English, which was at best most fragmentary and broken. However, it was far better than no means of communication and gave the two girls the only pleasure that they enjoyed. Perhaps it was not a remarkable coincidence that this night they were speaking of escape and planning to cut a hole in the back of their tent through which they might sneak away into the jungle after the camp had settled down for the night and their sentry should be dozing at his post. And while they conversed, the sentry before their tent rose and strolled away, and a moment later they heard a scratching upon the back of the tent. Their conversation ceased and they sat with eyes riveted upon the point where the fabric of the tent moved to the pressure of the scratching without.

Presently a voice spoke in a low whisper. "Memsahib Drinov!"

"Who is it? What do you want?" asked Zora in a low voice.

"I have found a way to escape. I can help you if you wish."

"Who are you?" demanded Zora.

"I am Bukula," and Zora at once recognized the name as that of one of the blacks that Abu Batn had forced to accompany him from the base camp.

"Put out your lantern," whispered Bukula. "The sentry has gone away. I will come in and tell you my plans."

Zora arose and blew out the candle, and a moment later the two captives saw Bukula crawling into the interior of the tent. "Listen, Memsahib," he said, "the boys that Abu Batn stole from Bwana Zveri are running away tonight. We are going back to the safari. We will take you two with us, if you want to come."

"Yes," said Zora, "we will come."

"Good!" said Bukula. "Now listen well to what I tell you. The sentry will not come back, but we cannot all go out at once. First I will take this other Memsahib with me out into the jungle where the boys are waiting; then I will return for you. You can make talk to her. Tell her to follow me and to make no noise."

Zora turned to La. "Follow Bukula," she said. "We are going tonight. I will come after you."

"I understand," replied La.

"It is all right, Bukula," said Zora. "She understands."

Bukula stepped to the entrance to the tent and looked quickly about the camp. "Come!" he said, and, followed by La, disappeared quickly from Zora's view.

The European girl fully realized the risk that they ran in going into the jungle alone with these half-savage blacks, yet she trusted them far more implicitly than she did the Aarabs and, too, she felt that she and La together might circumvent any treachery upon the part of any of the Negroes, the majority of whom she knew would be loyal and faithful. Waiting in the silence and loneliness of the darkened tent, it seemed to Zora that it took Bukula an unnecessarily long time to return for her; but when minute after minute dragged slowly past until she felt that she had waited for hours and there was no sign either of the black or the sentry, her fears were aroused in earnest. Presently she determined not to wait any longer for Bukula, but to go out into the jungle in search of the escaping party. She thought that perhaps Bukula had been unable to return without risking detection and that they were all waiting just beyond the camp for a favorable opportunity to return to her. As she arose to put her decision into action, she heard footsteps approaching the tent, and thinking that they were Bukula's, she waited; but instead she saw the flapping robe and the long-barreled musket of an Aarab silhouetted against the lesser darkness of the exterior as the man stuck his head inside the tent. "Where is Hajellan?" he demanded, giving the name of the departed sentry.

"How should we know?" retorted Zora in a sleepy voice. "Why do you awaken us thus in the middle of the night? Are we the keepers of your fellows?"

The fellow grumbled something in reply and then, turning, called aloud across the camp, announcing to all who might hear that Hajellan was missing and inquiring if any had seen him. Other warriors strolled over then, and there was a great deal of speculation as to what had become of Hajellan. The name of the missing man was called aloud many times, but there was no response, and finally the sheik came and questioned everyone. "The women are in the tent yet?" he demanded of the new sentry.

"Yes," replied the man. "I have talked with them."

"It is strange," said Abu Batn, and then, "Ibn Dammuk!" he cried. "Where art thou, Ibn? Hajellan was one of thy men." There was no answer. "Where is Ibn Dammuk?"

"He is not here," said a man standing near the sheik.

"Nor are Fodil and Dareyem," said another.

"Search the camp and see who is missing," commanded Abu Batn; and when the search had been made they found that Ibn Dammuk, Hajellan, Fodil, and Dareyem were missing with five of the blacks.

"Ibn Dammuk has deserted us," said Abu Batn. "Well, let it go. There will be fewer with whom to share the reward we shall reap when we are paid for the two women," and thus reconciling himself to the loss of four good fighting men, Abu Batn repaired to his tent and resumed his interrupted slumber.

Weighted down by apprehension as to the fate of La and disappointment occasioned by her own failure to escape, Zora spent an almost sleepless night, yet fortunate for her peace of mind was it that she did not know the truth.

Bukula moved silently into the jungle, followed by La; and when they had gone a short distance from the camp, the girl saw the dark forms of men standing in a little group ahead of them. The Aarabs, in their telltale thôbs, were hidden in the underbrush, but their slaves had removed their own white robes and, with Bukula, were standing naked but for G-strings, thus carrying conviction to the mind of the girl that only black prisoners of Abu Batn awaited her. When she came among them, however, she learned her mistake; but too late to save herself, for she was quickly seized by many hands and effectually gagged before she could give the alarm. Then Ibn Dammuk and his Aarab companions appeared, and silently the party moved on down the river through the dark forest, though not before they had subdued the enraged high priestess of the Flaming God, secured her wrists behind her back, and placed a rope about her neck.

All night they fled, for Ibn Dammuk well guessed what the wrath of Abu Batn would be when, in the morning, he discovered the trick that had been played upon him; and when morning dawned they were far away from camp, but still Ibn Dammuk pushed on, after a brief halt for a hurried breakfast.

Long since had the gag been removed from La's mouth, and now Ibn Dammuk walked beside her, gloating upon his prize. He spoke to her, but La could not understand him and only strode on in haughty disdain, biding her time against the moment when she might be revenged and inwardly sorrowing over her separation from Zora, for whom a strange affection had been aroused in her savage breast.

Toward noon the party withdrew from the game trail which they had been following and made camp near the river. It was here that Ibn Dammuk made a fatal blunder. Goaded to passion by close proximity to the beautiful woman for whom he had conceived a mad infatuation, the Aarab gave way to his desire to be alone with her; and leading her along a little trail that paralleled the river, he took her away out of sight of his companions; and when they had gone perhaps a hundred yards from camp, he seized her in his arms and sought to kiss her lips.

With equal safety might Ibn Dammuk have embraced a lion. In the heat of his passion he forgot many things, among them the dagger that hung always at his side. But La of Opar did not forget. With the coming of daylight she had noticed that dagger, and ever since she had coveted it; and now as the man pressed her close, her hand sought and found its hilt. For an instant she seemed to surrender. She let her body go limp in his arms, while her own, firm and beautifully rounded, crept about him, one to his right shoulder, the other beneath his left arm. But as yet she did not give him her lips, and then as he struggled to possess them the hand upon his shoulder seized him suddenly by the throat. The long, tapered fingers that seemed so soft and white were suddenly claws of steel that closed upon his windpipe; and simultaneously the hand that had crept so softly beneath his left arm drove his own long dagger into his heart from beneath his shoulder blade.

The single cry that he might have given was choked in his throat. For an instant the tall form of Ibn Dammuk stood rigidly erect; then it slumped forward, and the girl let it slip to the earth. She spurned it once with her foot, then removed from it the girdle and sheath for the dagger, wiped the bloody blade upon the man's thôb and hurried on up the little river trail until she found an opening in the underbrush that led away from the stream. On and on she went until exhaustion overtook her; and then, with her remaining strength, she climbed into a tree in search of much needed rest.

Wayne Colt watched the shadowy figure approach the mouth of the corridor where his cell lay. He wondered if this was a messenger of death, coming to lead him to sacrifice. Nearer and nearer it came until presently it stopped before the bars of his cell door; and then a soft voice spoke to him in a low whisper and in a tongue which he could not understand, and he knew that his visitor was a woman.

Prompted by curiosity, he came close to the bars. A soft hand reached in and touched him, almost caressingly. A full moon rising above the high walls that ring the sacrificial court suddenly flooded the mouth of the corridor and the entrance to Colt's cell in silvery light, and in it the American saw the figure of a young girl pressed against the cold iron of the grating. She handed him food, and when he took it she caressed his hand and drawing it to the bars pressed her lips against it.

Wayne Colt was nonplussed. He could not know that Nao, the little priestess, had been the victim of love at first sight, that to her mind and eyes, accustomed to the sight of males only in the form of the hairy, grotesque priests of Opar, this stranger appeared a god indeed.

A slight noise attracted Nao's attention toward the court and, as she turned, the moonlight flooded her face, and the American saw that she was very lovely. Then she turned back toward him, her dark eyes wells of adoration, her full, sensitive lips trembling with emotion as, still clinging to his hand, she spoke rapidly in low liquid tones.

She was trying to tell Colt that at noon of the second day he was to be offered in sacrifice to the Flaming God, that she did not wish him to die and if it were possible she would help him, but that she did not know how that would be possible.

Colt shook his head. "I cannot understand you, little one," he said, and Nao, though she could not interpret his words, sensed the futility of her own. Then, raising one of her hands from his, she made a great circle in a vertical plane from east to west with a slender index finger, indicating the path of the sun across the heavens; and then she started a second circle, which she stopped at zenith, indicating high noon of the second day. For an instant her raised hand poised dramatically aloft; and then, the fingers closing as though around the hilt of an imaginary sacrificial knife, she plunged the invisible point deep into her bosom.

"Thus will Oah destroy you," she said, reaching through the bars and touching Colt over the heart.

The American thought that he understood the meaning of her pantomime, which he then repeated, plunging the imaginary blade into his own breast and looking questioningly at Nao.

In reply she nodded sadly, and the tears welled to her eyes.

As plainly as though he had understood her words, Colt realized that here was a friend who would help him if she could, and reaching through the bars, he drew the girl gently toward him and pressed his lips against her forehead. With a low sob Nao encircled his neck with her arms and pressed her face to his. Then, as suddenly, she released him and, turning, hurried away on silent feet, to disappear in the gloomy shadows of an archway at one side of the court of sacrifice.

Colt ate the food that she had brought him and for a long

time lay pondering the inexplicable forces which govern the acts of men. What train of circumstances leading down out of a mysterious past had produced this single human being in a city of enemies in whom, all unsuspecting, there must always have existed a germ of potential friendship for him, an utter stranger and alien, of whose very existence she could not possibly have dreamed before this day. He tried to convince himself that the girl had been prompted to her act by pity for his plight, but he knew in his heart that a more powerful motive impelled her.

Colt had been attracted to many women, but he had never loved; and he wondered if that was the way that love came and if some day it would seize him as it had seized this girl; and he wondered also if, had conditions been different, he might have been as strongly attracted to her. If not, then there seemed to be something wrong in the scheme of things; and still puzzling over this riddle of the ages, he fell asleep upon the hard floor of his cell.

With morning a hairy priest came and gave him food and water, and during the day others came and watched him, as though he were a wild beast in a menagerie. And so the long day dragged on, and once again night came—his last night.

He tried to picture what the final ceremony would be like. It seemed almost incredible that in the twentieth century he was to be offered as a human sacrifice to some heathen deity, but yet the pantomime of the girl and the concrete evidence of the bloody altar and the grinning skulls assured him that such must be the very fate awaiting him upon the morrow. He thought of his family and his friends at home; they would never know what had become of him. He weighed his sacrifice against the mission that he had undertaken and he had no regret, for he knew that it had not been in vain. Far away, already near the Coast, was the message he had dispatched by the runner. That would insure that he had not failed in his part for the sake of a great principle for which, if necessary, he was glad to lay down his life. He was glad that he had acted promptly and sent the message when he had, for now, upon the morrow, he could go to his death without vain regrets.

He did not want to die, and he made many plans during the day to seize upon the slightest opportunity that might be presented to him to escape.

He wondered what had become of the girl and if she would come again now that it was dark. He wished that she would, for he craved the companionship of a friend during his last hours; but as the night wore on, he gave up the hope and sought to forget the morrow in sleep.

As Wayne Colt moved restlessly upon his hard couch, Firg, a lesser priest of Opar, snored upon his pallet of straw in the small, dark recess that was his bedchamber. Firg was the keeper of the keys, and so impressed was he with the importance of his duties that he never would permit anyone even to touch the sacred emblems of his trust, and probably because it was well known that Firg would die in defense of them they were entrusted to him. Not with justice could Firg have laid any claim to intellectuality, if he had known that such a thing existed. He was only an abysmal brute of a man and, like many men, far beneath the so-called brutes in many of the activities of mind. When he slept, all his faculties were asleep, which is not true of wild beasts when they sleep.

Firg's cell was in one of the upper stories of the ruins that still remained intact. It was upon a corridor that encircled the main temple court—a corridor that was now in dense shadow, since the moon, touching it early in the night, had now passed on; so that the figure creeping stealthily toward the entrance to Firg's chamber would have been noticeable only to one who happened to be quite close. It moved silently, but without hesitation, until it came to the entrance beyond which Firg lay. There it paused, listening, and when it heard Firg's noisy snoring, it entered quickly. Straight to the side of the sleeping man it moved, and there it knelt, searching with one hand lightly over his body, while the other grasped a long sharp knife that hovered constantly above the hairy chest of the priest.

Presently it found what it wanted—a great ring, upon which were strung several enormous keys. A leather thong fastened the ring to Firg's girdle, and with the keen blade of the dagger the nocturnal visitor sought to sever the thong. Firg stirred, and instantly the creature at his side froze to immobility. Then the priest moved restlessly and commenced to snore again, and once more the dagger sawed at the leather thong. It passed through the strand unexpectedly and touched the metal of the ring lightly, but just enough to make the keys jangle ever so slightly.

Instantly Firg was awake but he did not rise. He was never to rise again.

Silently, swiftly, before the stupid creature could realize his danger, the keen blade of the dagger had pierced his heart.

Soundlessly, Firg collapsed. His slayer hesitated a moment with poised dagger as though to make certain that the work had been well done. Then, wiping the telltale stains from the dagger's blade with the victims's loincloth, the figure arose and hurried from the chamber, in one hand the great keys upon their golden ring.

Colt stirred uneasily in his sleep and then awakened with a start. In the waning moonlight he saw a figure beyond the grating of his cell. He heard a key turn in the massive lock. Could it be that they were coming for him? He rose to his feet, the urge of his last conscious thought strong upon him—escape. And then as the door swung open, a soft voice spoke, and he knew that the girl had returned.

She entered the cell and threw her arms about Colt's neck, drawing his lips down to hers. For a moment she clung to him, and then she released him and, taking one of his hands in hers, urged him to follow her; nor was the American loath to leave the depressing interior of the death cell.

On silent feet Nao led the way across the corner of the sacrificial court, through a dark archway into a gloomy corridor. Winding and twisting, keeping always in dark shadows, she led him along a circuitous route through the ruins, until, after what seemed an eternity to Colt, the girl opened a low, strong, wooden door and led him into the great entrance hall of the temple, through the mighty portal of which he could see the inner wall of the city.

Here Nao halted, and coming close to the man looked up into his eyes. Again her arms stole about his neck, and again she pressed her lips to his. Her cheeks were wet with tears, and her voice broke with little sobs that she tried to stifle as she poured her love into the ears of the man who could not understand.

She had brought him here to offer him his freedom, but she could not let him go yet. She clung to him, caressing him and crooning to him.

For a quarter of an hour she held him there, and Colt had not the heart to tear himself away, but at last she released him and pointed toward the opening of the inner wall.

"Go!" she said, "taking the heart of Nao with you. I shall never see you again, but at least I shall always have the memory of this hour to carry through life with me."

Wayne stooped and kissed her hand, the slender, savage little hand that had but just killed that her lover might live. Though of that, Wayne knew nothing.

She pressed her dagger with its sheath upon him that he might not go into the savage world unarmed, and then he turned away from her and moved slowly toward the inner wall. At the entrance of the opening he paused and turned about. Dimly, in the moonlight, he saw the figure of the little priestess standing very erect in the shadows of the ancient ruins. He raised his hand and waved a final, silent farewell.

A great sadness depressed Colt as he passed through the inner wall and crossed the court to freedom, for he knew that he had left behind him a sad and hopeless heart, in the bosom of one who must have risked death, perhaps, to save him—a perfect friend of whom he could but carry a vague memory of a half-seen lovely face, a friend whose name he did not know, the only tokens of whom he had carried away with him were the memory of hot kisses and a slender dagger.

And thus, as Wayne Colt walked across the moonlit plain of Opar, the joy of his escape was tempered by sadness as he recalled the figure of the forlorn little priestess standing in the shadows of the ruins.

Lost in the Jungle

IT WAS SOME time after the uncanny scream had disturbed the camp of the conspirators before the men could settle down to rest again.

Zveri believed that they had been followed by a band of Oparian warriors, who might be contemplating a night attack, and so he placed a heavy guard about the camp; but his blacks were confident that that unearthly cry had broken from no human throat.

Depressed and dispirited, the men resumed their march the following morning. They made an early start and by dint of much driving arrived at the base camp just before dark. The sight that met their eyes there filled them with consternation. The camp had disappeared, and in the center of the clearing where it had been pitched a pile of ashes suggested that disaster had overtaken the party that had been left behind.

This new misfortune threw Zveri into a maniacal rage, but there was no one present upon whom he might lay the blame, and so he was reduced to the expedient of tramping back and forth while he cursed his luck in loud tones and several languages.

From a tree Tarzan watched him. He, too, was at a loss to understand the nature of the disaster that seemed to have over-taken the camp during the absence of the main party, but as he saw that it caused the leader intense anguish, the ape-man was pleased.

The blacks were confident that this was another manifestation of the anger of the malign spirit that had been haunting them, and they were all for deserting the ill-starred white man, whose every move ended in failure or disaster.

Zveri's powers of leadership deserve full credit, since from the verge of almost certain mutiny he forced his men by means of both cajolery and threat to remain with him. He set them to building shelters for the entire party, and immediately he dispatched messengers to his various agents, urging them to forward necessary supplies at once. He knew that certain things he needed already were on the way from the Coast—uniforms, rifles, ammunition. But now he particularly needed provisions and trade goods. To insure discipline, he kept the men working constantly, either in adding to the comforts of the camp, enlarging the clearing, or hunting fresh meat.

And so the days passed and became weeks, and meanwhile Tarzan watched in waiting. He was in no hurry, for hurry is not a characteristic of the beasts. He roamed the jungle often at a considerable distance from Zveri's camp, but occasionally he would return, though not to molest them, preferring to let them lull themselves into a stupor of tranquil security, the shattering of which in his own good time would have dire effect upon their morale. He understood the psychology of terror, and it was with terror that he would defeat them.

To the camp of Abu Batn, upon the border of the Galla country, word had come from spies that he had sent out that the Galla warriors were gathering to prevent his passage through their territory. Being weakened by the desertion of so many men, the sheik dared not defy the bravery and numbers of the Galla warriors, but he knew that he must make some move, since it seemed inevitable that pursuit must overtake him from the rear, if he remained where he was much longer.

At last scouts that he had sent far up the river on the opposite side returned to report that a way to the west seemed clear along a more northerly route, and so breaking camp, Abu Batn moved north with his lone prisoner.

Great had been his rage when he discovered that Ibn Dammuk had stolen La, and now he redoubled his precaution to prevent the escape of Zora Drinov. So closely was she guarded that any possibility of escape seemed almost hopeless. She had learned the fate for which Abu Batn was reserving her, and now, depressed and melancholy, her mind was occupied with plans for self-destruction. For a time she had harbored the hope that Zveri would overtake the Aarabs and rescue her, but this she had long since discarded, as day after day passed without bringing the hoped-for succor.

She could not know, of course, the straits in which Zveri had found himself. He had not dared to detach a party of his men to search for her, fearing that, in their mutinous state of mind, they might murder any of his lieutenants that he placed in charge of them and return to their own tribe, where, through the medium of gossip, word of his expedition and its activities might reach his enemies; nor could he lead all of his force upon such an expedition in person, since he must remain at the base camp to receive the supplies that he knew would presently be arriving.

Perhaps, had he known definitely the danger that confronted Zora, he would have cast aside every other consideration and gone to her rescue; but being naturally suspicious of the loyalty of all men, he had persuaded himself that Zora had deliberately deserted him—a halfhearted conviction that had at least the effect of rendering his naturally unpleasant disposition infinitely more unbearable, so that those who should have been his companions and his support in his hour of need contrived as much as possible to keep out of his way.

And while these things were transpiring, little Nkima sped through the jungle upon a mission. In the service of his beloved master, little Nkima could hold to a single thought and a line of action for considerable periods of time at a stretch; but eventually his attention was certain to be attracted by some extraneous matter and then, for hours perhaps, he would forget all about whatever duty had been imposed upon him; but when it again occurred to him, he would carry on entirely without any appreciation of the fact that there had been a break in the continuity of his endeavor.

Tarzan, of course, was entirely aware of this inherent weakness in his little friend; but he knew, too, from experience that, however many lapses might occur, Nkima would never entirely abandon any design upon which his mind had been fixed; and having himself none of civilized man's slavish subservience to time, he was prone to overlook Nkima's erratic performance of a duty as a fault of almost negligible consequence. Some day Nkima would arrive at his destination. Perhaps it would be too late. If such a thought occurred at all to the ape-man, doubtless he passed it off with a shrug.

But time is of the essence of many things to civilized man. He fumes, and frets, and reduces his mental and physical efficiency if he is not accomplishing something concrete during the passage of every minute of that medium which seems to him like a flowing river, the waters of which are utterly wasted if they are not utilized as they pass by.

Imbued by some such insane conception of time, Wayne Colt sweated and stumbled through the jungle, seeking his companions as though the very fate of the universe hung upon the slender chance that he should reach them without the loss of a second.

The futility of his purpose would have been entirely apparent to him could he have known that he was seeking his companions in the wrong direction. Wayne Colt was lost. Fortunately for him he did not know it; at least not yet. That stupefying conviction was to come later.

Days passed and still his wanderings revealed no camp. He was hard put to it to find food, and his fare was meager and often revolting, consisting of such fruits as he had already learned to know and of rodents, which he managed to bag only with the greatest difficulty and an appalling waste of that precious time which he still prized above all things. He had cut himself a stout stick and would lie in wait along some tiny runway where observation had taught him he might expect to find his prey, until some unwary little creature came within striking distance. He had learned that dawn and dusk were the best hunting hours for the only animals that he could hope to bag, and he learned other things as he moved through the grim jungle, all of which pertained to his struggle for existence. He had learned, for instance, that it was wiser for him to take to the trees whenever he heard a strange noise. Usually the animals got out of his way as he approached; but once a rhinoceros charged him, and again he almost stumbled upon a lion at his kill. Providence intervened in each instance and he escaped unkilled, but thus he learned caution.

About noon one day he came to a river that effectually blocked his further progress in the direction that he had been traveling. By this time the conviction was strong upon him that he was utterly lost, and not knowing which direction he should take, he decided to follow the line of least resistance and travel downhill with the river, upon the shore of which he was positive that sooner or later he must discover a native village.

He had proceeded no great distance in the new direction, following a hard-packed trail, worn deep by the countless feet of many beasts, when his attention was arrested by a sound that reached his ears dimly from a distance. It came from somewhere ahead of him, and his hearing, now far more acute than it ever had been before, told him that something was approaching. Following the practice that he had found most conducive to longevity since he had been wandering alone and ill-armed against the dangers of the jungle, he flung himself quickly into a tree and sought a point of vantage from where he could see the trail below him. He could not see it for any distance ahead, so tortuously did it wind through the jungle. Whatever was coming would not be visible until it was almost directly beneath him, but that now was of no importance. This experience of the jungle had taught him patience, and perchance he was learning, too, a little of the valuelessness of time, for he settled himself comfortably to wait at his ease.

The noise that he heard was little more than an impercep-tible rustling, but presently it assumed a new volume and a new significance, so that now he was sure that it was someone running rapidly along the trail, and not one but two—he distinctly heard the footfalls of the heavier creature mingling with those he had first heard.

And then he heard a man's voice cry "Stop!" and now the sounds were very close to him, just around the first bend ahead. The sound of running feet stopped, to be followed by that of a scuffle and strange oaths in a man's voice.

And then a woman's voice spoke, "Let me go! You will never get me where you are taking me alive."

"Then I'll take you for myself now," said the man.

Colt had heard enough. There had been something familiar in the tones of the woman's voice. Silently he dropped to the trail, drawing his dagger, and stepped quickly toward the sounds of the altercation. As he rounded the bend in the trail, he saw just before him only a man's back—by thôb and thorîb an Aarab—but beyond the man and in his clutches Colt knew the woman was hidden by the flowing robes of her assailant.

Leaping forward, he seized the fellow by the shoulder and jerked him suddenly about; and as the man faced him Colt saw that it was Abu Batn, and now, too, he saw why the voice of the woman had seemed familiar—she was Zora Drinov.

Abu Batn purpled with rage at the interruption, but great as was his anger so, too, was his surprise as he recognized the American. Just for an instant he thought that possibly this was the advance guard of a party of searchers and avengers from Zveri's camp, but when he had time to observe the unkempt, disheveled, unarmed condition of Colt he realized that the man was alone and doubtless lost.

"Dog of a Nasrâny!" he cried, jerking away from Colt's grasp. "Lay not your filthy hand upon a true believer." At the same time he moved to draw his pistol, but in that instant Colt was upon him again, and the two men went down in the narrow trail, the American on top.

What happened then, happened very quickly. As Abu Batn drew his pistol, he caught the hammer in the folds of his thôb, so that the weapon was discharged. The bullet went harmlessly into the ground, but the report warned Colt of his imminent danger, and in self-defense he ran his blade through the sheik's throat.

As he rose slowly from the body of the sheik, Zora Drinov grasped him by the arm. "Quick!" she said. "That shot will bring the others. They must not find us."

He did not wait to question her, but, stooping, quickly salvaged Abu Batn's weapons and ammunition, including a long musket that lay in the trail beside him; and then with Zora in the lead they ran swiftly up the trail down which he had just come.

Presently, hearing no indication of pursuit, Colt halted the girl.

"Can you climb?" he asked.

"Yes," she replied. "Why?"

"We are going to take to the trees," he said. "We can go into the jungle a short distance and throw them off the trail."

"Good!" she said, and with his assistance clambered into the branches of a tree beneath which they stood.

Fortunately for them, several large trees grew close together so that they were able to make their way with comparative ease a full hundred feet from the trail, where, climbing high into the branches of a great tree, they were effectually hidden from sight in all directions.

When at last they were seated side by side in a great crotch, Zora turned toward Colt. "Comrade Colt!" she said. "What has happened? What are you doing here alone? Were you looking for me?"

The man grinned. "I was looking for the whole party," he said. "I have seen no one since we entered Opar. Where is the camp, and why was Abu Batn pursuing you?"

"We are a long way from the camp," replied Zora. "I do not know how far, though I could return to it, if it were not for the Aarabs." And then briefly she told the story of Abu Batn's treachery and of her captivity. "The sheykh made a temporary camp shortly after noon today. The men were very tired, and for the first time in days they relaxed their vigilance over me. I realized that at last the moment I had been awaiting so anxiously had arrived, and while they slept I escaped into the jungle. My absence must have been discovered shortly after I left, and Abu Batn overtook me. The rest you witnessed."

"Fate functioned deviously and altogether wonderfully," he said. "To think that your only chance of rescue hinged upon the contingency of my capture at Opar!"

She smiled. "Fate reaches back farther than that," she said. "Suppose you had not been born?"

"Then Abu Batn would have carried you off to the harem of some black sultan, or perhaps another man would have been captured at Opar."

"I am glad that you were born," said Zora.

"Thank you," said Colt.

While listening for signs of pursuit, they conversed in low tones, Colt narrating in detail the events leading up to his capture, though some of the details of his escape he omitted through a sense of loyalty to the nameless girl who had aided him. Neither did he stress Zveri's lack of control over his men, or what Colt considered his inexcusable cowardice in leaving himself and Romero to their fate within the walls of Opar without attempting to succor them, for he believed that the girl was Zveri's sweetheart and he did not wish to offend her.

"What became of Comrade Romero?" she asked.

"I do not know," he said. "The last I saw of him he was standing his ground, fighting off those crooked little demons."

"Alone?" she asked.

"I was pretty well occupied myself," he said.

"I do not mean that," she replied. "Of course, I know you were there with Romero, but who else?"

"The others had not arrived," said Colt.

"You mean you two went in alone?" she asked.

Colt hesitated. "You see," he said, "the blacks refused to enter the city, so the rest of us had to go in or abandon the attempt to get the treasures."

"But only you and Miguel did go in. Is that not true?" she demanded.

"I passed out so soon, you see," he said with a laugh, "that really I do not know exactly what did happen."

The girl's eyes narrowed. "It was beastly," she said.

As they talked, Colt's eyes were often upon the girl's face. How lovely she was, even beneath the rags and the dirt that were the outward symbols of her captivity among the Aarabs. She was a little thinner than when he had last seen her, and her eyes were tired and her face drawn from privation and worry. But, perhaps, by very contrast her beauty was the more startling. It seemed incredible that she could love the course, loudmouthed Zveri, who was her antithesis in every respect.

Presently she broke a short silence. "We must try to get back to the base camp," she said. "It is vital that I be there. So much must be done, so much that no one else can do."

"You think only of the cause," he said, "never of yourself. You are very loyal."

"Yes," she said in a low voice. "I am loyal to the thing I have sworn to accomplish."

"I am afraid," he said, "that for the past few days I have been thinking more of my own welfare than of that of the proletariat."

"I am afraid that at heart you are still bourgeois," she said, "and that you cannot yet help looking upon the proletariat with contempt."

"What makes you say that?" he asked. "I am sure that I said nothing to warrant it."

"Often a slight unconscious inflection in the use of a word alters the significance of a whole statement, revealing a speaker's secret thoughts."

Colt laughed good-naturedly. "You are a dangerous person to talk to," he said. "Am I to be shot at sunrise?"

She looked at him seriously. "You are different from the others," she said. "I think you could never imagine how suspicious they are. What I have said is only in the way of warning you to watch your every word when you are talking with them. Some of them are narrow and ignorant, and they are already suspicious of you because of your antecedents. They are sensitively jealous of a new importance which they believe their class has attained."

"*Their* class?" he asked. "I thought you told me once that you were of the proletariat?"

If he had thought that he had surprised her and that she would show embarrassment, he was mistaken. She met his eyes squarely and without wavering. "I am," she said, "but I can still see the weaknesses of my class."

He looked at her steadily for a long moment, the shadow of a smile touching his lips. "I do not believe—"

"Why do you stop?" she asked. "What is it that you do not believe?"

"Forgive me," he said. "I was starting to think aloud."

"Be careful, Comrade Colt," she warned him. "Thinking aloud is sometimes fatal"; but she tempered her words with a smile.

Further conversation was interrupted by the sound of the voices of men in the distance. "They are coming," said the girl.

Colt nodded, and the two remained silent, listening to the sounds of approaching voices and footsteps. The men came abreast of them and halted; and Zora, who understood the Aarab tongue, heard one of them say, "The trail stops here. They have gone into the jungle."

"Who can the man be who is with her?" asked another.

"It is a Nasrâny. I can tell by the imprint of his feet," said another.

"They would go toward the river," said a third. "That is the way that I should go if I were trying to escape."

"Wullah! You speak words of wisdom," said the first speaker. "We will spread out here and search toward the river; but look out for the Nasrâny. He has the pistol and the musket of the sheykh."

The two fugitives heard the sound of pursuit diminishing in the distance as the Aarabs forced their way into the jungle toward the river. "I think we had better get out of this," said Colt; "and while it may be pretty hard going, I believe that we had better stick to the brush for awhile and keep on away from the river."

"Yes," replied Zora, "for that is the general direction in

which the camp lies." And so they commenced their long and weary march in search of their comrades.

They were still pushing through dense jungle when night overtook them. Their clothes were in rags and their bodies scratched and torn, mute and painful reminders of the thorny way that they had traversed.

Hungry and thirsty they made a dry camp among the branches of a tree, where Colt built a rude platform for the girl, while he prepared to sleep upon the ground at the foot of the great bole. But to this, Zora would not listen.

"That will not do at all," she said. "We are in no position to permit ourselves to be the victims of every silly convention that would ordinarily order our lives in civilized surroundings. I appreciate your thoughtful consideration, but I would rather have you up here in the tree with me than down there where the first hunting lion that passed might get you." And so with the girl's help Colt built another platform close to the one that he had built for her; and as darkness fell, they stretched their tired bodies on their rude couches and sought to sleep.

Presently Colt dozed, and in his dream he saw the slender figure of a star-eyed goddess, whose cheeks were wet with tears, but when he took her in his arms and kissed her he saw that she was Zora Drinov; and then a hideous sound from the jungle below awakened him with a start, so that he sat up, seizing the musket of the sheik in readiness.

"A hunting lion," said the girl in a low voice.

"Phew!" exclaimed Colt. "I must have been asleep, for that certainly gave me a start."

"Yes, you were asleep," said the girl. "I heard you talking," and he felt that he detected laughter in her voice.

"What was I saying?" asked Colt.

"Maybe you wouldn't want to hear. It might embarrass you," she told him.

"No. Come ahead. Tell me."

"You said 'I love you.' "

"Did I, really?"

"Yes. I wonder whom you were talking to," she said, banteringly.

"I wonder," said Colt, recalling that in his dream the figure of one girl had merged into that of another.

The lion, hearing their voices, moved away growling. He was not hunting the hated man-things.

12

Down Trails of Terror

SLOW DAYS DRAGGED by for the man and woman searching for their comrades—days filled with fatiguing effort, most of which was directed toward the procuring of food and water for their sustenance. Increasingly was Colt impressed by the character and personality of his companion. With apprehension he noticed that she was gradually weakening beneath the strain of fatigue and the scant and inadequate food that he had been able to procure for her. But yet she kept a brave front and tried to hide her condition from him. Never once had she complained. Never by word or look had she reproached him for his inability to procure sufficient food, a failure which he looked upon as indicative of inefficiency. She did not know that he himself often went hungry that she might eat, telling her when he returned with food that he had eaten his share where he had found it, a deception that was made possible by the fact that when he hunted he often left Zora to rest in some place of comparative security, that she might not be subjected to needless exertion.

He had left her thus today, safe in a great tree beside a winding stream. She was very tired. It seemed to her that now she was always tired. The thought of continuing the march appalled her, and yet she knew that it must be undertaken. She wondered how much longer she could go on before she sank exhausted for the last time. It was not, however, for herself that she was most concerned, but for this man—this scion of wealth, and capitalism, and power, whose constant consideration and cheerfulness and tenderness had been a revelation to her. She knew that when she could go no further, he would not leave her and that thus his chances of escape from the grim jungle would be jeopardized and perhaps lost forever because of her. She hoped, for his sake, that death would come quickly to her that, thus relieved of responsibility, he might move on more rapidly in search of that elusive camp that seemed to her now little more than a meaningless myth. But from the thought of death she shrank, not because of the fear of death, as well might have been the case, but for an entirely new reason, the sudden realization of which gave her a distinct shock. The tragedy of this sudden self-awakening left her numb with terror. It was a thought that must be put from her, one that she must not entertain even for an instant; and yet it persisted—persisted with a dull insistency that brought tears to her eyes.

Colt had gone farther afield than usual this morning in his search for food, for he had sighted an antelope; and, his imagination inflamed by the contemplation of so much meat in a single kill and what it would mean for Zora, he clung doggedly to the trail, lured further on by an occasional glimpse of his quarry in the distance.

The antelope was only vaguely aware of the enemy, for he was upwind from Colt and had not caught his scent, while the occasional glimpses he had had of the man had served mostly to arouse his curiosity; so that though he moved away he stopped often and turned back in an effort to satisfy his wonderment. But presently he waited a moment too long. In his desperation, Colt chanced a long shot; and as the animal dropped, the man could not stifle a loud cry of exultation.

As time, that she had no means of measuring, dragged on, Zora grew increasingly apprehensive on Colt's account. Never before had he left her for so long a time, so that she began to construct all sorts of imaginary calamities that might have overtaken him. She wished now that she had gone with him. If she had thought it possible to track him, she would have followed him; but she knew that that was impossible. However, her forced inactivity made her restless. Her cramped position in the tree became unendurable; and then, suddenly assailed by thirst, she lowered herself to the ground and walked toward the river.

When she had drunk and was about to return to the tree, she heard the sound of something approaching from the direction in which Colt had gone. Instantly her heart leaped with gladness, her depression and even much of her fatigue seemed to vanish, and she realized suddenly how very lonely she had been without him. How dependent we are upon the society of our fellow men, we seldom realize until we become the victims of enforced solitude. There were tears of happiness in Zora Drinov's eyes as she advanced to meet Colt. Then the bushes before her parted, and there stepped into view, before her horrified gaze, a monstrous, hairy ape.

To-yat, the king, was as much surprised as the girl, but his reactions were almost opposite. It was with no horror that he viewed this soft, white she-Mangani. To the girl there was naught but ferocity in his mien, though in his breast was an entirely different emotion. He lumbered toward her; and then, as though released from a momentary paralysis, Zora turned to flee. But how futilely, she realized an instant later as a hairy paw gripped her roughly by the shoulder. For an instant she had forgotten the sheik's pistol that Colt always left with her for self-protection. Jerking it from its holster, she turned upon the beast; but To-yat, seeing in the weapon a club with which she intended to attack him, wrenched it from her grasp and hurled it aside; and then, though she struggled and fought to regain her freedom, he lifted her lightly to his hip and lumbered off into the jungle in the direction that he had been going.

Colt tarried at his kill only long enough to remove the feet, the head, and the viscera, that he might by that much reduce the weight of the burden that he must carry back to camp, for he was quite well aware that his privation had greatly reduced his strength.

Lifting the carcass to his shoulder, he started back toward camp, exulting in the thought that for once he was returning with an ample quantity of strength-giving flesh. As he staggered along beneath the weight of the small antelope, he made plans that imparted a rosy hue to the future. They would rest now until their strength returned; and while they were resting they would smoke all of the meat of his kill that they did not eat at once, and thus they would have a reserve supply of food that he felt would carry them a great distance. Two days' rest with plenty of food would, he was positive, fill them with renewed hope and vitality.

As he started laboriously along the back trail, he commenced to realize that he had come much farther than he had thought, but it had been well worthwhile. Even though he reached Zora in a state of utter exhaustion, he did not fear for a minute but that he would reach her, so confident was he of his own powers of endurance and the strength of his will.

As he staggered at last to his goal, he looked up into the tree and called her by name. There was no reply. In that first brief instant of silence, a dull and sickening premonition of disaster crept over him. He dropped the carcass of the antelope and looked hurriedly about.

"Zora! Zora!" he cried; but only the silence of the jungle was his answer. Then his searching eyes found the pistol of Abu Batn where To-yat had dropped it; and his worst fears were substantiated, for he knew that if Zora had gone away of her own volition she would have taken the weapon with her. She had been attacked by something and carried off, of that he was positive; and presently as he examined the ground closely he discovered the imprints of a great manlike foot.

A sudden madness seized Wayne Colt. The cruelty of the jungle, the injustice of Nature aroused within his breast a red rage. He wanted to kill the thing that had stolen Zora Drinov. He wanted to tear it with his hands and rend it with his teeth. All the savage instincts of primitive man were reborn within him as, forgetting the meat that the moment before had meant

so much to him, he plunged headlong into the jungle upon the
faint spoor of To-yat, the king ape.

La of Opar made her way slowly through the jungle after
she had escaped from Ibn Dammuk and his companions. Her
native city called to her, though she knew that she might
not enter it in safety; but what place was there in all the world
that she might go to? Something of a conception of the immensity of the great world had been impressed upon her during
her wandering since she had left Opar, and the futility of
searching further for Tarzan had been indelibly impressed
upon her mind. So she would go back to the vicinity of
Opar, and perhaps some day again Tarzan would come there.
That great dangers beset her way she did not care, for La
of Opar was indifferent to life that had never brought her
much of happiness. She lived because she lived; and it is true
that she would strive to prolong life because such is the law of
Nature, which imbues the most miserable unfortunates with as
powerful an urge to prolong their misery as it gives to the
fortunate few who are happy and contented a similar desire
to live.

Presently she became aware of pursuit, and so she increased
her speed and kept ahead of those who were following her.
Finding a trail, she followed it, knowing that if it permitted her
to increase her speed it would permit her pursuers also to
increase theirs, nor would she be able to hear them now as
plainly as she had before, when they were forcing their way
through the jungle. Still she was confident that they could not
overtake her; but as she was moving swiftly on, a turn in the
trail brought her to a sudden stop, for there, blocking her
retreat, stood a great, maned lion. This time La remembered
the animal, not as Jad-bal-ja, the hunting mate of Tarzan, but as
the lion that had rescued her from the leopard, after Tarzan had
deserted her.

Lions were familiar creatures to La of Opar, where they
were often captured by the priests while cubs, and where it was
not unusual to raise some of them occasionally as pets until
their growing ferocity made them unsafe. Therefore, La knew
that lions could associate with people without devouring them;

and, having had experience of this lion's disposition and
having as little sense of fear as Tarzan himself, she quickly
made her choice between the lion and the Aarabs pursuing her
and advanced directly toward the great beast, in whose attitude
she saw there was no immediate menace. She was sufficiently
a child of nature to know that death came quickly and pain-
lessly in the embrace of a lion, and so she had no fear, but only
a great curiosity.

Jad-bal-ja had long had the scent spoor of La in his nostrils,
as she had moved with the wind along the jungle trails; and
so he had awaited her, his curiosity aroused by the fainter
scent spoor of the men who trailed her. Now as she came
toward him along the trail, he stepped to one side that she
might pass and, like a great cat, rubbed his maned neck against
her legs.

La paused and laid a hand upon his head and spoke to him in
low tones in the language of the first man—the language of the
great apes that was the common language of her people, as it
was Tarzan's language.

Hajellan, leading his men in pursuit of La, rounded a bend in
the trail and stopped aghast. He saw a great lion facing him, a
lion that bared its fangs now in an angry snarl; and beside the
lion, one hand tangled in its thick black mane, stood the white
woman.

The woman spoke a single word to the lion in a language
that Hajellan did not understand. "Kill!" said La in the language of the great apes.

So accustomed was the high priestess of the Flaming God
to command that it did not occur to her that Numa might
do other than obey; and so, although she did not know that
it was thus that Tarzan had been accustomed to command
Jad-bal-ja, she was not surprised when the lion crouched and
charged.

Fodil and Dareyem had pushed close behind their companion as he halted, and great was their horror when they saw
the lion leap forward. They turned and fled, colliding with the
blacks behind them; but Hajellan only stood paralyzed with
fright as Jad-bal-ja reared upon his hind feet and seized him,
his great jaws crunching through the man's head and shoul-

ders, cracking his skull like an eggshell. He gave the body a vicious shake and dropped it. Then he turned and looked inquiringly at La.

In the woman's heart was no more sympathy for her enemies than in the heart of Jad-bal-ja; she only wished to be rid of them. She did not care whether they lived or died, and so she did not urge Jad-bal-ja after those who had escaped. She wondered what the lion would do now that he had made his kill; and knowing that the vicinity of a feeding lion was no safe place, she turned and moved on along the trail. But Jad-bal-ja was no eater of man, not because he had any moral scruples, but because he was young and active and had no difficulty in killing prey that he relished far more than he did the salty flesh of man. Therefore, he left Hajellan lying where he had fallen and followed La along the shadowy jungle trails.

A black man, naked but for a G-string, bearing a message from the Coast for Zveri, paused where two trails crossed. From his left the wind was blowing, and to his sensitive nostrils it bore the faint stench that announced the presence of a lion. Without a moment's hesitation, the man vanished into the foliage of a tree that overhung the trail. Perhaps Simba was not hungry, perhaps Simba was not hunting; but the black messenger was taking no chances. He was sure that the lion was approaching, and he would wait here where he could see both trails until he discovered which one Simba took.

Watching with more or less indifference because of the safety of his sanctuary, the Negro was ill-prepared for the shock which the sight that presently broke upon his vision induced. Never in the lowest steps of his superstition had he conceived such a scene as he now witnessed, and he blinked his eyes repeatedly to make sure that he was awake; but, no, there could be no mistake. It was indeed a white woman almost naked but for golden ornaments and a soft strip of leopard skin beneath her narrow stomacher—a white woman who walked with the fingers of one hand tangled in the black mane of a great golden lion.

Along the trail they came, and at the crossing they turned to the left into the trail that he had been following. As they disappeared from his view, the black man fingered the fetish that was suspended from a cord about his neck and prayed to Mulungo, the god of his people; and when he again set out toward his destination he took another and more circuitous route.

Often, after darkness had fallen, Tarzan had come to the camp of the conspirators and, perched in a tree above them, listened to Zveri outlining his plans to his companions; so that the ape-man was familiar with what they intended, down to the minutest detail.

Now, knowing that they would not be prepared to strike for some time, he was roaming the jungle far away from the sight and stench of man, enjoying to the full the peace and freedom that were his life. He knew that Nkima should have reached his destination by this time and delivered the message that Tarzan had dispatched by him. He was still puzzled by the strange disappearance of La and piqued by his inability to pick up her trail. He was genuinely grieved by her disappearance, for already he had his plans well formulated to restore her to her throne and punish her enemies; but he gave himself over to no futile regrets as he swung through the trees in sheer joy of living, or when hunger overtook him, stalked his prey in the grim and terrible silence of the hunting beast.

Sometimes he thought of the good-looking young American, to whom he had taken a fancy in spite of the fact that he considered him an enemy. Had he known of Colt's now almost hopeless plight, it is possible that he would have gone to his rescue, but he knew nothing of it.

So, alone and friendless, sunk to the uttermost depths of despair, Wayne Colt stumbled through the jungle in search of Zora Drinov and her abductor. But already he had lost the faint trail; and To-yat, far to his right, lumbered along with his captive safe from pursuit.

Weak from exhaustion and shock, thoroughly terrified now by the hopelessness of her hideous position, Zora had lost consciousness. To-yat feared that she was dead; but he carried her on, nevertheless, that he might at least have the satisfaction of exhibiting her to his tribe as evidence of his prowess and, perhaps, to furnish an excuse for another Dum-Dum. Secure in his might, conscious of few enemies that might with safety to themselves molest him, To-yat did not take the precaution of silence, but wandered on through the jungle heedless of all dangers.

Many were the keen ears and sensitive nostrils that carried the message of his passing to their owners, but to only one did the strange mingling of the scent spoor of the bull ape with that of a she-Mangani suggest a condition worthy of investigation. So as To-yat pursued his careless way, another creature of the jungle, moving silently on swift feet, bore down upon him; and when, from a point of vantage, keen eyes beheld the shaggy bull and the slender, delicate girl, a lip curled in a silent snarl. A moment later To-yat, the king ape, was brought to a snarling, bristling halt as the giant figure of a bronzed Tarmangani dropped lightly into the trail before him, a living threat to his possession of his prize.

The wicked eyes of the bull shot fire and hate. "Go away," he said. "I am To-yat. Go away or I kill."

"Put down the she," demanded Tarzan.

"No," bellowed To-yat. "She is mine."

"Put down the she," repeated Tarzan, "and go your way; or I kill. I am Tarzan of the Apes, Lord of the Jungle!"

Tarzan drew the hunting knife of his father and crouched as he advanced toward the bull. To-yat snarled; and seeing that the other meant to give battle, he cast the body of the girl aside that he might not be handicapped. As they circled, each looking for an advantage, there came a sudden, terrific crashing sound in the jungle downwind from them.

Tantor, the elephant, asleep in the security of the depth of the forest, had been suddenly awakened by the growling of the two beasts. Instantly his nostrils caught a familiar scent spoor—the scent spoor of his beloved Tarzan—and his ears told him that he was facing in battle the great Mangani, whose scent was also strong in the nostrils of Tantor.

To the snapping and bending of trees, the great bull rushed through the forest; and as he emerged suddenly, towering

above them, To-yat, the king ape, seeing death in those angry
eyes and gleaming tusks, turned and fled into the jungle.

13

The Lion-Man

PETER ZVERI WAS, in a measure, regaining some of the
confidence that he had lost in the ultimate success of his
plan, for his agents were succeeding at last in getting to him
some of his much needed supplies, together with contingents
of disaffected blacks wherewith to recruit his forces to sufficient numbers to insure the success of his contemplated
invasion of Italian Somaliland. It was his plan to make a
swift and sudden incursion, destroying native villages and
capturing an outpost or two, then retreating quickly across
the border, pack away the French uniforms for possible
future use and undertake the overthrow of Ras Tafari in
Abyssinia, where his agents had assured him conditions
were ripe for a revolution. With Abyssinia under his control
to serve as a rallying point, his agents assured him that
the native tribes of all Northern Africa would flock to his
standards.

In distant Bokhara a fleet of two hundred planes—bombers,
scouts, and fighting planes—made available through the greed
of American capitalists, were being mobilized for a sudden
dash across Persia and Arabia to his base in Abyssinia. With
these to support his great native army, he felt that his position
would be secure, the malcontents of Egypt would join forces

with him and, with Europe embroiled in a war that would prevent any concerted action against him, his dream of empire might be assured and his position made impregnable for all time.

Perhaps it was a mad dream; perhaps Peter Zveri was mad—but, then, what great world conqueror has not been a little mad?

He saw his frontiers pushed toward the south as, little by little, he extended his dominion, until one day he should rule a great continent—Peter I, Emperor of Africa.

"You seem happy, Comrade Zveri," said little Antonio Mori.

"Why should I not be, Tony?" demanded the dreamer. "I see success just before us. We should all be happy, but we are going to be very much happier later on."

"Yes," said Tony, "when the Philippines are free, I shall be very happy. Do you not think that I should be a very big man back there, then, Comrade Zveri?'

"Yes," said the Russian, "but you can be a bigger man if you stay here and work for me. How would you like to be a Grand Duke, Tony?"

"A Grand Duke!" exclaimed the Filipino. "I thought there were no more Grand Dukes."

"But perhaps there may be again."

"They were wicked men who ground down the working classes," said Tony.

"To be a Grand Duke who grinds down the rich and takes money from them might not be so bad," said Peter. "Grand Dukes are very rich and powerful. Would you not like to be rich and powerful, Tony?"

"Well, of course, who would not?"

"Then always do as I tell you, Tony; and some day I shall make you a Grand Duke," said Zveri.

The camp was filled with activity now at all times, for Zveri had conceived the plan of whipping his native recruits into some semblance of military order and discipline. Romero, Dorsky, and Ivitch having had military experience, the camp was filled with marching men, deploying, charging and assembling, practicing the Manual of Arms, and being instructed in the rudiments of fire discipline.

The day following his conversation with Zveri, Tony was assisting the Mexican, who was sweating over a company of black recruits.

During a period of rest, as the Mexican and Filipino were enjoying a smoke, Tony turned to his companion. "You have traveled much, Comrade," said the Filipino. "Perhaps you can tell me what sort of uniform a Grand Duke wears."

"I have heard," said Romero, "that in Hollywood and New York many of them wear aprons."

Tony grimaced. "I do not think," he said, "that I want to be a Grand Duke."

The blacks in the camp, held sufficiently interested and busy in drills to keep them out of mischief, with plenty of food and with the prospects of fighting and marching still in the future, were a contented and happy lot. Those who had undergone the harrowing experiences of Opar and those other untoward incidents that had upset their equanimity had entirely regained their self-confidence, a condition for which Zveri took all the credit to himself, assuming that it was due to his remarkable gift for leadership. And then a runner arrived in camp with a message for him and with a weird story of having seen a white woman hunting in the jungle with a black-maned golden lion. This was sufficient to recall to the blacks the other weird occurrences and to remind them that there were supernatural agencies at work in this territory, that it was peopled by ghosts and demons, and that at any moment some dire calamity might befall them.

But if this story upset the equanimity of the blacks, the message that the runner brought to Zveri precipitated an emotional outbreak in the Russian that bordered closely upon the frenzy of insanity. Blaspheming in a loud voice, he strode back and forth before his tent; nor would he explain to any of his lieutenants the cause of his anger.

And while Zveri fumed, other forces were gathering against him. Through the jungle moved a hundred ebon warriors, their smooth, sleek skin, their rolling muscles and elastic step bespeaking their physical fitness. They were naked but for narrow loincloths of leopard or lion skin and a few of those ornaments that are dear to the hearts of savages—anklets and armbands of copper and necklaces of the claws of lions or leopards—while above the head of each floated a white plume. But here the primitiveness of their equipment ceased, for their weapons were the weapons of modern fighting men; high-powered service rifles, revolvers, and bandoleers of cartridges. It was, indeed, a formidable-appearing company that swung steadily and silently through the jungle, and upon the shoulder of the black chief who led them rode a little monkey.

Tarzan was relieved when Tantor's sudden and unexpected charge drove To-yat into the jungle; for Tarzan of the Apes found no pleasure in quarreling with the Mangani, which he considered above all other creatures his brothers. He never forgot that he had been nursed at the breast of Kala, the she-ape, nor that he had grown to manhood in the tribe of Kerchak, the king. From infancy to manhood he had thought of himself only as an ape, and even now it was often easier for him to understand and appreciate the motives of the great Mangani than those of man.

At a signal from Tarzan, Tantor stopped; and assuming again his customary composure, though still alert to any danger that might threaten his friend, he watched while the ape-man turned and knelt beside the prostrate girl. Tarzan had at first thought her dead, but he soon discovered that she was only in a swoon. Lifting her in his arms, he spoke a half dozen words to the great pachyderm, who turned about and, putting down his head, started off straight into the dense jungle, making a pathway along which Tarzan bore the unconscious girl.

Straight as an arrow moved Tantor, the elephant, to halt at last upon the bank of a considerable river. Beyond this was a spot that Tarzan had in mind to which he wished to convey To-yat's unfortunate captive, whom he had recognized immediately as the young woman he had seen in the base camp of the conspirators and a cursory examination of whom convinced him was upon the verge of death from starvation, shock, and exposure.

Once again he spoke to Tantor; and the great pachyderm, twining his trunk around their bodies, lifted the two gently to his broad back. Then he waded into the river and set out for the opposite shore. The channel in the center was deep and swift, and Tantor was swept off his feet and carried downstream for a considerable distance before he found footing again, but eventually he won to the opposite bank. Here again he went ahead, making trail, until at last he broke into a broad, well-marked game trail.

Now Tarzan took the lead, and Tantor followed. While they moved thus silently toward their destination, Zora Drinov opened her eyes. Instantly recollection of her plight filled her consciousness; and then almost simultaneously she realized that her cheek, resting upon the shoulder of her captor, was not pressing against a shaggy coat, but against the smooth skin of a human body, and then she turned her head and looked at the profile of the creature that was carrying her.

She thought at first that she was the victim of some strange hallucination of terror; for, of course, she could not measure the time that she had been unconscious, nor recall any of the incidents that had occurred during that period. The last thing that she remembered was that she had been in the arms of a great ape, who was carrying her off to the jungle. She had closed her eyes; and when she opened them again, the ape had been transformed into a handsome demigod of the forest.

She closed her eyes and turned her head so that she faced back over the man's shoulder. She thought that she would keep her eyes tightly closed for a moment, then open them and turn them stealthily once more toward the face of the creature that was carrying her so lightly along the jungle trail. Perhaps this time he would be an ape again, and then she would know that she was indeed mad, or dreaming.

And when she did open her eyes, the sight that met them convinced her that she was experiencing a nightmare; for plodding along the trail directly behind her, was a giant bull elephant.

Tarzan, apprised of her returning consciousness by the movement of her head upon his shoulder, turned his own to look at her and saw her gazing at Tantor in wide-eyed astonishment. Then she turned toward him, and their eyes met.

"Who are you?" she asked in a whisper. "Am I dreaming?" But the ape-man only turned his eyes to the front and made no reply.

Zora thought of struggling to free herself; but realizing that she was very weak and helpless, she at last resigned herself to her fate and let her cheek fall again to the bronzed shoulder of the ape-man.

When Tarzan finally stopped and laid his burden upon the ground, it was in a little clearing through which ran a tiny stream of clear water. Immense trees arched overhead, and through their foliage the great sun dappled the grass beneath them.

As Zora Drinov lay stretched upon the soft turf, she realized for the first time how weak she was; for when she attempted to rise, she found that she could not. As her eyes took in the scene about her, it seemed more than ever like a dream—the great bull elephant standing almost above her and the bronzed figure of an almost naked giant squatting upon his haunches beside the little stream. She saw him fold a great leaf into the shape of a cornucopia and, after filling it with water, rise and come toward her. Without a word he stooped, and putting an arm beneath her shoulders and raising her to a sitting position, he offered her the water from his improvised cup.

She drank deeply, for she was very thirsty. Then, looking up into the handsome face above her, she voiced her thanks; but when the man did not reply, she thought, naturally, that he did not understand her. When she had satisfied her thirst and he had lowered her gently to the ground again, he swung lightly into a tree and disappeared into the forest. But above her the great elephant stood, as though on guard, his huge body swaying gently to and fro.

The quiet and peace of her surroundings tended to soothe her nerves, but deeply rooted in her mind was the conviction that her situation was most precarious. The man was a mystery to her; and while she knew, of course, that the ape that had stolen her had not been transformed miraculously into a handsome forest god, yet she could not account in any way for his presence or for the disappearance of the ape, except upon the rather extravagant hypothesis that the two had worked together, the ape having stolen her for this man, who was its master. There had been nothing in the man's attitude to suggest that he intended to harm her, and yet so accustomed was she to gauge all men by the standards of civilized society that she could not conceive that he had other than ulterior designs.

To her analytical mind the man presented a paradox that intrigued her imagination, seeming, as he did, so utterly out of place in this savage African jungle; while at the same time he harmonized perfectly with his surroundings, in which he seemed absolutely at home and assured of himself, a fact that was still further impressed upon her by the presence of the wild bull elephant, to which the man paid no more attention than one would to a lapdog. Had he been unkempt, filthy, and degraded in appearance, she would have catalogued him immediately as one of those social outcasts, usually half demented, who are occasionally found far from the haunts of men, living the life of wild beasts, whose high standards of decency and cleanliness they uniformly fail to observe. But this creature had suggested more the trained athlete in whom cleanliness was a fetish, nor did his well-shaped head and intelligent eyes even remotely suggest mental or moral degradation.

And as she pondered him, the man returned, bearing a great load of straight branches, from which the twigs and leaves had been removed. With a celerity and adeptness that bespoke long years of practice, he constructed a shelter upon the bank of the rivulet. He gathered broad leaves to thatch its roof, and leafy branches to enclose it upon three sides, so that it formed a protection against the prevailing winds. He floored it with leaves and small twigs and dry grasses. Then he came and, lifting the girl in his arms, bore her to the rustic bower he had fabricated.

Once again he left her; and when he returned he brought a

little fruit, which he fed to her sparingly, for he guessed that she had been long without food and knew that he must not overtax her stomach.

Always he worked in silence; and though no word had passed between them, Zora Drinov felt growing within her consciousness a conviction of his trustworthiness.

The next time that he left her he was gone a considerable time, but still the elephant stood in the clearing, like some titanic sentinel upon guard.

When next the man returned, he brought the carcass of a deer; and then Zora saw him make fire, after the manner of primitive men. As the meat roasted above it, the fragrant aroma came to her nostrils, bringing consciousness of a ravening hunger. When the meat was cooked, the man came and squatted beside her, cutting small pieces with his keen hunting knife and feeding her as though she had been a helpless baby. He gave her only a little at a time, making her rest often; and while she ate he spoke for the first time, but not to her, nor in any language that she had ever heard. He spoke to the great elephant, and the huge pachyderm wheeled slowly about and entered the jungle, where she could hear the diminishing noise of his passage until it was lost in the distance. Before the meal was over, it was quite dark; and she finished it in the fitful light of the fire that shone redly on the bronzed skin of her companion and shot back from mysterious gray eyes that gave the impression of seeing everything, even her inmost thoughts. Then he brought her a drink of water, after which he squatted down outside her shelter and proceeded to satisfy his own hunger.

Gradually the girl had been lulled to a feeling of security by the seeming solicitude of her strange protector. But now distinct misgivings assailed her, and suddenly she felt a strange new fear of the silent giant in whose power she was; for when he ate she saw that he ate his meat raw, tearing the flesh like a wild beast. When there came the sound of something moving in the jungle just beyond the firelight and he raised his head and looked and there came a low and savage growl of warning from his lips, the girl closed her eyes and buried her face in her arms in sudden terror and revulsion.

From the darkness of the jungle there came an answering growl; but the sound moved on, and presently all was silent again.

It seemed a long time before Zora dared open her eyes again, and when she did she saw that the man had finished his meal and was stretched out on the grass between her and the fire. She was afraid of him, of that she was quite certain; yet, at the same time, she could not deny that his presence there imparted to her a feeling of safety that she had never before felt in the jungle. As she tried to fathom this, she dozed and presently was asleep.

The young sun was already bringing renewed warmth to the jungle when she awoke. The man had replenished the fire and was sitting before it, grilling small fragments of meat. Beside him were some fruits, which he must have gathered since he had awakened. As she watched him, she was still further impressed by his great physical beauty, as well as by a certain marked nobility of bearing that harmonized well with the dignity of his poise and the intelligence of his keen gray eyes. She wished that she had not seen him devour his meat like a—ah, that was it—like a lion. How much like a lion he was, in his strength, and dignity, and majesty, and with all the quiet suggestion of ferocity that pervaded his every act. And so it was that she came to think of him as her lion-man and, while trying to trust him, always fearing him not a little.

Again he fed her and brought her water before he satisfied his own hunger; but before he started to eat, he arose and voiced a long, low call. Then once more he squatted upon his haunches and devoured his food. Although he held it in his strong, brown hands and ate the flesh raw, she saw now that he ate slowly and with the same quiet dignity that marked his every act, so that presently she found him less revolting. Once again she tried to talk with him, addressing him in various languages and several African dialects, but as for any sign he gave that he understood her she might as well have been addressing a dumb brute. Doubtless her disappointment would have been replaced by anger could she have known that she was addressing an English lord, who understood perfectly every word that she uttered, but who, for reasons which he himself best knew, preferred to remain the dumb brute to this woman whom he looked upon as an enemy.

However, it was well for Zora Drinov that he was what he was, for it was the prompting of the English lord and not that of the savage carnivore that had moved him to succor her because she was alone, and helpless, and a woman. The beast in Tarzan would not have attacked her, but would merely have ignored her, letting the law of the jungle take its course as it must with all her creatures.

Shortly after Tarzan had finished his meal, a crashing in the jungle announced the return of Tantor; and when he appeared in the little clearing, the girl realized that the great brute had come in response to the call of the man, and marveled.

And so the days wore on; and slowly Zora Drinov regained her strength, guarded by night by the silent forest god and by day by the great bull elephant. Her only apprehension now was for the safety of Wayne Colt, who was seldom from her thoughts. Nor was her apprehension groundless, for the young American had fallen upon bad days.

Almost frantic with concern for the safety of Zora, he had exhausted his strength in futile search for her and her abductor, forgetful of himself until hunger and fatigue had taken their toll of his strength. He had awakened at last to the realization that his condition was dangerous; and now when he needed food most, the game that he had formerly found reasonably plentiful seemed to have deserted the country. Even the smaller rodents that had once sufficed to keep him alive were either too wary for him or not present at all. Occasionally he found fruits that he could eat, but they seemed to impart little or no strength to him; and at last he was forced to the conviction that he had reached the end of his endurance and his strength and that nothing short of a miracle could preserve him from death. He was so weak that he could stagger only a few steps at a time and then, sinking to the ground, was forced to lie there for a long time before he could arise again;

and always there was the knowledge that eventually he would not arise.

Yet he would not give up. Something more than the urge to live drove him on. He could not die, he must not die while Zora Drinov was in danger. He had found a well-beaten trail at last where he was sure that sooner or later he must meet a native hunter, or, perhaps, find his way to the camp of his fellows. He could only crawl now, for he had not the strength to rise; and then suddenly the moment came that he had striven so long to avert—the moment that marked the end, though it came in a form that he had only vaguely anticipated as one of several that might ring the curtain upon his earthly existence.

As he lay in the trail resting before he dragged himself on again, he was suddenly conscious that he was not alone. He had heard no sounds, for doubtless his hearing had been dulled by exhaustion; but he was aware through the medium of that strange sense, the possession of which each of us has felt at some time in his existence, that told him eyes were upon him.

With an effort he raised his head and looked, and there, before him in the trail, stood a great lion, his lips drawn back in an angry snarl, his yellow-green eyes glaring balefully.

14

Shot Down

TARZAN WENT ALMOST daily to watch the camp of his enemy, moving swiftly through the jungle by trails unknown to man. He saw that preparations for the first bold stroke were almost completed, and finally he saw uniforms being issued to all members of the party—uniforms which he recognized as those of French Colonial troops—and he realized that the time had come when he must move. He hoped that little Nkima had carried his message safely, but if not, Tarzan would find some other way.

Zora Drinov's strength was slowly returning. Today she had arisen and taken a few steps out into the sunlit clearing. The great elephant regarded her. She had long since ceased to fear him, as she had ceased to fear the strange white man who had befriended her. Slowly the girl approached the great bull, and Tantor regarded her out of his little eyes as he waved his trunk to and fro.

He had been so docile and harmless all the days that he had guarded her that it had grown to be difficult for Zora to conceive him capable of inflicting injury upon her. But as she looked into his little eyes now, there was an expression there that brought her to a sudden halt; and as she realized that after all he was only a wild bull elephant, she suddenly appreciated the rashness of her act. She was already so close to him that she could have reached out and touched him, as had been her intention, having thought that she would thus make friends with him.

It was in her mind to fall back with dignity, when the waving trunk shot suddenly out and encircled her body. Zora Drinov did not scream. She only closed her eyes and waited. She felt herself lifted from the ground, and a moment later the elephant had crossed the little clearing and deposited her in her shelter. Then he backed off slowly and resumed his post of duty.

He had not hurt her. A mother could not have lifted her baby more gently, but he had impressed upon Zora Drinov that she was a prisoner and that he was her keeper. As a matter of fact, Tantor was only carrying out Tarzan's instructions, which had nothing to do with the forcible restraint of the girl, but were only a measure of precaution to prevent her wandering into the jungle where other dangers might overtake her.

Zora had not fully regained her strength, and the experience left her trembling. Though she now realized that her sudden fears for her safety had been groundless, she decided that she would take no more liberties with her mighty warden.

It was not long after that Tarzan returned, much earlier in the day than was his custom. He spoke only to Tantor; and the great beast, touching him almost caressingly with his trunk, turned and lumbered off into the forest. Then Tarzan advanced to where Zora sat in the opening of her shelter. Lightly he lifted her from the ground and tossed her to his shoulder; and then, to her infinite surprise at the strength and agility of the man, he swung into a tree and was off through the jungle in the wake of the pachyderm.

At the edge of the river that they had crossed before, Tantor was awaiting them, and once more he carried Zora and Tarzan safely to the other bank.

Tarzan himself had crossed the river twice a day since he had made the camp for Zora; but when he went alone he needed no help from Tantor or any other, for he swam the swift stream, his eye alert and his keen knife ready should Gimla, the crocodile, attack him. But for the crossing of the woman, he had enlisted the services of Tantor that she might not be subjected to the danger and hardship of the only other means of crossing that was possible.

As Tantor clambered up the muddy bank, Tarzan dismissed him with a word, as with the girl in his arms he leaped into a nearby tree.

That flight through the jungle was an experience that might long stand vividly in the memory of Zora Drinov. That a human being could possess the strength and agility of the creature that carried her seemed unbelievable, and she might easily have attributed a supernatural origin to him had she not felt the life in the warm flesh that was pressed against hers. Leaping from branch to branch, swinging across breathless voids, she was borne swiftly through the middle terrace of the forest. At first she had been terrified, but gradually fear left her, to be replaced by that utter confidence which Tarzan of the Apes has inspired in many a breast. At last he stopped and, lowering her to the branch upon which he stood, pointed through the surrounding foliage ahead of them. Zora looked and to her astonishment saw the camp of her companions lying ahead and below her. Once more the ape-man took her in his arms and dropped lightly to the ground into a wide trail that swept past the base of the tree in which he had halted. With a wave of his hand he indicated that she was free to go to the camp.

"Oh, how can I thank you!" exclaimed the girl. "How can I ever make you understand how splendid you have been and how I appreciate all that you have done for me?" But his only reply was to turn and swing lightly into the tree that spread its green foliage above them.

With a rueful shake of her head, Zora Drinov started along the trail toward camp, while above her Tarzan followed through the trees to make certain that she arrived in safety.

Paul Ivitch had been hunting, and he was just returning to camp when he saw something move in a tree at the edge of the clearing. He saw the spots of a leopard, and raising his rifle, he fired; so that at the moment that Zora entered the camp, the body of Tarzan of the Apes lunged from a tree almost at her side, blood trickling from a bullet wound in his

head as the sunshine played upon the leopard spots of his
loincloth.

The sight of the lion growling above him might have shaken
the nerves of a man in better physical condition than was
Wayne Colt, but the vision of a beautiful girl running quickly
toward the savage beast from the rear was the final stroke that
almost overwhelmed him.

Through his brain ran a medley of recollection and conjecture. In a brief instant he recalled that men had borne witness to
the fact that they had felt no pain while being mauled by a
lion—neither pain nor fear—and he also recalled that men
went mad from thirst and hunger. If he were to die, then, it
would not be painful, and of that he was glad; but if he were not
to die, then surely he was mad, for the lion and the girl must be
the hallucination of a crazed mind.

Fascination held his eyes fixed upon the two. How real they
were! He heard the girl speak to the lion, and then he saw her
brush past the great savage beast and come and bend over him
where he lay helpless in the trail. She touched him, and then he
knew that she was real.

"Who are you?" she asked, in limping English that was
beautiful with a strange accent. "What has happened to you?"

"I have been lost," he said, "and I am about done up. I have
not eaten for a long while," and then he fainted.

Jad-bal-ja, the golden lion, had conceived a strange affection for La of Opar. Perhaps it was the call of one kindred
savage spirit to another. Perhaps it was merely the recollection that she was Tarzan's friend. But be that as it may, he
seemed to find the same pleasure in her company that a
faithful dog finds in the company of his master. He had protected her with fierce loyalty, and when he made his kill
he shared the flesh with her. She, however, after cutting off
a portion that she wanted, had always gone away a little
distance to build her primitive fire and cook the flesh; nor
ever had she ventured back to the kill after Jad-bal-ja had
commenced to feed, for a lion is yet a lion, and the grim and
ferocious growls that accompanied his feeding warned the

girl against presuming too far upon the newfound generosity
of the carnivore.

They had been feeding, when the approach of Colt had
attracted Numa's attention and brought him into the trail from
his kill. For a moment La had feared that she might not be able
to keep the lion from the man, and she had wanted to do so;
for something in the stranger's appearance reminded her of
Tarzan, whom he more nearly resembled than he did the
grotesque priests of Opar. Because of this fact she thought that
possibly the stranger might be from Tarzan's country. Perhaps
he was one of Tarzan's friends and if so, she must protect him.
To her relief, the lion had obeyed her when she had called upon
him to halt, and now he evinced no further desire to attack
the man.

When Colt regained consciousness, La tried to raise him to
his feet; and, with considerable difficulty and some slight assistance from the man, she succeeded in doing so. She put one of
his arms across her shoulders and, supporting him thus, guided
him back along the trail, while Jad-bal-ja followed at their
heels. She had difficulty in getting him through the brush to the
hidden glen where Jad-bal-ja's kill lay and her little fire was
burning a short distance away. But at last she succeeded and
when they had come close to her fire, she lowered the man to
the ground, while Jal-bal-ja turned once more to his feeding
and his growling.

La fed the man tiny pieces of the meat that she had cooked,
and he ate ravenously all that she would give him. A short
distance away ran the river, where La and the lion would
have gone to drink after they had fed; but doubting whether
she could get the man so great a distance through the jungle,
she left him there with the lion and went down to the river; but
first she told Jad-bal-ja to guard him, speaking in the language
of the first men, the language of the Mangani, that all creatures
of the jungle understand to a greater or lesser extent. Near
the river La found what she sought—a fruit with a hard rind.
With her knife she cut an end from one of these fruits and
scooped out the pulpy interior, producing a primitive but
entirely practical cup, which she filled with water from the
river.

The water, as much as the food, refreshed and strengthened Colt; and though he lay but a few yards from a feeding lion, it seemed an eternity since he had experienced such a feeling of contentment and security, clouded only by his anxiety concerning Zora.

"You feel stronger now?" asked La, her voice tinged with concern.

"Very much," he replied.

"Then tell me who you are and if this is your country."

"This is not my country," replied Colt. "I am an American. My name is Wayne Colt."

"You are perhaps a friend of Tarzan of the Apes?" she asked.

He shook his head. "No," he said. "I have heard of him, but I do not know him."

La frowned. "You are his enemy, then?" she demanded.

"Of course not," replied Colt. "I do not even know him."

A sudden light flashed in La's eyes. "Do you know Zora?" she asked.

Colt came to his elbow with a sudden start. "Zora Drinov?" he demanded. "What do you know of her?"

"She is my friend," said La.

"She is my friend also," said Colt.

"She is in trouble," said La.

"Yes, I know it; but how did you know?"

"I was with her when she was taken prisoner by the men of the desert. They took me also, but I escaped."

"How long ago was that?"

"The Flaming God has gone to rest many times since I saw Zora," replied the girl.

"Then I have seen her since."

"Where is she?"

"I do not know. She was with the Aarabs when I found her. We escaped from them; and then, while I was hunting in the jungle something came and carried her away. I do not know whether it was a man or a gorilla; for though I saw its footprints, I could not be sure. I have been searching for her for a long time; but I could not find food, and it has been some time since I have had water; so I lost my strength, and you found me as I am."

"You shall not want for food nor water now," said La, "for Numa, the lion, will hunt for us; and if we can find the camp of Zora's friends, perhaps they will go out and search for her."

"You know where the camp is?" he asked. "Is it near?"

"I do not know where it is. I have been searching for it to lead her friends after the men of the desert."

Colt had been studying the girl as they talked. He had noted her strange, barbaric apparel and the staggering beauty of her face and figure. He knew almost intuitively that she was not of the world that he knew, and his mind was filled with curiosity concerning her.

"You have not told me who you are," he said.

"I am La of Opar," she replied, "high priestess of the Flaming God."

Opar! Now indeed he knew that she was not of his world. Opar, the city of mystery, the city of fabulous treasures. Could it be that the same city that housed the grotesque warriors with whom he and Romero had fought produced also such beautiful creatures as Nao and La, and only these? He wondered why he had not connected her with Opar at once, for now he saw that her stomacher was similar to that of Nao and of the priestess that he had seen upon the throne in the great chamber of the ruined temple. Recalling his attempt to enter Opar and loot it of its treasures, he deemed it expedient to make no mention of any familiarity with the city of the girl's birth, for he guessed that Opar's women might be as primitively fierce in their vengeance as he had found Nao in her love.

The lion, and the girl, and the man lay up that night beside Jad-bal-ja's kill, and in the morning Colt found that his strength had partially returned. During the night Numa had finished his kill; and after the sun had risen, La found fruits which she and Colt ate, while the lion strolled to the river to drink, pausing once to roar, that the world might know the king was there.

"Numa will not kill again until tomorrow," she said, "so we

shall have no meat until then, unless we are fortunate enough to kill something ourselves."

Colt had long since abandoned the heavy rifle of the Aarabs, to the burden of which his growing weakness had left his muscles inadequate; so he had nothing but his bare hands and La only a knife with which they might make a kill.

"Then I guess we shall eat fruit until the lion kills again," he said. "In the meantime we might as well be trying to find the camp."

She shook her head. "No," she said, "you must rest. You were very weak when I found you, and it is not well that you should exert yourself until you are strong again. Numa will sleep all day. You and I will cut some sticks and lie beside a little trail, where the small things go. Perhaps we shall have luck; but if we do not, Numa will kill again tomorrow, and this time I shall take a whole hindquarter."

"I cannot believe that a lion would let you do that," said the man.

"At first I did not understand it myself," said La, "but after a while I remembered. It is because I am Tarzan's friend that he does not harm me."

When Zora Drinov saw her lion-man lying lifeless on the ground, she ran quickly to him and knelt at his side. She had heard the shot, and now seeing the blood running from the wound upon his head, she thought that someone had killed him intentionally and when Ivitch came running out, his rifle in his hand, she turned upon him like a tigress.

"You have killed him," she cried. "You beast! He was worth more than a dozen such as you."

The sound of the shot and the crashing of the body to the ground had brought men running from all parts of the camp; so that Tarzan and the girl were soon surrounded by a curious and excited throng of blacks, among whom the remaining whites were pushing their way.

Ivitch was stunned, not only by the sight of the giant white man lying apparently dead before him, but also by the presence of Zora Drinov, whom all within the camp had given up as irretrievably lost. "I had no idea, Comrade Drinov," he explained, "that I was shooting at a man. I see now what caused my mistake. I saw something moving in a tree and thought that it was a leopard, but instead it was the leopard skin that he wears about his loins."

By this time Zveri had elbowed his way to the center of the group. "Zora!" he cried in astonishment as he saw the girl. "Where did you come from? What has happened? What is the meaning of this?"

"It means that this fool, Ivitch, has killed the man who saved my life," cried Zora.

"Who is he?" asked Zveri.

"I do not know," replied Zora. "He has never spoken to me. He does not seem to understand any language with which I am familiar."

"He is not dead," cried Ivitch. "See, he moved."

Romero knelt and examined the wound in Tarzan's head. "He is only stunned," he said. "The bullet struck him a glancing blow. There are no indications of a fracture of the skull. I have seen men hit thus before. He may be unconscious for a long time, or he may not, but I am sure that he will not die."

"Who the devil do you suppose he is?" asked Zveri.

Zora shook her head. "I have no idea," she said. "I only know that he is as splendid as he is mysterious."

"I know who he is," said a black, who had pushed forward to where he could see the figure of the prostrate man, "and if he is not already dead, you had better kill him, for he will be your worst enemy."

"What do you mean?" demanded Zveri. "Who is he?"

"He is Tarzan of the Apes."

"You are certain?" snapped Zveri.

"Yes, Bwana," replied the black. "I saw him once before, and one never forgets Tarzan of the Apes."

"Yours was a lucky shot, Ivitch," said the leader, "and now you may as well finish what you started."

"Kill him, you mean?" demanded Ivitch.

"Our cause is lost and our lives with it, if he lives," replied Zveri. "I thought that he was dead, or I should never have come here; and now that fate has thrown him into our hands we would be fools to let him escape, for we could not have a worse enemy than he."

"I cannot kill him in cold blood," said Ivitch.

"You always were a weak-minded fool," said Zveri, "but I am not. Stand aside, Zora," and as he spoke he drew his revolver and advanced toward Tarzan.

The girl threw herself across the ape-man, shielding his body with hers. "You cannot kill him," she cried. "You must not."

"Don't be a fool, Zora," snapped Zveri.

"He saved my life and brought me back here to camp. Do you think I am going to let you murder him?" she demanded.

"I am afraid you can't help yourself, Zora," replied the man. "I do not like to do it, but it is his life or the cause. If he lives, we fail."

The girl leaped to her feet and faced Zveri. "If you kill him, Peter, I shall kill you—I swear it by everything that I hold most dear. Hold him prisoner if you will, but as you value your life, do not kill him."

Zveri went pale with anger. "Your words are treason," he said. "Traitors to the cause have died for less than what you have said."

Zora Drinov realized that the situation was extremely dangerous. She had little reason to believe that Zveri would make good his threat toward her, but she saw that if she would save Tarzan she must act quickly. "Send the others away," she said to Zveri. "I have something to tell you before you kill this man."

For a moment the leader hesitated. Then he turned to Dorsky, who stood at his side. "Have the fellow securely bound and taken to one of the tents," he commanded. "We shall give him a fair trial after he has regained consciousness and then place him before a firing squad," and then to the girl, "Come with me, Zora, and I will listen to what you have to say."

In silence the two walked to Zveri's tent. "Well?" inquired Zveri, as the girl halted before the entrance. "What have you to say to me that you think will change my plans relative to your lover?"

Zora looked at him for a long minute, a faint sneer of contempt curling her lips. "*You* would think such a thing," she said, "but you are wrong. However you may think, though, you shall not kill him."

"And why not?" demanded Zveri.

"Because if you do I shall tell them all what your plans are; that you yourself are a traitor to the cause, and that you have been using them all to advance your own selfish ambition to make yourself Emperor of Africa."

"You would not dare," cried Zveri, "nor would I let you; for as much as I love you, I shall kill you here on the spot, unless you promise not to interfere in any way with my plans."

"You do not dare kill me," taunted the girl. "You have antagonized every man in the camp, Peter, and they all like me. Some of them, perhaps, love me a little. Do you think that I should not be avenged within five minutes after you had killed me? You will have to think of something else, my friend; and the best thing that you can do is to take my advice. Keep Tarzan of the Apes a prisoner if you will, but on your life do not kill him or permit anyone else to do so."

Zveri sank into a camp chair. "Everyone is against me," he said. "Even you, the woman I love, turn against me."

"I have not changed toward you in any respect, Peter," said the girl.

"You mean that?" he asked, looking up.

"Absolutely," she replied.

"How long were you alone in the jungle with that man?" he demanded.

"Don't start that, Peter," she said. "He could not have treated me differently if he had been my own brother; and certainly, all other considerations aside, you should know me well enough to know that I have no such weakness in the direction that your tone implied."

"You have never loved me—that is the reason," he declared. "But I would not trust you or any other woman with a man she loves or with whom she was temporarily infatuated."

"That," she said, "has nothing to do with what we are discussing. Are you going to kill Tarzan of the Apes, or are you not?"

"For your sake, I shall let him live," replied the man, "even though I do not trust you," he added. "I trust no one. How can I? Look at this," and he took a coded message from his pocket and handed it to her. "This came a few days ago—the damn traitor. I wish I could get my hands on him. I should like to have killed him myself, but I suppose I shall have no such luck, as he is probably already dead."

Zora took the paper. Below the message, in Zveri's scrawling hand, it had been decoded in Russian script. As she read it, her eyes grew large with astonishment. "It is incredible," she cried.

"It is the truth, though," said Zveri. "I always suspected the dirty hound," and he added with an oath, "I think that damn Mexican is just as bad."

"At least," said Zora, "his plan has been thwarted, for I take it that his message did not get through."

"No," said Zveri. "By error it was delivered to our agents instead of his."

"Then no harm has been done."

"Fortunately, no; but it has made me suspicious of everyone, and I am going to push the expedition through at once before anything further can occur to interfere with my plans."

"Everything is ready, then?" she asked.

"Everything is ready," he replied. "We march tomorrow morning. And now tell me what happened while I was at Opar. Why did the Aarabs desert, and why did you go with them?"

"Abu Batn was angry and resentful because you left him to guard the camp. The Aarabs felt that it was a reflection upon their courage, and I think that they would have deserted you anyway, regardless of me. Then, the day after you left, a strange woman wandered into camp. She was a very beautiful white woman from Opar; and Abu Batn, conceiving the idea of profiting through the chance that fate had sent him, took us with him with the intention of selling us into captivity on his return march to his own country."

"Are there no honest men in the world?" demanded Zveri.

"I am afraid not," replied the girl; but as he was staring

moodily at the ground, he did not see the contemptuous curl of her lip that accompanied her reply.

She described the luring of La from Abu Batn's camp and of the sheik's anger at the treachery of Ibn Dammuk; and then she told him of her own escape, but she did not mention Wayne Colt's connection with it and led him to believe that she wandered alone in the jungle until the great ape had captured her. She dwelt at length upon Tarzan's kindness and consideration and told of the great elephant who had guarded her by day.

"Sounds like a fairy story," said Zveri, "but I have heard enough about this ape-man to believe almost anything concerning him, which is one reason why I believe we shall never be safe while he lives."

"He cannot harm us while he is our prisoner; and certainly, if you love me as you say you do, the man who saved my life deserves better from you than ignominious death."

"Speak no more of it," said Zveri. "I have already told you that I would not kill him," but in his treacherous mind he was formulating a plan whereby Tarzan might be destroyed while still he adhered to the letter of his promise to Zora.

15

"Kill, Tantor, Kill!"

EARLY THE FOLLOWING morning the expedition filed out of camp, the savage black warriors arrayed in the uniforms of French Colonial troops; while Zveri, Romero, Ivitch, and Mori wore the uniforms of French officers. Zora Drinov accompanied the marching column; for though she had asked to be permitted to remain and nurse Tarzan, Zveri would not permit her to do so, saying that he would not again let her out of his sight. Dorsky and a handful of blacks were left behind to guard the prisoner and watch over the store of provisions and equipment that were to be left in the base camp.

As the column had been preparing to march, Zveri gave his final instructions to Dorsky. "I leave this matter entirely in your hands," he said. "It must appear that he escaped, or, at worst, that he met an accidental death."

"You need give the matter no further thought, Comrade," replied Dorsky. "Long before you return, this stranger will have been removed."

A long and difficult march lay before the invaders, their route lying across southeastern Abyssinia into Italian Somaliland, along five hundred miles of rough and savage country. It was Zveri's intention to make no more than a demonstration in the Italian colony, merely sufficient to arouse the anger of the Italians still further against the French and to give the fascist dictator the excuse which Zveri believed was all that he awaited to carry his mad dream of Italian conquest across Europe.

Perhaps Zveri was a little mad, but then he was a disciple of madmen whose greed for power wrought distorted images in their minds, so that they could not differentiate between the rational and the bizarre; and then, too, Zveri had for so long dreamed his dream of empire that he saw now only his goal and none of the insurmountable obstacles that beset his path. He saw a new Roman emperor ruling Europe, and himself as Emperor of Africa making an alliance with his new European power against all the balance of the world. He pictured two splendid golden thrones; upon one of them sat the Emperor Peter I, and upon the other the Empress Zora; and so he dreamed through the long, hard marches toward the east.

It was the morning of the day following that upon which he had been shot before Tarzan regained consciousness. He felt weak and sick, and his head ached horribly. When he tried to move, he discovered that his wrists and ankles were securely bound. He did not know what had happened, and at first he could not imagine where he was; but, as recollection slowly returned and he recognized about him the canvas walls of a tent, he understood that in some way his enemies had captured him. He tried to wrench his wrists free from the cords that held them, but they resisted his every effort.

He listened intently and sniffed the air, but he could detect no evidence of the teeming camp that he had seen when he had brought the girl back. He knew, however, that at least one night had passed; for the shadows that he could see through the tent opening indicated that the sun was high in the heavens, whereas it had been low in the west when last he saw it. Hearing voices, he realized that he was not alone, though he was confident that there must be comparatively few men in camp.

Deep in the jungle he heard an elephant trumpeting, and once, from far off, came faintly the roar of a lion. Tarzan strove again to snap the bonds that held him, but they would not yield. Then he turned his head so that he faced the opening in the tent, and from his lips burst a long, low cry; the cry of a beast in distress.

Dorsky, who was lolling in a chair before his own tent, leaped to his feet. The blacks, who had been talking animatedly, before their own shelters, went quickly quiet and seized their weapons.

"What was that?" Dorsky demanded of his black boy.

The fellow, wide-eyed and trembling, shook his head. "I do not know, Bwana," he said. "Perhaps the man in the tent has died, for such a noise may well have come from the throat of a ghost."

"Nonsense," said Dorsky. "Come, we'll have a look at him." But the black held back, and the white man went on alone.

The sound, which had come apparently from the tent in which the captive lay, had had a peculiar effect upon Dorsky, causing the flesh of his scalp to creep and a strange foreboding to fill him; so that as he neared the tent, he went more slowly and held his revolver ready in his hand.

When he entered the tent, he saw the man lying where he had been left; but now his eyes were open, and when they met those of the Russian, the latter had a sensation similar to that which one feels when he comes eye to eye with a wild beast that has been caught in a trap.

"Well," said Dorsky, "so you have come to, have you? What do you want?" The captive made no reply, but his eyes never left the other's face. So steady was the unblinking gaze that Dorsky became uneasy beneath it. "You had better learn to talk," he said gruffly, "if you know what is good for you." Then it occurred to him that perhaps the man did not understand him so he turned in the entrance and called to some of the blacks, who had advanced, half in curiosity, half in fear, toward the tent of the prisoner. "One of you fellows come here," he said.

At first no one seemed inclined to obey, but presently a stalwart warrior advanced. "See if this fellow can understand your language. Come in and tell him that I have a proposition to make to him and that he had better listen to it."

"If this is indeed Tarzan of the Apes," said the black, "he can understand me," and he came warily to the entrance of the tent.

The black repeated the message in his own dialect, but by no sign did the ape-man indicate that he understood.

Dorsky lost his patience. "You damned ape," he said. "You needn't try to make a fool of me. I know perfectly well that you understand this fellow's gibberish, and I know, too, that you are an Englishman and that you understand English. I'll give you just five minutes to think this thing over, and then I am coming back. If you have not made up your mind to talk by that time, you can take the consequences." Then he turned on his heel and left the tent.

Little Nkima had traveled far. Around his neck was a stout thong, supporting a little bag of leather, in which reposed a message. This eventually he had brought to Muviro, war chief of the Waziri; and when the Waziri had started out upon their long march, Nkima had ridden proudly upon the shoulder of Muviro. For some time he had remained with the black warriors; but then, at last, moved perhaps by some caprice of his erratic mind, or by a great urge that he could not resist, he had left them and, facing alone all the dangers that he feared most, had set out by himself upon business of his own.

Many and narrow were the escapes of Nkima as he swung through the giants of the forest. Could he have resisted temptation, he might have passed with reasonable safety, but that he could not do; and so he was forever getting himself into trouble by playing pranks upon strangers, who, if they possessed any sense of humor themselves, most certainly failed to appreciate little Nkima's. Nkima could not forget that he was friend and confidant of Tarzan, Lord of the Jungle, though he seemed often to forget that Tarzan was not there to protect him when he hurled taunts and insults at other monkeys less favored. That he came through alive speaks more eloquently for his speed than for his intelligence or courage. Much of the time he was fleeing in terror, emitting shrill screams of mental anguish; yet he never seemed to learn from experience, and having barely eluded one pursuer intent upon murdering him he would be quite prepared to insult or annoy the next creature he met, especially selecting, it would seem, those that were larger and stronger than himself.

Sometimes he fled in one direction, sometimes in another, so that he occupied much more time than was necessary in making his journey. Otherwise he would have reached his master in time to be of service to him at a moment that Tarzan needed a friend as badly, perhaps, as ever he had needed one before in his life.

And now, while far away in the forest Nkima fled from an old dog baboon, whom he had hit with a well-aimed stick, Michael Dorsky approached the tent where Nkima's master lay bound and helpless. The five minutes were up, and Dorsky had come to demand Tarzan's answer. He came alone, and as he entered the tent his simple plan of action was well formulated in his mind.

The expression upon the prisoner's face had changed. He seemed to be listening intently. Dorsky listened then, too, but could hear nothing; for by comparison with the hearing of

Tarzan of the Apes Michael Dorsky was deaf. What Tarzan heard filled him with quiet satisfaction.

"Now," said Dorsky, "I have come to give you your last chance. Comrade Zveri has led two expeditions to Opar in search of the gold that we know is stored there. Both expeditions failed. It is well known that you know the location of the treasure vaults of Opar and can lead us to them. Agree that you will do this when Comrade Zveri returns, and not only will you not be harmed, but you will be released as quickly as Comrade Zveri feels that it would be safe to have you at liberty. Refuse and you die." He drew a long, slender stiletto from its sheath at his belt. "If you refuse to answer me, I shall accept that as evidence that you have not accepted my proposition." And as the ape-man maintained his stony silence, the Russian held the thin blade low before his eyes. "Think well, ape," he said, "and remember that when I slip this between your ribs there will be no sound. It will pierce your heart, and I shall leave it there until the blood has ceased to flow. Then I shall remove it and close the wound. Later in the day you will be found dead, and I shall tell the blacks that you died from the accidental gunshot. Thus your friends will never learn the truth. You will not be avenged, and you will have died uselessly." He paused for a reply, his evil eyes glinting menacingly into the cold, gray eyes of the ape-man.

The dagger was very near Tarzan's face now; and of a sudden, like a wild beast, he raised his body, and his jaws closed like a steel trap upon the wrist of the Russian. With a scream of pain, Dorsky drew back. The dagger dropped from his nerveless fingers. At the same instant Tarzan swung his legs around the feet of the would-be assassin; and as Dorsky rolled over on his back, he dragged Tarzan of the Apes on top of him.

The ape-man knew from the snapping of Dorsky's wrist bones between his teeth that the man's right hand was useless, and so he released it. Then to the Russian's horror, the ape-man's jaws sought his jugular as, from his throat, there rumbled the growl of a savage beast at bay.

Screaming for his men to come to his assistance, Dorsky tried to reach the revolver at his right hip with his left hand, but he soon saw that unless he could rid himself of Tarzan's body he would be unable to do so.

Already he heard his men running toward the tent, shouting among themselves, and then he heard exclamations of surprise and screams of terror. The next instant the tent vanished from above them, and Dorsky saw a huge bull elephant towering above him and his savage antagonist.

Instantly Tarzan ceased his efforts to close his teeth on Dorsky's throat and at the same time rolled quickly from the body of the Russian. As he did so, Dorsky's hand found his revolver.

"Kill, Tantor!" shouted the ape-man. "Kill!"

The sinuous trunk of the pachyderm twined around the Russian. The little eyes of the elephant flamed red with hate, and he trumpeted shrilly as he raised Dorsky high above his head and, wheeling about, hurled him out into the camp; while the terrified blacks, casting affrighted glances over their shoulders, fled into the jungle. Then Tantor charged his victim. With his great tusks he gored him; and then, in a frenzy of rage, trumpeting and squealing, he trampled him until nothing remained of Michael Dorsky but a bloody pulp.

From the moment that Tantor had seized the Russian, Tarzan had sought ineffectually to stay the great brute's fury, but Tantor was deaf to commands until he had wreaked his vengeance upon this creature that had dared to attack his friend. But when his rage had spent its force and nothing remained against which to vent it, he came quietly to Tarzan's side and at a word from the ape-man lifted his brown body gently in his powerful trunk and bore him away into the forest.

Deep into the jungle to a hidden glade, Tantor carried his helpless friend, and there he placed him gently on soft grasses beneath the shade of a tree. Little more could the great bull do other than to stand guard. As a result of the excitement attending the killing of Dorsky and his concern for Tarzan, Tantor was nervous and irritable. He stood with upraised ears, alert for any menacing sound, waving his sensitive trunk to and fro, searching each vagrant air current for the scent of danger.

The pain of his wound annoyed Tarzan far less than the pangs of thirst.

To little monkeys watching him from the trees he called, "Come, Manu, and untie the thongs that bind my wrists."

"We are afraid," said an old monkey.

"I am Tarzan of the Apes," said the man reassuringly. "Tarzan has been your friend always. He will not harm you."

"We are afraid," repeated the old monkey. "Tarzan deserted us. For many moons the jungle has not known Tarzan; but other Tarmangani and strange Gomangani came and with thundersticks they hunted little Manu and killed him. If Tarzan had still been our friend, he would have driven these strange men away."

"If I had been here, the strange men-things would not have harmed you," said Tarzan. "Still would Tarzan have protected you. Now I am back, but I cannot destroy the strangers or drive them away until the thongs are taken from my wrists."

"Who put them there?" asked the monkey.

"The strange Tarmangani," replied Tarzan.

"Then they must be more powerful than Tarzan," said Manu, "so what good would it do to set you free? If the strange Tarmangani found out that we had done it, they would be angry and come and kill us. Let Tarzan, who for many rains has been Lord of the Jungle, free himself."

Seeing that it was futile to appeal to Manu, Tarzan, as a forlorn hope, voiced the long, plaintive, uncanny help call of the great apes. With slowly increasing crescendo it rose to a piercing shriek that drove far and wide through the silent jungle.

In all directions, beasts, great and small, paused as the weird note broke upon their sensitive eardrums. None was afraid, for the call told them that a great bull was in trouble and, therefore, doubtless harmless; but the jackals interpreted the sound to mean the possibility of flesh and trotted off through the jungle in the direction from which it had come; and Dango, the hyena, heard and slunk on soft pads, hoping that he would find a helpless animal that would prove easy prey. And far away, and faintly, a little monkey heard the call, recognizing the voice of the caller. Swiftly, then, he flew through the

jungle, impelled as he was upon rare occasions by a direct-
ness of thought and a tenacity of purpose that brooked no
interruption.

Tarzan had sent Tantor to the river to fetch water in his
trunk. From a distance he caught the scent of the jackals and
the horrid scent of Dango, and he hoped that Tantor would
return before they came creeping up on him. He felt no fear,
only an instinctive urge toward self-preservation. The jackals
he held in contempt, knowing that, though bound hand and
foot, he still could keep the timid creatures away; but Dango
was different, for once the filthy brute realized his helplessness, Tarzan knew that those powerful jaws would make quick
work of him. He knew the merciless savagery of the beast,
knew that in all the jungle there was none more terrible than
Dango.

The jackals came first, standing at the edge of the little glade
watching him. Then they circled slowly, coming nearer; but
when he raised himself to a sitting position they ran yelping
away. Three times they crept closer, trying to force their
courage to the point of actual attack; and then a horrid, slinking
form appeared upon the edge of the glade, and the jackals withdrew to a safe distance. Dango, the hyena, had come.

Tarzan was still sitting up, and the beast stood eyeing him,
filled with curiosity and with fear. He growled, and the man-
thing facing him growled back; and then from above them
came a great chattering, and Tarzan, looking up, saw little
Nkima dancing upon the limb of a tree above him.

"Come down, Nkima," he cried, "and untie the thongs that
bind my wrists."

"Dango! Dango!" shouted Nkima. "Little Nkima is afraid of
Dango."

"If you come now," said Tarzan, "it will be safe; but if you
wait too long, Dango will kill Tarzan; and then to whom may
little Nkima go for protection?"

"Nkima comes," shouted the little monkey, and dropping
quickly through the trees, he leaped to Tarzan's shoulder.

The hyena bared his fangs and laughed his horrid laugh.
Tarzan spoke. "Quick, the thongs, Nkima," urged Tarzan; and

the little monkey, his fingers trembling with terror, went to work upon the leather thongs at Tarzan's wrists.

Dango, his ugly head lowered, made a sudden rush; and from the deep lungs of the ape-man came a thunderous roar that might have done credit to Numa himself. With a yelp of terror the cowardly Dango turned and fled to the extremity of the glade, where he stood bristling and growling.

"Hurry, Nkima," said Tarzan. "Dango will come again. Maybe once, maybe twice, maybe many times before he closes on me; but in the end he will realize that I am helpless, and then he will not stop or turn back."

"Little Nkima's fingers are sick," said the Manu. "They are weak and they tremble. They will not untie the knot."

"Nkima has sharp teeth," Tarzan reminded him. "Why waste your time with sick fingers over knots that they cannot untie? Let your sharp teeth do the work."

Instantly Nkima commenced to gnaw upon the strands. Silent perforce because his mouth was otherwise occupied, Nkima strove diligently and without interruption.

Dango, in the meantime, made two short rushes, each time coming a little closer, but each time turning back before the menace of the ape-man's roars and savage growls, which by now had aroused the jungle.

Above them, in the treetops, the monkeys chattered, scolded and screamed, and in the distance the voice of Numa rolled like far thunder, while from the river came the squealing and trumpeting of Tantor.

Little Nkima was gnawing frantically at the bonds, when Dango charged again, evidently convinced by this time that the great Tarmangani was helpless, for now, with a growl, he rushed in and closed upon the man.

With a sudden surge of the great muscles of his arms that sent little Nkima sprawling, Tarzan sought to tear his hands free that he might defend himself against the savage death that menaced him in those slavering jaws; and the thongs, almost parted by Nkima's sharp teeth, gave to the terrific strain of the ape-man's efforts.

As Dango leaped for the bronzed throat, Tarzan's hand shot forward and seized the beast by the neck, but the impact of the heavy body carried him backward to the ground. Dango twisted, struggled, and clawed in a vain effort to free himself from the death grip of the ape-man, but those steel fingers closed relentlessly upon his throat, until, gasping for breath, the great brute sank helplessly upon the body of its intended victim.

Until death was assured, Tarzan did not relinquish his grasp; but when at last there could be no doubt, he hurled the carcass from him and, sitting up, fell quickly to the thongs that secured his ankles.

During the brief battle, Nkima had taken refuge among the topmost branches of a lofty tree, where he leaped about, screaming frantically at the battling beasts beneath him. Not until he was quite sure that Dango was dead did he descend. Warily he approached the body, lest, perchance, he had been mistaken; but again convinced by closer scrutiny, he leaped upon it and struck it viciously, again and again, and then he stood upon it shrieking his defiance at the world with all the assurance and bravado of one who has overcome a dangerous enemy.

Tantor, startled by the help cry of his friend, had turned back from the river without taking water. Trees bent beneath his mad rush as, ignoring winding trails, he struck straight through the jungle toward the little glade in answer to the call of the ape-man; and now, infuriated by the sounds of battle, he came charging into view, a titanic engine of rage and vengeance.

Tantor's eyesight is none too good, and it seemed that in his mad charge he must trample the ape-man, who lay directly in his path; but when Tarzan spoke to him the great beast came to a sudden stop at his side and, pivoting, wheeled about in his tracks, his ears forward, his trunk raised, trumpeting a savage warning as he searched for the creature that had been menacing his friend.

"Quiet, Tantor; it was Dango. He is dead," said the ape-man. As the eyes of the elephant finally located the carcass of the hyena he charged and trampled it, as he had trampled Dorsky, to a bloody pulp, as Nkima fled, shrieking, to the trees.

His ankles freed of their bonds, Tarzan was upon his feet;

and, when Tantor had vented his rage upon the body of Dango, he called the elephant to him. Tantor came then quietly to his side and stood with his trunk touching the ape-man's body, his rage quieted and his nerves soothed by the reassuring calm of the ape-man.

And now Nkima came, making an agile leap from a swaying bow to the back of Tantor and then to the shoulder of Tarzan, where, with his little arms about the ape-man's neck, he pressed his cheek close against the bronzed cheek of the great Tarmangani, who was his master and his god.

Thus the three friends stood in the silent communion that only beasts know, as the shadows lengthened and the sun set behind the forest.

16

"Turn Back!"

THE PRIVATIONS THAT Wayne Colt had endured had weakened him far more than he had realized, so that before his returning strength could bring renewed powers of resistance, he was stricken with fever.

The high priestess of the Flaming God, versed in the lore of ancient Opar, was conversant with the medicinal properties of many roots and herbs and, as well, with the mystic powers of incantation that drove demons from the bodies of the sick. By day she gathered and brewed, and at night she sat at the feet of her patient, intoning weird prayers, the origin of which reached back through countless ages to vanished temples, above which now rolled the waters of a mighty sea; and while she wrought with every artifice at her command to drive out the demon of sickness that possessed this man of an alien world, Jad-bal-ja, the golden lion, hunted for all three, and though at times he made his kill at a distance he never failed to carry the carcass of his prey back to the hidden lair where the woman nursed the man.

Days of burning fever, days of delirium, shot with periods of rationality, dragged their slow length. Often Colt's mind was confused by a jumble of bizarre impressions, in which La might be Zora Drinov one moment, a ministering angel from heaven the next, and then a Red Cross nurse; but in whatever guise he found her it seemed always a pleasant one, and when she was absent, as she was sometimes forced to be, he was depressed and unhappy.

When, upon her knees at his feet, she prayed to the rising sun, or to the sun at zenith, or to the setting sun, as was her wont, or when she chanted strange, weird songs in an unknown tongue, accompanying them with the mysterious gestures that were a part of the ritual, he was sure that the fever was worse and that he had become delirious again.

And so the days dragged on, and while Colt lay helpless, Zveri marched toward Italian Somaliland; and Tarzan, recovered from the shock of his wound, followed the plain trail of the expedition, and from his shoulder little Nkima scolded and chattered through the day.

Behind him Tarzan had left a handful of terrified blacks in the camp of the conspirators. They had been lolling in the shade, following their breakfast, a week after the killing of Dorsky and the escape of his captive. Fear of the ape-man at liberty, that had so terrified them at first, no longer concerned them greatly. Psychologically akin to the brutes of the forest, they happily soon forgot their terrors; nor did they harass their minds by anticipating those which might assail them in the future, as it is the silly custom of civilized man to do.

And so it was that this morning a sight burst suddenly upon their astonished eyes that found them entirely unprepared. They heard no noise, so silently go the beasts of the jungle, however large or heavy they may be; yet suddenly, in the clearing at the edge of the camp, appeared a great elephant, and upon his head sat the recent captive, whom they had been told was Tarzan of the Apes, and upon the man's shoulder perched a little monkey. With exclamations of terror, the blacks leaped to their feet and dashed into the jungle upon the opposite side of the camp.

Tarzan leaped lightly to the ground and entered Dorsky's tent. He had returned for a definite purpose; and his effort was crowned with success, for in the tent of the Russian he found his rope and his knife, which had been taken away from him at the time of his capture. For bow and arrows and a spear he had only to look to the shelters of the blacks; and, having found what he wanted, he departed as silently as he had come.

Now the time had arrived when Tarzan must set out rapidly upon the trail of his enemy, leaving Tantor to the peaceful paths that he loved best.

"I go, Tantor," he said. "Search out the forest where the young trees have the tenderest bark and watch well against the men-things, for they alone in all the world are the enemies of all living creatures." He was off through the forest then, with little Nkima clinging tightly to his bronzed neck.

Plain lay the winding trail of Zveri's army before the eyes of the ape-man, but he had no need to follow any trail. Long weeks before, as he had kept vigil above their camp, he had heard the principals discussing their plans; and so he knew their objectives, and he knew, too, how rapidly they could march and, therefore, about where he might hope to overtake them. Unhampered by files of porters sweating under heavy loads, earthbound to no winding trails, Tarzan was able to travel many times faster than the expedition. He saw their trail only when his own chanced to cross it as he laid a straight course for a point far in advance of the sweating column.

When he overtook the expedition night had fallen, and the tired men were in camp. They had eaten and were happy and many of the men were singing. To one who did not know the truth it might have appeared to be a military camp of French Colonial troops; for there was a military precision about the arrangement of the fires, the temporary shelters, and the officers' tents that would not have been undertaken by a hunting or

scientific expedition, and, in addition, there were the uniformed sentries pacing their beats. All this was the work of
Miguel Romero, to whose superior knowledge of military matters Zveri had been forced to defer in all matters of this nature,
though with no diminution of the hatred which each felt for the
other.

From his tree Tarzan watched the scene below, attempting
to estimate as closely as possible the number of armed men that
formed the fighting force of the expedition, while Nkima, bent
upon some mysterious mission, swung nimbly through the
trees toward the east. The ape-man realized that Zveri had
recruited a force that might constitute a definite menace to the
peace of Africa, since among its numbers were represented
many large and warlike tribes, who might easily be persuaded
to follow this mad leader were success to crown his initial
engagement. It was, however, to prevent this very thing that
Tarzan of the Apes had interested himself in the activities of
Peter Zveri; and here, before him, was another opportunity to
undermine the Russian's dream of empire while it was still
only a dream and might be dissipated by trivial means; by the
grim and terrible jungle methods of which Tarzan of the Apes
was a past master.

Tarzan fitted an arrow to his bow. Slowly his right hand
drew back the feathered end of the shaft until the point rested
almost upon his left thumb. His manner was marked by easy,
effortless grace. He did not appear to be taking conscious aim;
and yet when he released the shaft, it buried itself in the fleshy
part of a sentry's leg precisely as Tarzan of the Apes had
intended that it should.

With a yell of surprise and pain the black collapsed upon the
ground, more frightened, however, than hurt; and as his fellows gathered around him, Tarzan of the Apes melted away
into the shadows of the jungle night.

Attracted by the cry of the wounded man, Zveri, Romero,
and the other leaders of the expedition hastened from their
tents and joined the throng of excited blacks that surrounded
the victim of Tarzan's campaign of terrorism.

"Who shot you?" demanded Zveri when he saw the arrow
protruding from the sentry's leg.

"I do not know," replied the man.

"Have you an enemy in camp who might want to kill you?" asked Zveri.

"Even if he had," said Romero, "he couldn't have shot him with an arrow because no bows or arrows were brought with the expedition."

"I hadn't thought of that," said Zveri.

"So it must have been someone outside camp," declared Romero.

With difficulty and to the accompaniment of the screams of their victim, Ivitch and Romero cut the arrow from the sentry's leg, while Zveri and Kitembo discussed various conjectures as to the exact portent of the affair.

"We have evidently run into hostile natives," said Zveri.

Kitembo shrugged noncommittally. "Let me see the arrow," he said to Romero. "Perhaps that will tell us something."

As the Mexican handed the missile to the black chief, the latter carried it close to a campfire and examined it closely, while the white men gathered about him waiting for his findings.

At last Kitembo straightened up. The expression upon his face was serious, and when he spoke his voice trembled slightly. "This is bad," he said, shaking his bullet head.

"What do you mean?" demanded Zveri.

"This arrow bears the mark of a warrior who was left behind in our base camp," replied the chief.

"That is impossible," cried Zveri.

Kitembo shrugged. "I know it," he said, "but it is true."

"With an arrow out of the air the Hindu was slain," suggested a black head man, standing near Kitembo.

"Shut up, you fool," snapped Romero, "or you'll have the whole camp in a blue funk."

"That's right," said Zveri. "We must hush this thing up." He turned to the head man. "You and Kitembo," he commanded, "must not repeat this to your men. Let us keep it to ourselves."

Both Kitembo and the head man agreed to guard the secret, but within half an hour every man in camp knew that the sentry had been shot with an arrow that had been left behind in the base camp, and immediately their minds were prepared for other things that lay ahead of them upon the long trail.

The effect of the incident upon the minds of the black soldiers was apparent during the following day's march. They were quieter and more thoughtful, and there was much low-voiced conversation among them; but if they had given signs of nervousness during the day, it was nothing as compared with their state of mind after darkness fell upon their camp that night. The sentries evidenced their terror plainly by their listening attitudes and nervous attention to the sounds that came out of the blackness surrounding the camp. Most of them were brave men who would have faced a visible enemy with courage, but to a man they were convinced that they were confronted by the supernatural, against which they knew that neither rifle nor bravery might avail. They felt that ghostly eyes were watching them, and the result was as demoralizing as would an actual attack have been; in fact, far moreso.

Yet they need not have concerned themselves so greatly, as the cause of all their superstitious apprehension was moving rapidly through the jungle, miles away from them, and every instant the distance between him and them was increasing.

Another force, that might have caused them even greater anxiety had they been aware of it, lay still farther away upon the trail that they must traverse to reach their destination.

Around tiny cooking fires squatted a hundred black warriors, whose white plumes nodded and trembled as they moved. Sentries guarded them; sentries who were unafraid, since these men had little fear of ghosts or demons. They wore their amulets in leather pouches that swung from cords about their necks and they prayed to strange gods, but deep in their hearts lay a growing contempt for both. They had learned from experience and from the advice of a wise leader to look for victory more to themselves and their weapons than to their god.

They were a cheerful, happy company, veterans of many an expedition and, like all veterans, took advantage of every opportunity for rest and relaxation, the value of both of which is enhanced by the maintenance of a cheerful frame of mind; and so there was much laughing and joking among them, and often both the cause and butt of this was a little monkey, now teasing, now caressing, and in return being himself teased or caressed. That there was a bond of deep affection between him and these clean-limbed black giants was constantly apparent. When they pulled his tail they never pulled it very hard, and when he turned upon them in apparent fury, his sharp teeth closing upon their fingers or arms, it was noticeable that he never drew blood. Their play was rough, for they were all rough and primitive creatures; but it was all playing, and it was based upon a foundation of mutual affection.

These men had just finished their evening meal, when a figure, materializing as though out of thin air, dropped silently into their midst from the branches of a tree which overhung their camp.

Instantly a hundred warriors sprang to arms, and then, as quickly, they relaxed, as with shouts of "Bwana! Bwana!" they ran toward the bronzed giant standing silently in their midst.

As to an emperor or a god they went upon their knees before him, and those that were nearest him touched his hands and his feet in reverence; for to the Waziri Tarzan of the Apes, who was their king, was yet something more and of their own volition they worshipped him as their living god.

But if the warriors were glad to see him, little Nkima was frantic with joy. He scrambled quickly over the bodies of the kneeling blacks and leaped to Tarzan's shoulder, where he clung about his neck, jabbering excitedly.

"You have done well, my children," said the ape-man, "and little Nkima has done well. He bore my message to you, and I find you ready where I had planned that you should be."

"We have kept always a day's march ahead of the strangers, Bwana," replied Muviro, "camping well off the trail that they might not discover our fresh campsites and become suspicious."

"They do not suspect your presence," said Tarzan. "I listened above their camp last night, and they said nothing that would indicate that they dreamed that another party was preceding them along the trail."

"Where the dirt of the trail was soft a warrior, who marched at the rear of the column, brushed away the freshness of our spoor with a leafy bough," explained Muviro.

"Tomorrow we shall wait here for them," said the ape-man,

"and tonight you shall listen to Tarzan while he explains the plans that you will follow."

As Zveri's column took up the march upon the following morning, after a night of rest that had passed without incident, the spirits of all had risen to an appreciable degree. The blacks had not forgotten the grim warning that had sped out of the night surrounding their previous camp, but they were of a race whose spirits soon rebound from depression.

The leaders of the expedition were encouraged by the knowledge that over a third of the distance to their goal had been covered. For various reasons they were anxious to complete this part of the plan. Zveri believed that upon its successful conclusion hinged his whole dream of empire. Ivitch, a natural born troublemaker, was happy in the thought that the success of the expedition would cause untold annoyance to millions of people and perhaps, also, by the dream of his return to Russia as a hero; perhaps a wealthy hero.

Romero and Mori wanted to have it over for entirely different reasons. They were thoroughly disgusted with the Russian. They had lost all confidence in the sincerity of Zveri, who, filled as he was with his own importance and his delusions of future grandeur, talked too much, with the result that he had convinced Romero that he and all his kind were frauds, bent upon accomplishing their selfish ends with the assistance of their silly dupes and at the expense of the peace and prosperity of the world. It had not been difficult for Romero to convince Mori of the truth of his deductions, and now, thoroughly disillusioned, the two men continued on with the expedition because they believed that they could not successfully accomplish their intended desertion until the party was once more settled in the base camp.

The march had continued uninterruptedly for about an hour after camp had been broken, when one of Kitembo's black scouts, leading the column, halted suddenly in his tracks.

"Look!" he said to Kitembo, who was just behind him.

The chief stepped to the warrior's side; and there, before him in the trail, sticking upright in the earth, was an arrow.

"It is a warning," said the warrior.

Gingerly, Kitembo plucked the arrow from the earth and

examined it. He would have been glad to have kept the knowledge of his discovery to himself, although not a little shaken by what he had seen; but the warrior at his side had seen, too. "It is the same," he said. "It is another of the arrows that were left behind in the base camp."

When Zveri came abreast of them, Kitembo handed him the arrow. "It is the same," he said to the Russian, "and it is a warning for us to turn back."

"Pooh!" exclaimed Zveri contemptuously. "It is only an arrow sticking in the dirt and cannot stop a column of armed men. I did not think that you were a coward, too, Kitembo."

The black scowled. "Nor do men with safety call me a coward," he snapped; "but neither am I a fool, and better than you do I know the danger signals of the forest. We shall go on because we are brave men, but many will never come back. Also, your plans will fail."

At this Zveri flew into one of his frequent rages; and though the men continued the march, they were in a sullen mood, and many were the ugly glances that were cast at Zveri and his lieutenants.

Shortly after noon the expedition halted for the noonday rest. They had been passing through a dense woods, gloomy and depressing; and there was neither song nor laughter, nor a great deal of conversation, as the men squatted together in little knots while they devoured the cold food that constituted their midday meal.

Suddenly, from somewhere far above, a voice floated down to them. Weird and uncanny, it spoke to them in a Bantu dialect that most of them could understand. "Turn back, children of Mulungu," it cried. "Turn back before you die. Desert the white men before it is too late."

That was all. The men crouched fearfully, looking up into the trees. It was Zveri who broke the silence. "What the hell was that?" he demanded. "What did it say?"

"It warned us to turn back," said Kitembo.

"There will be no turning back," snapped Zveri.

"I do not know about that," replied Kitembo.

"I thought you wanted to be a king," cried Zveri. "You'd make a hell of a king."

For the moment Kitembo had forgotten the dazzling prize that Zveri had held before his eyes for months—to be the king of Kenya. That was worth risking much for.

"We will go on," he said.

"You may have to use force," said Zveri, "but stop at nothing. We must go on, no matter what happens," and then he turned to his other lieutenants. "Romero, you and Mori go to the rear of the column and shoot every man who refuses to advance."

The men had not as yet refused to go on, and when the order to march was given, they sullenly took their places in the column. For an hour they marched thus; and then, far ahead, came the weird cry that many of them had heard before at Opar, and a few minutes later a voice out of the distance called to them. "Desert the white men," it said.

The blacks whispered among themselves, and it was evident that trouble was brewing; but Kitembo managed to persuade them to continue the march, a thing that Zveri never could have accomplished.

"I wish we could get that troublemaker," said Zveri to Zora Drinov, as the two walked together near the head of the column. "If he would only show himself once, so that we could get a shot at him; that's all I want."

"It is someone familiar with the workings of the native mind," said the girl. "Probably a medicine man of some tribe through whose territory we are marching."

"I hope that it is nothing more than that," replied Zveri. "I have no doubt that the man is a native, but I am afraid that he is acting on instructions from either the British or the Italians, who hope thus to disorganize and delay us until they can mobilize a force with which to attack us."

"It has certainly shaken the morale of the men," said Zora, "for I believe that they attribute all of the weird happenings, from the mysterious death of Jafar to the present time, to the same agency, to which their superstitious minds naturally attribute a supernatural origin."

"So much the worse for them, then," said Zveri, "for they are going on whether they wish to or not; and when they find that attempted desertion means death, they will wake up to the fact that it is not safe to trifle with Peter Zveri."

"They are many, Peter," the girl reminded him, "and we are few; in addition they are, thanks to you, well armed. It seems to me that you may have created a Frankenstein that will destroy us all in the end."

"You are as bad as the blacks," growled Zveri, "making a mountain out of a molehill. Why if I—"

Behind the rear of the column and again apparently from the air above them sounded the warning voice. "Desert the whites." Silence fell again upon the marching column, but the men moved on, exhorted by Kitembo and threatened by the revolvers of their white officers.

Presently the forest broke at the edge of a small plain, across which the trail led through buffalo grass that grew high above the heads of the marching men. They were well into this when, ahead of them, a rifle spoke, and then another and another, seemingly in a long line across their front.

Zveri ordered one of the blacks to rush Zora to the rear of the column into a position of safety, while he followed close behind her, ostensibly searching for Romero and shouting words of encouragement to the men.

As yet no one had been hit; but the column had stopped, and the men were rapidly losing all semblance of formation.

"Quick, Romero," shouted Zveri, "take command up in front. I will cover the rear with Mori and prevent desertions."

The Mexican sprang past him and with the aid of Ivitch and some of the black chiefs he deployed one company in a long skirmish line, with which he advanced slowly; while Kitembo followed with half the rest of the expedition acting as a support, leaving Ivitch, Mori, and Zveri to organize a reserve from the remainder.

After the first widely scattered shots, the firing had ceased, to be followed by a silence even more ominous to the overwrought nerves of the black soldiers. The utter silence of the enemy, the lack of any sign of movement in the grasses ahead of them, coupled with the mysterious warnings which still rang in their ears, convinced the blacks that they faced no mortal foe.

"Turn back!" came mournfully from the grasses ahead. "This is the last warning. Death will follow disobedience."

The line wavered, and to steady it Romero gave the command to fire. In response came a rattle of musketry out of the grasses ahead of them, and this time a dozen men went down, killed or wounded.

"Charge!" cried Romero, but instead the men wheeled about and broke for the rear and safety.

At sight of the advance line bearing down upon them, throwing away their rifles as they ran, the support turned and fled, carrying the reserve with it, and the whites were carried along in the mad rout.

In disgust, Romero fell back alone. He saw no enemy, for none pursued him, and this fact induced within him an uneasiness that the singing bullets had been unable to arouse. As he plodded on alone far in the rear of his companions, he began to share to some extent the feeling of unreasoning terror that had seized his black companions, or at least, if not to share it, to sympathize with them. It is one thing to face a foe that you can see, and quite another to be beset by an invisible enemy, of whose very appearance, even, one is ignorant.

Shortly after Romero reentered the forest, he saw someone walking along the trail ahead of him; and presently, when he had an unobstructed view, he saw that it was Zora Drinov.

He called to her then, and she turned and waited for him.

"I was afraid that you had been killed, Comrade," she said.

"I was born under a lucky star," he replied, smiling. "Men were shot down on either side of me and behind me. Where is Zveri?"

Zora shrugged. "I do not know," she answered.

"Perhaps he is trying to reorganize the reserve," suggested Romero.

"Doubtless," said the girl shortly.

"I hope he is fleet of foot then," said the Mexican, lightly.

"Evidently he is," replied Zora.

"You should not have been left alone like this," said the man.

"I can take care of myself," replied Zora.

"Perhaps," he said, "but if you belonged to me—"

"I belong to no one, Comrade Romero," she replied icily.

"Forgive me, Señorita," he said. "I know that. I merely chose an unfortunate way of trying to say that if the girl I loved were here she would not have been left alone in the forest, especially when I believe, as Zveri must believe, that we are being pursued by an enemy."

"You do not like Comrade Zveri, do you, Romero?"

"Even to you, Señorita," he replied, "I must admit, since you ask me, that I do not."

"I know that he has antagonized many."

"He has antagonized all—except you, Señorita."

"Why should I be excepted?" she asked. "How do you know that he has not antagonized me also?"

"Not deeply, I am sure," he said, "or else you would not have consented to become his wife."

"And how do you know that I have?" she asked.

"Comrade Zveri boasts of it often," replied Romero.

"Oh, he does?" Nor did she make any other comment.

17

A Gulf That Was Bridged

THE GENERAL ROUT of Zveri's forces ended only when their last camp had been reached and even then only for part of the command, for as night fell it was discovered that fully twenty-five percent of the men were missing, and among the absentees were Zora and Romero. As the stragglers came in, Zveri questioned each about the girl, but no one had seen her. He tried to organize an expedition to go back in search of her, but no one would accompany him. He threatened and pleaded, only to discover that he had lost all control of his men. Perhaps he would have gone back alone, as he insisted that he intended doing; but he was relieved of this necessity when, well after dark, the two walked into camp together.

At sight of them Zveri was both relieved and angry. "Why didn't you remain with me?" he snapped at Zora.

"Because I cannot run so fast as you," she replied, and Zveri said no more.

From the darkness of the trees above the camp came the now familiar warning. "Desert the whites!" A long silence followed this, broken only by the nervous whisperings of the blacks, and then the voice spoke again. "The trails to your own countries are free from danger, but death walks always with the white men. Throw away your uniforms and leave the white men to the jungle and to me."

A black warrior leaped to his feet and stripped the French uniform from his body, throwing it upon a cooking fire that burned near him. Instantly others followed his example.

"Stop that!" cried Zveri.

"Silence, white man!" growled Kitembo.

"Kill the whites!" shouted a naked Basembo warrior.

Instantly there was a rush toward the whites, who were gathered near Zveri, and then from above them came a warning cry. "The whites are mine!" it cried. "Leave them to me."

For an instant the advancing warriors halted; and then he, who had constituted himself their leader, maddened perhaps by his hatred and his blood lust, advanced again, grasping his rifle menacingly.

From above a bowstring twanged. The black, dropping his rifle, screamed as he tore at an arrow protruding from his chest; and, as he fell forward upon his face, the other blacks fell back, and the whites were left alone, while the Negroes huddled by themselves in a far corner of the camp. Many of them would have deserted that night, but they feared the darkness of the jungle and the menace of the thing hovering above them.

Zveri strode angrily to and fro, cursing his luck, cursing the blacks, cursing everyone. "If I had had any help, if I had had any cooperation," he grumbled, "this would not have happened, but I cannot do everything alone."

"You have done this pretty much alone," said Romero.

"What do you mean?" demanded Zveri.

"I mean that you have made such an overbearing ass of yourself that you have antagonized everyone in the expedition, but even so they might have carried on if they had had any confidence in your courage—no man likes to follow a coward."

"You call me that, you yellow greaser," shouted Zveri, reaching for his revolver.

"Cut that," snapped Romero. "I have you covered. And let me tell you now that if it weren't for Señorita Drinov I would kill you on the spot and rid the world of at least one crazy mad dog that is threatening the entire world with the hydrophobia of hate and suspicion. Señorita Drinov saved my life once. I have not forgotten that; and because, perhaps, she loves you, you are safe, unless I am forced to kill you in self-defense."

"This is utter insanity," cried Zora. "There are five of us here alone with a band of unruly blacks who fear and hate us. Tomorrow, doubtless, we shall be deserted by them. If we hope ever to get out of Africa alive, we must stick together. Forget your quarrels, both of you, and let us work together in harmony hereafter for our mutual salvation."

"For your sake, Señorita, yes," said Romero.

"Comrade Drinov is right," said Ivitch.

Zveri dropped his hand from his gun and turned sulkily away; and for the rest of the night peace, if not happiness, held sway in the disorganized camp of the conspirators.

When morning came the whites saw that the blacks had all discarded their French uniforms, and from the concealing foliage of a nearby tree other eyes had noted this same fact—gray eyes that were touched by the shadow of a grim smile. There were no black boys now to serve the whites, as even their personal servants had deserted them to foregather with the men of their own blood, and so the five prepared their own breakfast, after Zveri's attempt to command the services of some of their boys had met with surly refusal.

While they were eating, Kitembo approached them, accompanied by the head men of the different tribes that were represented in the personnel of the expedition. "We are leaving with our people for our own countries," said the Basembo chief. "We leave food for your journey to your own camp. Many of our warriors wish to kill you, and that we cannot prevent if you attempt to accompany us, for they fear the vengeance of the ghosts that have followed you for many moons. Remain here until tomorrow. After that you are free to go where you will."

"But," expostulated Zveri, "you can't leave us like this without porters or askaris."

"No longer can you tell us what we can do, white man," said Kitembo, "for you are few and we are many, and your power over us is broken. In everything you have failed. We do not follow such a leader."

"You can't do it," growled Zveri. "You will all be punished for this, Kitembo."

"Who will punish us?" demanded the black. "The English? The French? The Italians? You do not dare go to them. They would punish you, not us. Perhaps you will go to Ras Tafari. He would have your heart cut out and your body thrown to the dogs, if he knew what you were planning."

"But you can't leave this white woman alone here in the jungle without servants, or porters, or adequate protection," insisted Zveri, realizing that his first argument had made no impression upon the black chief, who now held their fate in his hands.

"I do not intend to leave the white woman," said Kitembo. "She is going with me," and then it was that, for the first time, the whites realized that the head men had surrounded them and that they were covered by many rifles.

As he had talked, Kitembo had come closer to Zveri, at whose side stood Zora Drinov, and now the black chief reached out quickly and grasped her by the wrist. "Come!" he said, and as he uttered the word something hummed above their heads, and Kitembo, chief of the Basembos, clutched at an arrow in his chest.

"Do not look up," cried a voice from above. "Keep your eyes upon the ground, for whosoever looks up dies. Listen well to what I have to say, black men. Go your way to your own countries, leaving behind you all of the white people. Do not harm them. They belong to me. I have spoken."

Wide-eyed and trembling, the black head men fell back from the whites, leaving Kitembo writhing upon the ground. They hastened to cross the camp to their fellows, all of whom were now thoroughly terrified; and before the chief of the Basembos ceased his death struggle, the black tribesmen had seized the loads which they had previously divided amongst them and were pushing and elbowing for precedence along the game trail that led out of camp toward the west.

Watching them depart, the whites sat in stupefied silence, which was not broken until after the last black had gone and they were alone.

"What do you suppose that thing meant by saying we belong to him?" asked Ivitch in a slightly thickened voice.

"How could I know?" growled Zveri.

"Perhaps it is a man-eating ghost," suggested Romero with a smile.

"It has done about all the harm it can do now," said Zveri. "It ought to leave us alone for awhile."

"It is not such a malign spirit," said Zora. "It can't be, for it certainly saved me from Kitembo."

"Saved you for itself," said Ivitch.

"Nonsense!" said Romero. "The purpose of that mysterious voice from the air is just as obvious as is the fact that it is the voice of a man. It is the voice of someone who wanted to defeat the purposes of this expedition, and I imagine Zveri guessed close to the truth yesterday when he attributed it to English or Italian sources that were endeavoring to delay us until they could mobilize a sufficient force against us."

"Which proves," declared Zveri, "what I have suspected for a long time; that there is more than one traitor among us," and he looked meaningly at Romero.

"What it means," said Romero, "is that crazy, harebrained theories always fail when they are put to the test. You thought that all the blacks in Africa would rush to your standard and drive all the foreigners into the ocean. In theory, perhaps, you were right, but in practice one man, with a knowledge of native psychology which you did not have, burst your entire dream like a bubble, and for every other harebrained theory in the world there is always a stumbling block of fact."

"You talk like a traitor to the cause," said Ivitch threateningly.

"And what are you going to do about it?" demanded the Mexican. "I am fed up with all of you and your whole rotten, selfish plan. There isn't an honest hair in your head nor in Zveri's. I can accord Tony and Señorita Drinov the benefit of a doubt, for I cannot conceive either of them as knaves. As I was deluded, so may they have been deluded, as you and your kind have striven for years to delude countless millions of others."

"You are not the first traitor to the cause," cried Zveri, "nor will you be the first traitor to pay the penalty of his treason."

"That is not a good way to talk now," said Mori. "We are not already too many. If we fight and kill one another, perhaps none of us will come out of Africa alive. But if you kill Miguel, you will have to kill me, too, and perhaps you will not be successful. Perhaps it is you who will be killed."

"Tony is right," said the girl. "Let us call a truce until we reach civilization." And so it was that under something of the nature of an armed truce, the five set forth the following morning on the back trail toward their base camp; while upon another trail, a full day ahead of them, Tarzan and his Waziri warriors took a shortcut for Opar.

"La may not be there," Tarzan explained to Muviro, "but I intend to punish Oah and Dooth for their treachery and thus make it possible for the high priestess to return in safety, if she still lives."

"But how about the white enemies in the jungle back of us, Bwana?" asked Muviro.

"They shall not escape us," said Tarzan. "They are weak and inexperienced to the jungle. They move slowly. We may always overtake them when we will. It is La who concerns me most, for she is a friend, while they are only enemies."

Many miles away, the object of his friendly solicitude approached a clearing in the jungle, a man-made clearing that was evidently intended for a campsite for a large body of men, though now only a few rude shelters were occupied by a handful of blacks.

At the woman's side walked Wayne Colt, his strength

now fully regained, and at their heels paced Jad-bal-ja, the golden lion.

"We have found it at last," said the man; "thanks to you."

"Yes, but it is deserted," replied La. "They have all left."

"No," said Colt, "I see some blacks over by those shelters at the right."

"It is well," said La, "and now I must leave you." There was a note of regret in her voice.

"I hate to say good-bye," said the man, "but I know where your heart is and that all your kindness to me has only delayed your return to Opar. It is futile for me to attempt to express my gratitude, but I think that you know what is in my heart."

"Yes," said the woman, "and it is enough for me to know that I have made a friend, I who have so few loyal friends."

"I wish that you would let me go with you to Opar," he said. "You are going back to face enemies, and you may need whatever little help I should be able to give you."

She shook her head. "No, that cannot be," she replied. "All the suspicion and hatred of me that was engendered in the hearts of some of my people was caused by my friendship for a man of another world. Were you to return with me and assist me in regaining my throne, it would but arouse their suspicions still further. If Jad-bal-ja and I cannot succeed alone, three of us could accomplish no more."

"Won't you at least be my guest for the rest of the day?" he asked. "I can't offer you much hospitality," he added with a rueful smile.

"No, my friend," she said. "I cannot take the chance of losing Jad-bal-ja; nor could you take the chance of losing your blacks, and I fear that they would not remain together in the same camp. Good-bye, Wayne Colt. But do not say that I go alone, at whose side walks Jad-bal-ja."

From the base camp La knew the trail back to Opar; and as Colt watched her depart, he felt a lump rise in his throat, for the beautiful girl and the great lion seemed personifications of loveliness, and strength, and loneliness.

With a sigh he turned into camp and crossed to where the blacks lay sleeping through the midday heat. He awoke them, and at sight of him they were all very much excited, for they had been members of his own safari from the Coast and recognized him immediately. Having long given him up for lost, they were at first inclined to be a little bit frightened until they had convinced themselves that he was, indeed, flesh and blood.

Since the killing of Dorsky they had had no master, and they confessed to him that they had been seriously considering deserting the camp and returning to their own countries; for they had been unable to rid their minds of the weird and terrifying occurrences that the expedition had witnessed in this strange country, in which they felt very much alone and helpless without the guidance and protection of a white master.

Across the plain of Opar, toward the ruined city, walked a girl and a lion; and behind them, at the summit of the escarpment which she had just scaled, a man halted, looking out across the plain, and saw them in the distance.

Behind him a hundred warriors swarmed up the rocky cliff. As they gathered about the tall, bronzed, gray-eyed figure that had preceded them, the man pointed. "La!" he said.

"And Numa!" said Muviro. "He is stalking her. It is strange, Bwana, that he does not charge."

"He will not charge," said Tarzan. "Why, I do not know; but I know that he will not because it is Jad-bal-ja."

"The eyes of Tarzan are like the eyes of the eagle," said Muviro. "Muviro sees only a woman and a lion, but Tarzan sees La and Jad-bal-ja."

"I do not need my eyes for those two," said the ape-man. "I have a nose."

"I, too, have a nose," said Muviro, "but it is only a piece of flesh that sticks out from my face. It is good for nothing."

Tarzan smiled. "As a little child you did not have to depend upon your nose for your life and your food," he said, "as I have always done, then and since. Come, my children, La and Jad-bal-ja will be glad to see us."

It was the keen ears of Jad-bal-ja that caught the first faint warning noises from the rear. He halted and turned, his great head raised majestically, his ears forward, the skin of his nose wrinkling to stimulate his sense of smell. Then he voiced a low growl, and La stopped and turned back to discover the cause of his displeasure.

As her eyes noted the approaching column, her heart sank. Even Jad-bal-ja could not protect her against so many. She thought then to attempt to outdistance them to the city; but when she glanced again at the ruined walls at the far side of the valley she knew that that plan was quite hopeless, as she would not have the strength to maintain a fast pace for so great a distance, while among those black warriors there must be many trained runners who could easily outdistance her. And so, resigned to her fate, she stood and waited; while Jad-bal-ja, with flattened head and twitching tail, advanced slowly to meet the oncoming men; and as he advanced, his savage growls rose to the tumult of tremendous roars that shook the earth as he sought to frighten away this menace to his loved mistress.

But the men came on; and then, of a sudden, La saw that one who came in advance of the others was lighter in color, and her heart leaped in her breast; and then she recognized him, and tears came to the eyes of the savage high priestess of Opar.

"It is Tarzan! Jad-bal-ja, it is Tarzan!" she cried, the light of her great love illuminating her beautiful features.

Perhaps at the same instant the lion recognized his master, for the roaring ceased, the eyes no longer glared, no longer was the great head flattened as he trotted forward to meet the ape-man. Like a great dog, he reared up before Tarzan. With a scream of terror little Nkima leaped from the ape-man's shoulder and scampered, screaming, back to Muviro, since bred in the fiber of Nkima was the knowledge that Numa was always Numa. With his great paws on Tarzan's shoulder Jad-bal-ja licked the bronzed cheek, and then Tarzan pushed him aside and walked rapidly toward La; while Nkima, his terror gone, jumped frantically up and down on Muviro's shoulder calling the lion many jungle names for having frightened him.

"At last!" exclaimed Tarzan, as he stood face-to-face with La.

"At last," repeated the girl, "you have come back from your hunt."

"I came back immediately," replied the man, "but you had gone."

"You came back?" she asked.

"Yes, La," he replied. "I traveled far before I made a kill, but at last I found meat and brought it to you, and you were gone and the rain had obliterated your spoor and though I searched for days I could not find you."

"Had I thought that you intended to return," she said, "I should have remained there forever."

"You should have known that I would not have left you thus," replied Tarzan.

"La is sorry," she said.

"And you have not been back to Opar since?" he asked.

"Jad-bal-ja and I are on our way to Opar now," she said. "I was lost for a long time. Only recently did I find the trail to Opar, and then, too, there was the white man who was lost and sick with fever. I remained with him until the fever left him and his strength came back, because I thought that he might be a friend of Tarzan's."

"What was his name?" asked the ape-man.

"Wayne Colt," she replied.

The ape-man smiled. "Did he appreciate what you did for him?" he asked.

"Yes, he wanted to come to Opar with me and help me regain my throne."

"You liked him then, La?" he asked.

"I liked him very much," she said, "but not in the same way that I like Tarzan."

He touched her shoulder in a half caress. "La, the immutable!" he murmured, and then, with a sudden toss of his head as though he would clear his mind of sad thoughts, he turned once more toward Opar. "Come," he said, "the Queen is returning to her throne."

The unseen eyes of Opar watched the advancing column. They recognized La, and Tarzan, and the Waziri, and some there were who guessed the identity of Jad-bal-ja; and Oah was frightened, and Dooth trembled, and little Nao, who hated Oah, was almost happy, as happy as one may be who carries a broken heart in one's bosom.

Oah had ruled with a tyrant hand, and Dooth had been a weak fool, whom no one longer trusted; and there were whisperings now among the ruins, whisperings that would have

frightened Oah and Dooth had they heard them, and the whisperings spread among the priestesses and the warrior priests,
with the result that when Tarzan and Jad-bal-ja led the Waziri
into the courtyard of the outer temple there was no one there to
resist them; but instead voices called down to them from the
dark arches of surrounding corridors pleading for mercy and
voicing earnest assurance of their future loyalty to La.

As they made their way into the city, they heard far in the
interior of the temple a sudden burst of noise. High voices were
punctuated by loud screams, and then came silence; and when
they came to the throne room the cause of it was apparent to
them, for lying in a welter of blood were the bodies of Oah and
Dooth, with those of a half dozen priests and priestesses who
had remained loyal to them; and, but for these, the great throne
room was empty.

Once again did La, the high priestess of the Flaming God,
resume her throne as Queen of Opar.

That night Tarzan, Lord of the Jungle, ate again from the
golden platters of Opar, while young girls, soon to become
priestesses of the Flaming God, served meats and fruits, and
wines so old that no living man knew their vintage, nor in what
forgotten vineyard grew the grapes that went into their making.

But in such things Tarzan found little interest, and he was
glad when the new day found him at the head of his Waziri
crossing the plain of Opar toward the barrier cliffs. Upon his
bronzed shoulder sat Nkima, and at the ape-man's side paced
the golden lion, while in column behind him marched his hundred Waziri warriors.

It was a tired and disheartened company of whites that
approached their base camp after a long, monotonous, and
uneventful journey. Zveri and Ivitch were in the lead, followed
by Zora Drinov, while a considerable distance to the rear
Romero and Mori walked side by side, and such had been the
order in which they had marched all these long days.

Wayne Colt was sitting in the shade of one of the shelters,
and the blacks were lolling in front of another, a short distance
away, as Zveri and Ivitch came into sight.

Colt rose and came forward, and it was then that Zveri spied him. "You damned traitor!" he cried. "I'll get you if it's the last thing I do on earth," and as he spoke he drew his revolver and fired point-blank at the unarmed American.

His first shot grazed Colt's side without breaking the skin, but Zveri fired no second shot, for almost simultaneously with the report of his own shot another rang out behind him, and Peter Zveri, dropping his pistol and clutching at his back, staggered drunkenly upon his feet.

Ivitch wheeled about. "My God, Zora, what have you done?" he cried.

"What I have been waiting to do for twelve years," replied the girl. "What I have been waiting to do ever since I was little more than a child."

Wayne Colt had run forward and seized Zveri's gun from the ground where it had fallen, and Romero and Mori now came up at a run.

Zveri had sunk to the ground and was glaring savagely about him. "Who shot me?" he screamed. "I know. It was that damned greaser."

"It was I," said Zora Drinov.

"You!" gasped Zveri.

Suddenly she turned to Wayne Colt as though only he mattered. "You might as well know the truth," she said. "I am not a Red and never have been. This man killed my father, and my mother, and an older brother and sister. My father was—well, never mind who he was. He is avenged now." She turned fiercely upon Zveri. "I could have killed you a dozen times in the last few years," she said, "but I waited because I wanted more than your life. I wanted to help kill the hideous schemes with which you and your kind are seeking to wreck the happiness of the world."

Peter Zveri sat on the ground, staring at her, his wide eyes slowly glazing. Suddenly he coughed and a torrent of blood gushed from his mouth. Then he sank back dead.

Romero had moved close to Ivitch. Suddenly he poked the muzzle of a revolver into the Russian's ribs. "Drop your gun," he said. "I'm taking no chances on you either."

Ivitch, paling, did as he was bid. He saw his little world tottering, and he was afraid.

Across the clearing a figure stood at the edge of the jungle. It had not been there an instant before. It had appeared silently as though out of thin air. Zora Drinov was the first to perceive it. She voiced a cry of surprised recognition; and as the others turned to follow the direction of her eyes, they saw a bronzed white man, naked but for a loincloth of leopard skin, coming toward them. He moved with the easy, majestic grace of a lion and there was much about him that suggested the king of beasts.

"Who is that?" asked Colt.

"I do not know who he is," replied Zora, "other than that he is the man who saved my life when I was lost in the jungle."

The man halted before them.

"Who are you?" demanded Wayne Colt.

"I am Tarzan of the Apes," replied the other. "I have seen and heard all that has occurred here. The plan that was fostered by this man," he nodded at the body of Zveri, "has failed and he is dead. This girl has avowed herself. She is not one of you. My people are camped a short distance away. I shall take her to them and see that she reaches civilization in safety. For the rest of you I have no sympathy. You may get out of the jungle as best you may. I have spoken."

"They are not all what you think them, my friend," said Zora.

"What do you mean?" demanded Tarzan.

"Romero and Mori have learned their lesson. They avowed themselves openly during a quarrel when our blacks deserted us."

"I heard them," said Tarzan.

She looked at him in surprise. "You heard them?" she asked.

"I have heard much that has gone on in many of your camps," replied the ape-man, "but I do not know that I may believe all that I hear."

"I think you may believe what you heard them say," Zora assured him. "I am confident that they are sincere."

"Very well," said Tarzan. "If they wish they may come with me also, but these other two will have to shift for themselves."

"Not the American," said Zora.

"No? And why not?" demanded the ape-man.

"Because he is a special agent in the employ of the United States government," replied the girl.

The entire party, including Colt, looked at her in astonishment. "How did you learn that?" demanded Colt.

"The message that you sent when you first came to camp and we were here alone was intercepted by one of Zveri's agents. Now do you understand how I know?"

"Yes," said Colt. "It is quite plain."

"That is why Zveri called you a traitor and tried to kill you."

"And how about this other?" demanded Tarzan, indicating Ivitch. "Is he, also, a sheep in wolf's clothing?"

"He is one of those paradoxes who are so numerous," replied Zora. "He is one of those Reds who is all yellow."

Tarzan turned to the blacks who had come forward and were standing, listening questioningly to a conversation they could not understand. "I know your country," he said to them in their own dialect. "It lies near the end of the railroad that runs to the Coast."

"Yes, master," said one of the blacks.

"You will take this white man with you as far as the railroad. See that he has enough to eat and is not harmed, and then tell him to get out of the country. Start now." Then he turned back to the whites. "The rest of you will follow me to my camp." And with that he turned and swung away toward the trail by which he had entered the camp. Behind him followed the four who owed to his humanity more than they could ever know, nor had they known could have guessed that his great tolerance, courage, resourcefulness, and the protective instinct that had often safeguarded them sprang not from his human progenitors, but from his lifelong association with the natural beasts of the forest and the jungle, who have these instinctive qualities far more strongly developed than do the unnatural beasts of civilization, in whom the greed and lust of competition have dimmed the luster of these noble qualities where they have not eradicated them entirely.

Behind the others walked Zora Drinov and Wayne Colt, side-by-side.

"I thought you were dead," she said.

"And I thought that you were dead," he replied.

"And worse than that," she continued, "I thought that, whether dead or alive, I might never tell you what was in my heart."

"And I thought that a hideous gulf separated us that I could never span to ask you the question that I wanted to ask you," he answered in a low tone.

She turned toward him, her eyes filled with tears, her lips trembling. "And I thought that, alive or dead, I could never say yes to that question, if you did ask me," she replied.

A curve in the trail hid them from the sight of the others as he took her in his arms and drew her lips to his.